W9-BSF-641

PRAISE FOR
IN HARM'S WAY

"A multilayered thriller . . . *In Harm's Way* delivers a likable protagonist with relationship problems, kid issues, job challenges, and the nagging suspicion that he'll never live up to his parents' expectations . . . Who among us can't relate?"
—*Houston Chronicle*

"[A] page-turner."
—*The Seattle Times*

"The multilayered plot and fast pacing makes this edge-of-your-seat crime novel crackle with suspense and unexpected twists."
—*Tucson Citizen*

"[A] worthy thriller . . . Ridley Pearson brings back Sheriff Walt Fleming as the hero of *In Harm's Way* . . . Sheriff Fleming makes for good company . . . he's terse, efficient, and a font of common sense."
—*St. Louis Today*

"An excellent thriller . . . a superb mystery."
—*The Mystery Gazette*

"A transfixing tale filled with secrets both large and small . . . riveting suspense."
—*Romantic Times*

KILLER SUMMER

"Pearson can plot a heist with ingenuity and delicious complexity . . . Once you're aboard . . . you're in this book for the whole ride."
—*St. Louis Post-Dispatch*

"Engaging . . . even the savviest readers will be fooled as Pearson drags poor Walt and friends through a series of clever twists and turns in this fast-paced nail-biter."
—*Publishers Weekly*

continued . . .

"[Pearson is] a master of that all-too-rare book: the read that is both exciting and intelligent . . . Pearson again demonstrates his skill producing dinner-delaying narratives."
—The Associated Press

KILLER WEEKEND

"Ridley Pearson has outdone himself with *Killer Weekend*."
—James Patterson

"A terrifying villain, an appealing protagonist, intricate plotting, and breakneck pacing . . . Ridley Pearson writes thrillers, the kind that try to yank you to the edge of your seat and keep you there. *Killer Weekend* succeeds."
—*Boston Sunday Globe*

"Ridley Pearson writes some of the tightest thriller fiction around. In the deftness of his conceptions, the care with details, and the quality of writing, he's fully worthy of comparison to Michael Connelly."   —Scott Turow

"This is a story built to keep you winded."
—*Rocky Mountain News*

"Consummate entertainment . . . I read *Killer Weekend* pretty much in one sitting—making it a strong bet others will, too."   —*The Baltimore Sun*

"Ridley Pearson packs a wallop in his newest thriller, *Killer Weekend*."   —*The Cincinnati Enquirer*

"If we had a Thriller Hall of Fame, Ridley Pearson would be a first-ballot certainty, both for his technical virtuosity and his intensely human stories. Does *Killer Weekend* maintain his standards? No, it sets new ones. Don't miss it."
—Lee Child

continued . . .

Titles by Ridley Pearson

In Harm's Way

Killer Summer

Killer View

Killer Weekend

Cut and Run

The Art of Deception

The Diary of Ellen Rimbauer
(writing as Joyce Reardon)

The Pied Piper

Beyond Recognition

Undercurrents

BOOKS FOR YOUNG READERS

*Peter and the Starcatchers
series* (with Dave Barry)

The Kingdom Keepers series

Steel Trapp series

IN
HARM'S
WAY

RIDLEY PEARSON

JOVE BOOKS   NEW YORK

THE BERKLEY PUBLISHING GROUP
Published by the Penguin Group
Penguin Group (USA) Inc.
375 Hudson Street, New York, New York 10014, USA
Penguin Group (Canada), 90 Eglinton Avenue East, Suite 700, Toronto, Ontario M4P 2Y3, Canada
(a division of Pearson Penguin Canada Inc.)
Penguin Books Ltd., 80 Strand, London WC2R 0RL, England
Penguin Group Ireland, 25 St. Stephen's Green, Dublin 2, Ireland (a division of Penguin Books Ltd.)
Penguin Group (Australia), 250 Camberwell Road, Camberwell, Victoria 3124, Australia
(a division of Pearson Australia Group Pty. Ltd.)
Penguin Books India Pvt. Ltd., 11 Community Centre, Panchsheel Park, New Delhi—110 017, India
Penguin Books (NZ), 67 Apollo Drive, Rosedale, Auckland 0632, New Zealand
(a division of Pearson New Zealand Ltd.)
Penguin Books (South Africa) (Pty.) Ltd., 24 Sturdee Avenue, Rosebank, Johannesburg 2196,
South Africa

Penguin Books Ltd., Registered Offices: 80 Strand, London WC2R 0RL, England

IN HARM'S WAY

A Jove Book / published by arrangement with Page One, Inc.

PRINTING HISTORY
G. P. Putnam's Sons hardcover edition / August 2010
Jove premium edition / August 2011

For Louise Marsh

Acknowledgments

Special thanks to Sheriff Walt Femling, his wife, Jenny, and their family. And to the residents of the Wood River Valley.

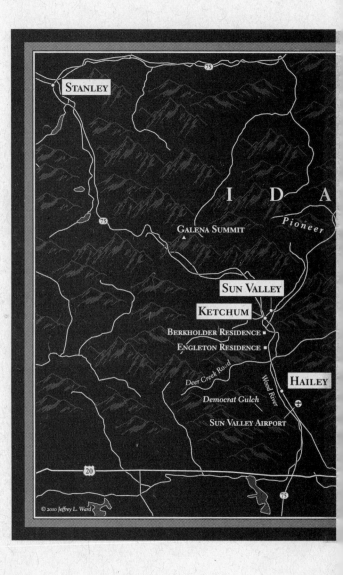

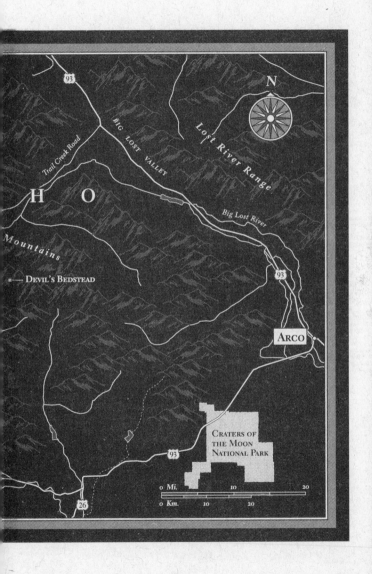

N

Lost River Range

Big Lost Valley

Trail Creek Road

Big Lost River

H O

Mountains

■— Devil's Bedstead

Arco

Craters of
the Moon
National Park

o Mi.   10   20

o Km.   10   20

IN
HARM'S
WAY

1

Glancing out the windshield and beyond the four-lane concrete bridge, Fiona spotted a log with flailing arms. Human arms. A child's arms, struggling up through the river's rushing water, held down by a tangle of branches.

Fiona instinctively reached out to block her passenger from hitting the dash while simultaneously slamming on the brakes. Her Subaru skidded, drifting into the breakdown lane just past the bridge. She set the emergency brake and released her seat belt in a single motion, her feet already on the asphalt. She crossed four lanes of busy traffic amid a flurry of horns and the high-pitched cries of biting rubber.

Over it all, she heard her passenger, Kira, calling out her name and she glanced back to see Kira hoisting her camera bag high in the air. Fiona gestured her back, but Kira ignored it and pressed forward, darting through gaps in the traffic. More tire squeals. A man crudely cursed from his black pickup as he avoided Kira by inches, careening off the roadway and onto the dirt shoulder, throwing up twin rooster tails.

Fiona ignored him, scampering down the bank, and waded into the shallow, painfully cold water at the river's edge. The fist-sized, slippery round stones of the river bottom made her look drunk as she charged into the more swiftly moving, knee-deep water. She glanced left, timing the approach of the floating logs, preparing to dive.

The limbs of the first of four logs struck her, knocking her off balance, and she fell. They scraped across her back, tearing her shirt and dragging her down under. She struggled out of the grasp of the tangled branches and gasped for air as she resurfaced. Finding her balance, she dodged the next log. And the next.

Barreling toward her came the final tree: the one with the human arms she'd seen upstream. It bore down on her, a tongue of torn wood aimed like a lance.

She no longer saw the arms thrashing. For an instant, she wondered if she'd seen them at all.

The approaching tree was well over a foot thick and likely weighed hundreds of pounds. Driven by the force of June runoff, it would hit her like a battering ram.

Kira, now at river's edge, again screamed, "F-i-o-n-a! No!"

From the same direction, Fiona heard a splash—the driver of the pickup now thundering out toward her.

The wide spread of pine boughs seemed aimed to sweep her off her feet once again. Distracted, she'd lost her chance to move out of the way. She counted down in her head . . .

Ten yards . . . five yards . . .

She drew a lungful of air and dove the four feet to the river bottom. Reached out and white-knuckled a mossy, large flat rock, keeping herself down. The limbs broomed over her, snagging her hair and yanking her head up and back. A chunk of hair tore loose. She screamed bubbles. Most of her shirt was torn off. She one-handed the rock, protecting her face as the remaining limbs scraped raw the flesh of her forearm.

In her blurred vision appeared a child's pale bare foot. Fiona let go of the rock, grabbed the ankle with both hands and followed up the leg to the child's waist, planting her feet in the maze of rocks on the river bottom and propelling herself up out of the water and into the snarl of tree branches. The tree limbs whipped and dug into her arms and face, demanding she release the child, but she would not let go.

At last, the tree passed and Fiona opened her eyes to see a little girl's terrified eyes gazing back at her. The girl blinked and coughed and Fiona felt tears spring to her eyes. *Alive!* The driver of the pickup appeared, lunging through the coursing water and extending an arm to Fiona, who held on to the crying child like life itself.

A smattering of applause arose from a small gathering of onlookers with their camera phones extended, all of whom had pulled to the side of the road to help. Behind them towered the greening mountains that surrounded Ketchum and Sun Valley, above them the azure sky that had helped name this place.

Fiona held the child high in an effort to screen her own face, hoping to keep herself out of sight of the cameras.

The girl's crying was steady now—a joyous sound. As Fiona briefly lost her balance to the uneven river bottom, the girl clutched her with an unexpected force.

"I won't let go," Fiona promised.

In the distance a siren wailed, an ambulance from St. Luke's Hospital less than a mile away. Someone had called 911. More applause as the pickup driver led her to dry ground and Fiona dropped to her knees, never relaxing her embrace of the child, who in turn pressed herself closer to her rescuer.

"You're okay. You're okay," Fiona whispered into the matted hair, as a dozen people rushed down the embankment and the pickup driver called out to give them room.

More cameras fired off shots, including her own, currently in Kira's hands. Too many cameras to ever control. She could imagine the images already being sent over the Internet. One moment, anonymous in a sleepy Idaho town. The next . . . out there.

Helpless to do anything about it, she understood that this moment represented the saving of one life and quite possibly the loss of another: her own.

2

Walt Fleming entered St. Luke's emergency room to the stares his sheriff's uniform typically provoked. Reaction was never neutral, and it affected him, to varying degrees. People were both afraid of and impressed by police. Everyone was guilty of some infraction, no matter how minor; it came down to how much of it they wore on their sleeves.

"Kenshaw!" he barked at the nurse behind the registration desk, never slowing a step. Despite his concern for the well-being of the child fished from the Big Wood River, he was impatient and tense about the condition of the child's rescuer.

"Observation two!" the nurse called down the hall after him.

The walls were beige, the ceiling lighting intense, the

complex aroma—medicinal disinfectant, bitter coffee—vaguely nauseating. He ran, did not walk, to Observation 2. He yanked back the privacy curtain, not waiting for permission.

"Oh, damn!" he barked out unintentionally upon seeing her. He stepped inside and drew the curtain closed behind him.

A nurse tending to an IV bag turned and was about to let loose on the intruder when sight of the uniform stopped her.

"Leave us a minute," Walt told the nurse as he met eyes with Fiona.

"I'm fine," Fiona said.

"Yeah, I can see that." She looked horrible.

The nurse gave Walt the once-over on her way out. She clearly had some choice words to offer, but contained herself.

Fiona wore a blue and white hospital gown—a loosely woven yellow blanket covered her from the waist down. Her face and arms were badly scratched, both carrying some butterfly bandages. Her scalp had been shaved in a spot about the size of a quarter over her left ear and was dressed with a small bandage. On her upper left shoulder he saw the glow of a bruise forming.

"They took some X-rays," she said, "against my better judgment. I really am fine. It's nothing. I realize I must look like hell, and you have no right to be—"

"You look good," he said. He'd rarely paid her any

kind of compliment about her looks. It hung in the air uncomfortably. "Alive is good," he added. Fiona would never win any beauty contests, but in his opinion she'd turn heads decades into the future. Her kind of tomboyish looks didn't need a surgeon's knife to remain interesting. She changed her looks frequently, using ball caps or haircuts. It was impossible to pin down her age, but she was over twenty-eight and under thirty-five if he was any judge. She took a lot of sun from her hours as a fishing guide, but she wore it well, not leathery the way some of the Ketchum women aged. In a strange way, her wounds added to her attractiveness, as if mystery were all she'd ever lacked.

"Given the options."

"What'd you do, fight a bear to get to her?"

"A fir tree, I think it was. Lots of nasty branches."

"That kind of goes hand in hand where trees are concerned—the branches thing. I heard the kid's fine."

"So I'm told."

"You're a hero."

"I may need your help with that," she said. "Sit."

Walt drew a rolling stool up to the side of the bed and rested his hands on the bed's stainless steel frame. He'd been reaching for her hand, but stopped himself.

She took his hand in hers, stretching the IV to do so. "Is this what you wanted?"

"Yeah." He absentmindedly glanced toward the pulled curtain.

She let go of his hand. "It's all right," she said, sensing his reluctance and misinterpreting it as embarrassment.

He regretted losing her touch, regretted having looked behind him, regretted that he couldn't see a few seconds ahead to know when to keep from doing something stupid.

"The IV," she said, following his eyes, "is nothing but a precaution. They have to charge you for something."

"The department's insurance will cover it."

"Nonsense," she said. "I wasn't on the job."

"You're always on the job."

"I'm a civilian employee—part time at that—who serves at the pleasure of the sheriff. That doesn't come with benefits, last I looked."

"Well, you didn't look carefully enough. You serve at my pleasure, and it's my pleasure that our policy will cover it. Have you ever seen the bill from an emergency room visit?"

"I'll withhold my objections until I know what we're talking about."

"That's better."

"So the 'Oh, damn'? Was that for my face?"

"General condition," he said. "The hospital gown. Lying there like that. Your face . . . I like your face. No complaints."

"The doctor said it won't scar. Some will heal faster than others, but they're nothing to worry about."

"You saved a life," he said.

"I need you to go to bat for me."

"Regarding?"

"Pam."

Pam was Fiona's other boss, the editor/owner of the *Mountain Express*, Ketchum/Sun Valley's weekly.

"Because?"

"There were a lot of people taking pictures."

"Heroic moments tend to get that."

"I don't want my picture to run."

"I doubt you'll have any say in the matter. For once your modesty, the way you stalk about, is going to lose out to the needs of the masses. Pam will run it on the front page, I would think."

"She can't," Fiona said defiantly.

"But she will, no matter how much you object."

"It's a giveaway. The front page hardly matters."

"A good front page, the more copies you give away, the more you can charge for your ads next time."

"Whose side are you on? I need you, Walt."

"It's false modesty: you saved a life."

"My picture cannot run in that paper." Her tone and demeanor had changed. The physical pain and shock behind her eyes had given way to anger.

"O . . . k . . . a . . . y. Maybe we should talk about this."

"I can't. That's not going to happen. I just need you to speak with her, to convince her."

"And you need me to do this because . . . ?"

"Because I'm her employee. I'm your employee. Employer to employer, I need you to talk to her and make up anything you want, any reason you want, just make sure no photo runs."

"If you were trying to win my curiosity, you've succeeded," he said. "What the hell is going on?"

She seemed ready to tell him something, but couldn't bring herself to do it.

"Talk to me," he said, his own voice now sharing her concern. He caught a glimpse of himself in one of the stainless steel fixtures. He had a wide face, slightly boyish, with kind eyes. His hair was short and graying prematurely. His ex-wife had once advised him to use "product" on his hair, but he'd resisted. He was suddenly revisiting that idea.

"I need you to convince her not to run any photos. I'm a civilian employee of your office—part time—and you want to protect my privacy. Make up anything you like."

"There's a little thing called freedom of the press."

"Which is why it can't come from me. From you it carries a lot more weight."

"My office can't make that kind of request without being able to back it up. I've never made such a request. And there have been plenty of times I didn't want a photo to run. We've blacked out eyes a few times. I could ask her for that—but I'd have to have a reason."

"That'll just cause more of a sensation," Fiona said. "That's worse than just running a picture."

"You're not giving me a lot of options here."

"Can't I get a favor with no strings attached? Please. Ask her not to run my picture."

Something had been nagging at Walt that now made a world of sense. Again, he voiced it without taking proper time to think through the consequences.

"This paranoia of yours . . . It doesn't happen to have anything to do with your always being on the other end of the camera, does it?" Her eyes grew intense. If what he'd seen a few seconds before was anger, this was now rage. "You take the pictures to make sure no one takes them of you? Is that it? Could that be any more insidious?"

"Please, stop," she said.

The nurse knocked on the frame. "I'm coming in there," she announced.

"I'll talk to her about it," Walt said, amazed by the relief that washed over Fiona's wounded face, and the warmth of her hand as she once again touched his.

3

Beatrice, Walt's three-year-old Irish spaniel, drooled onto Fiona's face on the front page of the *Mountain Express*, and then turned to lick Walt, who remained trapped behind the wheel of the Jeep. Walt pushed her into the backseat and told her to stay. He brushed the drool off the newspaper, but too late: Fiona, carrying the half-drowned child from the river, now had a teardrop beard that ran to her waist.

He pulled the Jeep Cherokee into the driveway behind his deputy's cruiser. The call of a bear attack had come in thirty minutes earlier. The property owner's insurance would want the police to sign off on the cause of the damage—it wasn't the first time for Walt. Garbage cans or vehicles with windows down were the most common targets of a wayward bear; rarely did the bear actually break into a kitchen and shred the place. This, Walt had to see.

Fiona's Subaru was parked beneath a portable basketball backboard. She'd been called in to document the damage. Sprinklers ran in the front yard, creating a haze behind which the densely green mountains rose magnificently. Every view here was worthy of a postcard.

The Berkholder residence, a 9,000-square-foot stucco home, occupied the back corner of a five-acre parcel at the end of a quarter-mile semiprivate drive. Their only neighbors—the Engletons—lived a half mile away. Fiona, who served as the Engletons' caretaker, lived in their guesthouse, meaning she could have walked over here.

He tossed the *Mountain Express* onto the car floor, annoyed by the reminder of his own failed attempt to keep Fiona's picture from appearing in it. He feared there would be hell to pay.

He cracked a window for Beatrice, told her to stay, and climbed out, in no great hurry to reach the front door. Thankfully his phone rang, stopping him alongside the *chick, chick, chick* of the sprinkler guns.

He instantly recognized the caller's number.

"Dad?"

"You don't have to sound so surprised."

"Pleasantly surprised is more like it. It's been a while, is all."

"Has it? I suppose it has. Honestly, I don't remember."

That's the point.

"To what do I owe . . . ?" Walt said.

"I've been approached as an intermediary, I suppose you could say. A detective with Crimes Against Persons, over here in Seattle. The guy knew I was your father and got hold of me through a mutual friend, Brent Staffer, a Bureau buddy of mine."

"Okay." Jerry never failed to remind his son he'd been a special agent for the FBI and that Walt had missed his own chance to serve a higher calling. He was also fond of reminding his son that he read the local Ketchum paper, tracked the stories involving Walt's department, and liked to rub it in when those jobs involved clearing a band of sheep from the highway or serving motorcade duty for a rock star on a weekend ski trip.

"He's trying to keep things low profile, very low profile, because of the personalities involved. Doesn't want so much as the record of a phone call. You get the point."

"I do." Walt dealt with plenty of the rich and famous—more than his father knew.

"He could call you on your cell number or maybe your home. He'd rather not call the shop. I mentioned that I knew you used that Internet thing—"

"Skype."

"That's the one. Said he could do it that way if you wanted."

"Did he say what it's about?"

"It's a homicide. He's a homicide dick. Boldt. We've talked about him before."

"We have," Walt said. In the world of homicide, Lou Boldt was a living legend—able to leap tall buildings in a single bound. He had a career clearance rate of eighty percent when the nearest competition was in the mid-sixties. He'd not only caught the Cross Killer, but the serial killer's copycat. Just the idea of speaking with Lou Boldt excited him—being involved with a case of Boldt's would be rare air.

"I'd be happy to speak with him," Walt said.

"Thought that was how you'd feel, but didn't want to put words into your mouth."

That's a first.

"I'm pretty sure I know the homicide," Jerry Fleming said. "Just guessing, but there's one been in the *Intelligencer* off and on for a week now. Makes sense that Boldt would have caught it. Woman assaulted. Beaten to death. Nothing sexual—at least not that's been reported. Reason it stays in the papers is both because of the beating she took—it was really bad, Walt—and because she had a history of dating people in professional sports."

"A call girl?"

"That's almost how it reads, but no, I don't think so. I'm sure Boldt can tell you. Dating, as in living with a guy for a few months. Basketball, football. Didn't seem to matter. She liked 'em big and strong. Liked the cameras and nightclubs. Papers rumored an affair with one of the team owners, but backed off it pretty quickly. She obviously got around. And then she gets herself pulverized, and of course everyone's thinking it's one of the jocks. That kind of testosterone-charged hammering those bucks can deliver."

"But me?" Walt asked.

"I don't know. I was asked if you'd take the call. If you'd keep it quiet. And I told him how I was sure you would but I'd ask."

"Absolutely," Walt said.

"That's all I needed."

"How are you?" Walt asked.

"I'll give him the green light and you can take it from there. Maybe this Skype thing keeps it the quietest."

"He can call me tonight. I'll leave it up. But how are you, Dad? How's it going?"

"He's an important man over here. You know that, right?"

"I know that," Walt said. He wasn't going to ask again; his father knew as much.

"Let me know if I can help out with it," Jerry said.

The line clicked.

"Dad?" Walt looked at the face of his phone: *Disconnected*.

No kidding, he was thinking, as he pocketed the phone.

Walt knocked and let himself in through the front door. A camera's flash caught his eye and he moved in that direction through a living room atop a spongy carpet. The Asian furniture contrasted with big canvases of contemporary art. He headed toward the strobing light with his father's description of the assault in his mind, half expecting to see a bloodied body beaten to a pulp on the kitchen floor though his conscious mind knew better—it had been called in as a bear attack. He was there to sign off on that assessment for the sake of any future insurance inquiry. Springtime brought the brown bears out of hibernation. They came down to the valley floor looking for water and were typically seduced by the aroma of garbage cans.

Walt whistled, seeing the extent of the damage.

Fiona glanced in his direction, but her eyes hardened and she went right back to her photography. He wanted to sort out their problems, but kept to business, heading over to deputy Tommy Brandon, who was on the phone.

Brandon hung up immediately. He wore XXL everything, a ten-hour beard that would have taken Walt six days to grow, and a smugness that came with being the go-to guy his whole life. Walt wasn't sure when Brandon's affair with his wife had begun, only that because of it Brandon owed him something beyond the apology he'd never gotten. Gail owed him attorneys' fees, by his way of thinking, but he'd never see anything. She owed their twin eleven-year-old daughters much more, but that would have to wait until the girls were older and realized the depth and degree of their mother's selfishness. For now, business as usual.

"So?" he asked Brandon.

"Picnic time at the Berkholders'," Brandon answered.

The kitchen cabinets hung open, their contents strewn across the countertops: cookies, coffee grounds, tea bags, crackers, broken jars, tomato sauce, jams, pickles—an extraordinary mess. The refrigerator hung partially open, with a slushy pile of leftovers, vegetables, and meats at its feet, as if it had vomited its contents onto the reclaimed barn wood flooring. The freezer oozed frozen lemonade, orange juice, and ice cream in a colorful creamy waterfall that caught each glass shelf.

Walt was no stranger to bear raids. His father ridiculed him for his responding to them as part of his job.

"Did you get the claw marks on—"

"Yes!" Fiona snapped, still refusing to look directly at him. "On the cabinets and the butcher block, both."

"The spill beneath the fridge?"

"Got it," she answered.

"Just for the record," Walt said, "I lobbied her hard. I thought I'd made—"

"Not hard enough," Fiona said.

Bewildered by the exchange, Brandon tried to slip away but Walt caught him.

"Access?" Walt asked his deputy.

Brandon led Walt down a short hallway to a four-car garage.

"Musta been left open, though the owner claims otherwise. Looks like the thing checked out the dog door"—the frame of the dog door had imploded into the hallway—"and maybe the door came open in the process. We found it like this."

Walt studied the door jamb, especially its metal hardware, and then did the same on the broken dog door. He looked into the whistle-clean garage—about the size of the first floor of his house—and its ship-deck-gray paint. He descended the three steps and went down on one knee, getting the light right.

"If she hasn't done so already," he said, "have Fiona get shots of the door hardware and some angles of the garage floor."

"Will do. But why does the insurance care about the garage floor?" Brandon asked.

"You ever been to one of these before?" Walt said.

"Sure."

"Open your eyes and use—"

"Your head," Brandon finished for him, quoting a Walt-ism.

"Exactly."

Brandon studied the door hardware and didn't have the courage to ask what he was supposed to be looking for.

"Fur," Walt said without looking back as he kept to the very edge of the garage floor. "Animal hair. A tight space like that dog door, we should have seen some caught in the screws or hinges."

He worked steadily toward the garage doors.

"Yeah, okay . . ." Tommy sounded confused.

"When was the last time you saw a bear pass over strawberry jam, broken glass jar or not?"

"Ah . . ."

"And since when doesn't a bear claw a door trying to get it open? It claws the cabinet—in the middle of the cabinet—but not the door?"

"But there *are* claw marks," Brandon protested.

"Check out the size of them," Walt said. "A bear that big doesn't tiptoe through a door. And he doesn't go through all the food and get back out without leaving tracks." Walt indicated the clean garage floor. "A flying bear, maybe?"

"Okay?" Brandon sounded unconvinced.

"Let's work the evidence," Walt said. "Chances are this was a two-legged bear."

"A *what*?"

"And I'd like to know why he went to all this trouble."

4

With his suit jacket waiting for him on the back of a chair inside the house, and a Seattle Seahawks apron protecting his shirt and tie, Walt pulled the barbecued pork loin off the grill, Beatrice drooling at his feet. It had been a long, poisonously quiet week. He expected to see Fiona later that night.

"I don't want dead pig," Emily said, her arms crossed, her eleven-year-old's face locked in determination.

"Don't do this," Walt said, collecting his wares onto the cutting board. "This is your dinner. You like bacon, don't you?"

"Yeah."

"Bacon is pork, same as this."

"Then why can't I have bacon?"

"It's the *same thing*," sister Nikki said.

"Because this is what I cooked for dinner," Walt answered. "I thought you'd like it. It's your favorite."

"Is not."

"I like it," Nikki said.

"You don't have to eat it, Em. But no ice cream with Lisa if you don't eat your dinner."

"That's not fair."

Nikki rolled her eyes. She didn't understand her sister any more than Walt did.

"It is what it is: no dinner, no ice cream. I had planned for the three of you to bike over to Fifteen Flavors. If you'd rather not . . . ?"

He managed to kick open the door while carrying the board. Beatrice, Emily, and Nikki followed, in that order.

Lisa charged through the front door, apologizing for being late. Walt conferred with her about the evening's rules, including bedtime and the ice-cream trip, all unnecessary since Lisa knew more about the girls' routine than he did.

"You look fancy," she said, as he got the apron off and the jacket on.

"My one and only suit."

"It suits you."

"Ha, ha. It's the Advocates dinner. Very swishy."

He hugged his daughters good night, getting barely anything out of Emily, and heaved a sigh as he closed the front door behind him. An early summer evening was a piece of heaven in Hailey, and this one was no exception. The sun tracked surprisingly high in the sky for seven p.m., skirting the tops of the valley's western mountains, its golden light taking on a magical, ethereal quality. Neighborhood lawn sprinklers ticked, the smell of burning charcoal hung in the air. Some kids rode by in a pack of speeding bicycles.

As he drove north, Walt composed something to say to Fiona, something to try to break the ice. She'd sent him an e-mail with photographs of the bear damage—no message. He'd called twice on the pretense of a follow-up, but she'd failed to call back. It wasn't the first time Fiona had gone off-grid—she occasionally disappeared for days at a time, unreachable, unpredictable—but this time it felt personal.

Sun Valley's Limelight Room, located in the Sun Valley Inn, was a four-star convention hall that had recently undergone a multimillion-dollar renovation. It was filled with lavishly appointed tables for three hundred dinner guests, a low stage, and a lectern. Two projection screens displayed PowerPoint slide shows of women at work, mixed with bullet lists of the accomplishments of the nonprofit established to support the battered and abused. Each table of ten had a sponsor. Walt was the guest of a retired general who, thankfully, had picked up the tab for the entire table. Fiona sat to Walt's left, with Kira Tulivich next to Fiona. Twenty-one-year-old Kira, adorable and gorgeous in a summer dress, had been the victim of

a savage assault two years earlier, and an important witness for Walt. Scheduled to give one of the evening's two
keynote addresses, Kira looked both nervous and out of
sorts as she studied the cutlery and tried to decide which
fork to use.

Walt elbowed Fiona in the ribs and gestured for her
to rescue her charge. Fiona directed Kira to the outside
fork and relief washed over the young woman's face.

"Thank you," Fiona whispered.

"Nice to hear your voice," Walt said, between bites.

"We can discuss this later," she said.

"But we won't, will we? Because you won't return my
calls."

"Later."

"I fought hard for you. Not hard enough, I know—
you told me that—but as hard as I dared. As sheriff . . . I
explained my delicate relationship with the paper." He ate
some more salad and watched her move hers around the
plate. "You never did tell me why it mattered so much.
The way you've treated me, I assume it was more than just
modesty or vanity. But for the life of me, I can't figure it
out."

"For the life of you, no," she said.

"But if it was so important—"

"What's done is done," she said, cutting him off.

"Doesn't feel that way."

"No, it doesn't, does it?"

"Why so angry?"

"Am I? I don't mean to be. Seriously. It's not with you."

"Of course it is."

"Not meant to be."

"I don't believe that," he said.

He looked up. Every face at the table was looking at them, listening to them. The others immediately returned to their food and they faked conversation, but Walt realized they'd all heard every word. Given the other guests at the table, it meant that most of the valley would know, word for word, everything said. It was the blessing and the curse of the Wood River Valley, and something that all residents willingly suffered as a trade-off to the lifestyle.

During the entrée, Fiona coached Kira on her talk, and finally the moment arrived when Kira was introduced.

"We are so grateful to have with us tonight," the evening's host began, "a young woman of extraordinary courage, poise, and intelligence. Kira Tulivich turned to Advocates following an ordeal that not only tested her own will to live, but resulted in the apprehension of domestic terrorists by our own Sheriff Walt Fleming, and put an end to a terrorist cell operating within our state. Hers is a story of strength, determination, and recovery, and we are honored to hear from her tonight. Won't you please join me in welcoming . . ."

Her formal introduction was overpowered by the thunderous applause as the guests spontaneously rose to their feet. Kira's story was already well known. This was her first public appearance since the incident, and the applause carried her from the table to the lectern, some of the women openly weeping. It took her three tries to quiet the crowd. Finally people sat. Kira cleared her throat with a sip of water and began her short and emotional speech.

Halfway through the speech, Walt felt fingernails scratching at his fist beneath the skirt of the tablecloth as Fiona's hand found its way into his. He looked over at her, but she never took her watery eyes off the stage. He missed the rest of the talk, his mind racing and unable to light on any single thought except that life brought unexpected pleasures and made it worth getting up in the morning. For the first time at such an event, he hoped the keynote speech would go on for hours.

Fiona withdrew her hand from his and grabbed her mobile phone, vibrating from within her purse. As she went to stop it, he saw her eyes light upon the screen and consternation grip her face. She slipped the phone back into her purse but their connection was gone. She didn't even seem to be hearing Kira's speech.

"You okay?" he whispered.

She looked at him, attempting, but failing, to wipe the crease from her brow. She nodded.

Kira said from the lectern, "I think the main thing I want to say is thanks to the Advocates. The physical healing was the easy part, as it turned out, but the—"

She stopped abruptly, locked in a stare.

Walt turned back, following her line of sight to one of

the hall's two center doors, just closing. His sheriff's instinct was to jump up and hurry into the hallway to see who was out there. But he kept to his seat.

Kira then searched and her eyes found Fiona, who nodded back at her reassuringly. Some heads turned in the direction of their table. Kira's eyes finally fell back to her notes and she continued speaking.

"But the emotional healing, the *real* healing," she continued, "well . . . it really does take a village."

Walt turned and reached out to both reassure and congratulate Fiona for her mentoring of the girl, but the chair stood empty, Fiona gone.

Eyes darting around the room, assuming Fiona had gone up to greet Kira as she left the stage, he found his vision blocked as an appreciative audience rose to its feet. Walt stood, tempted to climb up onto his chair, cursing his five-foot-seven frame.

Instead, he seized the moment, ducking out into the hallway, moving toward the restrooms—thinking Fiona might have gone there—but then, upon seeing a pair of bellmen outside, approached them.

"A woman?" Walt inquired. "Cream-colored top. Black purse. Maybe left just now."

"Didn't see her."

"Don't I know you?" the other bellman asked.

Walt ignored it, wondering if the kid had been in trouble or just knew his picture from the local paper. "How about a guy?" Walt said.

"Big guy? Yeah," said the first bellman.

A couple came out—the exodus was under way—and the guest handed the second boy his valet claim stub. The kid took off at a run.

"Yes, the big guy," Walt said, trying to hold the other boy's attention. The rush of people wanting their cars was suffocating. Walt presented his sheriff's shield, held down low. The boy caught sight of it. "The big guy," he repeated.

"Came and went. Wasn't inside more than, like, two minutes."

"How big?"

"Solid Snake," said the kid. "You know, Metal Gear, Sons of Liberty?" Reading Walt's bewilderment, he added, "PSP? Gaming?"

"Uhh."

"Huge, stupid huge. Ridiculous." A valet stub stabbed at the kid and he accepted it. "Sorry," he said to Walt. He took off.

Walt fought up-current against the departing guests and reentered the half-empty conference hall. He located his host and thanked him. He made his way toward the stage and awaited his turn with Kira.

"You seen Fiona?" Kira asked him immediately. Guests broke in, congratulating her. She shook hands with several of them. Walt wanted a private moment with her but wasn't going to get it.

"Restroom," he said. It was the only explanation that made any sense; Fiona wasn't leaving Kira in the lurch.

"You paused," he said. "You were looking toward the doors."

She shook her head as if by doing so she might convince him it hadn't happened.

"Please," he said.

"Roy Coats," she said, lowering her voice and naming the man who had raped her, a man Walt had watched die. "Just a flashback. They still happen. Why it had to be right then . . . but I suppose it was because I was talking about it. I don't talk about it much."

"Did he look like Coats?" Walt asked.

"No," Kira answered. "It *was* him."

"Ms. Tulivich . . . Kira?" A woman wearing too much perfume pushed in front of Walt and he lost his moment.

He turned and looked back toward the center doors, imagining how it must have felt for her to see an image of Roy Coats listening in on her recovery speech. He lived with his own demons: memories of bloody murder scenes he couldn't shake, traffic accidents, his killing a man in the backcountry, an incident with his father when he'd been nine years old. Things he didn't talk about. He envied her ability to talk to counselors, to free the demons, to break the silence of those terrors.

People milled around him and for a moment it was almost as if he wasn't there. He might have been a table or chair they were dodging. He'd internalized, he'd sunk beneath the surface and was kicking like mad to reach the air above.

Fiona wasn't returning; he knew it without checking for her. He couldn't imagine what would have taken her out of the room at that, of all moments. She had practically adopted Kira, had installed her into the Engletons' main house as her associate caretaker. Abandoning her in the last few lines of her talk seemed impossible. Unthinkable.

Or, he wondered, had Fiona also seen whoever had been at the back of the room?

He reached for his phone and called her. It jumped straight to voice mail—the phone was turned off.

He had a vision of her reacting to whatever message she'd read on her phone. Had the message—some kind of personal emergency—caused her to leave? Should he stop by her place on his way home? Or was that overstepping his bounds, given that she'd shut off her phone?

He slowed the Jeep at the highway entrance to the private road leading to the Engleton and Berkholder properties. He didn't need an excuse to check up on her, but she was also a woman who appreciated her space, and in the end he gave it to her, reluctantly.

Tie loosened, his suit coat slung over the back of a dining-room chair, Walt enabled the Skype software as he had for each of the past eight evenings and then checked on the girls.

He found Lisa asleep atop Nikki's bedcovers, a book in her lap. In her late thirties, Lisa still had the look of a woman much younger, and the energy to go with it.

Catching her in a catnap was a rarity. He gently shook her awake, the intimacy of the moment not escaping him. He hadn't felt the warmth of a sleeping woman in a very long time.

Walt nearly gave Nikki a goodnight kiss, but decided against it as she was such a light sleeper. He turned around and instead planted a kiss onto Emily's cheek. She could sleep through an earthquake. Lisa hopped up and adjusted the blinds and shut the door as they left together.

"Any problems?" Walt asked.

"Smooth as silk."

"Did Nikki say anything about Gail?"

"Didn't mention her. Not to me."

That was a first. Nikki was obsessed with using their marriage separation as an excuse. "Then you should be around more often," he said, realizing too late a man didn't say that to a happily married woman.

"It takes time."

"They'll never get over it. Nikki, she may not even get *past* it."

"Sure she will."

"Maybe Em's hiding it all, but she doesn't seem affected. She's moved on, I think."

"Nikki's the one to watch, for sure. What's the schedule this week?"

"There's a city council thing on Wednesday," he said, "and a Search and Rescue exercise on Thursday. A Chamber event on Friday night that I'm hoping to duck."

"Wednesday and Thursday are no problem and I'll keep Friday open just in case." She paused. "Listen, Walt, I have a favor to ask."

"Name it," he said.

"It's a big favor," she cautioned.

"Let me be the judge of that," he said.

"My neighbor's daughter. She's fifteen. Eight weeks pregnant. She's blaming it, or attributing it, or whatever, to her boyfriend. I don't know the boy, but I've seen him and he looks like a decent kid."

"It happens. Do you want to make sure he steps up?" Walt offered.

He wasn't familiar with the look on her face. She'd been helping with the girls since just after their birth, well before the separation. She'd learned to read his moods, knew when to keep her distance, when to try to get him talking; he'd learned that nothing ruffled Lisa, that she was one of those people who moved from good to better and back to good. She didn't complain. She didn't back down. But somehow she kept herself and everyone around her on an even keel. Her current expression of perplexity, concern, and fear was something new to him.

"Or maybe not," he said, when she failed to speak.

"I think it's the stepfather's." She wouldn't meet his eyes, her vision locked onto his neck.

"Oh . . . damn."

Lisa nodded gravely. "We have cats," she said, as if that explained something. "One of them . . . this is a long time ago . . . last summer sometime . . . wouldn't come in one night, and I spotted her next door and went over to get her. It was very late. Well past midnight. I heard the girl . . . her voice for sure, not her mother's . . . *engaged*? Is that how you put it? In the act, and not happy about it. My kitty was under that window, as if she . . . as if that voice, that girl's voice wouldn't let her leave. I didn't mean to stay. I wanted to pick up Clawsy and get out of there, but something wouldn't let me leave. Not voyeuristic! I don't mean that. But a need to help. He covered her cries. Tried to keep her voice down. Don't look at me like that: a woman knows the difference, believe me. I couldn't see in the window, and the curtain was pulled. But in between her sobs—*rhythmic* sobs—a hand smacked up onto the glass. A big hand. A man's hand. A hand wearing a wedding ring. It was not the hand of an eighteen-year-old boy."

The look had not left her face, but her eyes had teared up and presently she pursed her lips and dried her eyes on her shoulders.

"And she's blaming the boyfriend," he said.

"So two lives go down the drain, and the one that should, walks away. There's a nine-year-old sister. And a five-year-old after her. He's got them lined up, Walt. He's got himself taken care of for a long time."

"A paternity test would do it," he said.

"As if he'd ever allow that to happen."

"There are ways," Walt said.

"I haven't wanted to ask you, but there's a point where—"

"Don't be ridiculous. It would be criminal not to act."

"That's eventually what I came around to."

"Write down the names for me. I'll see what I can do."

He led her toward the dining room from where an unfamiliar chirping noise was coming.

"You're getting a call," Lisa said. "Skype. We have an account, too." She hurried to the room and pointed out a window on his computer screen. "You want to answer it?"

"Please," he said.

She clicked the mouse, scribbled down two names, and waved good-bye as she let herself out the back door.

The window on the computer's screen showed a big face, severe and intense with wide eyes and a 1950s flat-top haircut going gray. The face reminded Walt of a home plate umpire.

"Lou Boldt." The voice was not as gruff as Walt expected from such a face. Low, but soft-spoken.

"Walt Fleming. Good to meet you."

"Thanks for letting me give you a shout."

"No problem."

"I have a situation here."

"My father gave me the Cliffs Notes."

"The deceased's name is Caroline Vetta. Twenty-nine." Boldt ran through what he knew of the homicide and the deceased's connection to prominent Seattle sports figures.

"How can I help?"

"This girl was beat up badly. A person can make the

case that it's a crime of passion. That's why the lid is on it, because she was friendly with some very high rollers, and no one wants any false accusations made."

"Tricky for you."

"Yes, it is. Hard to get an interview with these guys without nine lawyers involved. The media gets hold of it and it's going to look like we've got a suspect. And we don't need that."

"Would you like me to interview someone? Is that it? Someone over here?" Walt sensed Boldt wasn't going to ask him outright; Walt was going to have to offer. "Is there a connection to my county?"

"Two connections," Boldt said. "And, to answer your question, no, I wouldn't dump that on you. The first guy is Marty Boatwright."

Walt took a deep breath. "Oh," he said.

"Owned the Seahawks until the sale eight years ago. Met Caroline when she was twenty-two. Some say that acquaintance continued until a few months ago."

"Don't know him personally. Have worked with his people some. He's generous in the community over here. Throws the kind of parties that sheiks and kings attend."

"Can you get to him?"

"Maybe. I know his head of security."

"The second is Vince Wynn."

"The sports agent? He has a place here?"

"I thought everyone had a place there," Boldt said. When he laughed, it was a big laugh, and the webcam shook. His image danced on the screen. "What is that nickname for Sun Valley?"

"Glitter Gulch," Walt said.

"That's the one."

"Wynn can't spend much time here. Didn't he just sign that pitcher to the Mets?"

"Four years, a hundred mil. And Wynn gets a pile of that for a few phone calls and dinners? I'd take it."

"And he got a piece of Caroline?" Walt asked.

"He was here in Seattle the night it went down. He entertained some clients at a club. She dated one— maybe more than one—of his football clients. Supposedly that's how they met, and maybe she worked her way up the food chain. This woman . . . my guess is we're going to find out there was commerce involved. A courier? A call girl? I don't know yet, but the way she moved around between these people . . . It's complicated. It's not normal, even in these circles. As to what the nature of this call is," Boldt said, "I'm thinking . . . my brass is thinking . . . that we could do this . . . I could do this . . . a lot quieter if it was done over there. It being your jurisdiction, I didn't want to wander in uninvited. And they don't want me making the first contact because we've got a leak here in my department we can't seem to find, much less plug."

"So I make the contact and set up an interview and you do it over here," Walt said.

"Over a weekend, maybe. Downtime. We have three TV news crews on us, basically twenty-four/seven, and a half dozen from radio, and both papers. Last I knew, all you had over there was a weekly. I could pretty much come and go as I please, which is not the case here."

"Works for me," Walt said.

"I don't want to make trouble for you."

"Open invitation," Walt said. "I can make the inquiries."

"The point being that these individuals would want this done as quietly as we do. It wouldn't even be low profile, it's *no profile* if they're willing."

"They should be all over that."

"That's what we're thinking."

"Consider it done."

"I owe you one."

"Not yet you don't."

"Thanks just the same."

"Leave this thing on in the evenings. When I know something, I'll ring you back."

"Freaking amazing technology, you ask me," Boldt said. "I thought slide rules were impressive." He moved even closer to the webcam, distorting his face while trying to work the keyboard. "Thanks again."

"No problem."

The window went black.

Walt tipped back in the chair. His father had condemned him for years for accepting the sheriff's office of a small Idaho county, had teased him unmercifully that his cases were about bears tipping over garbage cans while real law enforcement solved real crimes. And here he was, one week past what had the appearance of a bear raiding a kitchen, and a few minutes past a phone call with a legendary homicide cop dealing with a major crime. He hadn't realized how sweet vindication could taste.

5

Fiona picked a piece of popcorn off the leg of her paja-mas and popped it into her mouth. Her feet tucked to the side, she occupied the right side of the couch next to Kira, who wore an afghan over her shoulders. The Engletons' high-definition projector threw a six-by-six-foot image onto a screen that came down from the ceil-ing, making Meryl Streep's head about four feet tall.

"I've seen this at least three times," Fiona said, between bites.

"I love the last scene, when she's in the car and her eyes and her smile tell you everything that's going on and then she tells the driver to go."

"The best."

"And Anne Hathaway's outfits."

"Absolutely. And Stanley Tucci at the luncheon."

"Makes me want to cry," Kira said. "We should do this more often."

"No argument from me."

Fiona awaited the scene where Meryl Streep dumps jacket after jacket onto Anne Hathaway's desk, knowing there was no dialogue.

"I thought we should get away," she said.

"That sounds interesting. A weekend trip? Where to?"

"Maybe a week or two. Yellowstone, Glacier and back. Or maybe backpacking in the Sawtooths."

"I thought this is like the peak of the fly fishing season. Isn't this when you rake in the bucks?"

"I'm tired of fishing."

"Since when?" Kira took her eyes off the movie for the first time.

Fiona reached down and paused the film on a freeze frame of Anne Hathaway looking befuddled.

"And we need to bear-proof this place before we go. Michael and Leslie would want me to do everything possible."

"You're sick of fishing? Then why were you out until eleven o'clock last night? And the night before? Why did you tell me how incredible it was? Whoever you are, what have you done with Fiona? Give her back, please."

"Summer lasts, what, eight weeks?"

"Max."

"And I haven't taken five minutes for myself for the past two summers."

"And you're using me as an excuse?"

"Yes. I'm using you as an excuse."

"In which case you'll hate me in September when you realize how broke you are. In eight weeks you make about eight *months* of income. If you want to go, you should go without me."

"Without you? No. Not going to happen."

"I don't need a babysitter." She placed the bowl onto the coffee table in front of them. "I didn't mean that the way it sounded."

"I can take it."

"I appreciate everything you've done, everything you're doing for me."

"But you feel I'm overprotecting you."

"No. I don't. I didn't mean it to come out that way." She studied Fiona. "Is it the bear? You're worried about the bear? He attacks the garbage, not the house-sitter. You said so yourself."

"It might be better to just get out of here until they catch it."

"What is going on?"

"I just need to get out of here."

"Then go. Really! I'll be fine. You should go! You do nothing but work. You hold down three jobs. I don't know how you do it. Take the time off. I can handle things here. I promise I won't hide in the garbage cans at night."

"It would have to be both of us," Fiona said.

"But that's impossible. Really. I started, what, seven weeks ago? It's peak season. As if I'd get a two-week vacation. And no, you can't make a call for me. Everyone has been so nice to me. But I can't use it as an excuse forever. Right? Isn't that what I've been told over and over? That I have to get beyond it. Well, I think I am. I'm not going to accept special treatment. I want to be treated like everyone else. I'm sick of everyone treating me like I'm damaged goods. It happened. It's over. And I want to get over it."

"Good stuff," Fiona said, unable herself to lose the sordid images of Kira's abduction and sexual abuse that had been captured on video. Indelible. Inexcusable. Even knowing the monster who'd done it was dead did little to help.

"Seriously. I mean it," Kira said.

"So we'll stay."

"I think you should go if you want to."

"I'm good."

"What's going on? I don't get you."

"What if it wasn't a bear?"

"Excuse me?"

"The sheriff has put together a pretty convincing case—circumstantial, but convincing—that the Berkholders' kitchen attacker was not a bear. My photography played into that. Bears are dirty creatures. They leave tracks. None were found. The sheriff thinks some guy made it look like a bear—even brought a bear claw along with him—but that it was just a guy trying to steal food."

"A guy."

"Maybe living in the woods around here."

"Now you're creeping me out." She stared at Fiona long and hard. "That's why the pajama party, isn't it? That's why you want to bear-proof the place? Bear-proof, or creep-proof?"

"I think we'd both be smarter to stick together and just get away from here."

"Why would you lie to me?"

"I didn't lie. I just didn't want to get you all worked up about something that's probably nothing. And now you are."

"The woods?"

"That's what he thinks. This time of year—summer—people move into the national forest. Vagrants. Outlaws. People who can't afford to have, or don't want, an address. The sheriff's office puts the number into the hundreds."

"Hundreds?"

"Totally off the radar. Just out there camping somewhere."

"And stealing food from people's houses."

"Cheaper than buying."

"Every summer?"

Fiona nodded sadly.

"You don't scare that easily." Kira wore her suspicion openly. They were sisters now. Fiona wasn't supposed to hide anything.

Fiona averted her eyes. "Don't go there."

"Where?"

"Please."

"We'll bear-proof it," Kira said. "Maybe the handgun course comes in handy now."

"You know how I felt about that."

"Once my father gets a bug up his butt . . ."

"So you said."

"The whole purpose of the course was to teach you to know what you're shooting at before you so much as finger the trigger."

"I still don't like it."

"I sleep better knowing it's there."

"But I don't. And think about it. It's not right," Fiona said. "A gun shouldn't have that kind of power."

"But it does, and if there's a prowler . . ."

"You . . . me . . . both of us . . . We don't need this. Not ever again. Why would we elect to stay here? Come with me. We kill some time while Walt—the sheriff— sweeps the woods. It's safe again, and we return."

"I won't give him that power. Some faceless dude who's stealing pancake batter? We talked about this. *You* convinced me: 'Once a victim, never again a victim.' I'm not giving some phantom the power to make me leave."

"And if it's not a phantom?" Fiona asked.

The two exchanged looks. For a moment it appeared Kira was about to ask a question, but she censored herself.

"He hit a house a half mile from here," she said. "Who would be dumb enough to hit the next-door neighbor?"

"These guys are not rocket scientists."

"You're not telling me something. I can see it, and don't try to convince me otherwise."

"If you stay, I stay," Fiona said.

"That's bullshit. I'll be fine."

"What about moving back in with your par—"

"No way. Not even for a week. I'm done there. You know how I feel about that."

"But one week?"

"I love them, but I'm not living with them. My father's look is . . . tragic. He can't help himself. It's like it happened to him. It's like secondhand smoke or something."

Fiona reached for the DVD's remote control. Kira leaned forward and placed her hand onto Fiona's.

"Thank you," she said. "I know you're trying to protect me. I know how awful you'd feel if anything happened. But nothing's going to happen. I'm in charge of my life now. I *have* a life now. You made that happen. You, the Advocates, my parents, this whole valley. But I'm not running from some dude stealing soup cans. 'Once a victim, never again a victim,'" she repeated.

"But there's also, BS is BS. 'Being smart is being safe.'"

"I'm staying," Kira said. "Unless you're kicking me out?"

"Yeah, right," Fiona said. She touched the remote and the movie continued.

Kira settled back into the couch and pulled the bowl of popcorn into her lap. "I love it when they go to Paris," she said.

But not Yellowstone, Fiona was about to say. She didn't.

6

With Beatrice leading the way, Walt, Fiona, Tommy Brandon, and Guillermo Menquez followed a game path through a dark forest of fir, white pine, and aspen on a north-facing slope. Beatrice was not actually leading, but following a scent from a can of evaporated milk found by Fish and Game Deputy Ranger Menquez a hundred yards from the Berkholders' stucco home. That the can carried a scent, and that that scent led them deeper into the woods, encouraged Walt that they were onto something.

"No bear tracks that I've seen," Menquez said. He was a stocky man with a thick mustache and an oily face.

"No scat," Walt said, agreeing. "No fur caught in the shrubs or on the stumps of old branches—"

"Show-off," Fiona said.

Walt ignored it. "No evidence that any of the food in the kitchen had been consumed." He expected Beatrice to lead them to a camper, a squatter, and Menquez, a bear expert, was along in case they encountered one—or, if Walt's theory proved right, the "bear" required a translator. The Hispanic population had exploded in the valley over the past decade. Increasingly, his office and Fish and Game dealt with Mexicans squatting in the national forest while moving from one menial job to another. With the collapse of the economy had come whole settlements of twenty, forty, sixty day laborers in illegal campsites. Fiona was along to record whatever was found, and because for the past several days she'd come out of her cocoon to repeatedly badger Walt about finding and removing whatever—*whoever*—was living in the woods near the Engletons'.

Walt extended his arm, stopping the others, and dropped to one knee, focusing on the brown pine straw that covered the barely discernible trail.

"Brandon! A stick," he said, reaching back with an open palm.

Tommy Brandon found a fallen limb, cracked off a dry branch, and delivered it to Walt like a nurse to a surgeon. Walt reduced it further.

"Photo, please."

Fiona sneaked forward and made several pictures of the area in front of Walt. "It might help," she said, "if I knew what I was photographing."

"Right here," he said, using the tip of the stick to

gently lift the edge of a fallen leaf. He pushed the leaf away, pinched it, and tossed it behind him. "Another photo," he said.

"What is that?" she asked. She zoomed in on the pine straw and for the first time saw through the lens that half a dozen of the brown needles were cracked and broken. "You couldn't have seen that," she mumbled.

"Here," he said, using the stick to point out a small frown of discoloration. "It's a toe impression," he said. "A boot or Vibram sole—something stiff and inflexible. Not a running shoe." He looked down at his own boot. "Size ten or eleven. We're lucky it hasn't rained in the past couple of weeks." He looked up the trail and whistled for Beatrice to stop. Once the dog was looking at him, Walt made a hand gesture and she sat on the side of the trail. "We don't want her disturbing things. It's a man." He looked behind him. Then he took hold of Fiona's hiking boot and lifted it up and moved it. "He's over a hundred and . . ." He sized up Fiona, "twenty pounds, and less than one-eighty."

"Jesus," she gasped, amazed he nailed her weight.

"Six feet or a little more."

Fiona glanced back at Brandon, who nodded as if to reassure her that the sheriff was for real.

"Beatrice," Fiona stated. "You saw a change in Beatrice as she passed by here."

"Very good, Ms. Kenshaw," Walt said.

"Her nose? Her tail? What?"

"Both," Walt answered. "She's my Geiger counter.

She's the one in charge at the moment, and she knows it. Look at her up there."

The dog sat proudly on the side of the trail, with an expression that seemed to ask what was keeping them.

"You ever seen anything cuter than that?" Walt said. "She's impatient with us!"

"Truthfully, I'm a little freaked out," Fiona said.

"It's what I do," Walt said. "What Bea and I do. No big deal."

"Unless you happen to see it in action," Fiona said. "The height? How do you get that?"

Brandon answered. "Shoe size combined with weight. Big feet, not very heavy. Tall and thin."

"Not Hispanic," Menquez said. "Not very likely if he's over six feet."

"No, Gilly," Walt said. "How do you feel about going off trail?"

"Point the way," Menquez said.

Brandon, reading a topo map, said, "There's a half-acre bench ahead, maybe two hundred yards."

"Water source?" Walt said.

"An intermittent stream, spring fed on the backside of the bench."

Walt looked up into the trees. "Running northwest to southeast," he said.

"Exactly," Brandon answered.

"You *are* showing off, aren't you?" Fiona said to Walt. "You've been here before."

"Doubtful," said Brandon before Walt could answer.

Walt silenced her with a look. "We go in silent," he said, addressing them all. "Brandon, you'll go upstream from this side." He pointed. "Gilly, we'll give you a head start. You're to the north and I want you to come up over the lip and onto the bench the same time as I do. We'll use channel six. I'll give you two clicks. If you're in position, you'll return with two; if you need another minute, three clicks; two minutes, four."

Menquez nodded and took off into the woods without anything more said. He moved as silently as a cat.

"You," Walt said to Fiona, "will stop when I motion for you to stop. I want you behind a tree in case any shots are fired. You're not to move until I call for you. The best way you can help me right now is not to think; just follow orders. I know that runs against your grain—against your brain—but . . ."

"No problem. I get it."

"Okay. Good." He addressed Brandon. "Let's go."

Walt received three clicks from Menquez, kept an eye on his watch, and sent the two-click signal a minute later. As two clicks were returned, Walt pushed up the final incline and popped out through the forest into the gleaming sunshine. The effect on his eyes was as if he'd left twilight and stepped into the glare of spotlights. He slipped on his aviators, picking up Menquez in his peripheral vision.

Brandon, who'd beaten them both to the site, stepped

out from behind a tree near the trickling stream fifty
yards to Walt's left.

At the back side of the small clearing, near the stream
and against the hill in a copse of aspens, was a fire ring
of stones producing steam, some litter, a lean-to, and a
small stack of sticks and firewood. The men came at it
from three sides, an adrenaline-charged spring to their
steps.

Walt dropped to a knee, placed his hand first on the
firestones, then into the steam and charred wood at its
center. He held up five fingers on his right hand: *five
minutes.* He silently signaled Brandon, directing him up
the hill. Brandon took off.

Walt turned around and motioned at the woods, and
Beatrice came running toward him at full speed. He
dropped her into a sit with a second hand signal, re-
charged her nose with the can of evaporated milk, and
pointed into the woods.

"Find it!" he whispered.

The dog hurried off in the same direction as Brandon
had gone.

Walt stirred the litter with a stick, looking for an
expiration date, but found nothing.

"Our boy?" Menquez asked, studying the inside of
the open lean-to. "Someone . . . *two people* . . . bedded
down here. Recent enough that the wind hasn't disturbed it."

Walt joined him. "Like last night," he said.

"Be my guess."

"Two? That doesn't fit."

He was reaching for the handheld radio as Brandon spoke. "I see two individuals," he said harshly, keeping his voice low. "Bea had a dead reckoning. It's a couple. They're on a trail maybe a half mile ahead, traversing to the south. Up and over into Greenhorn. You want me to pursue?"

"Stop them if you can," Walt said. "We're on our way."

He called to Fiona, and a moment later they were off at a run.

The couple were in their late twenties. The granola set. He wore a red bandana over his hair; she carried a CamelBak and backpack. They had a bitch Labrador that got along well with Beatrice. The dogs chased each other around the woods, throwing pine straw and growling.

"Just the one night," he answered.

"We got off late this morning," she said. "We're going to circle around the end of Greenhorn and head out that trail."

"And in what condition did you find the campsite?"

"The litter wasn't ours," the man said. "We burned what we could—"

"And I packed out some," the girl added.

"But there was just too much of it," the young man complained.

"Can I see the trash you packed out?" the sheriff asked.

The woman surrendered a plastic bag and Walt dumped it and rummaged through it. She stared long and hard at Fiona.

Brandon said, "Have you seen anyone in the last day or so? Single male?"

"No," the man answered.

"Wildlife?" Menquez asked.

"Nothing bigger than a squirrel," the woman said. "What's this about?"

"When you arrived to the campsite," Brandon said, "what condition did you find it in? Did you get any sense for how long it had been abandoned?"

"Not long," Walt said, holding up a single-serve soy milk box on the end of a stick.

"I packed that out because it's lined with some kind of foil and doesn't burn well," she said. "We found a bunch of that melted stuff in the fire ring."

Fiona ran off a series of photographs at Walt's request. Walt had pushed the melted globs into their own pile.

"Very conscientious of you," Menquez said. "Wish more campers had your sense of responsibility."

"Expiration date," Walt said, "is November."

"Juice is usually six months," Fiona said. No one questioned her. "It would have sold in late May or June."

"But not July?"

"Iffy," she said. "It's possible, but that's a popular brand. I doubt it stays on the shelves that long. You could check."

"The Berkholders," Walt said, speculating.

"Soy milk's irradiated. Could be a pantry item," Fiona said. "Why not?"

"What's going on?" the woman camper repeated. "Are you looking for someone?" She met eyes with her partner, who appeared anxious.

"We could use some help," Brandon said.

"Hey," the woman said, addressing Fiona, "I know where I know you. Aren't you . . . ? Didn't you save that kid, that drowning kid?"

"Anything you can tell us," Fiona said—Walt making note of her choice of pronouns—"will be kept strictly confidential, and could really help us. This is important. This is the county sheriff. He's out here personally, just to give you some idea. Think about that."

The woman checked with the man again. He shook his head nearly imperceptibly, but Fiona caught it.

"What?" Fiona asked. "Please. Help us."

"I was," the woman said. The man shook his head more vehemently, cutting her off. "We're all grown-ups here," she clarified. "I was sunbathing. No shirt. You know," she said to Fiona. "It was a glorious afternoon. One thing led to another. Jimmy and I . . . we enjoyed the fresh air together. Out there in the middle of the clearing. On a Therm-a-Rest. I may have gotten a little vocal, I think." She blushed. "The point being that both of us . . . we both thought we heard something. Up the hill. We were still . . . and I . . . . you know . . . I didn't want to . . ."

"Stop," said Jimmy.

The woman laughed nervously and shrugged.

"But we both heard him," Jimmy said.

"It was probably just a deer," she said.

"Was not!" said Jimmy. "And you know it."

"This is yesterday afternoon?" Walt said, clarifying.

"Four o'clock maybe," the woman said. "The sun was still very hot."

"He was returning to the campsite?" Walt proposed to his team.

"Maybe he's rotating between two or three," Menquez said. "We see a lot of that. With the five-day limit, they stay clear of us by moving every five days. Not much we can do about it."

"Him?" Walt asked the man.

"She won't admit it now," Jimmy said, "but she was the one who said it felt like someone was watching."

The woman looked a little sheepish. She looked at Fiona. "Sometimes you just get this sixth sense, you know, that someone has their eye on you. You know what I'm talking about. And it always gives me the creeps. Or nearly always. I felt it yesterday, and to be honest, I don't know, maybe it's just where we were, the setting and all, but it kind of turned me on."

"Jesus," Jimmy groaned, "Kind of? Why don't you just describe every detail?"

"That's why we didn't stop," she said. "I didn't exactly feel like stopping."

"Can we stop now?" Jimmy asked. "Please?"

"My deputy will take down your statement."

"You've been very helpful," Fiona said. "I know that's not easy."

"Is there some creep out here?" Jimmy asked. "Is that what you're telling us?"

"Honestly, if I were you," Walt said, "I might try the Pioneers or the Boulders. Someplace north."

"You see?" he said to the woman, blaming her for all their trouble. He called for their dog and started off down the trail.

The woman stayed behind and gave Brandon their names and phone numbers.

"Sorry about that," Brandon said.

"Oh, well," she said. "He'll get over it."

"I can sit on this campsite," Menquez offered. "Maybe we get lucky and he comes back."

"Observation only," Walt said. "No action. These guys . . . A guy like this, Gilly . . ."

"Yes, I understand, Sheriff. If he's the one breaking into people's houses, I would want backup. Don't worry."

"Couldn't you sweep the area?" Fiona asked. "The other campsites?"

"Could, I suppose, but there's just too many," Walt said. "It would take too much manpower, too many resources for just petty theft and vandalism."

"But what if he knows that?" she complained. "What if he's counting on that?"

"Then he's right," Walt said. He whistled for Bea. The dog arrived with a deer bone in her mouth.

With the woman down the trail, the four stared at the pale white bone in the dog's mouth. It represented a violent death. No one spoke what was on their mind, if anything, but Walt looked down the trail toward the hiker, hoping that she and Jimmy would heed his advice.

7

Fiona waved her finger through the gauzy column of steam rising from the teacup alongside her computer, breaking apart and swirling into separate coils. She considered trying to photograph the image, to capture it, to stop it in time. This was the part of photography that fascinated her: the stoppage of time, owning a particular moment. Forever. Leave composition and color to others, she thought of herself as an archivist.

She dragged a shot of the Berkholders' vandalized refrigerator to her "best-of" folder, admiring how it offered something new to the collection.

As she clicked the computer mouse, she heard a synchronous thud against the cottage's outside wall. At first she allowed herself to believe it was the aspen tree on the southwest corner; the tree grew incredibly close to the wall, often banging against it when the wind blew.

But there's no wind tonight, she thought.

And though the woods were full of such sounds—unexplainable creaks and cracks—she'd come to discern a difference between the sounds of nature and the sounds of animals in nature. The sound hadn't resulted from a tree limb falling, or a pine tree splitting; it had sounded more like something slapping the cottage's clapboard siding.

Bear! She spun in her chair, her elbow bumping the mug and sloshing some tea onto the table. She jumped up. Something—*someone?*—moved off quickly through the woods, snapping twigs and swooshing branches. She lunged forward, killing the interior lights and switching on the outside floods. The computer monitor cast a glow into the room as she raced to the wall and peered out a window. But too late. If there had been anything out there it was long gone, amid the harsh shadows knitting in the woods.

It can't be!

A deer or elk antler making contact with the wall—that made sense. But the escape into the woods had sounded like something big and fast, which brought her back to a bear. The bear. Except that Walt had now convinced her that the destruction at the Berkholders' had not been the work of a bear, but instead an itinerant who'd vandalized the place and had worked hard to make it look like the work of a bear.

It can't be. Her chest was tight, her throat constricted. Heat flooded through her, immediately followed by a penetrating cold.

A man, out there creeping around her cottage.

Not possible.

She glanced to the front door and then threw herself across the room to the phone, stabbing the intercom button.

"Kira! Pick up! Pick up!"

"Yeah?" Kira said over the main residence's speakerphone. A television played in the background.

"Lock the doors. Pull the blinds. And leave the phone on while you're doing it."

"What's going on?"

"Just do it! Right now! There's a . . . bear," she said. "I think there was a bear outside my window just now."

"No way!"

"Kira. Now!"

"Okay, okay."

She heard the girl moving through the rooms, pulling drapes and dropping blinds. Then footfalls returned toward the phone.

"I don't see how pulling blinds is going to make any difference to a bear," Kira said.

"Are the doors locked?"

"Yes."

"Okay."

"You sound so . . . freaked out."

"Do I? Sorry. It just scared me, was all."

It can't be. Not again.

"I think it's cool. I wouldn't mind seeing a bear for real."

"Do not go near the doors or windows."

"Jeez . . . Chill."

"You have the baseball bat?"

"P . . . le . . . ase," Kira said, drawing the word out dramatically.

"I'm coming over. Get the bat and stand by the front door and get ready to unlock it for me."

"What? Seriously? Why? You don't need to do that, Fiona. I'm fine. I don't need a babysitter."

"I know *you* don't," Fiona said. She paused, looking near the front door for her running shoes. "But I think I do."

8

The young man wasn't prepared for the formality of the interview room, just as Walt had hoped. He was accompanied by his father, who was fit and ruggedly handsome, and his attorney, Terry, for whom Walt had a great deal of respect. The boy shared his father's good looks, broad shoulders, and deep voice, though the combination belied his boyish, naïve eyes.

Terry Hogue, a sizable, well-dressed man with a commanding presence, displayed the calmness of an academic. "As to the nature of the inquiry, Sheriff, I'd like to restate that my client, Mr. Donaldson, is here of his own volition, that is, voluntarily, and has not been charged with any crime."

"That's correct, Terry."

"That Mr. Donaldson is willing to cooperate with

your investigation, if any, and that nothing said here today is being recorded and may not be used against him."

"Agreed."

"That said," Hogue continued, "I've asked my client to clear his answers with me before responding, so he may seek my advice, which I'm here to give. We apologize in advance for any delays that may cause."

"Understood."

"It's all yours," Hogue said.

"Mr. Donaldson . . . may I call you Brian? Brian, are you in a relationship with Dionne Fancelli, of eighteen Alturas Drive?"

The nervous boy looked to Hogue, who nodded his assent.

"Yeah. Me and Di are boyfriend, girlfriend."

"And we're all aware of Ms. Fancelli's medical condition," Walt said. "That is, that she's pregnant, with child."

The boy nodded regretfully, without checking with Hogue. The father fidgeted in his chair.

"Sheriff," Hogue said, "let's be clear that acknowledging the young woman's medical condition by no means implies my client's role in that matter."

"Which is why we're here, Terry. Right?"

"We're here as a result of your invitation," Hogue clarified.

"Have you had sexual intercourse with Ms. Fancelli?" Walt asked the boy.

The boy looked to Hogue, who spoke for him. "My

client will not comment on the physical nature of his and Ms. Fancelli's friendship."

"I assume we're all aware that Ms. Fancelli is claiming the child is your client's," Walt said to the attorney, since Hogue was the one answering.

"We're aware of the claim," Hogue said, "but again, we are making no statement about the physical or sexual nature of their relationship."

"We're also all aware that Ms. Fancelli is fifteen."

Silence.

"I will assume Mr. Hogue has briefed you on the quirky nature of Idaho law," Walt said to the boy. "Idaho accepts sexual relationships between adolescents of similar ages. But you must be at least eighteen years old in Idaho to have consensual sex with an adult, that is a person eighteen or over. You are over eighteen, Brian. And therefore, if you have penetrated Ms. Fancelli, orally, vaginally, or anally, you are in violation of state law."

Hogue seemed on the verge of stepping in, but resigned himself to allow Walt to continue, apparently wanting to see where this was going.

"With the girl's claim of penetration, the state can therefore charge you in this matter, leaving it for the courts to decide. There is no physical proof required, although you may or may not be aware that Ms. Fancelli has retained electronic correspondence—e-mails and texts—in which she discusses your sexual relations with her, and your replies to those e-mails contain no denials. To the contrary, in fact."

"Where are we going with this, Walt?"

"We'd like to take a swab."

"Absolutely not," Hogue said. "Show us a court order, and my client will oblige."

Walt met eyes with Hogue. "I'm requesting your client provide a swab voluntarily and that he aids this office in obtaining a hair or some other sample from Ms. Fancelli that contains the young woman's DNA. Perhaps he is already in possession of something along these lines."

"This is ridiculous!" the father said, nearly coming out of his chair. "They haven't got anything! No way this is happening."

Hogue, without breaking eye contact with Walt, motioned for the man to remain in his chair, and implicitly, to remain quiet.

"I don't get it," Brian said.

The father couldn't help himself. "He wants you to do his work for him. Let's get out of here."

Hogue turned on the father. "You may leave the room, or you can remain and be quiet, but that's the last we're going to hear from you right now."

The father huffed, but stayed in his seat.

"Let me get this straight," Hogue said. "You're requesting my client's participation and cooperation in certain aspects of your evidence collection and in keeping with the confidentiality of the current interview, you're implying any evidence acquired as a result of this cooperation . . . ?"

"Is therefore off the books," Walt said. "Not that we're keeping any books. Not at the moment."

A puzzled Hogue looked him over, still maintaining eye contact. "You'll leave the room, please. Both of you."

"Me?" said the father.

"Yes," said Hogue.

The two got up and left the room.

Once the door was firmly shut, Hogue spoke. "You have another suspect."

"I need the boy's cooperation," Walt said.

"You're aware that if and when you come back for any physical evidence from my client, I will fight any reference to—"

"My case against your client, at that point, would be dicey at best. I would have prejudiced the evidence. I'd probably lose the possibility of a court case against him."

"No probably about it."

"What a pity," Walt said.

Hogue sat back, rubbed his big hand against his maw and chuckled. "Never a dull moment with you, Walt."

Walt showed no expression.

"The girl's DNA," Hogue said. He mulled it over. "You suspect the father."

"Never a dull moment with you, Terry."

"How certain are you?"

"Certain of what, counselor? I don't believe we've discussed any other suspects."

"If you want the girl's DNA, and my client's as well, then you must have, or have access to, the fetus's DNA. How is it that you have the child's DNA but not the mother's?" Again, he was thinking aloud.

Walt's lack of expression remained implacable.

"If you burn me on this, Walt . . . You've always played fair with me."

"Can't teach an old dog new tricks."

"We'd be taking a big risk."

"A risk that I would prejudice my evidence, that your client would skate. I need a hair from her. A cigarette butt. A love stain. He needs to volunteer it to me."

"And I repeat: you're implying you can get . . . what . . . amnio fluid but not the girl's DNA? How's that happen?" He took a moment. "You have a witness. You possess the means to obtain a court order to collect the amnio fluid, but are less confident you can win the DNA of a minor."

"You don't need to trouble yourself, counselor, with what I do or do not have. What I need is your client's cooperation."

"And you'll have it."

"I thought it might work out that way."

A knock on the door interrupted them.

"Sorry to interrupt," a female deputy said, leaning her head in the door. "We've got shots fired out Lake Creek."

Walt immediately stood, extending his hand to Hogue. "Do what you can," he said.

"You'll be hearing from me," Hogue answered.

9

"She's not answering," Deputy Linda Chalmers reported.

"Try again," Walt said.

"I've already . . . Why do we need photography anyway? It's a couple of shells in the grass."

Walt answered that with a glare.

"Yes, sir."

He was in a fix. He'd requested Fiona be called onto the scene, more out of a personal want, and now saw no way to back out of the request without making his original intentions obvious. He marched to the back of the Cherokee, as if put out to do this himself, took his camera from an emergency backpack he kept there, and walked back into the darkened lawn. He shot off a series of photos of the spent shell casings, adding his pen into the grass for scale.

Chalmers was first officer, having responded to a dispatch, the result of an Emergency Center's receipt of a neighbor's 911 call. Chalmers shadowed Walt to the Jeep and back to the lawn.

"Warning shots?" Walt said.

"No, sir. That's the thing. He made no apologies. Said he was firing right at him."

"Him?"

"The intruder. He said 'him,' yes, sir."

"In the direction of the neighbor's?"

"That's correct."

"Any reports of the shots landing?"

"No, sir. Judging by his breath, that doesn't surprise me. There's the suggestion of alcohol."

"The name again?"

"Vincent Wynn," Chalmers said.

Walt froze. Wynn was on Boldt's short list of potential interviews.

"*The* Vince Wynn?"

"Some kind of big shot. Acts like it, at least. I think he thought I should know who he is, and honestly, sir, I don't have a clue. Most of the celebrities up here, they don't want you to know who they are. How're you supposed to pretend you don't know Tom Hanks? I love Tom Hanks! I would violate my marriage vows for Tom Hanks. But this nincompoop? I'm sorry, no clue."

It was more words out of Deputy Chalmers than Walt had ever heard. She was clearly nervous, and concerned he might slight her for not knowing Wynn.

"He's a sports agent. Big-time sports agent."

"That would explain it."

"In that world, his world, he's Tom Hanks."

"Not with that face he isn't. You don't mind me saying so."

"I don't mind," Walt said.

"Can I stop calling Ms. Kenshaw, sir, now that you've taken the pictures yourself?"

"You may. Why don't you get me everything you can on Mr. Wynn? Any past grievances filed by neighbors. Traffic violations. Parking tickets. Run him."

"Done," she said, hurrying off.

Walt knocked on the patio door frame, since the door was open to the night. No screen door. Mosquitoes lasted about ten days in late June; then the cold nights stopped their cycle. A moth or two might wander inside, but Vince Wynn didn't seem too worried.

He was on his mobile phone, his hand wrapped around a heavy cocktail glass filled halfway with a dark liquid.

"Okay. Gotta go," he said, pocketing the phone.

"Vince Wynn," he introduced himself, switching the drink to his left hand and shaking hands with Walt.

"I'm a fan of some of your players," Walt said, believing he could loosen up Wynn before the liquor. "Suganuma Sakatura to the Mariners. One of the all-time great trades."

"Thank you."

"And that four-way with the Braves and Phillies."

"You follow baseball, I see."

"Play a little. Softball. Leagues, you know?"

"Let me guess." He sized up Walt. "Catcher or out-field? I'm going with catcher."

Walt shook his head. "You are a pro."

"It's what I do."

"And me," Walt said, "I chase down complaints when neighbors hear a gun being shot in their backyard."

"My own backyard, but point taken."

"I'm not going to argue with you," Walt said, still trying his best to sound awestruck. "You nearly talked Steinbrenner out of A-Rod. I'm supposed to argue with that?"

"I wasn't close. That got all blown out of proportion."

"And tonight," Walt said. "How close were you tonight?"

"Excuse me?"

"There are laws about the discharge of firearms within a prescribed distance of a residence."

"It was a prowler."

"So you said."

"The guy was on my property. Sneaking around out there." He threw the drink forward to point and sloshed the contents of the glass onto his hand.

"Let me guess," Walt said. "The call just now? Your lawyer?"

Wynn licked the booze off his wrist. "Yeah, my lawyer. But it's not him I was shooting at. It was Martel Gale," Wynn said. "You follow football?"

"Not so much. I've never heard of Martel Gale. Should I have? I'm a batboy through and through."

"New Orleans Saints. Pro Bowl center linebacker.

Phenomenal quickness. Great hands. And vision—it's all about speed and vision for a linebacker. Gale had it."

"Had," Walt noted. "Retired?"

"Imprisoned. Recently paroled. I'm on a list server," Wynn said. "It's a state DOJ thing from Louisiana. Because I'm at risk—a possible target. Turns out Gale was paroled two weeks ago. When he was convicted, the court awarded performance bonuses he was owed—a lot of money—to be donated to worthy causes, a halfway house for battered women, a legal fund for victims of abuse. I oversaw the distribution of that money. Gale took issue with that. Blames me. Thinks I cheated him. He thought the bonuses should have been donated to his savings account. Hence the threats and me being on the list server. Hence the e-mail I got that he'd been paroled. Never mind that they sent it out two weeks late."

"And you have reason to believe Martel Gale is here in Sun Valley?"

"Mark my words: it was Gale out there tonight. If I hit him, lock me up, Sheriff. If I killed him, throw a parade. Check him out. You can do that, right? Look up his victims—the conditions of his victims. Look up a girl named Caroline Vetta."

"The homicide in Seattle," Walt said, a spike of heat flooding him. He'd been looking for a way into a discussion of Boldt, and Wynn had just handed it to him.

"Impressive."

"I'd wanted to talk to you about that."

"Me? Why would you want to talk to me about Caroline?" Back on his heels.

"Was she on the list server?" Walt asked, beginning to draw tangents. "Did she have reason to fear Martel Gale?"

"Any woman alive has reason to fear Gale. He eats 'em for breakfast. Treats 'em like his personal punching bags. Did Gale know her? Wouldn't surprise me. He attracted the lookers like flies to shit. But if she was on the list, it didn't do her any good, did it? The alert came two weeks late. You believe that shit?"

"There's a Seattle detective, a Sergeant Boldt, would like a word with you, in private, about Caroline Vetta. He's suggesting you meet over here, not in Seattle, in order to avoid the press."

Wynn coughed a laugh. "Shit, you guys are all a piece of work. You're telling me I've got to get back on the horn with my lawyer?"

"If you want to involve your lawyer," Walt said, "I think that might be agreeable. The idea is to keep it out of the press, not to pull an end run on you."

"As if the cops care."

"This one does, apparently. He can do it in front of all the cameras if you'd prefer."

He looked up from the drink. "I don't see why we can't do something. Let me make a call and get back to you."

"Works for me." The man drank the liquor like it was water. "Do you have reason to believe Martel Gale is in Sun Valley?"

"You already asked me that."

"And you said you shot at him, not that you knew he was here."

"Listen, several women could have testified against him for all I know. Right? And why not Caroline? She could have been one of the girls. Maybe he paid her back." The way he looked up over the rim of the glass sent a charge through Walt. He needed to make sure Boldt talked to this one.

"The sooner you can let me know about meeting with the detective, the better. He's going to fly over specially for this."

"Am I supposed to be honored? Let him do what he's got to do."

"I'd like to inspect your weapon," Walt said.

"Pity, it's in the bedroom safe, and hell if I didn't forget the combination. That's what I was on the phone to my lawyer about. I knew you fellas would probably want to see it, and I didn't want to piss anyone off, but it's in there locked up and I won't have the combination until tomorrow sometime, when my office is open."

"About the time your lawyer's plane lands?" Walt asked.

"Cynicism from a county sheriff?"

"Why make it more difficult than it has to be?"

"So the lawyers earn their money, I guess."

"You can't go firing a gun in your backyard."

"So you said. Gale was out there. I wasn't taking any chances."

Walt heard the man's name and thought of his wife.

It was Gail out there. He'd never be fully free of her, which was the hardest part to adjust to—like one of those stomach microbes from Mexico.

If he had a killer loose in the valley, he needed to know about it.

"Could have been a hiker," Walt said. "Could have been a neighbor."

"Gale did Caroline," Wynn said. "I was next on the list. Trust me. A guy like that settles scores. Football players. Hell, they remember the smallest shit from the previous season, and they make the player pay the next time they face him across a scrimmage line. It's the way the game's played. It's who they are."

"In which case you've either wounded him or escalated the terms. And your gun's locked in your safe," Walt said. "And you forgot the combination."

Wynn glanced into the house and back at Walt. "That is problematic," he said. "Maybe you could leave that smokin' hot deputy at my front door all night."

"Deputy Chalmers is married with five kids. Her husband runs a martial arts school in Hailey. Her eldest is eighteen and has his black belt."

Wynn didn't seem to hear. Walt had lost part of him back at the mention of Boldt.

"A second weapons violation will result in felony charges. Neither of us wants or needs that. Forgetting the combination to the safe may be a good thing."

"I see someone out there, and I'll shoot first, ask questions later. Take my chances the judge is a sports fan." He wasn't threatening, just stating fact. "A guy like that comes after you, you don't get a second chance. Ask Caroline. Ask the other women he sent to the emergency room. His nickname in the league was Gale Force. Guy handed out concussions like business cards. Ask Trent Green, Kurt Warner. We call those guys a snake bite: all it takes is one hit to kill you."

Gail Force. Walt wiped the smirk off his face, wondering why he'd never thought of that one himself.

"No more guns."

"How about a machete or a baseball bat?"

"Try the phone next time. That's why we're here."

"To protect and serve. Right, Sheriff?"

"Right."

"So protect me."

"Try the Yellow Pages."

"Find Gale, you'll do us all a favor."

"Let me know about setting up the thing with Boldt. The sooner, the better."

"Two-eighty?" Wynn said as Walt turned to leave.

The comment spun him around.

"Your batting average. You're a switch hitter," he said. "Calluses." He indicated Walt's hands.

Walt looked down at his palms. "Maybe I'm a gardener," he said.

"Yeah, I can see that," Wynn said sarcastically. "Two-eighty," he repeated confidently.

"Two eighty-five," Walt answered. Impressed, but trying not to show it.

10

The temptation proved too great and Walt made the turn at the split rail fence at the side of State Highway 75. He drove through the overbuilt log gate and turned left up the hill toward a stand of fir.

He approached the Engleton guesthouse thinking up an excuse for the visit. He stopped and returned to the Cherokee to retrieve his camera.

Movement caught his eye and he looked toward the main house in time to see a woman's silhouette standing in a downstairs window. It was Kira. She held something in her hand across her chest—a baseball bat, he realized.

Fiona opened the cottage's door wearing a T-shirt, navy blue sweatpants, and rubber flip-flops. Her hair was held off her face by a pair of plastic clips.

"Problems?" she asked.

"You weren't answering calls," he said.

"No," she replied.

"We had a situation: a guy throwing shots in his back-yard, believing a client of his was coming after him. I needed some pictures. Took them myself, no big deal."

"A broker? I wouldn't want to be a money manager in this town right now. I can't imagine the amounts people must have lost."

"No, not a money guy, a sports agent. Thought some ex–football jock was creeping around his backyard, and decided it was safer to shoot him than to say hello." He offered her his camera, making it clear it was a profes-sional, not personal, visit. Wasn't sure why he felt that so important.

She staggered back a step, off balance. He caught her by the elbow and held on.

"You're saying he saw this . . . football guy?" she said.

"No. The whiskey might have done the seeing, I think. It was more likely a neighbor."

"Come in," she said, accepting the camera. "Want me to print these for you?"

"Please." He stepped inside.

"Coffee?" she asked.

"Yes, please."

"Sit," she said.

"It's a nice place," he said.

"Have you never been here?"

"No."

"How pathetic of me. I can't believe it's your first time."

It was done up as an English cottage. Leslie Engleton had great taste and deep pockets.

"I was worried about you," he said, blurting it out.

"Me? That's nice of you. But I'm fine. Just quiet. You know me." She filled the kettle. "I do that now and then."

She got the stove lit under the kettle and sat down in front of a laptop at the breakfast table. She fished around in a box of wires at her feet and connected his camera to the computer.

"Yours?" he asked, admiring a photo of a black woman on a porch holding a small terrified child.

"Yes. Just after Katrina."

"Powerful."

"Thanks. So who was this guy with the gun? This sports guy?"

"Believe me, you don't care. Just another guy with a gun who shouldn't have been drinking. I gave him a warning."

She seemed about to say something, but didn't.

"No prowlers, I take it?" he asked.

"For the record, I tried to get Kira to take a trip with me. And that was before the campsite and the hikers. I'd just as soon not be here. For her sake, not mine," she added emphatically—a little too emphatically, he thought. "She doesn't need any more scares."

He recalled seeing Kira with the bat and made sense of it.

"Gilly's a good tracker," Walt said. "I think we'll catch this guy."

"You'd get no complaint from me. But seriously, did he know it was this football guy? How weird is that?"

The water was beginning to boil. She returned to the stove.

"He has a history with this guy."

"What kind of history?"

"Money. You're certainly the curious one tonight," he said.

"I like staying up on your cases, knowing what you're doing."

"Since when?" he asked.

"Since . . . I don't know. I just do. Particularly this prowler at the Berkholders' or now at this other guy's."

"Could have been the same guy, I suppose, though that's a long way to travel."

"Not so very far."

"That, and the Berkholders' home was empty at the time. With so many homes empty in this community, why hit one where there's a chance of running into some-one?"

"Better stocked. Fresh food."

"So, you're the detective now?" He waited. "Hey, that was a joke."

"Ha, ha."

"Listen, Gilly and I found a spot with the grass beaten down outside the Berkholders'. This guy scouted the place, and timed it so no one was home. You don't have anything to worry about here."

"Which is why you parked the Jeep at the top of the hill where you can't miss it?"

"You noticed that," he said.

"Earth to Walt: I have a photographer's eye. I don't miss much."

"No, you don't, do you?"

His photographs had downloaded. She worked the laptop. Walt stood and looked over her shoulder, impressed with how she modified each one.

"That's amazing," he said.

"You can do anything to a picture. You know that."

"*You* can. Not me."

"Is it typical of squatters?" she asked. "Scouting a place like that?"

"Probably not."

"No, I didn't think so."

"Keeping all the lights on is good," he said. "He'll stay away, if he hasn't left the area already." He paused. "Why do we make everything about the office? I didn't come here to give you my camera. I thought about that at the last moment."

"Then why did you come here?"

He barely hesitated. All the time spent thinking about this moment, the right situation, and it came down to no thought at all.

He bent down and kissed her on the lips. Her eyes

expressed her surprise, but her lips, warm and sweet with wine, pressed to his more tightly, and then her eyes shut and her hands came around his head, and her body shook as if caught in guttural laughter.

He pulled back and she held on to him saying, "Don't . . . don't you dare stop," kissing him hungrily.

Her chair went over backward, Walt throwing his arms around her and saving her from the fall, the weight and warmth of her pressed to him as he eased her to the floor, her hair spread like a fan on the throw rug. She was laughing, in fact, like a child opening an unexpected, yet long anticipated, gift. Their bodies touching, hands beginning to explore and delight, she worked her fingers past his ears, holding his face an inch away from her own and managed to growl, "Why . . . so . . . long?"

Walt answered with smiling eyes, his fingers trapping a tear as it spilled down her cheek.

"Do we dare do this?" he whispered.

"You're damn right we do," she answered breathlessly, tugging the shirttail from his waistband and running her hands up his back, delivering chills.

Time arrested all thought. Walt fell away from himself, from his planning and predetermining. They knocked a vase off the coffee table. She laughed harder, and slapped his hand as he reached to right it, grabbing and guiding his fingers lower on her. Scared and elated, both present and absent, he felt her respond to his touch, her legs parting, her warmth overwhelming. The scent of her, sacred and mysterious, engulfed him, intoxicating. Dizzy with her, overwhelmed, underprepared, and fearing inexperience, he fell victim to her, suddenly finding himself past any point of reason or thought, driven by human hunger and a forceful need to join her.

When it was over, when the flush beneath her collarbone flared and her bare flesh rippled with gooseflesh, she opened her eyes to the ceiling and smiled devilishly, chortling to herself.

"Oh my God," she said. She took him by the hair and tugged and laughed privately again and said more softly, "Oh my God."

He answered not with words—couldn't find any; they'd all deserted him—but with a squeeze of her hand and by lying next to her and hooking his ankle over hers so that their feet embraced as their bodies just had. They stared at the ceiling together.

"You must promise me," she said, "that you'll never pretend that didn't happen. It's all I ask."

"Promise."

Five minutes passed into ten. She offered little touches as if making sure he was still there beside her, as if reassuring herself. "There are moments you never forget," she said. "This is one of them."

"Agreed."

"I'm not saying it has to happen again. I'm not saying it won't. I'm just saying . . . it had to happen now and it did and we can't have any regrets."

"No. None. Not from me," he said.

"You don't have to court me, but you mustn't ignore me."

"Never. Not possible."

"And I promise to keep it professional in public. I know that can't be easy for you. I don't want you worrying about that."

"I'm not even *thinking* right now. I'm certainly not worrying about anything, except disappointing you, because I never want to, I don't intend to. If I could wrap up all the happiness in the world into a package, if I could give you that, I would. Whatever the word means to you, whatever it is you want—I would give you that."

"Then you'd wrap up yourself," she said, her fingers absentmindedly finding his face and the tips of her fingers searching his expression like a blind person's. Finding a grin, they pulled away, satisfied.

"I know you can't stay," she said, "but I want you to, you're welcome to as long as you can. I'd like to fall asleep in your arms. I'd like to never wake up."

"I'd like to take a shower with you," he said. "To soap you all over."

"Now?"

"Why not?"

Later, he could hear the water still bubbling in the kettle, the chorus of night creatures—crickets, frogs, and things that go chirp in the dark; beneath it all he heard the steady, comforting sound of a cat purring and his eye finally lighted on the tabby balled up by a pillow on the loveseat, so still he'd not seen it.

"What's its name?" he asked.

"Her," she said. "Angel."

He nodded.

"It never hurts to have an angel around," she said. She wore a terry-cloth robe pulled tightly around her slim waist as she fixed them both tea and brought him a cup. He wore his uniform again, its shoulders damp from his wet hair.

She sat cross-legged on the couch.

He stared at her. The cat got up and climbed into her lap.

"I like this about you," he said.

"The silence?"

"Umm."

"Me, too." She hesitated. "You were like an eighteen-year-old tonight."

"Had a few, have you?"

She threw her spoon at him and hit him in the chest. He caught it as it fell and placed it on the coffee table.

"Don't overthink this," she said.

"It's tempting," he said, "but no. I don't plan to."

"You're welcome here anytime. Standing invitation."

"Standing, as in the shower?"

"Don't get fresh."

"Please?"

She laughed.

"I've heard you laugh more tonight than in two years of knowing you."

"Maybe you haven't known me."

"Maybe not," he admitted. "Although in the Biblical sense—"

"Shut up! If I had another spoon to throw, I would."

He passed her the spoon. Her eyes shone brightly as she teased a second throw, and she set it down.

He sighed contentedly.

They stared.

"I want you to know," she said, "I'm serious about this. But it doesn't mean you have to be. This is your free pass out of jail. Tonight. Right now. No harm. No foul. But if you don't take the pass, if you stay in jail and decide to roll the dice, that's something else entirely."

"Understood," he said. He didn't want a pass. He wanted to sleep here. He wanted to tell her he'd dreamed of this, fantasized about it and that it had exceeded all he'd imagined because one couldn't imagine how at ease he felt with her. He felt transformed. If not for the kids, he'd run away with her if she'd have him, and it struck him that she would have him, that she'd have agreed, and he nearly laughed.

"Go home," she said.

"Are you always this bossy?"

"Only when I'm afraid of losing something."

"Not going to happen."

He placed down the cold teacup, crossed to kiss her on the cheek, but she offered him her lips and they kissed until the cat climbed off her lap in disgust.

11

Walt received Wynn's handgun the following afternoon and spent thirty minutes with the man's attorney arranging the terms for a Boldt interview. He impounded the handgun, pending Wynn's voluntary completion of a one-day weapons course the following week.

He reached Boldt by Skype that night, explaining he'd heard back from NFL owner Marty Boatwright, and that both interviews were now arranged. Boldt said he'd make travel plans and get back to him.

He watched the Disney Channel with his daughters, read with them at bedtime, and caught up with e-mails while Beatrice licked herself at his feet. It was the first normal evening he'd had in a while and he promised himself to make more of them. He'd quickly come to see that Fiona was right about his intolerance of silence, though dared not test it. He kept himself busy with simple tasks until utterly fatigued and fell asleep in a bed he'd once shared with Gail. Beatrice snored before he did. He slept without any recollection of dreaming.

The following day, a Tuesday in July, Terry Hogue was announced from the front desk. He complimented Walt on the decorated 1867 rolling block Remington rifle hung in a glass box on the wall. They discussed firearms for ten minutes, Walt feeling no need to push the attorney.

Finally, Hogue withdrew a sealed plastic bag and pushed it across Walt's desk. Inside was a pair of black lace underwear.

"They belong to Dionne Fancelli."

"Not exactly what I'd expected," Walt said.

Hogue slid a signed and notarized document to Walt. "His statement as to how this undergarment came into his possession and that it was passed directly to you."

Walt read the letter carefully. "A love souvenir."

"Their second, and last time," Hogue said. "I questioned the boy repeatedly, Walt. They've had sexual intercourse twice. Other stuff along the way, sure. But only twice, the last time eight months ago. He's willing to cooperate fully. It's not him. I happen to believe him, in case you care."

"I care."

"I thought you might."

"What I told you before—that was straight. I'm not after him."

Hogue produced a second plastic bag. This one contained a cotton swab.

"So that completes our end of the deal," Hogue said. "I guess I should wish you good luck. My client would welcome the dismissal of him as a person of interest."

"Has she said anything to him about problems at home?"

"He knew there were problems," Hogue said. "The two times they attempted sexual intercourse failed miserably. And it wasn't him, it was her. She became so overwhelmed emotionally that he withdrew, despite protection."

"And they didn't try after that."

"No. And they didn't talk about it. He brought it up only once. She blew up at him. They didn't speak for days. He doesn't know enough to have spotted the warning signs. He just thought she was too young and that he was stupid for having tried."

"He was right."

"Indeed."

"Okay," Walt said, accepting a second letter pertaining to the swab.

"If we can help you get the bastard, Walt . . ."

"Thank you. My guess is, you already have."

Walt had the two bags packaged and shipped to the Meridian lab, knowing it would be several weeks, if he was lucky, before getting the reports.

The prenatal sample from the mother would have to be done in the next few weeks—between the tenth and thirteenth week—and would be more problematic. Past the fourteenth week an amniocentesis was the only option, a procedure that would put the fetus at some degree of risk and one he therefore wouldn't push for. He had to work quickly with the courts.

He attended a Rotary Club lunch, met with his two investigating deputies to review cases, and answered a dozen e-mails before heading home to Lisa and the girls.

He was in the Cherokee when he overheard a radio call from his dispatcher. A prowler had been reported at the Roger Hillabrand residence. Hillabrand, a defense contractor, continued to hold an interest in Fiona, and had for a time been a suspect in another of Walt's cases. More important, he lived within a mile—as the crow flies—of the Engleton ranch; less than a mile from the wilderness campground Guillermo Menquez was keeping an eye on.

Deputy Chalmers responded to the dispatcher's call, and a moment later, Walt announced that he would oversee the complaint. Chalmers would respond ASAP, bypassing the gate to keep it closed and climbing the two-mile driveway on foot, alert for the intruder. If she reached the house before Walt, she was to inform Hillabrand Walt was en route.

He called Lisa and let her know he was going to be late. Nikki took the phone.

"Why do our faces look backward in the mirror?" she asked.

"It's bedtime, sweetheart. I can try to explain it in the morning."

"But how come?"

"It has to do with the way light reflects."

"Like when the doctor hits your knee?"

"No, that's 'reflex.'"

"But that's what you said."

"Spelled different. Different word."

"Sounds the same."

"Yes, it does. Like hear and here—one's listening, one's a place."

"Reflects is a place?"

"I'll explain tomorrow."

"Promise?"

There it was, that word that had impacted his life more than any other. Bobby. Gail. His badge. His father. He heard his own breathing through the phone's earpiece. He said good night, a lump forming in his throat for reasons unknown. Was this the silence about which Fiona had warned? From which he ran? Was he supposed to call her?

Ten minutes later he reached the reinforced entry gate at the base of the Hillabrand estate—two hundred acres of private property contiguous with the Cold Springs run of the Sun Valley ski mountain. Perched atop an 8,000-foot-high mountaintop, two miles up a gravel road, stood Hillabrand's 10,000-square-foot log "cabin," a monument to a bachelor with too much money and just enough sense to hire a tasteful architect.

"It's my fault," Hillabrand said. He wore a crisply pressed, sky blue polo shirt, creased blue jeans, and

forest green Keens. With his leathery tan, blue eyes, and
wry smile, he had to fight off comparisons to Robert
Redford. "I got absorbed with work. I'd left all the
lights off, so the place was dark as a graveyard—an open
invitation, I'm afraid. I heard something . . . and had a
look . . ." He led Walt down a confusing set of hallways
and reached a hotel-sized kitchen. He pulled back a curtain on the kitchen's Dutch split door.

"He'd been working on this door. Tried to jimmy it."
He opened the door and showed Walt where a crude
tool had been used in an attempt to open the door. "I
switched on the outside light. Got a quick look. Six feet,
broad shoulders. No face. Only his back. Jeans. Dark
sweatshirt. He was gone in a flash. Very fast."

"Hair color?" Walt was taking notes.

"No. Ball cap, I guess."

"You must have a weapon in this place," Walt said.
Hillabrand was a former army general who'd retired into
an NGO. He employed a security detail of service vets
fiercely loyal to him.

"Of course. Did I pursue him into the woods? Come
on, Sheriff. Give me some credit."

"You called your own people first, I take it?"

"You really take a dim view of me, don't you?" He
leaned back. "No. I called nine-one-one and reported
the intruder. I don't keep a posse around me, you know?
Is that what you think? I have staff. Of course I do. But
they keep regular hours."

"Deputy Chalmers will remain with you, preferably in a windowless room—a second-story room will do."

"You have to be kidding me," Hillabrand said.

"A man of your . . . position, sir . . . our first job is your protection." Walt contrasted this with his response to the similar situation at Vince Wynn's residence. He'd assumed any gunshots had driven the intruder away in Wynn's case, but he realized he'd made it personal as well, and that was a bad development.

"You think this was . . . nonsense. I thought . . . the Berkholder thing . . ."

"And that may be all it is, but this is the way we're going to do it."

Chalmers stood at the ready. Hillabrand motioned for her to follow him, and they left. Walt went out the kitchen door, his flashlight on, trained onto the dewy grass.

Tracking wasn't a hobby for him, and it wasn't a professional requirement. It was a study, a science, a passion. He held the Maglite's bluish halogen bulb close to the lawn and watched as a million pearls of dew lit up and sparkled. In their midst, like a string of lakes, were lightless oval shapes, each a footprint of the intruder. He stayed to the side, following them down the curve of the lawn to the edge of the forest and from there into the ever darker woods, alert for displaced leaves, freshly broken twigs, and the bent shafts of plants and wildflowers. Lower and lower down the hill he went, hunched and attentive, excited by the puzzle solving. There were stretches where he lost all signs of the man, wishing he'd brought Beatrice along with him, instead of leaving her in the Cherokee. Tempted to go back and get her, he doubted she'd pick up a scent from the ground alone, and couldn't trouble himself to return.

Five minutes stretched to twenty. It was a steady descent, the intruder avoiding and crossing the occasional game trail. It felt as if he knew where he was going, that this was scouted terrain. And as the invisible path that Walt followed stopped descending and began to traverse the north-facing hill, finally swinging higher and beginning to climb now, he was aimed for the ridge that dropped down into the drainage where the Berkholders and Engletons lived. The drainage where, on the opposing north-facing slope, the campground had been discovered.

A jolt of deepening concern rattled him. Fiona lived over there. As he crested the ridge and briefly glimpsed the lights below, the Engleton ranch called out as a destination. Due to terrain, and without going down to the highway, it was impossible to get from where Walt stood to the other side of the drainage without crossing the Engleton property.

Halfway between Hillabrand's house and the Engletons', he debated his options, favoring returning to the Cherokee, where he had a shotgun and an emergency backpack with a bigger flashlight, batteries, the satellite phone, and warm clothing. It might take him an extra five to ten minutes, because of the climb and then the drive off Hillabrand's mountain, but it seemed worth it.

His legs, aching from the descent and climb, carried him well. He charged back up the mountain, zigzagging in order to set a sustainable pace, and picking up the first game trail he encountered. Wild animals, for the most part, made sensible, if sometimes meandering, routes through forest and across wilderness. Walt followed this trail for two hundred yards and then cut back through the trees, quickly gaining elevation. Minutes later, he reached Hillabrand's out of breath. He radioed Chalmers and told her to allow Hillabrand to move around his house but to stay with him for the time being.

"I picked up his trail and believe he may be heading into the next drainage. I'm headed for the Engleton place."

He called for backup on the way. His closest patrol was nearly twenty minutes away. He directed them to approach without siren or lights, expecting to have completed the first part of his rounds by the time they arrived.

Beatrice knew when Walt was excited. She shot between the seats, her paws on the center console, and licked Walt below the ear.

"Back off!" Walt shouted.

The dog whimpered and backed up, but the thumping of her tail against the backseat, in concert with the pounding of Walt's heartbeat in his ears, gave away her enthusiasm.

Hillabrand's two-mile driveway was crushed stone

and steep with a half dozen hairpin switchbacks. As fast as Walt drove, it wasn't fast enough. He one-handed his phone to dial Fiona's number from his contact list, wondering why he hadn't programmed a speed dial number for her. It made perfect sense that he should have her number set as a speed dial, and yet it seemed too personal at the same time, and he wondered if he was afraid to be seen dialing her via the shortcut, and if so what caused such fear in him. His sense of Fiona and him, of Gail and Brandon, could get so tangled up that it seemed impossible to unknot. He couldn't risk exposing himself to another person the way he had with Gail. It had left him raw and vulnerable in a way he hadn't felt since adolescence, and that was too many years behind him to offer any guidance. As a teen he had stumbled and crashed his way through his early relationships, not understanding himself enough to have much to offer. By adulthood, in his twenties, his focus had been on building a career for himself, with little time or energy to devote to the otherworldly nature of getting inside Gail's skin. They'd made love, they'd had laughs, they ate meals together and attended parties, but never with too much talking, never fully explaining themselves to the other the way he expected relationships were supposed to function. That his only fully invested relationship had collapsed, unexpectedly on his part, left him with the sinking feeling it could happen again far too easily.

The phone rang in his ear. He urged her to pick up. Then the click of the voice mail and his cursing into the car, and Beatrice whimpering again. He skidded to a stop before Hillabrand's reinforced gate and waited for its electronic eye to detect the Cherokee's motion and open. The steel bar climbed and Walt threw a rooster tail behind as he sped out and into a dirt-spewing fishtail turn and down the canyon road, his thumb finding the green button on his cell phone, and redialing her number.

He'd never figured out how a few minutes could stretch into hours, but that was how it felt. The short drive took too long. The Cherokee climbed up the Engleton driveway and Walt jammed the brakes. He hesitated, then shut the engine off and climbed out, running for Fiona's front door.

He pulled up just short of the door, his chest tight despite the fact that there were no signs of any problems here.

He knocked lightly, and when she failed to answer, knocked louder.

No answer.

He called out. "Fiona! It's me!"

A ringing in his ears. The chorus of a summer evening: insects and frogs.

How far to press this?

He stepped around to the side of the cottage as a light breeze stirred the trees. The wood-slat Venetian blinds were pulled, but he pressed an eye to the edge.

It was the sitting area. He flashed back to the two of them on the floor, her legs hooked in his, the back of her head pressed against the leg of the coffee table and thumping softly—that chortle of hers, both satisfied and amused as she arched her back, her nails digging into him. For a moment he didn't breathe. Given the angle, he could barely make out the couch but he thought he saw her curled up on it.

He rapped softly on the window. She'd invited him back anytime. He wanted to see her. He wanted the door opened.

She didn't move. Maybe it was nothing but a blanket and pillows, he thought. He went to the next window, but couldn't get a decent angle there either. His knuckle hovered next to the glass. He withdrew it and returned to the front door and knocked lightly one last time.

No answer.

He faced a choice of kicking in the door or checking the area and leaving. The temptation to bust it down was overwhelming—but was it to satisfy his need or hers? Why the hell wouldn't she answer him? Had she reconsidered? Was that even her on the couch?

He stepped away and walked the perimeter of the cottage, then circled the main house, also dark. He knocked on the front door and the back, but was not answered. From the back patio he looked down over the small pond, its surface gently stirred by the light breeze.

He looked up the hill to the general area where he'd been standing only twenty minutes earlier. Hillabrand's intruder would have passed through the property without going out of his way to circle well around.

He studied the steep incline of the mountain, recalling the campsite. It seemed a plausible destination.

He called dispatch on his radio. "Find Gilly Menquez for me. Fast." He provided a radio channel number for Menquez to use to reach him and then switched his handheld to that channel.

He returned to the Cherokee, not quite able to put the vehicle in gear and leave the Engleton property. He called Fiona's cell phone for a third time. Voice mail.

Again he fought the temptation to kick in her door. She took her privacy seriously, ardently savored her downtime. If she was staying on the couch and not coming to the door, then all his shouting in the world wouldn't make her admit him. To violate that might create an insurmountable wall between them. Along with this came the realization his decision was not professional, but personal. He disliked himself for it. He was supposed to know better.

He cranked the engine, put the Cherokee in gear, and backed up. His headlights suddenly illuminated a young woman—Kira Tulivich—hiding behind a tree just beyond the cottage, a baseball bat firmly in hand. She stood within striking distance of where Walt had had his face pressed to the cottage window. He felt a shiver. *What the hell?* He slammed on the brakes.

But a voice called out over the police band radio. "Sheriff, we've been unable to raise Ranger Menquez. I called his home. His wife hasn't heard from him. He's late and she's worried."

When Walt looked up again, Kira was gone. He accelerated and arrived at the end of the Engleton driveway. Instead of turning right toward the highway, he swung the wheel left, pointing the Cherokee up the hill in the general direction of the abandoned campsite.

"Tell backup they'll find my Cherokee up the old mining road across from Red Top and to catch up to me on the trail. Channel six," he said.

Beatrice beat her tail against the backseat furiously again, somehow understanding they were going for a hike.

An evening thunderstorm had moved through an hour earlier, leaving raindrops like strung crystal beads on the cottage windows. Moonlight now peeked out from behind fast-moving clouds, throwing shadows into the woods like light from behind a slowly moving fan.

Fiona saw men in those shadows. She couldn't tear herself away from the window, had been unable to do so for days now. She stared out over the back of the couch for hours at a time, like a cat or dog, her imagination running wild. She'd been here before, nearly in this same situation, forcing her to question how it was that she might face such a thing twice in one lifetime when some women—most women—never experienced it even once. Did she invite it upon herself, as some had suggested? Did she ask for it, subconsciously want it? If so, what kind of twisted individual did that make her? How could she not know her own self?

She fell into a trance of self-hatred and confusion, her eyes glazed over for minutes at a time, not seeing, not hearing, yet unable to tear herself away. She thought this must be the same sick attraction that people had to horror films. Morbid curiosity. She had projects to complete. Phone calls to return. She needed a shower. Some food. But there she sat, legs tucked up into her chest, chin on the back of the couch. The terror she'd experienced a few nights before had been the anomaly; she rarely felt such things anymore. They'd been burned out of her, as if her body had developed an immunity to fear. It was not that she felt brave—far from it. Numb more aptly described her. Resolved. For all the work, all the so-called progress, the countless hours poured into not seeing herself as a victim, she had little to show for it. An e-mail along with one thud on a wall, and she'd recoiled, reverted, regressed. She'd failed to find her way out, knowing with absolute certainty what this was about, whom this was about.

That was why, when the sound of a car came up the driveway, when its engine idled a long thirty seconds before shutting off, she knew in a moment of clarity what was coming, and yet felt helpless to prevent it. She didn't believe in fate; destiny was, to an extent, something one could control. There were external forces and powers, certainly, and these were things to be reckoned with. But there was also determination and hard work and, from somewhere in the distant reaches of her mind, this idea of *faith*. For all the times she'd told herself to fight back if ever given this chance, she now felt more inclined to accept the inevitable. Monsters were real.

She knew this firsthand.

A knock on the door.

She held her legs more tightly.

Noises in the bushes.

When Walt's face pressed to the glass, sliced into stripes by the blinds, staring into the darkened room, she suppressed a laugh, covering her mouth and slumping down to where she hoped he might not see her.

The gap between what she'd anticipated and seeing Walt was too enormous, too much for her to bridge at a moment's notice. Instead, she froze, hoping he might go away. And then, by the time she'd come to her senses and wanted to see him, longing for his company, she was far too embarrassed to move. How could she possibly explain herself when her one great wish in life, the sum of all her effort, was to never have to explain herself to anyone? To be accepted for who she was, not who she'd been.

He tapped on the glass. She willed him to go away.

And this particular time her will proved the stronger. She thought she heard the door to the main house close, but didn't get up to look. She knew she owed him, if not an explanation, at least an excuse, but didn't pick up the phone.

The motor came back to life and the Cherokee's backup lights shone brightly against the blinds. Slats of light flooded the room as she hung her head, cursing herself for squandering such a chance.

The sound of the motor mixed with the hum of the refrigerator and the rush of blood across her eardrums, and finally faded completely. For the next twenty minutes she sobbed beneath a blanket. Entirely alone.

As the low rumble of a vehicle broke the silence, she knew it had to be him, and she mentally thanked him for giving her a second chance. She hurried to a mirror and worked on her face, wondering if it could be salvaged. A car door thumped shut. She did the best she could: some tissue to the eyes, some lipstick, and she headed to the door to greet him.

Walt and Beatrice ascended the hill trail, the dog working ahead of him, swinging left and right in unpredictable patterns, her nose to the ground. The only discernible sounds were her huffing and snorting as she vacuumed the pine straw. He would never understand how the seemingly random nature of a dog's scenting could produce results, but he'd witnessed it too many times to doubt its success. The only command he'd given her had been "Find it," a birding command that had been honed and modified by trainers to have her search out a human scent, dead or alive. She could do so with laser precision. Given her current agitated state, she had not yet locked onto any scent of importance, a fact that had Walt looking over his shoulder back at the lights of the Engleton place, and up the slope toward the ridge that led to Hil-labrand's. Without Gilly's silence, the more intelligent strategy would have been to work Beatrice up that ridge, attempting to pick up the intruder's scent. But Gilly's well-being trumped any such notion.

He pushed himself more quickly up the hill, burdened by the added weight and encumbrance of the emergency backpack and by carrying the shotgun in his right hand. His radio called him—backup was just arriving to the Cherokee, fifteen to twenty minutes behind him.

Beatrice stopped abruptly and lifted her head. Walt paused as well, watching her. She scented the air, looked back at him, her eyes iridescent in the glare of his head-lamp, and then continued on. *False alarm.*

A quarter mile later he broke off trail and Beatrice extended her search area, ensuring they weren't leaving a scent behind. Soon, she was working ahead of him again, her paws crunching, her nose sucking and snorting. She would disappear for a few minutes and then circle back to measure his pace and reestablish herself. He would cluck for her, letting her know he'd seen her. It was too dark, and he was in too big a hurry to do any tracking; he left all the work up to her.

His thoughts wandered back to Fiona and a series of mental photographs in his mind's eye: the dark shape of her huddled on the couch; the chair misplaced in the center of the room; the absolute dark of the place—both the cottage and the main house without a single light inside, but the motion-sensing exterior lights working;

the calm of the pond; the night sounds all around him. Had he seen her car? He thought it had been there, but couldn't remember its exact location. Why had Kira been hiding behind that tree with a baseball bat?

Beatrice circled back from the dark and nudged his hand: she'd found something. How long had she been gone? One or two minutes. Walt picked up his pace, and in her excitement she rushed ahead of him and out of the glare of his headlamp.

Thirty seconds later, she reappeared and returned to nudge his hand, her tail beating furiously.

"Good girl! Find it! Find it!"

He was jogging now, the backpack bouncing, the funnel of light in front of him setting everything in the forest in motion as shadows stretched and danced. His boots crunched on the trail, his breathing was raspy and heightened.

He recognized his location. He was just below the level ground of the illegal campsite. Bea had led him around to the northern edge.

There, ahead of him, was the unmistakable shape of a human form, its back to a tree. Unmoving. He whistled Bea away—imagining it as a crime scene before he reached the corpse. She jerked as if a rope had been attached, returning to his side and heeling. He reached down and patted her head.

Gilly Menquez came into the beam of the headlamp. *Something in his hand at his side. A gun?*

A bottle of wine.

Empty.

Walt came to a stop in front of the man. Menquez was snoring. Passed out. Walt nudged him with the toe of his boot. Menquez snorted but didn't awaken.

Walt's eyes drifted back into the dark forest, imagining the lights of the Engleton place, the black pearl of the small pond cut into the hill. Anger welled up in him. He staggered back and slumped against a tree, his radio already in hand.

12

Fiona came awake to the rough sensation of Angel licking her hand. The bird songs told her it was early morning. As she blinked repeatedly to clear her eyes, as her fingers uncurled and absentmindedly stroked Angel, she became acutely aware of a hangover headache, dry mouth, and blurred vision. She tried to sit up, but the pain in her head cautioned her to take her time. She reached back and felt a long horizontal knot along the base of her skull, then looked up to see the edge of her kitchen counter directly above and connected the two. To her left, the collapsible footstool was overturned, and this too fit into the picture.

Angel took the opportunity to climb onto her chest and settle into a deep and satisfied purr, and Fiona continued to scratch her behind the ears. She tried to think back, to solve the mystery of finding herself lying on the floor with a lump on her head, but nothing came to her. Only silence where an image should have been. From that silence came the sound of a car, but that had turned out to be Walt—or was that even the right night? Had there been a second car that same night, had it been an altogether different night?

She lifted Angel off and eased her to the floor and tried again to sit up, this time managing to wedge her elbows under her. Her vision woozy, she felt nauseated, on the verge of throwing up. And though the pain drummed intensely at the back of her skull, radiating down through her and provoking the urge to retch, she identified the vertigo and the unexplained silence as the source of her fear. For the fear overcame her like a wave and drowned her. As she vomited, she hoped the purge might clear her head and help her to reorient her-self—to remember something, anything. But it was as if someone had placed her there on the floor, had played some awful trick on her, abandoning her with no hints or clues about the cause of her condition, that she was the object of a joke gone horribly awry.

The smell of the vomit disgusted her and made her move. She sat up, pushed away from it, and struggled forward onto hands and knees. If she hadn't felt the bump she would have sworn she was severely hungover and wouldn't have been surprised to find a near-empty bottle on the coffee table. A few times in her life she'd drunk herself into blackouts, although not since college.

She couldn't imagine she'd done this to herself, but at that point she would have welcomed any explanation. Anything would have been better than the mental silence that stretched as an empty bridge between her present condition and whatever had come before.

She struggled to her feet and, keeping a hand out on the back of a stool, a wall, and a doorknob, found her way into the bathroom, where she undressed and showered. The blurriness of her vision came and went, and when she threw up for a second time, she told herself to get to the hospital. Not trusting her own ability to drive, she called over to the main house, hoping for Kira, but she never picked up.

With the hospital less than a mile away, she moved slowly toward her Subaru, only to realize she was wearing only her bathrobe. She turned and admired her cottage as if seeing it for the first time. The driveway of Mexican pavers formed a kind of courtyard between the main house and her cottage and there was something there, something that connected everything. Again she tried to fill the void of what had come before the fall— for having found no bottle or evidence of drink, she assumed she'd tripped over the footstool. Her brain was functioning enough to tell her that the only viable explanation for the knot on her head was that she'd been walking backward at the time. Away from something. And that it must have been something compelling to keep her attention off the footstool behind her.

But as she drove off the property, even these thoughts

became difficult to recall. She couldn't firmly place where she'd been when she woke up. She touched her hair and found it wet, but didn't remember having taken a shower.

She clutched the wheel more tightly, white-knuckled, focusing on the car and road like when she'd driven solo for the first time. That was her only glimmer of hope: she could recall the moment with absolute clarity—sixteen years old and terrified, her father in the passenger seat.

She convinced herself she wasn't going out of her mind—only that she'd just lost a very important piece of it, a piece she hoped like hell to reclaim.

13

Looking out his back window at the sway of the aspens in a light breeze, Walt recalled a time when his two girls had played just as they were now, but with another woman by their sides. He was grateful for Lisa's help, her tireless patience, her willingness to both discipline and comfort the girls, but he would have preferred Gail despite all her failings as a mother. The night before, he and the girls had watched a DVD that had landed on his office desk, a documentary about a Mongolian camel who wanted nothing to do with her offspring. The story had had a happy ending: a prayer, a reunion of mother and child, and a weeping camel. There would be no happy ending for his family, for his daughters. From now on the girls would be shuttled between two lives, two very different households, and no matter how hard he tried to explain it, it would be up to them to sort it all out, to make sense of the fractures they would encounter for years to come. He hoped to be the glue to hold it all together, to mend the fractures or at least keep them from widening. He could keep the day-to-day routine working; he knew routine, respected its importance. But watching Lisa laugh and play with them—on their level—he couldn't help but see Fiona out there—all four of them out there, laughing and teasing and rebuilding something. It was absurd to make such a jump, but now that he'd crossed one line, the other wasn't so hard, the distance not so great.

He'd clear a day soon and take the girls camping—although they'd probably prefer the shopping malls in Boise. Or maybe shopping and a movie and a motel with a pool.

"You okay?" It was Lisa. He hadn't seen her approaching.

"Yeah. Good. Real good," he said.

"You looked a little zoned."

"I think I just came to an important realization," he said. "I've been laboring under this notion that the girls and I need to suffer because Gail's gone. You showed me something out there just now."

"Me?"

"Fun is fun," he said. "We're going to start having fun around here."

"I like the sound of that," Lisa said, "and I know the girls will too."

"Thank you," he said to her, making sure she felt his sincerity. "You've practically been living here for far too long. That's going to change."

"No problem," she said. She turned to call the girls. Walt caught himself glancing at the wall phone and thinking of Fiona.

Two nights had passed since the Hillabrand intruder, and still nothing but a few voice mails back and forth. She'd been pleasant enough but not gushing, and he'd expected gushing. She wasn't feeling well but didn't want him visiting. He tried to take it in stride. It wasn't easy.

He debated leaving her yet another message, but couldn't imagine a more adolescent move.

He returned to the office and sat at his desk, unable to keep his eye off the phone and e-mail. He read over a proposal currently in front of the county commissioners to privately host the Dalai Lama in Sun Valley, an outdoor event expected to draw an audience of between twenty and fifty thousand, with at least ten thousand coming from out of town. There was no way his small office could manage the traffic and simultaneously guarantee the Dalai Lama's safety; no way he was going to turn over that responsibility to a private security firm, as was being proposed. He nearly began drafting an e-mail, but changed his mind. It could wait.

He reviewed other paperwork instead. A man held in their drunk tank had suffered convulsions and was attempting to sue the county. A suspected rapist needed transfer to Ada County. He signed some paperwork, sent a few e-mails, and made several calls. But each time he reached for the phone, he thought of her, and debated driving out to her place again.

Nancy, his assistant, stood in his doorway. "A body's been found. Mile marker one twenty-five. Some kids, an Adopt-A-Highway crew, discovered it. Tommy Brandon responded and called it in. Says it isn't pretty."

Walt checked the clock. He was scheduled to pick up the Seattle detective, Boldt, at the airport.

"Okay, tell him I'm on my way," Walt said. "And have someone meet that flight and get the sergeant settled, will you, please?"

"No problem."

Typically, news of any death ran a feeling of dread through him as he always thought first of his late brother. But that wasn't the case. He was instead unusually grateful to be called away from his desk, to be rid of the monotony. On the way out the door, he took one last look at his desk phone. Longing.

"And call Kenshaw," he added, trying to make it sound like an afterthought. He appreciated the excuse to contact her. "Tell her to bring her gear and meet us. Same with the coroner. And Barge Levy. And you'd better check with Meridian to test their availability." The state crime lab would be involved if there was a determination of foul play.

On his way to the Jeep Cherokee, he identified a lightness to his step, and tried to suppress it.

Several cars and trucks lined the breakdown lanes on both sides of State Highway 75. Fiona's Subaru was not among them.

Parked on the shoulder behind Brandon's cruiser were two pickup trucks, one with six Boy Scouts in the truck bed, all armed with pokers and Day-Glo garbage bags. He felt bad that they'd discovered the body, and urged Brandon to release them and get them "the hell away from here."

Brandon had cobbled together a police tape barrier using a real estate sign, a lug wrench, and a broken ski pole as fence posts. Walt spotted the body at the epicenter of the confined area.

He ordered Beatrice to stay in the Jeep. She smeared her nose against the glass, drawing Chinese characters, desperate to join him.

The lower third of the thousand-foot mountain, a scree field of broken red rock, terminated thirty yards from the highway, where it joined a field of brown, sun-baked weeds and buffalo grass. The open eyes of the dead body, had there been any, would have looked up at the red of the rock, the full saturation of the evergreens, and an impossibly blue sky that was the hallmark of high mountain living.

"Some kind of face-lift," Walt said, approaching the body. It had been severely preyed upon.

"I haven't messed with him," Brandon said. "Wanted to wait for you. But it's pretty obvious we won't be matching that face with any missing person reports."

Walt neared the haphazardly installed police tape.

"There's a set of tire tracks, so tread lightly," Brandon said.

"I see 'em."

Walt dodged the tire treads, and kneeled. "It's a truck. A pickup maybe." He studied the lay of the grass. "Three . . . no, four . . . kids and an adult approached the body. That is, if you came in from over there." He pointed.

"I did."

Walt parted some grass and used a stick to lift some of the matted weeds.

"The predators were a family of fox and a dog the size of a Labrador. The dog was running. Might have been after the fox, not our John Doe."

The body appeared to have been tossed into a tangle of twigs and weeds that ran along the base of the scree field, which was piled four feet high in places and stretched out sixty yards or more.

Instead of eyes, two blood-black holes stared up. A piece of the nose was missing. He'd been a big man— six-four or -five, two-seventy. Fit. Wide shoulders. Huge thighs in what had to be custom-tailored jeans.

Walt declined to move the body until he had some decent photos.

As if on cue, Fiona's Subaru pulled up. She climbed out, waved at Walt, and went around back to collect her gear.

He remembered her saying that their moment together wouldn't interfere with their professional work, but there was something wrong about her not answering any of his calls or e-mails and now showing up all sunny and bright. In fact he resented it, and had Brandon not been there, he would have rushed over to her and demanded some answers. It was then he realized he was going to be the one to have a hard time keeping this professional.

As Walt stood there, his mind reeling, Brandon had the good sense to direct her around the side of the roped-off area and to help her over the security tape.

She looked tired but determined to appear otherwise.

"Hi, there!" she said, as if they were neighbors running into each other in the supermarket.

"Uhhh," Walt said.

"Good God!" She staggered back as she spotted the body among the sticks and debris. She glanced sharply at Walt, back to the body, over at Brandon. Back to the body. She looked afraid and confused and as if she might be sick. "Dear God." She took another step back, kneeled, and retched.

When she looked up, she had tears in her eyes.

He took one quick step toward her, wanting to comfort her, but caught himself like a runner coming off the blocks before the gun.

"You okay? Should have warned you. Sorry about that. You don't have to do this," he said.

Brandon looked at him like he was crazy. Walt never excused anyone from a crime scene, especially not the photographer.

"Someone's got to take the pictures," Brandon said,

speaking what he was thinking. Brandon lacked the social filter that came on standard model human beings. He tended to say whatever entered his head.

"I'm okay," she said. "I can do it."

"You don't look okay," Walt said.

"You get used to it," Brandon said, trying for sympathetic but sounding brutish.

Her tears hit Walt the hardest. He'd forgotten how horribly a dead body could impact the uninitiated.

She busied herself, keeping her attention on the contents of her camera bag as she switched lenses and checked filters. Her hands shook to where she dropped a lens. She scrambled to recover it, blowing onto and fogging its glass and inspecting it, but all with the exaggerated movements of someone who knew she was being watched.

Walt heard a car door shut and, turning in that direction, felt the hair rise on the nape of his neck as a silhouette of a massive figure stood on the pavement's edge. Behind the man, a sheriff's cruiser had joined the breakdown lane and now the commanding silhouette made sense, and Walt raised a hand toward Sergeant Lou Boldt. He experienced both exhilaration and dread. The teacher had walked in on his unfinished science project.

Torn between wanting to comfort Fiona and welcoming the sergeant, Walt moved toward the highway. Boldt came down the embankment. He was broad-shouldered, somewhere in his late forties, his graying, close-cropped haircut a throwback to the 1950s. His head appeared oversized, a condition emphasized by his short neck. A pair of reading glasses hung around that neck, bouncing off a red tie and crisp white shirt, framed by a brown sport coat, threadbare at the sleeves. As he drew closer to Walt, a warmth filled his pale gray eyes. He reminded Walt of a husky or wolf. They shook hands vigorously, like long-lost friends, Boldt towering over Walt. His voice was deep but surprisingly gentle for such a big man.

"I hope I'm not intruding."

Walt thought how much more impressive the man was in person, compared to a chat window on a computer monitor.

"Not at all," Walt said. Both men knew he was lying.

"Never been one to sit around a motel room."

"I know the feeling."

"You mind?" he asked, nodding toward the crime scene.

Walt waved him forward and glanced at Fiona, wondering how she was doing. Wondering if she'd give him some look, some sign that she was indeed the same woman who'd freely—hungrily—shared herself with him only a few days before. But she maintained her professional demeanor, her head in her gear—or maybe she was still too overcome by the sight of the body to look up.

Boldt accepted introductions and then went silent, almost reverent, as he approached the body. He didn't comment on the amateur job of the tape barrier. He didn't make small talk with Fiona or Brandon. Instead, he looked left and right, studied the ground as Walt had done, took in the tangle of branches and brambles that partly concealed the body.

"Don't let me get in the way," he finally said to Walt.

"Happy to have you," Walt lied, wishing he'd had a few minutes more alone with the body before Boldt had arrived.

Boldt stepped closer, moving slowly and deliberately. "I hate outdoor scenes," he said. "Give me a nice small apartment any time."

"A lot of variables," Walt said.

"Far too many."

The man's precaution impressed Walt. The tentativeness of each step. The scrutiny of his surroundings.

Brandon caught Walt's eye and raised an eyebrow, also impressed.

"Coyotes?" Boldt asked.

"A family of fox and a good-sized dog," Walt answered.

"Did that hawk have a role in it?" Boldt asked.

He'd caught Walt by surprise, a situation that brought a flush to his face. Boldt pointed out a matted mess of reddish feathers and blood-stained down ten yards south, at the edge of the tangle of avalanche debris.

"Red-tail," Walt said, identifying it immediately. "Looks fresh. You're right."

He instructed Brandon to bag the dead bird, and Brandon looked anything but thrilled.

"You think he was thrown in there?" Walt asked.

"Kind of looks it," Boldt said. "Are those tire tracks from a pickup truck?"

"We'll need to pull a tape to confirm it, but I'd say so."

"He's a big boy," Boldt said. "Hell of a throw from that distance."

"Got that right."

"Odd place to dump a body if that's what we're looking at," Boldt said, one eye cast toward the highway. "All the open country you've got around here, and a person chooses the side of the highway."

"He could have been hiking. Could have come down the side of the mountain. But there are no real trails along this stretch. And if he'd been bushwhacking, his socks, where they're exposed, would be covered in cheat grass and be carrying good old Idaho dust. The socks are way too clean. He's a mess—don't get me wrong. But he wasn't hiking."

"I like the way you think," Boldt said.

A guy like Boldt would never see the accident first. He would look for foul play, invent it from a dozen different scenarios and then slowly and willingly backtrack to settle on accidental death or natural causes, but only much later.

"Maybe . . ." Walt said, "someone did him in the vehicle, panicked, and dumped him here. More an act of passion."

"Works for me." He didn't sound at all convinced, and Walt wondered why he'd thrown that out there. Better to keep his lips zipped around Boldt.

As Boldt moved to his right, dropped to a knee, and then stood back up, Walt's resentment over the intrusion gave way to admiration. It was like watching a big-league hitter at batting practice.

"Listen," Boldt said, "do what it is you do. Don't let me interfere."

"We would normally wait for Fiona—Ms. Kenshaw—to give us the go-ahead," Walt replied. "When she's through with him in this position, we'd roll him and look for ID and go inch by inch for evidence."

"I'm making you uncomfortable," Boldt said.

"Dead bodies make me uncomfortable, not visiting detectives."

Fiona relaxed the camera. "I'm done until I can get closer."

"Gloves?" Walt asked Boldt, producing a pair of surgical gloves and offering them to his guest. But Boldt waved him off and, reaching into the pocket of his sport coat, withdrew a pair.

"I'm going to play up the significance of the tire tracks and try to work them into the story, so for now, Fiona, give me whatever you can of the tracks, and stay well clear of them if possible. Brandon, you'll help me roll the body. We'll go after it from the other side. Fiona, make sure to get close-ups of the sticks and all this stuff around him."

"What's all this rock and debris from? Landslide?" Boldt asked.

"Snow slides," Walt explained. "Each winter we see slides all along here. A number of deer and elk are found as it melts each spring."

"Lovely."

"The slides shove all the year's deadfall, the smaller live trees, you name it, down ahead of them. Rock, scree, and everything else piles up here at the bottom."

"Looks like a bomb hit," Boldt said.

"Pretty close to that."

Boldt processed what he'd been told, filing it away. You could see the guy thinking. Over his entire career, Walt had investigated a dozen suspicious or criminal deaths. Boldt probably handled that many per month in a bad month, and had been doing so for a quarter century.

Brandon established a route up through the detritus and led the way for Fiona, who climbed tentatively. Walt could tell by the way she moved that she still wasn't herself. She should have taken his offer to walk away from this one; he could have faked his way through some pictures.

"You noticed the red-tail," Walt said. "The hawk," he clarified. "Anything else I've missed?"

Fiona was down on one knee taking pictures, partially obscured by the upended branches. Head down, she was either adjusting a setting on the camera, or struggling for composure.

"Could it be an accidental death?" Boldt asked. "This location?"

"Absolutely."

"But the boots and clothes don't look exactly right," Boldt said, searching for what Walt had been getting at.

"They'd stop me from making too hasty a ruling, if that's what you're asking."

"It is." For the first time in several minutes, Boldt stepped closer to the pile of bramble and sticks. "I might bag his head and hands and feet," Boldt allowed, clearly reluctant to say anything. "Paper bags. Prior to rolling him. Moving a person that size . . . moving him out of there is going to be an adventure. Bound to shake a few leaves off the tree."

"Tommy!" Walt called out.

"Paper bags," Brandon said. "Got it."

"Back of my Cherokee if you don't have them. Left side. In the backpack."

"I'm on it."

Fiona met eyes with Walt through the tangle of twigs, still looking slightly pale and definitely disoriented. He wished there were something he could do for her. He wanted to dismiss her and allow her to get away from looking close-up through a lens at the man with the missing eyes. Her own eyes were distant and unfocused; he wasn't sure she even saw him.

"Maybe that's enough," he said to her. "We can take it from here."

She shook her head. "I'm good," she said.

"A big guy like this doesn't go down easy," Boldt said.

"No."

"The head wound, right at the scalp line? There's not enough blood."

"Postmortem? Maybe occurred when they tossed him."

"*They* is the operative word. A guy that size, it would take two."

"Might have been robbery," said Brandon, returning with the paper bags and tape. "Check out the tan line on his left wrist."

"Yes, I saw that, too," Boldt said. "Not just a missing watch, but a big watch—a very big watch."

"A TAG Heuer maybe. Something like that. You tell him about the break-ins?" Brandon asked.

Walt dressed down his deputy with a single look. He had no intention of running down every active case.

"He's referring to a pair of B-and-E's in the area. Made to look like bears. Probably some itinerants. We get a lot of that in summers, more so this year because of the economy."

"But doubtful he was out hiking," Boldt said, repeating what he'd been told.

Boldt looked up the inhospitable scree face of the mountain. Low cumulus clouds moved swiftly north to south against the static edge of the mountain peak. It was disorienting; for a moment it appeared the mountain was moving, not the clouds.

Walt wasn't buying the hiking theory. There were no established trails up there where the trees met the scree field. He didn't expect a city cop to understand it, but he wasn't going to repeat himself. He could invent a story to explain the tire tracks: the driver could have veered off road to avoid hitting a deer, the tracks having nothing to do with the body; or a driver might have spotted the body and, not knowing what it was, driven over for a closer look and then taken off; or the pickup might have dumped the body.

"Get the name of the Boy Scout leader, the guy driving those kids, and let's get them out of here," Walt instructed Brandon. "We don't want them seeing us rolling him. This is bad enough already."

Maybe the medical examiner would be able to tell a better story. "Bruising might fill in some of this," Walt said.

"True enough."

He and Boldt moved through the thicket of tumbled debris and approached the body from uphill.

"Brandon!" Walt shouted. "Get a tarp. Back of the Cherokee."

Brandon waved.

More cars slowed. He saw people using their cell phones to take pictures. Boldt saw it too as they waited for the tarp. He pointed out a dirt track that led to a nursery south of their position.

"We'll canvass the area and put something out on the radio," Walt said. "This is the one and only road up and down the valley. We could easily have a witness to the truck running off the shoulder."

When Brandon returned with the tarp, the three men positioned it and then rolled the body. The back of the skull was staved. The blunt force had been delivered by something fairly wide, long, and solid.

"Well, there's our cause of death," Boldt said.

"Those jeans are worth a week's pay," Brandon said, spotting the leather tag on the belt loop. "And those boots are Van Gorkoms. Custom made, Mountain Trekkers. Fifteen hundred a pop."

"Ouch," Boldt said. "So the guy was a clotheshorse."

"Apparently not the only one," Walt said. "I've never heard of Van Gorkoms."

"He's wearing what? Size fifteen?" Brandon said. "Guys like him and me, we can't buy stuff off the rack."

"But you don't wear Van Gorkoms," Boldt said.

"Me? A saddlemaker in Shoshone makes my hiking boots. They're okay but they don't last, and they give me blisters when I'm breaking them in."

"I don't think the detective actually cares, Tommy."

A fade line on the back pocket of the blue jeans suggested a wallet, but as Walt searched for it, he came up empty-handed.

"Missing billfold, missing watch," Boldt said.

Walt shook his head.

"A carjacking gone bad?" Boldt suggested.

"Probably the best explanation we're going to get on what we've got," Walt said, hating to admit it.

"It was *his* vehicle, you're saying." Brandon sounded impressed. "A hitchhiker maybe, or someone fakes a breakdown and gets this guy to pull over. Guy gets out to help and gets a tire iron on the back of the skull for being the Good Samaritan. They get a wallet, a watch, and an SUV, and the whole thing's over in three minutes."

"They hit him a little hard, and dump the body as quickly as possible," Boldt said.

The sleeves of the dead man's shirt were both torn, and Walt reached to open the one on the left arm wider, revealing a sloppy tattoo. It looked like two initials: KK. He tore the shirt slightly wider: another poorly delineated tattoo of a fat-cheeked cherub beneath a storm cloud blowing up a storm.

Walt thought he heard Fiona gasp as she took several more shots of the overturned body. Drawn by the sound, Walt looked over at her, but she wouldn't come out from behind the camera. Her hands were shaking too much for the shots to be any good. He shouldn't have asked her for the close-ups. He'd been thoughtless and cruel, and he wished it was just the two of them so he could apologize.

"That's enough pictures," he said—too little, too late. He wanted her out of here. "You can wrap it up. If you can, have them to me sometime tomorrow morning."

"No problem, Sheriff."

If Brandon caught her use of his title instead of his Christian name, he did a good job of hiding it, though Walt heard how wrong it sounded coming from her mouth. Walt didn't want Brandon having anything on him and wondered if he'd already fallen behind in the count.

Fiona replaced the lens cap and negotiated her way back toward her car, going the long way around to avoid the cordoned-off area.

"That sure looks like a prison tat," Boldt said. "Suggests his prints will ID him."

"I know who it is," Walt declared as it added up for him.

"He looks familiar to me, too," Brandon said, believing Walt meant to name a local man. "But I can't place him."

"New Orleans Saints," Walt said. He knew Brandon was a football fan.

"Goddamn, you're right! The Gale Force. Marvin Gale. Linebacker."

"Martel," Walt said, "not Marvin."

He and Boldt had previously discussed Vincent Wynn's accusations surrounding the paroled linebacker.

"That's him?" Boldt said, sounding gravely disappointed. He nodded, assessing the size of the man and adding in the crudely drawn tattoos. "Of course."

"I think we can rule out a carjacking," Walt said.

He felt her before he took her in. Fiona, standing on the shoulder of the highway by her Subaru, the wind tossing her hair, arms at her sides, shoulders sagged in resignation. Overcome by the sight of death, no doubt. Saddened. But she also seemed to be waiting. *For him?* he wondered. He hoped. He ached to go to her, to leave this, to say something.

She climbed into the car and drove away.

14

Walt and Boldt approached the nursery on foot, down a dirt track a quarter mile south of the body. The sun shone brightly, sparking off the plastic tarps of the six 50-foot-long hothouses, curved over the garden beds like small Quonset huts. A beat-up green pickup truck was parked at the end where the track widened into a bulb. A miniature backhoe sat outside a barn shed big enough for two vehicles. Next to the shed stood an old, half-sized Airstream trailer with dirty windows and an open padlock hanging from a rusted hasp.

Walt pounded on the door, as Boldt wandered over and looked inside the nearest hothouse.

"Heck of an operation," Boldt said.

"Nothing much grows here without a lot of help and a

little luck," Walt said. "Twenty below in the winter. High nineties in the summer. Dry as a bone."

The door was answered by a sleepy-eyed woman in her midthirties who'd seen too much sun and too little of the hairdresser. Her forest green golf shirt carried a logo of a tree beneath which was stitched: GOLDEN EAGLE NURSERY.

"Help you, Sheriff?"

"Hope so," Walt said.

She descended the rough wooden steps, shorter than Walt, sinewy and lean.

"Maggie Sharp," she said, shaking his hand.

Walt introduced Boldt as a colleague from Seattle.

"Just visiting," Boldt said.

"What's up? What's with all the cars up there?"

"We're wondering if any time in the past couple of days you saw a pickup truck go off the west shoulder of the highway?"

"Up there? I don't know . . . No."

"Anything you can tell us would help," Walt said, sensing the woman's hesitation. "You won't be involved personally."

"Wasn't my truck," she said, as Boldt walked over to the vehicle.

"No," Walt said. "Wider tires than your Chevy." Boldt looked over, silently impressed Walt had already scouted the truck. "There's no law against driving off the road," Walt said, forcing a smile.

"Wasn't me," she said, her tone unnecessarily defensive.

"I think we've already established that."

"So?"

"You're the closest to the area. Maybe you saw some people up there? Something—anything—going on."

"At night perhaps," Boldt said, having joined them.

"I don't work nights here. Who said I work nights?"

Boldt and Walt met eyes.

Boldt said, "A neighbor of yours, someone in . . . Golden Eagle . . . thought they saw a pickup on the left side of the road, but seeing how this road of yours leads in here, we're thinking they might have seen your truck and confused it with the truck we're interested in."

Walt shot Boldt a quizzical look: where had he come up with that piece of fiction?

"Is that right?" Her eyes told them both she was buying herself time.

"Lights on vehicles can play tricks with the eye at night," Walt said. "Depth perception. If it was your truck and not the truck we're interested in, that helps."

"Why would I be here at night?" Maggie Sharp asked. "It's not like anyone's paying overtime around here. I work a ten-hour shift, five days a week. Six o'clock comes around, I'm gone. I appreciate the job and all, don't get me wrong. Not a lot of jobs going around right now. I'm not complaining. I'm just saying if it was after six, it wasn't me."

"Okay," Boldt said. "That makes sense enough. How 'bout your boss? One of your coworkers?"

"At night? Listen, if there was a freeze warning or something, maybe. And the sheriff can tell you, we get hard freezes every month of the year. But a lot fewer since global warming. Right? And none in the past month or so. It's a hot summer. Hot and even drier than usual."

"These things hold up in the thunderstorms?" Walt asked, looking out across the hothouses.

"They do okay," she said.

"We had a pretty decent storm a couple nights back," he recalled. "Hailed, didn't it?"

Her eyes narrowed; she sensed a trap but couldn't see it clearly. "I can't speak for the owner," she said. "All I can tell you is if someone saw a pickup after six it wasn't me. Wasn't mine. Okay?"

"Okay."

"So we should talk to the owner," Boldt said. "About a truck being seen here at night."

"No. I mean, sure. That's up to you, right? What do I care?"

And yet she did seem to care. Both men sensed her misgivings.

"If you remember anything," Walt said, "we're in the book."

"Yeah, I think I can find you." The smile didn't work on her face, as out of place as the attempted confidence in her voice.

The men thanked her. Walt and Boldt walked back up the road toward the highway.

"How'd you know it wasn't her truck?" Boldt asked.

"You're walking on it," Walt said. "Noticed on the way in that there were only two trucks using this very much. A pickup with narrower rubber—hers—and a dually, probably a delivery truck. There are some other tracks mixed in, but they're older for the most part and they're all passenger cars, not pickups."

"More to this country sheriff thing than I might have thought," Boldt said.

"I take a lot of heat from my father. He's ex-Bureau, as you maybe already know. He thinks I'm wasting my time here. A big day for us is a bar brawl."

"To each their own. You have kids?"

"Two girls. Twins. Eleven going on fifteen."

"Good place for them, I imagine."

"Why I'm here."

"Not everybody gets that," Boldt said.

"You?"

"Boy and girl about the same age. If I could figure out how to live in a place like this?" he said, looking into the sky. "Yeah. No-brainer. So I get it."

"If you ever feel like retiring," Walt said. He meant it more as a joke but he thought how valuable a person like Boldt would be on a contractual basis, and it gave him some new ideas. He'd taken to the guy immediately. He'd prepared himself for some holier-than-thou city detective; was stunned to find the man so approachable.

"What'd you think of her?" Boldt asked.

"Not much. Afraid of something. The badge, I suppose. Get a lot of that up here. You?"

"Same. Wasn't buying her."

"So adamant about not working nights."

"Yeah. So we know two things," Boldt said.

"She saw something, and she saw it at night," Walt said. "And that's a problem for her."

"And us."

"And us," Walt agreed.

Boldt stopped near the middle of the dirt track and spun slowly in a full circle. "Jeez," he said. He drew in a deep breath, and took in so much air he coughed. "You've got to be kidding me."

Walt took in the panorama of sage-covered hills, evergreens, and blue sky. "Forget to look sometimes," he admitted.

"No property in sight with any kind of view."

Walt realized Boldt had been assessing the likelihood of witnesses.

"I don't often canvass," he explained. "We'll work the local media. Put the word out. My guys will go door-to-door in Golden Eagle, Rainbow Bend, and maybe some of Gimlet—all nearby subdivisions. There're a couple private ranches tucked up behind the mountain on this side. That's why there aren't any trails up there—there's a lot of deeded ground." They reached the highway shoulder and turned north toward the cars scattered off the road. "A truck going off the highway at night," Walt said. "This stretch is lousy with elk and deer. We see more than a fair share of accidents and rolls right here."

"You think he may have been on foot?" Boldt asked.

"Someone swerves away from a deer and hits this guy on the side of the road?"

"Maybe swipes him. Guy goes down headfirst," Walt said. "It wouldn't take much."

"Then why wouldn't Martha Stewart back there tell us what she saw?"

Walt bit back a smile.

"We're going to get along okay," Walt said.

"I'll be out of your hair day after tomorrow," Boldt reminded.

"What if I beg?" Walt said.

Boldt grinned. The two men walked north, cars slowing to rubberneck the cop cars. Walt needed to assemble a team to walk the field, alert for cigarette butts, beer cans, litter of any kind.

Then he remembered that the Boy Scouts had been collecting litter at the time of the discovery, and he took off running up the road, reaching for his radio and calling through to Brandon.

Boldt trailed behind, in no particular hurry, already scheming how he might extend his stay.

15

Along with three deputies, Walt moved carefully through the litter strewn across the plastic sheets taped to the motor pool's garage floor. The four piles of trash were kept separate, in quadrants designated by blue painter's tape. Piece by piece, the bits of highway-side litter—beer cans, cigarette butts and packs, newspaper, fast food, and even a withered condom or two—were carefully dragged and moved away from where the four bright orange bags had been dumped.

It did not escape Walt that these piles possibly represented his best and only chance at nailing a killer, that a bunch of well-meaning children had collected what might be his only hard evidence in the case.

It was seven p.m., well past Walt's usual office hours, something not lost on his subordinates, and no doubt adding to their concerted efforts. The mood, originally lightened with trash jokes, had turned serious as time wore on. Walt kept his head down, using a wooden poker to separate the garbage into three different piles: useless; personal; possible DNA. Corn chip bags and fast food went into "useless"; anything with handwriting or printing into "personal"; empty beer and soda cans, cigarette butts, the condoms into "possible DNA." The Boy Scouts had done a thorough job, and though Walt had assigned five of his deputies into the same field to collect evidence, he didn't anticipate them finding much.

Nancy had stayed late as well, without any discussion. She arrived at Walt's side carrying a piece of paper in her right hand, and Walt knew what it was without asking. On this day there was only one piece of paper, one piece of information, that would bring her out to the garage in person.

"ALPS?" he called across the garage, his voice reverberating off the corrugated steel roof. *Automated Latent Print System.*

She nodded. "It's him," she said.

Walt churned, an odd combination of dread and relief: pleased that he'd gotten it right, disturbed by the confirmation. *Martel Gale.*

"Notify Boldt," he said. "See if he wants to grab dinner."

Walt couldn't remember the last time he'd sat down to dinner one-on-one with another guy, never mind that it was a business dinner. Somehow that didn't matter. It wasn't political. It wasn't family. It wasn't required. He'd chosen to be here.

Boldt was a commanding presence, whether standing over a dead body or sitting across the table at Zou 75, an upscale Asian restaurant on the north end of Hailey's Main Street. His size accounted for much of it, as did his being easily mistaken for Brian Dennehy, that sense of celebrity that he carried. But more than that, it was the intensity that he radiated, a kind of force field that made even the loudest talker whisper instead, that caused children to stare and adults to speculate on who this person might be.

Walt, accustomed to drawing looks whenever he wore the uniform, knew to ignore the gaping; but with Boldt at the table, he became all the more aware that the two of them were the center of attention.

They waded through the requisite small talk, some sharing about family, their mutual love of the outdoors and Whidbey Island, a place Boldt liked to vacation and where Walt occasionally visited his father. Very occasionally.

"I read the transcript of one of your lectures," Walt said. "'The Victim Speaks If You're Willing to Listen.'"

"Don't hold it against me. I'm not much of a speaker."

"I found it interesting, and I have to say I practice most of what you preach."

"I've got nothing new to say, believe me. Rehashing old ideas is all."

"What does Martel Gale tell us, now that we know it's him?"

"We covered some good scenarios earlier," Boldt said. "The watch and the wallet could be a smoke screen, could be for real."

"Vincent Wynn threatened to kill the man and take his chances with the courts," Walt reminded. They'd reviewed this during an earlier Skype conversation.

"I have to say it plays several ways when we factor in Caroline Vetta. Maybe Caroline's killer is dead. Or maybe he's an easy scapegoat. Or maybe Wynn or Boatwright had their own reasons for taking out Gale that had nothing to do with Caroline. Or maybe it had everything to do with Caroline—that one of them attributed her death to Gale and brought their own brand of justice to the table."

"We have six pieces of trash that might carry DNA," Walt said. "That's discounting the beer and pop cans because they can be so tricky for the lab. Twelve, including the cans."

"Too expensive to run those without a suspect," Boldt said.

Walt shrugged, not sure he wouldn't resort to that at some point. The existence of a national DNA database for felons made it all the more tempting.

"Then there's your B-and-E's," Boldt said. "The possibility this guy ran into the wrong guy in the woods."

"We should conclude our canvassing tomorrow," Walt said. "Maybe we pick up something. And our plea to drivers will be on the morning news. There's a good chance someone saw something. It's a busy highway. But I'm not holding my breath."

"You want to sit in on my interview with Wynn tomorrow, it's fine with me."

"Appreciate it. Let's see about that. We're withholding Gale's identification. I'd like to keep that quiet for a day or two, which would allow you to interview both Boatwright and Wynn without them the wiser. Maybe I'll accompany you—drive you—and talk to some of his neighbors. With that threat he made, made to my face, it would be irresponsible not to pursue. But the interview is yours. Gives you the upper hand."

"If you change your mind."

"Thanks."

"The tire tracks?"

"The tread is being cross-referenced. We got some markers on one of the right-side tires: if we find the truck we can tie it to the scene, but we're a long way from pulling a sales receipt and identifying a suspect. A long way."

They worked through their entrées. Boldt ordered a glass of milk, and as it arrived drew more curious looks from the neighboring tables. Walt had a second beer.

"What am I missing?" Walt asked. "What am I not doing that you would do?"

"I'm not looking at this critically," Boldt said.

"But if you were?"

"But I'm not. Listen, I respect jurisdiction, believe

me. That work you did on that dirt driveway? I couldn't have done that. You're better at this than I am."

"False modesty aside, anything else occur to you?"

Boldt ate some more of his teriyaki chicken and pushed aside the pickled seaweed. "I work with a criminal psychologist, a woman named Daphne Matthews who has a way of drilling down into a victim along the same lines I do, but all from inside the head instead of the evidence. A case like this, with so many moving parts, the possible relationship to Caroline Vetta, the complication with Wynn's threat . . . If it was in my house, I'd bring her in and have her work up Gale. She's been working Vetta since that happened, and maybe she'd pick up an overlap. Who knows? But in terms of police work—the grunt stuff—I'm right with you so far. I wouldn't lose sight of that nursery, though, like you. It moves down my list, especially with limited manpower and resources."

"Can we ask her to look into Gale, or is that something I shouldn't ask?"

"It relates to Vetta as far as I'm concerned. I can ask her to do that. Absolutely."

"I've only worked with a profiler a couple of times, and only once when I had a suspect in custody."

"She's not a profiler. Not exactly. What's interesting about Matthews is she's able to tell you who the victim was, where the victim was emotionally in and around the death. She can run a background on a suspect and give you a percentage of probability that's uncanny. She has a heck of a track record."

"All of that would help."

"Yeah, it couldn't hurt."

"You'll make the call?"

"I will," said Boldt.

"You ought to try the seaweed," Walt said. "It's way better than it looks."

"Not a chance," Boldt said, sipping the milk and savoring it as if a fine wine.

16

"You don't look comfortable," the woman said.

Fiona glanced around the office at the medical school degrees, the photos of views from several different mountain peaks—her eye critical of the photography.

"I'm not."

"You've been to counseling before?"

"I have. A few years ago. It wasn't fun."

"This isn't then," the woman cautioned. She was small and thin and her gray hair was cut like a man's. For an instant Fiona wondered about her sexual orientation, then wondered why she would think such a thing.

"The thing is . . . It's just that there's this blank spot and I want it back. I thought everything would come back within a day or two."

"Sadly, no. Head injury can affect memory, both short

term and long term. I define short term as the past thirty minutes. Even though only a little over a day, the blank spot you're talking about would be considered long term."

"I don't remember what happened . . . where I was, what was going on. I don't even remember falling down. Just waking up with Angel licking me."

"Not unusual."

"It is if you're on my side of it."

"Yes, and we can address that anxiety. I meant strictly medically speaking."

"I don't want to address it. I want it back."

"And it will come back. It nearly always does. I've had patients who've been in traffic accidents lose anywhere from a few minutes up to several months before the accident, but it has always come back. There are exercises you can do."

"And if it's not entirely *physical*?" Fiona asked.

"Emotions can block memory. Absolutely. If that's what you're asking. Fear can alter memory. A man comes into a bank waving a gun at five people and you'll get five different explanations of what happened. Very common."

"And if the man then pistol-whips one of the five?"

"Are you suggesting someone hurt you? Someone caused your injury?" The woman leaned forward in her chair and spoke more softly. "It says . . . I read it was an accident."

"It was an accident, I'm sure. But I don't remember, that's all."

"You're safe here, Fiona. You can talk to me. Nothing

leaves this room that you don't want to have leave this room. You need to know that. To trust that."

"It's nothing like that."

Katherine studied her thoughtfully. "How are you sleeping?"

"Not great."

"Memory is affected by sleep and fatigue as well."

"These exercises . . . can they bring back those missing minutes?"

"They will help you retain your current memories. The best thing for those missing minutes is to get you back on track, to get the injury behind you and your life moving forward. The brain has an amazing capacity to fill in, to catch back up. To reboot. You were unconscious for a period of time. How long, we don't know. You awoke and it was morning?"

"Yes."

"So you'd been out the entire night."

"I'd been sleeping."

"We don't know that. What you call sleep may have been the result of the trauma. That kind of concussion, severe head injury, can do strange things to memory. What's the last thing you recall that night? If we establish the bookends, we may be able to fill in the in-between."

"A car in the driveway. I remember that. The voice of a friend of mine, I think, but I can't say for sure."

"Can you check with this friend? Ask if he or she came to see you?"

"He. I suppose so."

"He may have talked to you. Do you think . . . Is it possible that—"

"No. Not him. No. He didn't push me or hurt me or anything, if that's what you're going to ask."

"And you're sure?"

"Positive."

"Then I'd ask him."

Fiona nodded.

"Do you remember having a conversation with him?"

"No. It's more like I hear him calling me. I'm not sure that isn't wishful thinking. It's all very dreamlike. Doesn't seem so real, you know?"

"I'd check with him."

"Yeah."

"Is there a reason you haven't done that already?"

Fiona felt a spike of heat in her face and hoped Katherine wouldn't see it. But the woman didn't miss much.

"Are these the emotions you were referring to?" Katherine asked.

"It's complicated," Fiona said.

"The point being that there can easily be two elements to the memory loss: physical and emotional. If you can get past the emotional, the physical may repair faster."

"What if I don't want to know?"

"Can memory loss protect us? Absolutely. Discounting the physical, organic element to such loss, we believe that's a major factor: obscuring the memory of the original incident, the painful, physical trauma. It's too much to face at first. The body has to heal, has to put distance between itself and the accident, before the brain allows us to relive it. But it does come back. It will."

"And if it's too much to face? What then?"

"I get the feeling, Fiona, that you know much more than you're sharing. It's okay to share your fears. Your suspicions. That's what I'm here for. Please don't prejudge yourself. Don't think you can shock me or that I'll judge you in any way for what you're thinking. It doesn't work like that. I'm here to help. I'm equipped to deal with whatever you may throw at me. I want to help you. Please."

Fiona stared back through fearful eyes.

"The man involved. Tell me about him."

"No, thank you."

"You said he's a friend. More than a friend?"

"Yes, but just recently."

"The night—"

"No. But recent."

"And you're afraid to ask him if he came by, if he called for you. I can see that. You don't want to sound needy. You don't want to sound injured or damaged."

"It isn't that."

"Then it's . . . ?" Katherine viewed her compassionately.

"Complicated," she said. "I explained that."

"He's married? Something like that?"

"No. I mean, yes, but no . . . not like that."

"You're sure?"

"I'm good."

"To the contrary, you wouldn't be here if you were

good. I could suggest we meet again soon. That you contact your friend and see if anything he tells you helps at all. I can prescribe a sleep medication if you—"

"No, thank you."

"As you wish."

Fiona glanced at her wristwatch.

"I have plenty of time," Katherine said. "But I'm a student of body language and I can tell when a patient wants out."

"It shows?"

"You could have gotten most of this off the Internet, maybe did, for all I know. That leads me to believe you came here wanting more than the Wikipedia version of memory loss. You've suggested there could very well be an emotional component, and yet are reluctant to discuss what that may involve. You were pushed or hit, and you have memory of a man calling your name, and I must say you display some of the indications of an abused or battered woman, including your steadfast refusal that this friend of yours could ever do such a thing to you. That's textbook, Fiona."

"I know that."

"Because?"

"Because I know that," she said.

"From experience," Katherine said. "Correct me if I'm wrong."

Fiona stared angrily. "You're wrong," she said.

"Okay, I'm wrong."

"It's complicated."

"That doesn't forgive anything. Nor does it usually explain it."

"No, I don't imagine so. You probably get that a lot."

"My work is to untangle the complicated. To simplify. To help you to simplify, actually. Your brain can tie a knot across your memory, Fiona. We work together to untie that knot and the memory may very well return much quicker."

"And if I don't want the memory?"

"Will you block it forever? No. I would doubt that."

"No, I didn't think so."

"Do you want my help?"

"I thought I did. Now, I'm not so sure."

"You have to want it."

Fiona set her jaw.

"Fear is so elusive," Katherine said. "It's a bit of a magician. It can make itself appear much larger than it actually is. It's our unwillingness to look at it, to confront it, that allows this inflated presence. Most of the time, when we face our fears we let the air out and realize there wasn't much to it after all."

"And when it's justified?" Fiona asked.

"Well, then it's more . . . complicated."

"Exactly," Fiona said.

"But talking about it is where to start. Keeping these things inside, given your current situation, isn't going to help anything. I'll be honest with you: your memory is going to come back—that's my prediction based on a good deal of experience. Talking to me may or may not precipitate that return. But your sharing your fears with me, your discussion of the emotional context will greatly improve how you handle the memories when they do return—this I can promise. You don't need to do this alone."

"But I do," she said.

"I'm here," Katherine said. "Day or night, I'm here."

Fiona bit her lower lip because she felt it quivering, felt her eyes well. She stood from the chair, offering her back to Katherine, and tried to keep calm as she walked out of the room.

17

"You okay?" Boldt asked from the Jeep's passenger seat. Beatrice half-slept in the backseat, rolling a lazy eye as the men spoke.

"Yeah. Sorry. I petitioned the court about acquiring a DNA sample and was turned down. It's a child abuse case."

"The toughest there are."

"Right. So I'm a little out of sorts."

"Understandably. Any way around it?"

"Maybe. Might be. I have an article of clothing—a pair of panties. But ultimately I need the embryo's DNA and that's apparently not going to happen."

"And another scumbag remains out there."

"Something like that."

"You can always lie to the bastard and hope he comes

apart, though such guys rarely do. And never discount the value of a fine piece of entrapment. Any felony will do."

Both men laughed into the windshield.

"The offer still stands for you to sit in on the Boatwright interview."

"We're good," Walt said.

"You don't have to drive me around. I can rent a car."

"It's my pleasure. I thought I might canvass the neighbors or his employees about any knowledge of Gale or visits to the house. I'd like to start eliminating potential suspects. That is, with your permission."

"Don't need my permission," Boldt said. "Other way around. I'm the guest here, and I appreciate your helping me out."

"I wouldn't mind talking to Matthews," Walt said, "if you think that's possible."

"Easily arranged."

"I can pay her if necessary. Bring her over here, if you think that's possible."

"No need for that," Boldt said. "I'm sure she'll be happy to help out. If you nail down a suspect and the suspect is a tough nut you might want to bring her over. She's extremely good at reading people and leveraging weaknesses in personalities. But that's for down the road."

Walt could see Boldt went somewhere else, staring out the side window. At first he thought the landscape had grabbed him, overcome him the way it could. But the longer the silence went on, the more Walt suspected

something else was going on, that he'd triggered something without having any idea about what he'd done.

"Hell of a place you live, Sheriff," Boldt finally said at
the end of a long sigh.

No man in his seventies looked like Marty Boatwright
without the help of plastic surgery. His watery eyes and
the chicken skin on the backs of his hands gave him away.
He greeted both men, meeting the Jeep in the driveway,
then escorted Boldt inside. As Walt parked the Cherokee,
he imagined Boldt would likely take that to the bank—
guys like Marty Boatwright didn't greet anyone in their
driveway; the impending interview had rattled the man
and had put him on the defensive before it began.

The 11,000-square-foot log home sat on three acres
carved out of a hill, giving Boatwright an unobstructed
view of the Warm Springs side of the Sun Valley ski area.
The property was terraced into two cascading drops,
both supported by four-foot stone walls, with a narrow
creek falling down waterfalls and collecting into a half-
acre pond at the bottom, just this side of the helicopter
pad that had drawn the scorn of his neighbors.

On the bib of lawn that supported a large flagstone
terrace and dining patio, a garden worker struggled with
an invasive tube root in the first of three successive flower
beds. A wheelbarrow topped with fresh soil sat alongside
a tarp and a variety of garden tools.

"How's it going?" Walt said, immediately sensing the

man's unease. Not an atypical reaction. He tried to soften the moment. "I have the same problem in my backyard," Walt said. "Can't stop the things."

"I transplanted one indigenous aspen seven years ago, and there's not a day I don't curse the decision. If I'd gone with one from a nursery . . . They don't send out tap roots like them natives. The indigenous . . . their suckers come up everywhere, and most of the time I let them be, but not when they invade my flower beds."

"You're replanting."

"I am." The man seemed more relaxed.

"In July." Walt tried to sound interested instead of accusatory.

"Mr. Boatwright wanted it done."

"Bad timing."

"Tell me about it. Too hot in the days to get anything decent started. The lilies were doing fine in my opinion. I'll fill it with annuals and worry about it next spring."

"The other beds too?"

"Who knows? You follow the NFL?"

"Baseball."

"Well, let me tell you something, you work for Mr. Boatwright, you learn that he's the coach and quarterback all in one. He says you go deep, you go deep, or you're on the bench. In my case that means the unemployment line. So I go deep."

"I hear you." Walt considered his approach. "You ever get to meet any players?"

"You kidding? Place is like a hotel."

"Anyone I'd know of?"

The gardener seemed proud of his insider's position. "Head coach and a couple of assistants up here last weekend. I hear the commissioner's coming in for the wine auction this year. You know these guys, Sheriff. Dinner parties every night. Jump in the jet. Fly back. He's a human yo-yo, and he's not getting any younger."

The guy liked to talk. Walt wasn't complaining. "Any players?"

"He interviewed a couple wide receivers back around the time of the draft. An offensive lineman, the kid that book was written about—*The Blind Side*—about the same time. No one too recently, at least that I know about." Leaning on his shovel, the heavily suntanned man seemed grateful for the respite. "But you'd have to check with Mary—his executive secretary. She should be around here someplace. Her office is on the lower level of the north wing."

"I'd probably need a map."

"Got that right."

"Is he a good guy to work for?"

"I actually report to Debbie, one of Mary's three assistants. I don't actually deal with Mr. Boatwright. Debbie's all right. They basically give me an open budget. It's the dream job. I'm overpaid, I get great benefits, and I'm pretty much left on my own."

"Wanna trade?" Walt said. He won a chuckle. "Anything a sheriff should know about Mr. Boatwright that I don't already know?"

"I told you, it's a dream job."

"I'm interested in a linebacker. A retired linebacker. He would have come by sometime in the past couple days. Big guy, obviously. Might have been alone. Might have been wearing jeans and a leather jacket. Name of Martel Gale."

"The Gale Force? Shit, I'd have recognized him, I think. Loved watching that guy hit. Listen, I don't see that many of the guests, and to tell you the truth, I don't pay that much attention unless I happen to get a look and recognize someone. I like the sport, so I'm kind of a major fan, but I don't know half the faces of the guys who come here. The girls, that's different. Hard not to look at the girls, you know what I mean?"

"Girls, or women?"

"I've said enough. I should get back to work."

Walt didn't look over his shoulder immediately, but he'd seen a flicker in the man's eyes and suspected he'd caught someone eyeing them both. Mary, perhaps, or one of the three assistants.

Walt felt tempted to ask about Caroline Vetta, but he lacked a photo and it was Boldt's business, not his.

"You think you could check with Debbie, informal like, if Gale has been around in the past week?"

"I suppose." He sounded surprised.

"I could do it," Walt said, not sure that he could, "but all I'm interested in is trying to get an autograph for my nephew, trying to catch Gale while he's still in town, and when a sheriff asks something it becomes a big production and it's not like that, so it makes it kind of difficult."

"I can see that."

"I've already asked Vince Wynn but he's not on such good terms with Gale."

The gardener turned away and went back to the struggle with the root.

"I shouldn't be loafing," he said.

Was it the mention of Wynn? Walt wondered. Or had the man received a second signal from within the house?

"Nice talking to you," Walt said.

"I'll ask if I can," the gardener told the dug-up flower bed.

"I'm sure I'm not telling you anything you don't already know," Walt said, "but I was told water stops tap roots. You put the offending tree on an island and that's the end of it."

The gardener lifted his head and eyed the only stand of aspen, in rough grass between the lawn and the driveway.

"I might be able to work with that," he said.

"Just a thought," Walt said. But his mind had made a leap to Boatwright and Wynn and the dead man, Gale. Like the trees, if he and Boldt could keep the men from extending their reach to their handlers and attorneys, maybe they'd have half a chance to get some piece of the truth out of them. The secret might be to isolate them, but Walt had no idea how to go about that, given e-mails and cell phones, and the intricacies of both men's businesses. Unless he could find a way to turn one against the other. One of the two must at least have heard from Gale, whether or not they had a connection to the man's death. Given Boatwright's reliance on a team of personal secretaries, there might even be a paper trail to follow.

He walked the grounds wondering if Gale had done the same some night after being refused an audience with Boatwright, wondering if that was what had happened to Wynn the night the agent had fired his gun into the dark.

Boldt climbed into the Jeep forty minutes later and Walt started up the motor and drove off the property.

"Everyone has secrets," Boldt finally muttered. "But this guy. What a piece of work. My guess is he's got a couple vaults full of them."

"It went that well, did it?"

"Treated me like I was the water boy."

"Is there a connection to Caroline Vetta?"

"He knows a heck of a lot more than he's telling," Boldt said, "that's for sure. But he's done so many deals for so many years, has told so many lies, that he's an expert. Or maybe he's so old he believes them."

"Are you done with him?"

"You're kidding, right?"

"Any chance you'll subpoena his personal calendar?"

"Gale?"

"That's what I was thinking," Walt admitted. "I'm

told the secretaries run his life, manage every minute of his time. Surround him."

"It may very well come to that," Boldt said.

Boldt lowered the window and put his hand outside, his fingers outstretched in the wind.

Beatrice sat up and nosed the back window, and Walt put his window down as well.

Boldt raised his voice over the wind. "I subpoena someone like that and it'll be a lot of court time before it's finally ruled upon and I'll only be refused. Everyone's a football fan, including judges."

"But we both want, both need, the same thing: his personal calendar. So if I could find a way to get a look at his book, you'd benefit too. I'd make sure of that."

"Have you got an angle?"

"No. Not yet. But maybe Wynn will give me one—give *you* one. If he can connect Gale to Boatwright . . . Well, one of the judges here, he's the home plate umpire for our softball league."

"What's that got to do with the price of oil?" Boldt asked.

"Hates football," Walt said.

Beatrice barked into the wind.

For a moment, Walt thought it might have been Boldt.

18

Despite the three full face-lifts, Marty Boatwright's neck flesh flapped like a luffing sail as he dialed out on his mobile phone. A tall man with flinty eyes and a cleft chin, he'd been mistaken for a Douglas most of his adult life, first Kirk and then Michael. It had been explained to him by one of his lawyers that mobile phones were digitally encrypted and therefore impossible to casually eavesdrop upon, and though the government could monitor any conversation on any phone, stiff warrant requirements meant mobile phones were the safest from unwanted ears. So this call was made mobile to mobile.

"It's me," he said, as Vince Wynn answered.

"Hey, Marty."

"That cop was just here."

"Coming here next."

"I didn't tell him shit. Let my boys do the talking."

"Okay."

"They don't know shit about her. Nothing but a fishing trip as far as I can tell. Seems like they think it was all sex and power whoring and how maybe there were fees involved. Means she must have deposited the money. Can you believe that? What kind of dumb shit would bank the money?"

"Caroline—"

"No names, you asshole!"

"—may have been a lot of things, but she was not dumb."

"You'll be scratching that on a cell wall you don't get your act together."

"I'm fine, Marty."

"We both know what this is about."

"Yeah."

"And whatever happened to her . . . She . . . We talked about this."

"Yeah."

"But it doesn't have to involve us. Doesn't involve us."

"No. That's right."

"So keep it that way."

"Of course."

"He's clever, this cop. Looks big and thick but he's anything but. He's more Howie Long than Lyle Alzado."

"Got it."

"Consider your answers carefully, that's all I'm saying."

"I'm good, Marty."

"If you're so good, what the hell were you doing shooting your gun off the other night?"

Silence.

"You thought I wouldn't hear about that? The whole town's heard about that. What kind of a dumbass thing—"

"It was a personal security matter, Marty. A disgruntled former player. They were warning shots is all."

"Who?"

"Never mind."

"Keep the damn gun in the closet, asshole. We don't need any more attention than we've already got. This thing . . . *her* . . . People are going to jail for this shit. Jail, I'm talking about."

"I'm aware of that."

"Not me. You hear me? Not me!"

"So noted."

"Stick to one-word answers. Don't get creative. That mouth of yours. And you're under no obligation to—"

"Stu's here," Wynn said. "He'll do all the talking."

"Stu? Well, tell him hello for me."

"I'll do that."

"He's a wolf in sheep's clothing. Be careful with this guy, for your own sake."

"I will be. I negotiate for a living, Marty. No one ever knows what the hell I'm thinking."

Marty Boatwright coughed out a laugh. Half his lung came up. Once it started he couldn't stop it. He shut down the call without signing off and sank into his desk chair and weathered the storm of old age, his eyes and nose running, the Depends warming at his crotch.

Prison. No way.

19

"This isn't charity," Boldt stated as Walt pulled the Jeep up to the wrought-iron gate blocking Vince Wynn's driveway. Walt rolled down his window and announced himself to a speaker key code box.

"Far from it," he said.

"You'd like in on this interview. That's why the escort."

"Not entirely true," Walt said. "I'm interested in Wynn for Gale. Absolutely. He threatened the man to my face. And I'm curious as to how he reacts to your questioning about Vetta. Absolutely."

"I don't see a guy like Vince Wynn dumping a body alongside a highway, especially not the busiest road you've got. The bottom of a construction site maybe, but more likely he'd drive him, or more likely pay someone to drive him, a long way into the wilderness and leave him for the scavengers."

"Agreed. But I can see him clubbing him from behind. Wynn's too smart to take on a guy like Gale face-to-face. You hit him when his back's turned. You make sure he's not getting back up."

"He could have been jacked, Sheriff. We talked about this. Lured out of the vehicle maybe. Struck from behind. It's more and more difficult to see it otherwise. We've got to find that SUV."

Gale's missing SUV, a rental from Avis, had been the topic of much discussion. City and sheriff patrols were searching parking lots, motels, and campgrounds. State police had been notified and a BOLO—a Be On Lookout—had been issued in the six-state region surrounding Idaho. Walt had hoped for results by now and, along with Boldt, secretly feared they'd lost the vehicle for good.

"You think it was staged to *look* like a carjacking," Boldt said.

"I think guys like Wynn know what guys like us expect to see. An agent at his level, he's all about selling an impression of something that maybe isn't true, maybe isn't all it's made out to be."

"So he gives us what we want. I'd buy that."

"Plays into our comfort zone."

"A carjacking gone wrong," Boldt said, nodding.

"It's all after the fact," Walt said. "He's all boozed up and he does the guy and then has to backfill. But a guy like that reads the paper up here. He knows what kind of crime we see and how often we see it. We had a carjacking not six months ago where a man was struck with a tire iron while changing a tire. Wasn't exactly like Gale, but close enough. The doer finished changing the tire and drove off in the car, having no idea the driver had already alerted OnStar. We were given GPS coordinates and had the guy in custody within the hour."

"And the body?"

"Stuffed into a culvert twenty feet from the car. Wynn could easily have read about it and pulled a copycat."

Boldt said, "If he's the killing type."

The gate opened electronically and Walt drove through, parking by a basketball backboard.

"Which is what we've come here to find out."

"Indeed it is."

"If Caroline Vetta got him started, broke his cherry, then doing Gale wouldn't have mattered much to him."

A wry smile overcame Boldt. "You and Matthews would like each other," he said. He took a long look at the house and Walt thought he was using it as his introduction to Wynn. "You're welcome to join me if you'd like."

"I'd just confuse things," Walt said. "Only two can dance at a time. I'll leave the advance work up to you. Maybe we'll pull a Columbo on him and double-team him after you're done, hit him with Gale five minutes after he's done fending off Vetta."

"Sounds like a plan." Boldt climbed out. "You want to take off, I could call you. I hate to take up your time."

"No worries. I'm going to put it to good use."

The closest neighbors had a sport court behind the house that integrated tennis, basketball, volleyball, and a backboard onto a single slab of asphalt. Walt crossed it and an apron of green grass to reach a single-story adobe house with four wings running in an X from a central living area, the back of which was a twenty-foot-high wall of tinted glass that faced the ski mountain. He found the front door at the apex of a horseshoe driveway that housed what appeared to be a centuries-old pagoda through which the same stream that passed through Wynn's estate gurgled in and among an Asian rock garden.

The woman who answered the door could have been going on sixty but looked more like forty, and showed no signs of work having been done. She was all yoga and juice drinks and acupuncture, wearing stonewashed blue jeans and a tight-fitting T-shirt. There was no hiding her surprise at discovering a uniformed sheriff at her front door.

"Hello?"

Walt introduced himself by rank.

"Gwen Walters. I know your face from the papers," she said. "I voted for you!"

Walt thanked her. He got that a lot, but wondered how often it was true.

"I wanted to ask you a few questions, if you have a minute?"

"Of course." She motioned him inside. "Tea? Juice?"

"I'm fine."

Sunlight flooded the living room. The outside patio was about the size of Walt's city lot. They took seats at a teak table in padded chairs covered in Sunbrella fabric.

"Vince Wynn," Walt said.

"Yes," she said. "I thought as much." She squinted, and squirmed uncomfortably in the chair. "The shooting?"

"Yes. Among other things."

"I'm not a gossip, Sheriff. And I respect my neighbors' privacy. It's important to all of us."

"I agree."

"Vince is something of a celebrity in his own right."

"Yes, he is."

"Though my husband calls all agents bloodsuckers. He's in the film business, my husband. Not that you'd know him. An effects director."

"Mr. Wynn claimed he had a trespasser. The other night? The shooting?"

"I wouldn't know about that," she said.

"The shooting or the trespasser?"

"I didn't see anyone." She looked off into the sky, then back at Walt, still squinting, now choosing her words carefully. "Vince is very . . . social. I suppose in his business one needs to entertain a great deal."

"It's busy up there," Walt said.

"It is."

"At all hours."

"Yes. All hours. A lot of . . . partying."

"Men guests? Women guests?"

"Guests. Many guests."

"The gun incident. Was that a first?"

"Vince . . . How do I put this? The entertaining can go quite late. Can get . . . I think he enjoys a party as much as the next person. Sometimes it gets a little rowdy, a little late and a lot loud. And if I had to guess, I'd say Vince doesn't have the best control of his temper."

"Hot-headed."

"I'm painting the wrong picture."

"Fights?"

"Shouting. Arguments. But they could be phone calls for all I know. He seems to be on the phone more than he's off, and he likes to take calls outside, I've noticed. And his work is confrontational by nature, isn't it? All that dealing. And the sums! Mark, my husband, keeps up on all of it. A sports fan. Loves living next to Vince. But my God, some of the numbers."

"Arguments," Walt said.

"He can be loud," she said.

"Drugs?"

She squinted, looked pained to speak.

"Have you seen drug use in the home?"

She hesitated and finally nodded. Walt felt a jolt of adrenaline—if he could get her to say it, he had probable cause to search Wynn's home.

"Is that a yes?"

She nodded again.

"I need a verbal answer."

"He's my neighbor."

"He lives a matter of yards from your kids," he said, keeping in mind the sports court.

She tilted her head and looked at him curiously.

"The basketball court. I'm assuming—"

"Teenagers. Two boys and a girl."

"A neighbor like that doesn't make for the best role model," Walt said.

"Don't patronize me, Sheriff."

He was losing her. He'd been so close.

"Does he . . . interact with them at all?"

"He's great with the boys. Gets them autographed balls and things. But Vince is . . . proud of his working out. Likes to go around bare-chested. Personally, it kind of grosses me out, and I don't love for my daughter to see that."

"The night of the gunshots?"

"I called nine-one-one, if that's what you're after, yes. Or maybe you already know that." She studied him thoughtfully and won nothing back. "It scared the devil out of me and Mark. The drinking. Gunshots. I mean, we're not very far away."

"The drug use." Walt made it a statement.

Gwen Walters seemed ready to say something, but didn't.

Walt fumbled with his shirt pocket and produced a photo of Gale and laid it on the table.

"Have you seen him before?"

She shook her head. "I have to say he looks vaguely familiar, but no, I can't say I know him."

"A guest of Mr. Wynn's? Familiar from that?"

Another shake of the head. "I couldn't say for sure. There are so many."

"But recently?"

"No, not recently."

"How about her?" Walt said, following this with a copy of a newspaper photograph of Caroline Vetta.

The woman had been mid-sip of some iced tea when she froze in that position, her eyes trained onto the photo. She placed the glass down, looked at Walt, and then back to the photograph. "I couldn't say," she repeated far less confidently.

"She visited Mr. Wynn?"

"I couldn't say," she said yet again. "There are . . . Vince has a lot of friends. Many of them are women."

"But she looks familiar to you," Walt said.

"Is it Caroline?" the woman asked.

"It is." Walt worked to keep any reaction off his face, while inside he'd gone electric. *First-name basis.*

"Different hair when we knew her. It changes her face dramatically."

"You knew her as an acquaintance of Mr. Wynn's?"

"She came here often for a while. Last year, this was. Ended around Christmas, I think. We heard about what happened to her. Poor thing. She was a sweet girl. Pretty as a picture."

"How would you define their relationship? Warm? Hostile?"

"Same as any other, I suppose. On again, off again."
A light filled her eyes. "You don't think . . . ?"

Walt kept any reaction off his face.

"Vince?" She bordered on outrage.

"What do you think? Is it possible?"

"We had them down to dinner. Barbecues. Vince was always so entertaining. The stories he has."

"And Caroline?"

"Caroline was good with men. Flirtatious. Attractive."

She appraised him and he thought he saw her nod faintly, though he may have imagined it. The veins in her neck rose.

"The question that needs to be asked," Walt continued, "is whether Mr. Wynn ever displayed his temper in her company. Did the arguments you overheard ever involve Ms. Vetta?" The questioning was better left for Boldt but there was no turning back.

"Vince argues with *everybody*, Sheriff. He's confrontational by nature."

"Including Ms. Vetta."

"Of course! Yes. Okay? They argued. Vince is never afraid to take a position. No shrinking violet, he."

Walt heard the word wrong. *Shrinking violence.* He took a second to process it correctly. And another few to collect his thoughts. "Did he ever hit or threaten her in your presence? And I caution you to carefully consider your answer."

"Vince threatens everyone," she said matter-of-factly.

"He swears, he boasts, and he takes on anyone he wants to take on. It's who he is. He enters the room, you know it. Some people are just like that."

"I need a straight answer," Walt said. "Caroline Vetta was brutally beaten to death. I need you to keep that in mind."

Gwen Walters, overcome, struggled to keep her lips from shaking. She hung her head, nodding. "I get it. Poor thing." Then she shook her head. "But did I see Vince actually hit her? No. Nor did I see him hit anyone else. Not ever."

"But you heard things," Walt speculated.

"We're neighbors. Neighbors know a lot more than they ought to."

It struck Walt then, hit him in the chest. He'd played it wrong from the start. Wynn knew something about this family they didn't want known. The kids? Bedroom secrets? Drug use on their part? Who knew? But she had something to hide, to keep hidden, the same as Lisa's neighbor, the same as Wynn, and she wasn't about to open that valve because the water could flow both directions.

She stood from her chair, suddenly a different woman. Extended her hand.

"Sheriff," she said.

"She's dead," Walt said.

"I don't envy you your job. If I think of something," she said unconvincingly.

They shook hands; hers was bloodless and cold and she quickly withdrew it.

Not another word passed between them. As he re-entered the cathedral of light and made his way to the front door, he marveled that people lived this way.

He stopped there at the threshold, turned, and met eyes with her. Said nothing, but also didn't move. Time suspended.

"For what it's worth, their relationship, Caroline and Vince, seemed more business than pleasure. My husband wondered aloud, more than once, if she wasn't more mistress than girlfriend, if you know what I mean?"

"A call girl."

"A paid companion. When they were together it felt different. That's all. Like they shared a secret but not the kind of secret couples share. I can't explain it."

"I think you explained it very well," he said. And he thanked her.

"I need you," Boldt said, as he and Walt stood talking beneath Vince Wynn's basketball hoop.

"It went that bad?" Walt asked. "You want to double-team him?"

"Dodge ball. There's a lawyer named Evers. Real piece of work. Wynn wants to put the Vetta death on Gale. Keeps it neat and clean."

"Does he know about Gale?"

"Not that I could tell, but he's no one to play poker with."

"Did he blame Gale outright?"

"His lawyer wouldn't let him go that far, but he would have if he'd been left on his own. Gale's identity as your John Doe is going to leak. If we're going to go after Wynn before Evers circles the wagons, now's the time."

"How do you want to handle it?" Walt didn't want to come off as naïve, but also wanted to show the man respect.

Boldt said, "They were very well rehearsed for Vetta. Not so sure that would prove to be the case with Gale. I'd hint at the evidence—ask to see his vehicles, a subscription to the local paper, hint at hairs and fibers evidence and work to confirm the last time the two met."

"Get him back on his heels."

"And then maybe I'll interrupt and revisit Vetta. A guy like this, he's a multitasker and his work is a constant pressure cooker. We're never going to win anything close to a confession, but maybe he shows us a few cracks we can exploit later."

"He agreed to meet you in the first place because he doesn't want the publicity. That's in our favor. I take it we have hairs and fibers from the Vetta scene?"

"I like the way you think," Boldt said. "Feel free to play that if you need it." Boldt slapped him on the back.

Wynn appeared surprised as he opened the door revealing the two. "Harris?" he called into the house.

Harris Evers was balding and was one of those city people who didn't look comfortable when dressing down for the role of country folk. His jeans carried creases, his bare ankles were the color of copy paper, and his black leather belt with its industrial clasp was intended for a pair of fancy trousers.

"Sheriff?" Evers said.

"Wondered if I might have a few words with your client."

"Concerning?"

"You might call it a follow-up on the shots fired the other night."

"I think not," Evers said.

"You are aware your client, Mr. Wynn, threatened an individual to my face, said he'd kill the man and take his chances with the courts." Evers shot a furtive glance in Wynn's direction, his disappointment impossible to disguise.

Walt continued. "That individual is dead. Yesterday, Martel Gale was discovered on the side of Highway Seventy-five."

"Now wait a goddamned minute!" Wynn said, practically levitating off the floor. "You're telling me Gale is dead?"

"And you threatened to kill him."

"I . . . oh, damn . . . That was just bull. That was just me being me."

"You said it to my face," Walt reminded.

Evers tensed, eyes darting. "How about we all sit down a minute?"

"How about our friends here go back to wherever they came from?" Wynn said, his temperature rising.

"We can go the formal route," Walt said, "but I can't

promise that *Sports Center* and *Pardon the Interruption* won't hear a certain agent is under investigation."

Wynn muttered, "You piece of—"

"Vince!" Evers waved everyone into the living room. They sat down around an elephant saddle coffee table beneath a Dale Chihuly chandelier in a living room with a full view of the ski mountain a mile away.

Walt could think of a dozen ways to begin the questioning, but he heeded Boldt's advice about working the evidence, wandering into territory that wasn't entirely familiar to him and hoping Boldt would come to his rescue if necessary.

"How many baseball bats do you own, Mr. Wynn?"

"What?"

"Baseball bats."

"What kind of a question is that?"

"Pretty simple one. Some people collect electric guitars," Walt said. "Wine. Demi Moore has a three-story Victorian house in Hailey filled with nothing but dolls. A couple hundred dolls. Has a house-sitter that lives there and takes care of her doll collection. I'm thinking a guy like you, in your position, you probably own more than your fair share of baseball bats. Am I wrong?"

Wynn checked with Evers, who nodded. "I have an autographed collection."

"Would that be here, in Idaho? Or Los Angeles?"

"Both. It's divided between my houses and my office."

"Sheriff," said Evers, "this is pertinent because . . . ? Are we talking murder weapon?"

Walt ignored him. "How many bats?"

"Maybe a dozen here."

"And how about vehicles? How many registered or otherwise vehicles do you own here in Idaho?"

Wynn squinted. "Including motorcycles?"

"You have access to that information," Evers said. "My client doesn't have to answer that. Look it up."

"Three," Walt said, "not including the four motorcycles. A Porsche, a vintage Roadster, and a Ford F–one hundred."

"So why ask?" Wynn said.

"Sheriff Fleming and I share interests in the Vetta case, which is open and ongoing," Boldt said.

"When was the last time you or your employees drove the F–one hundred?" Boldt asked Wynn.

"My pickup? No clue. No idea. I don't drive it all that much. Once a week, maybe. My employees have their own trucks. They don't drive mine."

"Vince," Evers said. "You don't answer unless I say so." He understood the mistake Wynn had just made, whether his client did or not. By taking his employees out from behind the steering wheel, he'd just implicated himself if his truck offered any physical evidence. It was a major victory and Boldt shot Walt a satisfyingly congratulatory look.

"The last time you drove it?" Walt said.

"No, Vince. That's enough about the truck," Evers said.

"What?" Wynn snapped at his attorney. To Walt he said, "I drove the dirt bikes over to the Copper Basin. That was maybe ten days ago. Me and a friend. Left after lunch, were back around sunset. Came over Trail Creek at sunset. So that's what: nine, nine thirty? It was a Thursday. Two Thursdays ago."

"Not since."

"Not since."

"Have you had any tire work done to the truck in the interim period?"

"Jesus!" Wynn said.

"You will *not* answer that!" Evers advised.

Wynn was starting to get the idea.

"We're happy to cooperate, Sheriff," the attorney said. "But if you seek specifics like this, I will advise Vince not to answer until he and I can study and discuss his alternatives."

Walt noticed that Boldt sat back in his chair, and took it as a sign he was trying to look comfortable, trying to establish they would be there a while, though Walt now doubted it.

"You put the blame for Vetta onto Gale," Boldt said.

"I think it makes sense, yes," Wynn replied.

"So who killed Gale?" Boldt asked.

"How the fuck should I know?"

"After the incident the other night, your discharge of the handgun, did you have any contact with Martel Gale? And I should warn you, we have records of his communications."

Wynn's puzzled look turned toward his attorney.

"My client won't answer that," Evers said. "Gentlemen, I need time with my client. If you want to continue this—"

"I would suggest a trip down to my offices," Walt said. "Should we say, one hour?"

Wynn's agitation flared in his cheeks. "You *want* this to leak. You want this on television."

"I want answers," Walt said, correcting him.

"We should point out that our departments see a correlation between the two deaths," Boldt added, "and will continue cooperating and sharing resources and evidence."

"This is totally out of hand!" Wynn said. "You guys are way off base."

"Coach us up, Mr. Wynn," Boldt said. "By all means."

"I threatened him. I was pissed off, okay? I was *scared*. The guy is—was, whatever—a fucking freak of nature. The last I saw him, he was jacked so high on steroids he was the fucking Incredible Hulk, and I mean *after* the guy turns green. Okay? Like that. But does that mean I did the guy? Gimme a fucking break!"

"To your knowledge," Walt said calmly, "has your pickup truck had any tire work done in the past two weeks?"

"No, no, no," Evers said, interrupting any chance that Wynn might answer. "We're not getting into details like that."

"Why? What do I care?" Wynn said. "No. Okay? No tire work that I know of."

"Vince!" Evers chastised. "This is not how this is going to be done."

"You stated earlier," Boldt said, "that you came straight here from Seattle, correct?"

"Yeah? So?"

"Upon your arrival to your home here, were you then, or are you now, aware of any of your possessions having gone missing?" Boldt inquired.

Wynn checked with Evers.

Walt reminded, "It's here or in Hailey."

Evers nodded to his client.

"No," Wynn said.

Boldt scribbled down a note.

"Okay," Evers said, "we are done here. We will comply with any warrants or written requests as you present them."

"Harris, we are *not* making a circus out of this," Wynn said. He addressed both Walt and Boldt. "I have not seen or spoken to Gale in over a year. Beginning and end of statement. I don't know squat about his death or his even being here."

"Yet you shot at him the other night," Walt said.

"I shot at *someone*."

"You told me it was Gale."

"I told you I thought it was Gale," said the negotiator.

"And now he's dead."

"Good riddance."

"Vince, please!"

"You believed Gale was in the area?" Boldt asked.

"I got that list server notice," Wynn said. "That was enough for me. I figured Caroline was probably on that list, and I knew what had happened to her. I wasn't taking any chances."

Walt thought obtaining the names on the list server would prove difficult if not impossible, but it seemed worth the effort. If Gale had indeed been seeking revenge, then his likely victims would be on that list.

"We'll ask that you not leave the county without checking with my office," Walt said.

"That's bullshit!" Wynn said. "I've got a dozen deals going. I'm due in L.A. on a moment's notice."

"Check with my office before leaving," Walt said, addressing the attorney.

"I did not do Gale!" Wynn said, exasperated.

Boldt leaned forward. "Tell us everything you know about your relationships with Caroline Vetta and Martel Gale right here, right now, and you have a chance to make this go away. But my sense of things is this is probably your last chance to do this quietly."

"You're threatening my client?" Evers said. "Am I hearing this right?"

"I'm trying to save you a trip to Seattle," Boldt said. "But I think I'm about done doing you any favors." He stood.

Walt rose from the couch, wondering how he might pull off obtaining a search warrant before Wynn thought to bleach every baseball bat in his collection, wondering what his father would think about his working hand in hand with a cop like Lou Boldt. And then wondering why that mattered to him in the first place.

20

An image rose within the dreamlike swirl of color and the echo of a distant voice. Ethereal, foreboding, it felt more ghost than angel, and she turned away from it.

"I'm sorry." A man's deep voice that she experienced as penetrating, cold, sexual, and dangerous. She clawed away from him, dragging herself on hands and knees, sensing the retreat was more memory than experience. She caught a glimpse of herself, naked but for a cotton thong, rushing to escape. Then felt him catch hold of her ankle and drag her back. She reached out, grabbing the leg of a chair, only to bring it down on top of herself.

"Take me back to that moment." A woman's voice as gentle and forgiving as silence. Where it came from, she had no idea. Was God a woman with a voice like a summer breeze? Why did she feel so compelled to comply, to do whatever this voice asked of her?

"Is there someone in the room with you?" The woman again.

"I owe you that. Much more than that." The man's voice now, his silhouette blocking the glow from a window. She knew that window—it existed in her present memory.

"I see a window," she heard herself say. "He's standing in front of a window."

"Tell me about him."

But as she looked again, she flinched and ran from what she saw, what she heard. She stepped back, arms out behind her like angel wings.

"He says he's sorry." She identified this as her own voice. But she couldn't be sure if anyone heard or who it was intended for.

"Sorry for . . . ?" The woman again, gently pressing. Always pressing.

"He's lying. He always lies."

"You know him?"

"Yes."

"Not a stranger?"

"No way."

"He's in the room with you?"

"Yes. I . . ." The silhouette distended and broke into two black blobs. The ephemeral quality suddenly made her doubt its authenticity.

"Do you recognize him?"

"Recognize? Him? Oh, yeah."

"Is he saying anything else?"

"He's . . . coming toward me. Coming for me. No! No! Not again! Not that! He'll kill me! He'll kill me this time. I've got to—"

A bell rang. A small bell. The kind her grandmother kept on the fireplace mantel and told stories about, tall tales of India and elephants, and she could practically smell the incense burning. Her eyes came open to soft lighting and the barely discernible image of a thin woman with graying hair sitting stiffly in a chair opposite her. Her grandmother? But no; she was long dead.

Her scalp itched. She felt pearls of sweat on her upper lip that tasted of salt as she licked them off. And then she identified the source of the incense: a small ceramic dish to the left of the thin woman.

"Whoa," she said. "Did I go under?"

"I believe so. Yes, Fiona."

"Did I say anything?"

"We'll get to that," Katherine said. Fiona took in the surroundings of the office and for a moment didn't recall coming here to this session. "Whoa," she said again.

"It can be a little surprising the first time," Katherine said.

"I'm totally disoriented."

"Understandable. You were somewhere else just now."

"I don't remember a thing."

"As it should be. We can work on that."

"Did I remember anything? Do you know how I hit my head? Do you know what happened?"

"The important thing is that *you know* what happened."

"I do? I remembered?"

"I believe so, yes."

"And did I tell you anything useful?"

"It's all useful. We don't want to get ahead of ourselves."

"There was a man. I think he was speaking to me . . . saying something to me . . . though I don't know what, exactly."

Trying to connect what she was being told with an unwilling memory, Fiona felt as if she were reaching into dark water.

"Don't force it," Katherine said. "There's no rush. The point is: you'll get there if you need to. You'll find it if it's important."

"Of course it's important. There's a piece of my life missing."

"Maybe for good reason."

"The only reason is because I hit my head."

"Not necessarily. We've discussed this."

"Protecting myself from myself? I don't buy that."

"And I'm not selling, just trying to help you to work this out."

Fiona felt herself cooling off. Whatever it was, it had to be something major for her to have gotten this worked up about it. But what, she had no idea.

"I need this," she said.

"We generally have what we need. The general misperception is that we need what we want."

"Be careful what you wish for."

"Words to live by," Katherine said.

"Can we try again?"

"Not today. Soon enough, though."

"Thursday's session?"

"We'll see."

"I need to know." She hung her head. It was everything she could do not to cry.

21

"No, I'll handle it," Walt said into his BlackBerry, staring at the dairy case in Atkinson's Market. "I'm heading that way anyway."

On the other end of the call, Tommy Brandon said nothing.

Walt understood the source of his deputy's confusion: he rarely, if ever, refused the offer of help. Overburdened and overworked, he welcomed, even preached the need for such initiative. But here he was, pushing back on Brandon. And there was Brandon, not understanding—*or understanding too well*, Walt thought. Brandon was no slouch; he probably saw right through Walt's justification.

He cursed Brandon's efficiency. In studying topographic maps and Google Earth images of the area around the location of Gale's body, all in an effort to widen their canvassing, Brandon had made an interesting, and possibly damaging discovery: the Engleton property—where Fiona lived—was technically immediately adjacent to the crime scene, if one discounted four hundred feet of elevation. Looking from high above, only the blur of the scree field separated them.

If Gale had not been tossed from a pickup truck, then he had likely fallen to his death from the eastern edge of the Engleton property, though the condition of his clothes did not suggest he'd been hiking. The contradictions needed clarification.

Someone needed to question Fiona—and quite possibly Kira—and Walt was not leaving that to anyone else.

He reviewed his exchange with Brandon, searching for a believable if inelegant way out.

"She has some photos of the scene for me," he said, realizing, upon reflection, how stupid it sounded: Fiona e-mailed her photographs to the office. He had to end the conversation—quickly.

"Listen, I'm in Atkinson's trying to buy string cheese. Nikki is very picky, and I can't for the life of me remember which brand it is she likes. For her, there's only the one. I'll take the Engleton place. You divvy up the rest and we'll hope someone saw something."

"Got . . . it," Brandon said, intentionally clipping his words so that Walt would not miss his unspoken message.

A man stepped up and, without so much as looking at

the shelves, snagged a carton of milk from the case and dumped it into his cart, on top of several twelve-packs of beer and a half dozen bags of beef jerky.

Walt recognized him immediately from his driver's license photo: Dominique Fancelli, stepfather of Dionne Fancelli, the pregnant high-schooler. A dozen options crowded Walt's mind: confrontation, arrest, intimidation. Maybe he could steer him out back and just beat the shit out of him and take his chances with voters. Paying no attention to the string cheese, Walt placed it into his cart, his eyes never leaving the man.

He pushed his cart, following the man down the paper aisle. Watched him load up on paper towels and toilet tissue and consider an air freshener. Stood there watching, hoping the man might turn and provoke him. Not much could test his patience, but this man had Walt's heart going arrhythmic in his chest.

Fancelli continued toward the checkout lanes and Walt followed as if on surveillance, holding back yet fully focused on the target. Reminding himself how unprofessional it would be to confront the man, Walt turned his cart away and headed for the fresh bread beneath the Country Bakery sign. He was considering a loaf of raisin bread when Fancelli appeared in his peripheral vision, leaving with a bag of groceries in hand. A teenage girl, no older than thirteen, passed him on her way into the store, and Fancelli ogled her bare legs and tank top. Before Walt could even make sense of it, he'd abandoned his cart and rushed through the swinging door.

Fancelli was halfway across the parking lot, zeroing in on a tricked-out pickup truck, swinging the bag like a schoolboy.

"Fancelli!" Walt marched in long, stiff strides, reaching the man as he turned around. Fancelli's eyes flared at sight of the uniform. His brow furrowed. The bag slowed its pendular motion.

Walt invaded the man's space, putting his face to Fancelli's, unbothered by their height difference.

"How's Dionne doing?" he asked, a bit breathlessly.

Fancelli leaned away but did not take a step back, his eyes creased, his lips suddenly bloodless and thin. His nostrils flared.

"Give her my best."

The man's head nodded, nearly imperceptibly.

Walt stepped away and offered him his back as he returned to the store.

"No problem," Fancelli croaked out.

Walt stopped and looked over his shoulder at the man, visions of Emily and Nikki playing before his eyes. For all the reasons bullets were manufactured, this seemed a way to put one to its best possible use. He caught his hand actually touching the grip of his sidearm. He turned back and walked on, a fraction of a second gone, but a lifetime passed.

He arrived at the top of Fiona's driveway to the yellow profusion of the Engleton flower beds, the air gauzy and charged with a glow of late afternoon. He was slightly out of breath and light-headed, anticipation roaring in his ears.

Knocked on the cottage door. Stepped through as she answered.

"I've missed you. You've been awfully quiet." The hopeful yet sad look in her eyes prompted him. He took her chin in his right hand, placed his left on her hip as if dancing. She didn't object, and though he saw distance in her eyes as he kissed her, she returned his offer as if he was somehow the answer she'd been awaiting. As they spun, she shoved the door closed with the palm of her hand and they crashed across the coffee table and fell to the couch, this time without a hint of amusement. She infused the act with a seriousness, a disconnected commitment, and he sensed the danger of the moment, but was unable to hold himself back. If talk had been required, it was too late for both of them. If he'd thought himself bulletproof, he was not. She closed her eyes tightly as he joined her, a mask half of pleasure, half of pain that caused him to reconsider, but again, he couldn't stop. He fell atop her with a gasp, surprised and alarmed by his urgency and the unshakable knowledge that somewhere in the middle of their frantic actions she might have asked him to stop if she'd been so inclined.

"Wow," she said, confusing him, because she sounded so happy. "I ought to answer the door more often."

"I didn't plan that," he said.

"Which makes it all the more wonderful."

"It's not really me, to do something like that."

"Well, then maybe you'll change." She kissed him.

"Maybe I already have."

She left him, collecting and dragging her clothes with her to the back of the cottage. A few minutes later she had a pot of hot water going, and they were both dressed and it was, for a moment, as if nothing had happened. Her cheeks and chest were flushed as she sat down next to him. She looked out from behind sleepy eyes and he wanted her again, right there. But he behaved himself, containing himself to the tea and a few minutes of delicious silence that they shared with the fading gurgle of the cooling tea kettle.

"Tell me this was a social call," she said.

He felt a painful spike in his chest. The uncommon urge to lie. A matter of days, and he was already corrupted, prepared to compromise his ethics for this woman. The danger sign flashed for the second time in a matter of hours: she was getting to him. If he went forward unguarded, unchecked, he needed to accept that some of this was irreversible, that the flip side of such happiness and heart-pounding excitement was the abyss.

"Not entirely," he said, prepared for her to distance herself, glad when she didn't. "Brandon noticed on the map that this place, and the Berkholders', to a lesser degree, are in fairly close proximity to the body site." He added, "As the crow flies, which bodies do not." He'd thought he might win a smile out of her, but she'd gone cold and he thought back to their work on the body and again regretted keeping her on the scene for so long. He was about to apologize for that when she spoke.

"So what does that involve?"

"Asking you and Kira if you'd seen anyone matching Gale's description, which I think you just might happen to have pointed out when we found the body. I'll talk to Kira briefly—"

"She's not around."

"—or not, and then look around the place and call it good. Same at the Berkholders'. Really it was just an excuse to see you."

"You saw a lot of me," she said, cupping the mug of tea and offering him a vexing look of encouragement.

"This is getting complicated," he said.

"It is."

"More so for you than me."

"Certainly not true. You have the girls to think of. I understand that. It can't be easy. It's the beast in the room we're not discussing. Why is that?"

"Some of this can wait."

"For . . . ?"

He grimaced.

"You think this isn't serious? It's been two years in the making. It's very serious. To me, that is. If it isn't serious to you, that's important for me to hear. I'm a big girl. I get it."

"It's serious."

"Yes, it is. So the girls are a big part of it, and I want you to know that I defer to you on how we—if there is a 'we'—handle it. They don't need to know, shouldn't know until we're awfully sure where this is going. Once I become part of their lives, if I become part of their lives, it's not fair to them to retreat, so we'd better be awfully sure we know what we're doing. Do you know what you're doing?"

"I'm looking forward, not back. I'm trying to keep my pulse down because every time I look at you it runs out of control. I'm seeing a future instead of fearing one and I'm hungry for the first time in what seems likes years." He considered this. "You want to get something to eat?"

"I thought you have to canvass."

"When will Kira be back?"

"I don't keep her calendar."

"I'll walk around the premises. No sign of the bear-man, right?"

"Kira will tell you she hears things, but that's Kira."

"And you? Do you hear things?"

She turned away, and he thought maybe he'd embarrassed her and he wondered how he'd managed. Gail had been out of his life long enough, and the girls had dominated his attention, that he'd forgotten about how dealing with a woman was so incredibly different.

"It may take me a while to get good at this," he said. "I've lived in a bubble for too long. It may take me a while to remember that all women are not eleven-year-olds."

He got the smile he'd been hoping for earlier.

"Some of us are seventeen," she said.

"Point taken.".

"Have a look around. I'll clean up and we'll grab some dinner. That is, if you want?"

"It was my idea."

"Take your time. Give me fifteen minutes."

A woman who could clean up in fifteen minutes? He'd hit the mother lode.

"Back shortly," he said.

Sunset was still two hours out, but dusk had begun as a change to the quality of light, the mountains stretching long shadows across the narrow valley and turning the air a dusty gray. Walt walked the perimeter of the property, admiring the garden beds all dominated by a profusion of vibrant lilies, and the meticulous landscaping, briefly envious of the wealth on display. The valley was a playground for trust funders, and there were times that kind of inherited, unearned money made him crazy. His tracker's eye caught evidence of activity up the hill toward the east ridge, where he found a dump pile of dried twigs and leaves. He circled high above the house and cottage, then around and down a grassy slope overlooking a small teardrop pond. He walked the back side of the house, arriving at the attached garage, and peered in through the window to notice a vehicle missing from the first of the three bays.

He decided to mention the empty bay when he reconnected with Fiona.

"Does Kira use that car?"

Fiona gave him a sideways glance and crossed the

drive. She keyed in a code and the first of the garage doors opened, revealing the empty space. Put her hands on her hips but said nothing.

"No, the vehicles are off-limits, except in emergencies. Though she must have taken it, because I'm sure it wasn't stolen or anything. I could call her and ask, but I tried calling her earlier and her phone wasn't picking up."

"Not a big deal," he said, wandering into the garage and admiring the two luxury cars in the other bays. He caught sight of a sheet of paper taped on the butt end of a tool cabinet. "LoJack," he said.

"What?"

"Looks like the Engletons subscribe to a LoJack service. GPS boxes that can track cars down if they're stolen."

"That sounds like Michael. Should I call them and ask?"

"Can if you want. I don't want to get Kira in any trouble. She's had enough of it as it is. And to add insult to injury, if she's taken off, then she's probably lost her job."

Fiona stood still as Walt wandered the garage.

"You think I should call the company first?" she asked.

"I think if you call, the Engletons will hear about it for sure, because there could be charges involved with tracking down a vehicle. I'll bet Kira's car is in the shop and she borrowed this one and didn't dare tell you about it."

"Probably."

"I'd track *her* down first, you know?"

"Good idea."

He held the door for her as she got into his Jeep, and

she paused there a moment as if not knowing what to do. "You have to be careful," she said.

"Why's that?"

"I could get used to this."

"Not such a bad thing."

"You spoil me, I'll be spoiled."

"When you leave food on the shelf unattended, it spoils. When you pay attention to someone, they only get better."

"I never would have figured you for a sweet-talker."

"I suspect there are things about both of us that we have yet to learn. Isn't that supposed to be the fun part?"

She didn't answer. She pulled the door and he helped it shut, and only as he glanced at her through the windshield, as he came around the front of the Jeep, did it occur to him that with that statement he'd somehow bruised her. And he realized he had a lot to learn.

22

Fiona returned from her dinner with Walt and marched straight to the phone through a haze caused by constant flirting, two glasses of wine, and her unspoken concern for Kira. Her first instinct was to call Katherine, to try to find out if the anxiety she felt could be a result of her memory lapse, but she didn't want to be overanalyzed and she didn't need someone to question a decision she'd already made. So she Googled the name of the company on the sheet in the garage and asked how to go about tracking down a missing vehicle.

Angel rubbed warmly against her calf. Fiona reached down and cradled her in her lap and wondered if Angel and Beatrice would get along and whether or not it would ever come to that.

The man on the other end of the call spoke in a heavily

accented Indian English that she found hard to understand. She repeated herself often, briefly losing track of
her purpose, and finally determined that the company
distinguished a missing vehicle from a stolen vehicle, and
only offered their service for stolen vehicles.

The request to trace a stolen vehicle had to come from
a police department. She was advised to report the vehicle as stolen and to tell the police department to make
the request with their company as soon as possible. Vehicles reported within the first three hours of theft were
statistically proven to suffer the least amount of damage
and vandalism.

She hung up. Tried Kira's cell phone for the ump-
teenth time in the past two days and listened as it went
directly to voice mail, disconnecting without leaving a
tenth message only to have it never returned.

She considered calling Kira's parents, but knew of the
strained relationship there and didn't want to get the
girl in trouble over nothing. But was it nothing? Was it
a coincidence that Kira had been missing since Fiona
had awakened from her comatose nightmare? Had she
not tripped? Had Kira pushed her? Had Kira panicked
and fled without calling an ambulance? What kind of
argument could have preceded such an act? And why
had Katherine said that the apology revealed by her hyp-
notism had come from a man and not a woman, if Kira
had been the one apologizing? And why would Kira
possibly have to apologize?

They both avoided driving the Engletons' vehicles

because of insurance coverage. Fiona had a hard time believing Kira would take one of the cars; if she had, then it spoke volumes about Kira's mind-set at the time. Finding the truck was more important than ever.

She felt a twinge of guilt. Why had she intentionally avoided telling Walt the missing vehicle was a pickup truck?

She locked the door to the cottage, grabbed up her camera and reconnected it to the laptop, quickly working through the shots of the Gale crime scene, her finger finally hovering over the mouse as a series of shots appeared on-screen: muddy tire impressions.

Walt had made it clear a pickup truck had left the tire impressions at the crime scene.

The missing pickup truck? she wondered.

She double-clicked the first of the four images and it opened in its own window. She leaned in to take a closer look.

23

"No photo to go with it," Deputy David Blompier reported from the other side of Walt's desk. He was balding, with an amiable face and bulging belly. He was under a second caution to begin a workout regimen and Walt feared he'd soon have to be suspended for failing to act upon the warning.

Walt was looking at a printout of Martel Gale's bank account transaction report, forwarded through by e-mail, from Purchase Bank in River Ridge, Louisiana.

"Gale used his ATM card a day after he died," Walt noted.

"Withdrew the full four-hundred-dollar limit. Then again, the next business day: another four hundred."

"And no photo."

"Sawtooth National has stickers on their ATMs saying

there are cameras in use, but there aren't any. Remember? It came up last year in—"

"—that poacher case. Chasing that guy down. Yeah, I remember," Walt said.

"His killer?" Blompier asked.

"We're a long way from making that jump," Walt said. "But it's certainly possible. It's good work, David."

"Thanks. All I did was—"

"Get hold of the bank and find out if there's a way to real-time monitor their ATM use. You looking for any OT pay?"

"Absolutely."

"Let me know what the bank says."

"Yes, sir."

"And David?" Walt caught him at the door. Blompier turned in profile—a sight to behold.

"Yeah?"

"Hit the gym, and lay off the doughnuts. Last warning. You have to pass the course on the third try or it's an automatic suspension."

"Yes, sir."

"My hands are tied on this."

"Yes, sir."

"We need you. You understand?"

"Got it."

Walt fingered the page, wondering if the body had been found and robbed, or Gale's wallet had been taken by his killer. His phone rang as if in response. Dr. Royal

McClure, an M.D. who served as his medical examiner, informed him the results of the autopsy were in.

Walt called Boldt's cell and reached him on Main Street, where he'd been window-shopping. He picked him up and they drove north together.

"I'm glad you stayed," Walt said, from behind the wheel of the Jeep.

"My wife gave me a reprieve. I figured I'm already here, why not tack on a long weekend. Don't get this chance every day. I haven't been over here in years, probably won't be back anytime soon."

Walt knew the truth—Boldt suspected Gale's death tied into Vetta's and knew that once he left the area, obtaining information would be increasingly difficult. He'd been anxiously awaiting the results of Gale's autopsy and blood tox results.

Neither man mentioned or discussed any of this, and Walt wondered why not, but at the same time felt hesitant to broach the subject himself. The events of the past week had made him increasingly aware of, and sensitive to, the existence of secrets big and small and the role they played in his and other people's lives. In some ways everyone was acting out a role, keeping a face on a much more complicated identity: health issues, relationships, fantasies, fears, phobias—so often held in check just below the surface, and the person living the lie, mole-whacking to keep the truths from surfacing at inopportune moments.

Walt parked in front of the medical building adjacent to the hospital and they entered.

Dr. Royal McClure's age was deceptive. The white hair and liver spots suggested sixty, but he was fit and bright-eyed. He had an excitable manner and a calming voice, the two somehow working in concert to give the impression of a facile mind at work in a laid-back personality. He had rotated into the county's mandatory medical examiner service a few years back, and had done such a good job Walt had put him on contract.

They were spared the body-on-a-gurney routine. McClure only brought out the body if Walt asked—which he rarely did—knowing Walt preferred an office visit to the hospital's morgue.

"In the preliminary," McClure began after introductions had been made, "I told you about the blunt trauma to the parietal and occipital plates of the skull." He reached back and touched the back of his own head. "And my suspicions were borne out: that was indeed the cause of death. The guy was struck hard. It's a clean blow. Something smooth. No bark or detritus in the hair or scalp. A single blow.

"There's nothing much more to give you. Clean tox. No drugs or alcohol, tobacco, pot, nothing. Guy was a churchgoer, as far as I can tell. What I do have is speculative, or at least inconclusive, but nonetheless interesting, at least to me, which is why I thought you might want to hear it face-to-face."

"Absolutely," Walt said.

He placed down a stack of Fiona's photographs. "Shots of the head injury and identifiers, including several tattoos. And, from the clothing," he said, removing a plastic bag from a file box and laying it on his desk, "soil caught in the back pockets of both pant legs and both shoes. And not just soil, but clean soil. Clean soil and peat moss, would be my guess, though you may want the lab to run an analysis to nail that down more accurately. But my point is, it's not your average dust bowl variety soil we typically see around here. Right? It's more like garden variety."

"Nursery?" Boldt said, drawing a sharp look from Walt.

"Why not? Sure. Nursery. It looks like what my wife and I use in our vegetable garden: black compost soil mixed with peat moss to hold in moisture. What it is *not* is the typical roadside dirt you see around here. It's far more refined than that, and there's no pebbles, leaf material, sticks. It's clean."

"That's helpful," Walt said. "Very helpful."

"Which leads me to the only other thing I've got," McClure said. "And honestly, I probably wouldn't have noticed without the soil, or maybe I would have, who knows?" He laughed self-consciously, his self-deprecating humor one of the qualities Walt appreciated most about him. Rare in a doctor. "Earwax," he said, fishing out a small plastic petri dish from the same cardboard box. The petri dish contained four cotton swabs on paper sticks.

"Earwax," Walt repeated.

"Pollen," Boldt said, craning his huge body over the desk for a closer look.

"The blue ribbon goes to the sergeant," McClure said. "Very good, Detective."

"We've used it a couple times. Once in a floater."

"Pollen most often adheres to sinus membranes, ante-mortem, and/or the cerumen—which is doc-speak for earwax—postmortem." He pronounced it "mor-tem," lending finality to the sound of the word. "I retrieved the cerumen, but found nothing in the sinuses. Ergo—"

"He was dragged through a garden or a flower bed, or thrown from a truck into a pile of debris," Walt said.

"I'd go along with the former, but would lay doubt at the foot of the latter," the doc said. "You can see by the strong orange color that the pollen was thick and apparently consistent. It had to be abundant."

"This time of year?" Boldt asked. "Isn't it a little late?"

"In nature, yes," McClure said. "I'd agree. Quite late. But we have a very shortened growing season here, Detective. Extremely short. I would imagine any number of vegetables, or other flowering plants might be pollinating at this time, but I'm not a botanist. Sunflowers, maybe? The lab may be able to identify the pollen for you. But I thought its existence worth bringing to your attention." He delivered this to Walt, who nodded and reached out to examine the petri dish.

"I'll put a rush on it," Walt said.

"The only other thing worth mentioning, and I think you'll find this of some interest, is that a good number of the contusions and abrasions are also postmortem. Though scuffs on his knees and face are antemortem."

"A struggle?" Walt said.

"If I had to guess, I'd say the blow from behind was enough to kill him, but possibly failed to do so right away. He went down. His brain hemorrhaged, but in those few conscious seconds it took the pressure on his brain to overcome him, maybe he managed to turn and get in a few blows on his attacker. They may have fought. I don't know. His hands and forearms and mouth, all suggest such a struggle, an exchange of blows perhaps. Then the initial trauma caught up to him—any of the rest of us would have gone unconscious with such a blow, I think—it's something of a medical miracle if he did not, but he was thick-boned and his skull may have protected him somewhat. His brain swamped, and he died."

"And was dragged through a garden," Walt said.

"Or a nursery," Boldt added.

"The lab work should help you there," McClure said. "I'll pack it up and get it off."

"I'll have one of my guys drive it down there this afternoon," Walt said, a video of the struggle playing out in his mind's eye, and the disturbing realization that Vince Wynn had showed no signs of having been in such a struggle.

"If there was a struggle," McClure said, artfully awaiting the attention of the two, "a guy this size might have gotten in some serious blows. It might be worth checking the emergency room."

"Or twenty-four-hour convenience stores," Boldt said, eyeing Walt. "Have you got any of those here?"

"Good suggestions," Walt said.

As he and Boldt were approaching the Jeep, Boldt stopped and waited for Walt to turn. "The woman at the nursery—"

"Maggie Sharp."

"—was wearing a lot of makeup. You notice that?"

"I did."

"Struck me funny at the time, an outdoor person like that bothering with cosmetics. But if she was covering something?"

"And while you were thinking that, I was thinking about Boatwright. The caretaker was tearing up a perfectly good garden and replanting it, supposedly at Boatwright's request."

"That certainly plays a little differently now."

"Blunt trauma," Walt said. "I keep coming back to a baseball bat. Marty Boatwright's a football guy, and he's old. I don't see him clubbing Gale from behind."

"His gardener maybe? An ax handle."

"What if Wynn was right? What if Gale was here poking around old wounds? Wynn scares him off so he moves on to Boatwright. Caretaker sees a trespasser and takes a club to the back of the guy's head without introductions. Boatwright realizes who it is, and for whatever reasons of his own, doesn't want anything to do with this and tells him to dump the body and remake the garden, because in the struggle the garden got trashed."

"There'd be an evidence trail a mile long," Boldt said. "If Boatwright or his man owns a pickup truck, I'd start there. His man's clothes and house would be next."

"Be interesting if Boatwright's name turned up on the same list server as Wynn: people considered at risk from Gale. That list would help us out."

"I had a case down there that involved a home for boys. I had contact with some people. I could make a few calls."

"It's not your case," Walt said. "I couldn't ask you to do that."

"You didn't. Not that I heard. And as far as that goes, Gale's death could easily tie to Caroline Vetta, and that means I'm interested."

"Boatwright is not going to open his doors for us," Walt said. "And replanting a garden hardly gives me probable cause."

"The lab identifies what kind of plant made that pollen and we've got front-row seats either at the nursery or Boatwright's."

"I can nudge them to hurry it up. But they won't get started until Monday at the earliest. And only then if I twist a few arms."

"Looks like you and I are entering a long-distance relationship, Sheriff. And you know how those turn out."

"In all honesty, it's been a pleasure."

"Back at you."

Walt moved for the car door. Boldt stayed where he was.

"It's none of my business," Boldt said. "How do I say this? Your father . . . when we talked . . ."

"My father can be a real asshole."

"He took a kind of holier-than-thou attitude, not with me, but about you. Like I could teach you something by coming over here. As I said, it's none of my business."

"I apologize."

"My point being, he was wrong. Dead wrong. I could give him a call, as a follow-up, let him know how it went over here. Wouldn't want to do that without your permission. Wouldn't want to tread where I shouldn't."

The pit in Walt's stomach told him more about himself than he wanted to acknowledge.

"Tread wherever you'd like," he said, feeling the warmth of sweet satisfaction flooding him. "Kind of wish I had a wire in place for that phone call."

Boldt barked out a laugh. When he climbed into the Jeep, the vehicle sagged to his side and then leveled. Boldt clipped into the seat belt, let out a sigh, and said, "I'm going to miss this place."

24

"This is a pleasant surprise," Walt told Fiona as he entered his office to find her waiting for him.

"I told Nancy it had to do with photographs," she said, hoisting her camera case. "I lied."

"A social visit?" He kissed her on the cheek. The return kiss was tepid at best. He moved around to behind his desk, thinking of little else.

"I wish. No. It's . . . I need a favor, and I'm not sure it's fair to ask. I don't want to take advantage of our . . . you know . . . the other night, but at the same time, I need something."

He stood and eased his office door shut and returned to the chair next to her, forgoing the seat behind the desk.

"Talk to me," he said.

"I . . . the thing is . . ." She met his eyes and then looked quickly away.

"We're both adults here."

"It isn't that," she said. "It's . . . We don't really know each other," she said. "Not all that well."

He felt it in the center of his chest, not like a knife but more like a medical procedure where all the blood, all the life, was being drawn out of him into a syringe, while he sat there watching it.

"That's what we do. Right? From here on out. Get to know each other better. Share the stuff you never share. It's what makes the bond unique. Worth so much. I want to know you. I want to know all about you."

Her eyes welled. "You might be surprised."

"Try me. I like surprise."

For an instant he saw in her a hope or dream, but something passed like a shadow between them and then that look was gone, replaced by something more protective and even suspicious. He'd had similar moments in interrogations when the suspect seemed ready to download, only to clamp down and turn inward. He'd lost her. Rather than push, or fish, which was his nature, he sat back and tried to appear the model of patience.

"I called the company. The one that can trace the pickup. Michael and Leslie's pickup."

He kept his mouth shut, measuring her fragility in her sideways looks and the whispering quality of her voice.

"They said I have to file a police report. Report it as a stolen vehicle. Without that they won't trace it."

"Pretty common with these companies," he said. "They want it to be for real. It's not a service to track down your missing teenager."

"But that's just it: that's what I need. To track down Kira."

"Meaning?"

"I haven't seen her in a couple of days, Walt. That happens sometimes. We can go most of a week without overlapping. But the pickup truck being gone. That's not good. She knows the rules. The last thing I want is for her to get into trouble with Michael and Leslie and maybe lose the house-sitting thing. But if I want to track her down, I have to report it as stolen, and if I report it as stolen—"

"The Engletons find out about it."

"*Exactly.*"

"But if I were to make the call . . . ?"

"Something like that. Yes."

"No problem."

"What? Really?" He watched the load come off her: her head raised, her shoulders seemed higher, straighter.

"Not a big deal," he said. "I can have Nancy make the call."

"But does it . . . I don't know. Could you get into trouble?"

"I can't imagine how. We make these kinds of calls often enough. It's really not a big deal."

"It is to me."

"Well then, consider it done."

Her eyes softened.

"Have you tried something old-fashioned, like calling her?"

"Voice mail."

"I don't love the idea of her going missing at a time we're searching the woods in your area."

"I know."

"Do you think there's any chance . . . any possibility that her departure is related to—?"

"No!" she said sharply, cutting him off. "I think she just took off in the truck. She's still just a kid. There was already stuff brewing between us. She was mad that I left the Advocates dinner when I did."

"That surprised me as well."

"And she apparently had a flashback in the middle of her talk—"

"Yes, she told me."

"And that freaked her out, and I think she was counting on me being there for her. And I wasn't. And I feel bad about that, but it is what it is."

He hoped she might explain her sudden departure that night, but she chose not to—and that was how he thought of it: that she made a decision not to share with him, and he took that as a bad omen. He nearly said so. Might have, had she not cut into his thoughts.

"I just want to find her and get that truck back before it blows up on her."

"Did you try her parents?"

"That relationship . . . it's complicated."

He thought she sounded more like a psychologist than herself. "So I'll make the call. We should hear something by the end of the day. It doesn't take them long."

"Should I wait?"

"No. It'll be a few hours at the least. Maybe tomorrow. I'll call you."

"It's really nice of you," she said, her eyes softening.

"Happy to do it."

"I could repay you with a dinner."

"I'm with the girls the next few nights. With Boldt here, I've been distracted. First job, and all that."

"Is he gone?"

"Leaving in the morning."

"How's that been?"

"Interesting. We're kind of working together at the moment."

"On the Gale thing?"

He eyed her. "Good memory."

"Easy name to remember."

"Tell me about it," he said. Every time he spoke of the dead man he thought of his ex-wife. "Boldt was a big help to me. We've got some solid leads."

"From canvassing my place, no doubt," she said, forcing a smile behind it. A smile that didn't come easily.

"Exactly. I've suspected you for some time." He lowered his voice playfully. "I might need another one-on-one just to clear you."

"Talk to my attorney," she said, biting back a grin. She pulled herself out of the chair, leaned forward, and kissed him.

"Thank you," she repeated. She pulled his head to her lips and whispered. "I like your interrogation techniques. Like them *a lot*."

She left him there, firmly rooted in the chair, his neck still tingling from the sensation of her lips across his ear.

That afternoon the courts dealt Walt a crushing defeat by refusing him access to Dionne Fancelli's medical information and therefore preventing him from obtaining a DNA sample of the child she was carrying. He had her underwear, possibly carrying her DNA; he had a swab from the accused teen, but he lacked the DNA of the child in question. The state, increasingly aggressive in possible abuse and paternity cases, was nonetheless inconsistent. He was debating strategy when Nancy's voice came over the intercom.

"I have a reporter from *The Statesman*, Pam from the *Express*, and a couple of the TV stations all on hold. Hit us all at once."

"Concerning?"

"Martel Gale."

Walt swallowed. Gale's identity had not been released. He had expected the information might leak but not so quickly, and he had to wonder if this was somehow Harris Evers's doing, Vince Wynn's attorney. He couldn't imagine Wynn wanting the news public, but it seemed too coincidental.

"Issue a no comment."

"Got it."

His mind reeled. A sports celebrity death would bring the national news next. That, in turn, would bring pressure from the Hailey mayor, state congressman Clint Stennett, and soon, the governor. The cushion he'd hoped for was now gone. The longer the case dragged out, the worse it would get, the more demands he'd receive for an arrest. A good reporter would soon make the connection between Gale and Wynn and Boatwright, and possibly to Caroline Vetta, making his investigation all the more difficult. A good investigative reporter was a real pain in the ass because he or she could beat you to the information, had none of the legal restrictions imposed on law enforcement, and often had more resources at his disposal. One call from Nancy, and it sounded in Walt's ears like a starting pistol. He abhorred the idea that the investigation had just become a race, but there was no denying it.

He shot off an e-mail to Boldt, hoping to give him a heads-up. His office would be the next to be contacted. He called his PIO into his office.

As the office's public information officer, Deputy "Even" Eve Sanchez had the looks and the brains to be a crowd-pleaser. She was bilingual, beautiful, and young. The cameras liked her and so did Walt.

He briefed her on Gale and detailed the "potential land mines." They'd spoken about the case periodically over

the past few days, but not with the specifics of his suspicions and the Boldt interviews with Boatwright and
Wynn—all information she needed. They would take a
public position of "ongoing investigation" and therefore
"no comment." But McClure's office needed to be warned,
and Tommy Brandon and Fiona both needed debriefings
with Eve. They scheduled to meet twice daily and he
promised updates as he had them. For the time being he
would not take any questions or interviews, but when
pressed by her, agreed to join her at a press conference the
following morning at ten a.m. She would meet him at his
house later in the evening to prep him.

With Sanchez gone, he called Royal McClure to warn
him and asked Nancy to bring Fiona and Brandon in as
soon as possible.

He searched e-mails and his own notes about the
case, mentally reviewed discussions he'd had with Boldt,
and tried to see loose ends that needed tying off.

One that came to mind was the emergency room admissions for the night of Gale's death. If they offered anything promising, he'd want to lock them down. The
Louisiana list server for anyone affected by the Gale pros-
ecution loomed large. It was just the kind of thing a
reporter would scoop him on. He fired off a second e-mail
to Boldt asking if he could pull strings as he'd offered.

He hung up from another call with Nancy—requesting the emergency room log for the night in question—
and felt dizzy.

He needed food. He needed time.

He ordered takeout, called Lisa, and asked her to stay with the girls.

Nancy entered his office waving a sheet of paper.

"Emergency room records," she said, placing it before him.

Walt straightened the sheet and read. Two admissions, one a child with a broken ankle, the other an ax wound to the leg. He stared at the page, unable to divorce himself from his father's jabbing sarcasm about how unreal his son's job was when compared to one in a major city. Each hospital in Seattle probably saw a dozen emergency room admissions a night, some several dozen.

"This is it?" he said.

"You're looking at it."

"Not much help."

"No, I didn't think so."

He ran his hand through his hair.

"One of the guys was going to look into the convenience stores and drugstores—Chateau, and the Drug Store, in particular—and see if anyone remembers anything on that night. Can you chase that down?"

"Not a problem."

"Wait!" he said, holding the page now, wishing he could choke it. "Midnight to midnight," he said.

"Excuse me?"

"He was found on the fourteenth, and we bagged him on the fourteenth. But Royal couldn't give us a predictable time of death. Temperature drops too much each night. He was guessing he'd been there at least a day, and that seemed supported by the degradation—the predation to the face and limbs. So, let's say he went lights-out the twelfth or thirteenth."

"O . . . k . . . a . . . y?" she said cautiously, accustomed to being his sounding board and knowing to stay out of his way.

"Which is why I asked for the twelfth," he said, shaking the sheet of paper. "But it's a midnight start. It's a true day, and if Gale was killed—"

"Late night the twelfth," she said, unable to help herself.

"Exactly. Then we should be looking at the thirteenth, not the twelfth."

"I'll call."

Impatience got the better of him over the next twenty minutes. He would try answering an e-mail, only to find himself holding down the backspace key and starting over. He looked over his "hot list" of follow-ups to accomplish before the press conference, but felt stymied.

His computer rang a tone. He saw notice of an e-mail from Boldt and read it. The detective had managed to contact a man in the Louisiana Attorney General's office, a deputy A.G. by the name of Robert "Buddy" Cornell. Cornell believed he could scare up at least the e-mail addresses for those people on the Gale list server, and hoped to have it to Boldt by Monday morning.

Walt pounded out a thank-you and sent it off.

Nancy was standing in his doorway holding another sheet of paper. She looked different, like she'd tasted something funny. Gone was the playful Dr. Watson who'd sparred with him twenty minutes earlier.

"You need some food or something," he said. "You want to go home, I can handle it from here."

She said nothing as she stepped forward and slid the piece of paper across his desk, the St. Luke's Wood River Medical Center banner across the top.

"That's better," he said, noting right away that there had been ten—no, eleven!—emergency room admissions on the thirteenth.

He glanced up from the emergency room report at Nancy, who stood staring down at him, still as pale as a sheet.

"I'm telling you," he said, "you do not look well."

"Second from the bottom," she said, watching as his eyes found the printed line.

His stubby finger traced across the page. He looked up at Nancy, back to the page, back to Nancy.

"Head injury," he said.

She nodded.

Despite his concern, he wasn't ready to make that call.

25

Recognizing the caller ID as the sheriff's office central number, Fiona answered her mobile phone, expecting to hear Walt's voice. She was disappointed to discover it was Nancy, his secretary. Standing in the cottage's small galley kitchen, she glanced out the window over the sink into the stand of aspen trees and the blinding shock of lilies mixing with the white bark.

"Nancy?"

"I need a little clarification on something. We just got the GPS coordinates for the pickup truck you requested—"

"Oh, thank God."

"Thing is, the coordinates have it on the Engleton property."

"What?"

"There's like a five-yard possibility of error or some-thing, so . . . I'm not exactly sure how to proceed with this. You want me to send a dep—"

"No, no!" she said, hurrying to the far side of the liv-ing room and looking toward the main house. "I can't believe this. I'm *so* sorry. Let me look around and get back to you. Does it show *where* on the property? Does it get that detailed?"

"There's a hybrid view: satellite image laid on top of the mapping software. It shows the truck as in the main house. Like the living room. But there's that margin of error."

"I'll look."

"Call me back, would you, please?"

"Promise. Give me five minutes." She disconnected the call and slipped the phone into a pocket absentmind-edly. She crossed the driveway, oblivious to the chitter-ing of tree squirrels and a red-sailed paraglider working the thermals above a northern ridge. To her there was only the garage. The closer she drew to it, the more trepidation.

Maybe the device had been removed from the truck and left in the garage, and if so, what did that say about the truck's disappearance? She and Walt had checked the garage, had stood in the empty bay.

She rose to tiptoe and peered through the garage door's glass pane, looking in on the truck bed. Parked right where it belonged. She felt foolish and embarrassed to have put Walt up to the GPS search. Kira had obviously taken the truck and returned it, and Fiona found herself overcome with anger, furious at the girl for putting her through the worry and concern.

She marched to the front door of the home and found it locked. She knocked loudly, pounding on the door. Kira didn't answer. She tried the handle again, and stormed back across to the cottage to get her key. Returning, she opened the door and barged inside.

"Kira! Kira?" She marched room to room, growing madder by the minute. *"Kira!"* Hit the stairs running. Up a flight, two doors to the right. Threw open the door.

Empty. No sign of Kira, no different than the room had appeared the last time she'd checked. A twinge of fright ran through her. It hadn't occurred to her some-one other than Kira might have returned the truck. Someone other than Kira might be inside. The mountain man, for instance—was he the one she'd apparently mentioned while under hypnosis? The one who'd given her the concussion?

She moved stealthily, creeping along the hallway toward the elegant stairway leading to the ground-level living room. Clinging to the handrail, she took each step carefully, turning her head side to side to take in everything around her. Her "damn you, Kira" attitude had reversed, and she was now once again concerned for the missing girl's well-being, panicked over her own situation, wondering how she'd allowed her emotions to dictate. Nancy would have sent a deputy had she asked; in her determination to protect Kira and the Engletons, she'd acted hastily and stupidly.

She hesitated at the bottom of the stairs. She heard the low hum of the twin Sub-Zero refrigerators, the ticking of the ship's clock on the mantel. Ringing in her ears, and the thump of her own blood coursing past her eardrums. The house was enormous, multiple levels with several wings, a wine cellar, a sauna, a workout gym. On the one hand, she felt terrified; on the other, if Kira had returned the truck, she wanted to talk to her before the sheriff's office did.

The front door called to her. She would feel safer once outside. Instead, she rounded the bottom of the unsupported, curving cherrywood staircase, and moved down a hallway lined with closets and family photos to a back stairwell that she followed lower to the split level. She searched the weight room, the his/her bathrooms, and the sauna. Two guest bedrooms. A utility/storage area. The laundry. She returned upstairs and made her way into the south wing, a guest wing consisting of a pair of two-bedroom suites. Checked all the closets and all four bathrooms.

As she returned to the living room, she was filled with an added sense of dread, the feeling of being watched. She snatched up a leaded crystal cube—a philanthropic award given to Michael and Leslie by a California hospital—clutching it like a baseball, but wielding it as a weapon carried high at her shoulder.

"I know you're in here," she said softly, knowing no such thing. "I can *feel* you." Feeling too much to know what she felt.

She eyed the wide hallway leading to the garage. It stretched out beyond her, suddenly much longer. More closets and a pantry lined it—a person could hide behind any of the doors, waiting. She tried to slow her breathing, to calm herself, but it was useless. She pressed her back to the wall and edged toward the first of the doors, jumped across the hall and backed up to the opposing wall. She kept the glass cube held high, visualized herself smashing it into a stranger's face. She tacked her way down the hall, wall to wall, ever alert. Reached the garage door and threw it open.

It bounced off the stopper and came back at her and she blocked it with her toe. A box freezer in the garage groaned and Fiona suddenly viewed it as a coffin and moved toward it cautiously, slipping past the pickup truck that shouldn't have been there. With her back to the freezer, her fingers deciphered its latch and forced it open and she lifted its springed lid blindly, finally gathering the courage to peer behind her and see nothing but bricks of frozen meat in white paper wrappers.

Now, finally, she felt her nerves settling. Her last great fear was that she would find Kira in the truck. She gathered her courage, climbed onto the side rail, and, holding to the exterior mirror with her left hand and still clutching the glass cube in her right, pressed her eyes to the glass and tried to see inside. She moved front seat to back. Empty.

She climbed into the truck bed and hesitated only briefly before popping the lid on the Tuff-Box toolbox mounted below the cab's rear window. *Tools.* A jumper cable. No body. She sat down into the truck bed and released an audible sigh, waited for her light-headedness to pass, and collected herself. Slowly, the anger at Kira reentered her, and it was everything she could do to suppress it.

She owed Nancy a phone call. She owed Walt an explanation. But her imagination got the better of her. She'd been fixated on trying to explain what had happened to her, where Kira had gone, the body at the bottom of the mountain.

Knowing Nancy was expecting her call, she moved quickly now, suddenly energized, freed of the weight of her prior fears. It was almost as if she'd rehearsed it, the way she went about it so methodically.

She found the blank sheets of paper and the Scotch tape in Michael's office. The acrylic paint in Leslie's painting studio. She tripped the garage door on her return, and climbed into the truck and found the keys in the center island's cup holder. She slipped the key into the ignition and left the driver's door open and the key alarm sounding as she placed the taped-together sheets of copy paper behind each of the truck tires, mixed the eggplant purple paint with some water, and meticulously applied the paint to the tire rubber as if she'd done it a hundred times. She climbed behind the wheel and backed up the truck, and then collected the four strips of paper and liked three of the four she saw. She repeated the procedure for the front right tire and then wiped down all four tires with a wet rag and parked the truck and shut the automatic door, returning to her cottage, where she generated photographs of the truck tire impressions from the Gale crime scene.

The scale was wrong and so she reprinted two of the photographs, this time enlarging the photos to where she got less of the impression, but a wider width.

Then, placing the photographs next to the impressions she'd taken from the garage, she studied the tread pattern and took out a tape measure from her kitchen junk drawer, and noticed her hands shaking as she counted the rows of tread pattern and tried to calculate the widths. At last she turned around the photo to her right and moved it along the taped-together copy pages, and gasped at what she saw.

She jumped and let out a cry as the phone in her pocket buzzed, jolting her. She reached for it, knowing who it would be before ever checking the caller ID.

Her thumb hovered, wondering whether to answer it or not.

26

Walt sat facing the computer screen on his dining-room table when he heard the rhythmic tap of footfalls on his front porch steps. He was sending an e-mail to Boldt and hoping to Skype with the detective, to talk through the facts of the case and see if they converged for Boldt as they did for him. The tire impressions had come back from the lab as a BFGoodrich-branded tread—the Radial Long Trail. The pollen collected from Gale's earwax had been identified as coming from a yellow lily. He'd witnessed Boatwright's gardener digging up a flower bed. To mix blood into the soil? If he went after a man like Boatwright, he would need more than pollen and some hunches—an army of attorneys was more like it.

The footfalls stopped and Walt prepared himself for

the doorbell or a knock. At nine thirty p.m., it was late for a visitor, and the longer the pause continued, the more convinced he became that an insecure Fiona awaited him at the door. He pushed back his chair and closed the distance to the front door quickly, not wanting to lose her, throwing it open and feeling his expectation crushed as he stood facing a stranger.

"Hello?" he said.

In her late twenties or early thirties, the woman had a tired look about her, stringy brown hair, wore no makeup, had seven empty holes running up the spine of her left ear.

"Sheriff?" A husky, smoker's voice.

"Yes. May I help you?"

"I need to speak with you."

"I keep office hours. If you don't mind—"

"Away from the office," the woman said, interrupting. "A friend knew where you lived. I'm sorry about this."

He motioned her inside, and then to the couch. He offered her something to drink, hoping she wouldn't accept and she asked for coffee— "Any kind of coffee. Instant's all right."

He used his coffee press to make two cups and served her in a Simpsons mug. His was a State Farm.

Beatrice combat-crawled across the floor to the woman's feet and sighed to make sure to be noticed. The woman bent down and petted her and Bea set up camp, climbing to a sitting position and placing just her jaw onto the edge of the couch for convenience.

"I'm sorry," the woman said, "but it's wrong of me to come here. But I can't be seen at your office, or at least I don't want to be seen at your office."

"You don't have to apologize."

"It's about the man. The dead man."

Walt kept his outward appearance calm, though his insides were anything but.

"Martel Gale."

"Martel, yes. I didn't know his last name at the time."

"You knew him," Walt said. He sipped the hot coffee in part to maintain the image of nonchalance.

"Sheriff, I'm a member of NA—Narcotics Anonymous. The whole idea is anonymity, so my being here is radically wrong. But when I saw the story in the paper. When they ran the photograph of him—that football one—I felt an obligation to come forward."

"I'm glad you did."

"He visited our group last Tuesday night. It was a speaker night so there wasn't a lot of sharing, but he stuck around for coffee at the end and I talked to him. We get a lot of guests and like them to feel welcome."

Walt wondered if Martel Gale's good looks had had anything to do with her welcome.

"He stuck around awhile," she continued, "and we got to talking and though he didn't come right out and say it, I think he was here in Sun Valley for the ninth step."

"You know, I'm familiar with twelve-step programs—AA most of all—and believe me, we appreciate their success, but I'm not familiar with the particular steps."

"You might call it atonement," she said. "'We make direct amends to such people wherever possible except when to do so would injure them or others.' Basically, it's our chance to remove excess baggage and clear the way for our full recovery."

"I realize there is the assumption of anonymity," Walt said, choosing his words carefully, "but with Mr. Gale dead I'm hoping we can look beyond that and you can tell me as much as you know."

"And I would, except the last part of the step kind of prevents that. I mean, I have no way of knowing who such information might injure, and it's wrong for me to come here and talk about this in the first place, much less accidentally harm or injure someone by doing so. That's for the addict to decide. I'm not about to play Higher Power."

"Let's back up a moment," Walt said. He kept all urgency out of his voice, found his professional self, no matter how odd it felt to engage inside his own house. "He came to your meeting. You two met after the meeting. Did you happen to go somewhere? Did this all take place at the meeting itself?"

"We might have gone for a cup of coffee. At Tully's."

"And from what he told you, you came to believe he was here in town for the ninth step."

"Yes."

"So he would have been meeting with someone," Walt said.

"More than one," she blurted out before squinting at him accusingly.

"The point is," Walt said, "we don't harm or injure people . . ."

"Ellen."

"Ellen. We . . . the sheriff's office . . . our job is just the opposite. We protect people. In this case it's too late to protect Mr. Gale. Our job—my job—becomes explaining his death. And as you can imagine, that can often be a tall order, as it is in this case, given Mr. Gale's status as a visitor to our valley and something of an unknown. Add to that his celebrity status as a sports figure, and it gets more complicated."

"Which is one of the reasons I couldn't come to your office. I *do not* want my name or face on the news. No one knows I used, Sheriff. Not my boss, not my family. NA saved my life, but if I'm outed—"

"That's not going to happen."

"You'd be surprised how easily it does happen."

"You are safe here."

"Until I find some reporter was camped in the bushes."

She was right. Reporters occasionally hounded his home. Her anonymity wasn't perfectly safe anywhere.

"I thought about calling," she said. "But it seemed like the cowardly thing to do. Not that I expect that to make any sense to anyone but me. The point being: I'm here, but I don't think I can help all that much."

"What gave you the impression he was here for the ninth step?" Walt asked, afraid he was already losing her.

"I've said too much."

"Did he mention names?"

"No! Of course not."

"But he did say something."

"He said he was here to fix things, and we talked about a couple of the other steps and I pretty much could figure he was here for the ninth."

"Did he ask your help in finding someone?"

"How could you possibly know that?" she asked.

"Most everyone has post office boxes. Getting a real address can be tricky."

She eyed him suspiciously. "I'm saying a lot more than I intended to." She placed the coffee down and gave Bea another pat on the head. "I should probably go."

He had nothing to go on. A first name. Might not even be her real name. He couldn't let her go.

"Was his mood angry or vengeful?"

"Him? No. Just the opposite. Are you kidding? He was contrite. We're all contrite by the ninth. When you're using, you walk all over the people you care about the most. Steal from them. Lie to them. Cheat on them. Do whatever it takes to stay high. Use getting high as an excuse to do whatever you feel like. Drugs are incredibly convenient in that way, Sheriff. You can do basically whatever you want and it's always the drug's fault, never yours. And doing all that makes you feel shitty—pardon my French—so you get high to forget about it, and around and around we go."

"But I imagine some grudges build up along the way. Jealousies, or anger at those who stop helping or call you out."

"You've been around it," she said. "I can tell."

"We see just a little bit of substance abuse in my line of work."

She laughed and rubbed Bea out of nervousness. "I guess that's right," she said uncomfortably.

"But not Martel Gale," he said.

"He was a recovering addict. He had his proverbial shit together as far as I could tell. Long way to come to make amends. Most people write a letter. Some dare to make a phone call—and believe me, that's not easy. Traveling halfway across the country to do it in person? That's someone you care about. Trust me. Or *someones* I guess, in his case. He was all fucked up when he was using: steroids and HGH and any kind of performance enhancer out there. Massive quantities, to hear him tell it. Totally raged. Poisoned by it. A maniac. Testosterone overdose. Put his fist through car windows. Shit like that. Incredible Hulk stuff. A real terror."

"You'd think that might carry some anger with it," he said, thinking of Vince Wynn firing blindly into the dark hoping to hit Martel Gale. "Some rage."

"He wouldn't have come here if that was still lingering. Doesn't make sense. Just the opposite. He didn't come here to blame, believe me. He came here to take the heat, even if it should be shared. He came here to make it right."

"And someone didn't want to hear him?"

"How should I know?"

"Did he express any concern, any reservations?"

"We all have reservations, Sheriff. It's terrifying to expose yourself like that, to go up to another human being and admit your shortcomings and take responsibility for the wrongs you've committed."

"And if you surprise them?" he asked.

"What's that?"

"What happens when you're clearing your shelf and the other person didn't know, wasn't aware of half the stuff you did?"

"It happens, if that's what you're asking."

"I can't imagine that goes down terribly well."

"It can be awkward. To say the least."

"Dangerous?"

"I suppose."

Walt considered all he'd heard.

"I'm not saying that's what happened here," she said quickly.

"But if Martel Gale arrived unexpectedly to someone who didn't know he'd been harmed by the guy during his addiction, that could be embarrassing or even difficult for the person on the receiving end."

"Which is why the step is very clear about that. You don't ninth-step someone if it's going to injure or harm them or if there's any threat of that."

"But if you didn't know."

"You know," she said confidently. "Some of us have short lists, some incredibly long. But you give every person a lot of thought. You share with your sponsor. You work out who needs to be stepped and who doesn't."

"Your sponsor."

"Sure. At least I did."

"How would I find Martel Gale's sponsor?"

"You wouldn't. You won't. That's what the A is about in the name."

"But how could I?"

"You can't."

"A man died here. May have been killed."

"I'm aware of that. Why do you think I'm here?"

"They could contact me," Walt said. "If the sponsor wanted to. If someone told him or her that I needed to talk to them."

"Probably wouldn't."

"But might."

"Might, I suppose."

Walt waited for the offer. It didn't come. The two stared at each other across the coffee table. Bea's tail thumped against the leg of the table.

"Please," Walt said. "I know that if it's anything like AA, it's a small world. People know people, anonymous or not. And Gale. His sponsor knows what happened to him by this point. All I need is someone to make an introduction."

"His home group is New Orleans. A prison group at that."

Walt lodged the information. *A prison group.* He could research this without her.

"You could maybe make a call," he pleaded, wanting to attack it from as many sides as possible.

"It's true, we all know someone who knows someone."

"It's a man's life. Or the loss of one."

"I know that, Sheriff." She placed down the mug. "That's really good coffee," she said.

27

"Are you sure about this?" Brandon asked from the passenger seat of the Jeep.

"It's a regular Monday game. Wynn's in the group. Two birds, and all that. We've got the NA member's statement and maybe the pollen. It feels like it's coming together."

"Are you going to bust the game?"

"No, although it would give me a reason to get them down to the office and interrogate them formally. I wouldn't mind that. But no one would back up the charges. I'd look like a moron." He barely hesitated. "Are you going to marry her?"

"What? Aren't you asking the wrong person?"

"Gail doesn't always put the girls first, Tommy. You

know that. I may need your help here. I think it's something we have to think about."

"We?"

"It has to be figured out, Tommy. Eleven-year-olds
know perfectly well what you and their mother are doing
in that trailer, and that I don't appreciate it."

"And do they know what you and your photographer
are doing?"

The Jeep swerved. Walt flashed a punishing look over
at Brandon. "You have no idea what you're talking about."

"No?"

"No."

"Okay. Then I take it back."

"I'm perfectly capable of maintaining a private life
without exposing my daughters to every aspect of it."

"If you say so."

"Dangerous ground, Tommy."

"Wasn't me who brought it up. Wasn't me who made
the call to LoJack without a stolen vehicle report."

Walt had left the company his direct number but somehow they'd reported back to the main office and Brandon
had taken the call.

"If you two are serious, then fine, help me out. If
not . . . It's too much for them to handle right now."

"Listen, I know this is . . . I know it's not easy on any
of us. I hear you. Okay?"

For all his bravado, Brandon suddenly seemed more
like a kid. A good, solid deputy. Trustworthy. Brave to
the point of stupidity. But young. Walt respected him,

even enjoyed his company, but now, thanks in part to Fiona, he thought he saw him more clearly and he nearly laughed. Gail had ridden the first horse out of the barn, and at some point she was going to realize it wasn't yet broke. Tommy needed some miles.

Walt pulled the Jeep up to Boatwright's ostentatious gate and was about to buzz the box when the garden worker—the caretaker—Walt had spoken to before approached from the other side of the wrought iron, wearing a plastic spray tank on his back, goggles, and a face mask. He pulled down the mask.

"I'll tell him you're here," he said.

"Rather you didn't do that."

"He's got guests, Sheriff."

"He's hosting the Monday night poker game. That gives me enough to come onto the property. I only want to talk to him. This becomes a hassle, it will only get more complicated."

"I'm supposed to just let you in? I'll be looking for a job in the morning."

"You don't let us in, you'll be looking for a lawyer. Don't worry, he won't fire you."

"You don't know Marty Boatwright."

"I can be pretty persuasive."

The man tripped the gate and it swung open and Walt drove through.

"Those are BFGoodrich on that pickup," Brandon said. "Same as the lab report just came back."

Walt caught sight of the pickup, pulled off onto the

grass alongside a flower bed. He wondered if he would have caught the make of the tires the way a gear-head like Brandon had.

"Nice catch," he said.

Brandon, still steaming over their earlier discussion, didn't respond immediately. Finally he said, "You want me to do anything about it?"

Walt felt a pressure at his temples, and found himself wondering what Boldt would have done, a needless distraction. He had testimony that at least circumstantially connected Martel Gale to Boatwright and Wynn; he had the pollen and the flower bed being dug up on the property; and now he had a pickup truck with the same brand of tires that had left impressions by Gale's body.

"It's not like we can lift impressions without a warrant," Walt said, remaining behind the wheel as the caretaker stood impatiently alongside the vehicle. He looked to be straining to hear what was being said, a losing proposition. "Not if we want to beat Boatwright's attorneys. Guys like this . . . we have to tread so carefully, Tommy."

"They're Goodrich, Sheriff. I can read them from here."

"We don't want them knowing we know that. We don't need them changing the tires on us. Destroying possible evidence. I think we leave it for now."

"We could call in for a warrant."

"Judge Alban plays volleyball Monday nights, and Sitter has his own poker game. Neither is going to appreciate my interrupting them. We'd have to drive back down valley to get the warrant, providing either would issue it, and we'd need more than a tire brand that's on a few million vehicles for one of them to sign off on a guy like Boatwright. And in the meantime, if Boatwright gets word of what we're up to, then we'd likely lose the evidence anyway."

"So? Then what are we doing here?"

"Gale's fellow NA-er mentioned he was here to ninth-step—to make amends. I called Wynn's neighbor back and pressed her about the drug situation at Wynn's, something she'd given me on my first interview. She gave up how her husband has been in this Monday night game often enough and that there is always pot."

"Pot? Who cares about pot, Sheriff?"

"Listen, I know it's not the perfect situation, but guys like Boatwright and Wynn . . . they protect their privacy. You find Mr. Green Jeans and chat him up. Let him sweat a little."

"Got it."

"We'll compare notes."

Brandon climbed out of the Jeep. "Can I talk to you a minute?" he called out to the caretaker.

"Front door?" Walt asked the man, who suddenly looked a little frantic.

"Back patio," the caretaker said.

That made things easier for Walt—he wouldn't need an invitation inside.

Walt let himself through a split-rail fence gate and circled behind the house. The back patio was the size of a tennis court and included a hot tub. He was spotted by

Boatwright, who made a hand gesture, but it was too late. Walt arrived beneath a twelve-foot green umbrella where the eight men sat around a teak table cluttered with glasses of beer and wine and ashtrays cradling Cuban cigars. Walt spotted the smoking joint as it was whisked from an ashtray and vanished into a hand before being tossed into the grass.

"Gentlemen," he said.

"Don't you knock, Sheriff?" asked Marty Boatwright.

"Your caretaker told me where to find you." Technically, Walt could spin this into an invitation if pressed to do so.

Walt recognized Alex Macdonald, Richie Fabiano, and Vince Wynn, but it was the two-time Cy Young Award winner next to Alex who caused Walt's throat to tighten. He'd watched him pitch for the Red Sox all through his childhood, and the fact that he was now standing five feet away from him, that the man was looking at him, *smiling* at him, nearly stopped Walt's heart. The Sun Valley celebrities—politicians, film stars, pop stars—never affected him in the least. But a two-time Cy Young winner? He nearly had a coronary.

"You know Mandy Halifax, Sheriff?" Wynn asked, having caught the look of astonishment on the sheriff's face.

To Halifax, Wynn explained, "Our sheriff is a catcher, and captain of a league-winning team. Bats two-eighty-five."

"Pleased to meet you," Halifax said.

Walt came around the table and shook the man's

hand, briefly feeling like an eight-year-old, only to realize this hand had been the one that had grabbed the
joint off the table.

"Mr. Boatwright, Mr. Wynn, a word in private?"
Walt said.

"It's Marty, Sheriff. These guys call me a lot worse
than that, but Marty will do."

The group enjoyed that. Boatwright had been drinking, as had Wynn. Walt caught a look that transpired
between the two; it was a look of coconspirators, causing
him to wonder how much he was reading into it, and how
much was legitimate. For an instant he saw an Agatha
Christie–like plot of the two of them teaming up against
Martel Gale, and realized his regular reading consisted of
too many of his daughters' mystery books.

Boatwright struggled to stand. Halifax jumped up to
help him out of his chair, and Walt thought how well the
action fit with what he knew of the man. Mandy Halifax
went beyond legend to sports god. He wished he could
think of a way to involve Halifax in the questioning just
to spend more time with him.

With Halifax out of his chair, Walt made a point of
retrieving the smoldering joint, snuffing it out, and placing it into a glassine evidence bag. He took out a pen
and labeled it.

The joviality died around the table.

Boatwright grabbed one of the wine bottles and carried it with him, causing the others to bark with laughter.

"I'd look out for him," Macdonald shouted to Walt.

Wynn walked side by side with Boatwright and saw him inside to a sunroom off the kitchen. He grabbed a wineglass and returned with it, and Boatwright poured himself a glass of red wine.

"I have a very good hand, Sheriff," Boatwright said. "First decent hand of the night. You screw up my luck and you'll be sorry."

"Marty!" Wynn chided. To Walt, Wynn said, "Marty's not feeling any pain tonight."

"Can't piss but a thimble full," Boatwright said. "Can't get a hard-on without riding a goddamn paint shaker. Don't talk to me about feeling no pain."

Wynn rolled his eyes, trying to apologize for the man.

"Martel Gale came here to Sun Valley to make amends with you two," Walt said. "To make amends, not to threaten, not to make any financial claims. We're in the process of tracking down his communications, and we're going to find he contacted both of you, or at least your assistants or secretaries, and that could conceivably put you in a bind, so I'm here to let you get out ahead of it."

"Slow down, Sheriff," Wynn said, looking as blind-sided as Walt had hoped.

Boatwright's face reddened. His watery eyes dancing, he reached for the wine, but Wynn touched his forearm and stopped him.

"Who wants to go first?" Walt asked.

"You know my situation," Wynn said.

"Mr. Evers? You want to go that route?"

"It's not a 'route,'" Wynn complained.

"Deny it," Walt said. "Deny that he contacted you." He looked between both men.

"Martel Gale was a human time bomb," Boatwright said.

"Shut up, Marty," Wynn said. "You don't need to say anything. You're drunk. You shouldn't say anything."

"Was," Walt said, "as in the past, or in the present?"

"What's the difference?" Boatwright said, slurring his words. "Trouble is trouble."

"And how did you react to that trouble?" Walt asked.

"Marty!" Wynn said.

"Yeah, yeah," Boatwright said to Wynn. "I know. I know."

"Speaking for myself, I was not contacted by Martel Gale," Wynn said. "The last time I spoke with him, I think I told you, was just after the sentencing. This is maybe two years ago. And Marty, I'm going to strongly urge you not to say anything. You'll thank me in the morning."

"Yeah, yeah," Boatwright said. He raised his rheumy eyes to Walt. "The hell you looking at?"

"The list server notice was the first I'd heard about Gale in a long time," Wynn continued, carefully sticking to his original statement.

"Gale showed up here, didn't he, Mr. Boatwright?" Walt convinced himself he would never have Boatwright as vulnerable again.

"Marty, don't answer that."

"I'd like to speak with Mr. Boatwright alone, please, Mr. Wynn."

"No," Wynn said. "Not going to happen."

"Let me explain how this plays out," Walt said, patting his pocket that contained the joint. "Marijuana in plain view is enough to get drug charges on all of you, so you will be booked into jail. My booking reports are a matter of public record. They'll be sent to the press tomorrow morning and will be posted on our website. You'll spend the night at Public Safety, in jail. It's also likely to win me probable cause to search not only Mr. Boatwright's home, but yours as well, Mr. Wynn, as I have witnesses to repeated drug use at your residence. So there are a couple ways to play this. I admit it. But you may want to consider just how badly you piss me off before withholding your cooperation." He looked between the two men, the fight in them gone. "You can stay if you want, but if you play lawyer, you're out of here. Understood?"

Wynn nodded reluctantly.

"Here's what we know," Walt said, controlling the anger he felt. "Martel gets a Get Out of Jail card, and the next week Caroline Vetta goes down hard. Ten days later, Gale himself is dead. It's either sweet justice or coincidence or incredibly convenient. I'm supposed to figure out which, and for whom. You boys hold some of the answers. And I'm going to have those answers."

Wynn was too professional to give anything back to Walt. He remained outwardly calm, showing what might have passed for surprise. Boatwright swam in the wine. Walt wasn't sure he'd even heard him.

"Don't want to keep my guests waiting," Boatwright said.

"You did or did not hear from Martel Gale prior to the discovery of his body?" Walt asked.

Boatwright glared at Walt, checked over with a disapproving Wynn, and rolled his eyes back in his head. "Guy was a terror, Sheriff. Sorry he's dead, but I'm not sorry he's out of my life."

"I'd like an answer to the question," Walt said.

"I'm sure you would."

Walt heard the tinkle of metal coming from the direction of the patio, knew by the sound it was a dog approaching. He turned back expecting to see Boatwright's dog. But Boatwright didn't own a dog. It was Beatrice, nosing the carpet, working scents the way she'd been trained. Brandon must have left a car door open or put a window down. There wasn't much that could keep Bea from Walt, including, apparently, an open door on a patio.

A nosy dog at any time, Bea was locked on a scent. He knew that random-looking yet methodical movement of hers—she was working. He held back his temptation to stop her as her paws tapped out on the stone and she circled the poker table, then made a Bea-line straight for Walt.

But it wasn't to Walt. Nose to the ground, she sniffed her way directly to Wynn, then hurried to Walt and tapped his hand with her wet nose. She backed up, sat down, and looked up at her master, tail wagging.

For a moment, Walt stood there frozen, looking at his

dog, then Wynn's shoes, then back at his dog. Bea had just spoken to him as surely as if she'd used English, but the code was lost on Boatwright and Wynn. Only Walt and Beatrice understood what had been said. Walt processed the message, his heart thumping in his chest, knowing better than to speak until he knew what to say.

Boatwright and Wynn picked up on the change in Walt. A silence hung among the three, broken only by Bea's rapid panting, and the sound of male voices coming from the patio.

"I don't like dogs," Boatwright finally said. "Get that thing out of my home."

"Mr. Wynn," Walt said, his voice eerily calm. "I wonder if I might have a look at your shoes?"

"What?" Wynn said, looking down at his hand-sewn Italian loafers.

"Your shoes."

"No," he said, taken aback. "What for?"

In his limited dealings with Wynn, Walt saw panic flash across the man's face for the first time. It didn't last long, but it had been there. "I'd like a look at your shoes, if I might."

"You might not," Wynn said, eyeing the dog. He gathered his wits. "You have a search warrant, Sheriff?"

"Based on the possession of marijuana, I can get one if I need one. It's your call. We went over that." He directed this to Boatwright, assuming the man would find the idea of jail and a crime scene team in his home repugnant.

No one spoke.

Walt broke the silence. "I should be able to have them back to you in a day. No more."

"You want to take my shoes?" Wynn said, clarifying. "Are you out of your mind? I'm supposed to go home, what, barefoot? What the hell, Sheriff?"

"Two days at most," Walt said.

He met eyes with Wynn, impressed with the man's ability to so quickly dismiss the panic. He saw now only contempt and irritability, the hallmarks of a professional negotiator.

"I don't think so. Thanks anyway."

Walt winced. "Have it your way." He reached for his radio's mike clip.

"Vince," Boatwright said, "I'm not leaving that hand on the table. And I'm not putting up with some god-damned night in jail. Give the man your shoes."

"Can't do that, Marty," Wynn said.

"I'll loan you some slippers to get you home."

Wynn's pained expression told Walt plenty. Walt had jammed him up and both men knew it. Walt was going to have the man's shoes.

"I will keep everyone here," Walt explained, "and sep-arated, until the warrant is issued and the crime scene unit is in place. The CS unit drives up from Meridian, just FYI. And they won't begin that drive until sometime after nine a.m."

Boatwright said sternly, "Give the man the shoes, Vince. Don't be an asshole. That's Mandy Halifax out there. He's a guest in my home."

The two men locked into a staring contest, Wynn
clearly considering his diminishing options. He could anger
Boatwright and make Walt jump through the warrant
hoop, and still end up surrendering the shoes, or he could
give them up now.

"That dog had no business being in your house,"
Wynn explained to the drunken Boatwright.

Walt felt a shiver. How, exactly, had Beatrice escaped
the Jeep? It crossed his mind that it might not have been
accidental, in which case Bea sniffing out blood evidence
could be questioned in a court of law. He kept his mouth
shut.

"You're not thinking clearly," Boatwright told Wynn.
"You're not listening to me. These men are my guests.
This is my home. Give the man the goddamned shoes."

The frustration and anger on Wynn's face gave way to
resignation and he kicked off the loafers. But he was not
a happy man.

Back in the Jeep, now driving through town, Walt
finally dared to voice what had been bothering him. Beatrice stood partially between them, front paws on the
cup holders.

"Tommy, you understand how I approach this work?"

"Sheriff?"

"We don't invent evidence. We don't spin the truth.
Not in my office."

"Not sure what you mean."

"I never want one of my deputies lying for me, giving
false testimony."

"Sheriff?"

"So I'm not going to ask you, because I don't want the answer." Walt reached over and rubbed Beatrice's head.

Brandon looked from the dog to the sheriff. "Okay. Got it."

"You should have checked with me before trying something like that, Tommy."

"Got it."

"It was brilliant, mind you," Walt said. "But the courts would take a dim view of it."

"Moon's coming up," Brandon said. "Gonna be full in a couple days."

"Nothing prettier," Walt said.

"She's a good dog."

"She is."

Beatrice's tail started thumping. She knew they were talking about her.

"But she doesn't open car doors," Walt said.

Nothing but the whine of the tire rubber.

"You want me to talk to Gail about how to handle things, I will."

"I shouldn't have dumped that on you."

"True story."

"I'll handle it," Walt said.

"Appreciate that, Sheriff."

Walt craned his neck to get a look through the windshield at the moon growing over the edge of the mountaintops. "Nothing prettier."

28

"Drop me off near Grumpie's," Brandon said.

"Because?" Walt asked.

"I got a call while you were inside. From Bonehead."

The public knew "Bonehead" Miller as a colorful bartender at Ketchum's local hamburger haunt. The sheriff's office knew him as a two-time offender now working off the public service hours of his sentence acting as a criminal informant, a CI.

"Concerning?"

"Drop me off and I'll let you know."

If one of his daughters had spoken to him with that tone Walt would have chided her, and he considered doing so now because once that contempt for authority crept into a department, it was hard to weed out. But his relationship with Brandon demanded special handling,

something everyone in the office had come to understand. How far he allowed Brandon to stray, and how
hard Brandon pushed, would ultimately determine the
deputy's longevity with the office, and quite possibly
Walt's career, for he was beginning to sense that if a real
challenge were to come at the ballot box it would come
from within his own ranks. Who better than a young,
experienced Marlboro Man like Tommy Brandon? He
mused at the irony that someday Gail might end up the
sheriff's wife for a second time, and wondered if she
would be the one to push her lover to stage the challenge.

Brandon had street cred like few of Walt's other deputies. People warmed to him easily and he to them. He
regularly turned arrests and even convictions into criminal informants for the office. Most of the rumors and
hard information came through either Brandon or Eve
Sanchez. As he watched Brandon swagger across Warm
Springs Road and cut around to the back of the clapboard shack that was Grumpie's, he wondered if by being
this information conduit, Brandon didn't possess too
much power, wondering what, if anything, he might do
about it.

Brandon sent a text message and waited by the putrid
Dumpster behind the burger joint, the garbage smoldering in the summer heat.

Bonehead Miller was aptly named for his protruding

forehead and deep-set eyes. His dirty blond, shoulder-length hair was tucked up under a Cardinals baseball cap. He wore a soiled apron over a sleeveless undershirt, show-ing off some faded tattoos. He had one silver tooth—all the rest chipped—and a goatee and soul patch that looked like a wire brush for an outdoor grill.

There were no introductions. He handed Brandon a cheeseburger with catsup, pickles, pepperoncini, and Swiss wrapped in butcher paper, and Brandon ate as Bonehead talked.

"So I'm on the clock, right?"

"Mmm," Brandon answered, using his finger to catch a drip.

"You'll like this. I expect you to knock a couple hours off for this one."

Bonehead always expected more than he would receive.

"Of course," Brandon said through the food, lying. *You'll get what I think it's worth, asshole*, he was thinking. Twice in for drugs was all-in for drugs as far as he was concerned. He had no room in his world for the Bone-head Millers.

"There's this guy been in here a couple times and I asked around with my buddies and he's pretty much making the rounds far as I can tell. Rat fuck of a guy. Makes me look like fucking Donald Trump. Smells bad. A woodsman. I heard you were looking for a woodsman, a meth cooker. I hear right?"

"Keep . . . talking," Brandon said with his mouth full, savoring the best burger in town. It was half gone.

"Looks like Tom Hanks in that one where he's washed onto that island."

"*Cast Away*," Brandon said.

"That's the one. Comes in here smelling like piss and woodsmoke, orders a burger and beer, and lays down a hun. Wouldn't have thought nothing of it but Raven over at the Chute happens to mention some moron laying down a Franklin for a beer and we get to talking and it's gotta be the same asshole."

"Franklin, as in Ben Franklin, as in a hun," Brandon said, just to get his facts straight.

"That's what I'm saying. Thing is, it was like the same day, dude. So this guy's laying down the Franklins just to be seen laying them down. Right? What a jerk."

"And this interests me because . . . ?"

"Fuck if I know. It just don't make sense to me, and you're always telling me you want to hear about the shit that don't make sense."

"True enough."

"You're looking for a cooker, right?"

"I didn't say anything." Brandon scrunched up the butcher paper and tossed it over his shoulder into the Dumpster without looking. They were always looking for meth cookers. They were also looking for the guy who had tossed the Berkholders' place to look like a bear attack. One and the same? Or two different guys?

"You don't want it," the guy said, "what do I care? Maybe Jimmy Johns wants it."

Johns was a Ketchum deputy.

"Don't bite the hand that feeds you, Bonehead. You'll get credit for this if it pays off."

"Pays off how?"

"Get the word out that I'd like to talk to this guy if he shows up somewhere. Can you do that?"

"I can do that."

"Do that, you'll get more credit. You got it?"

"I got it. Could be your meth cooker, right?"

"Could be."

"Worth five hours, right?"

"Could be."

"He's been around. I can get him for you."

"Do that." Brandon pulled out a five-dollar bill. "For the burger," he said.

"On the house."

"Can't accept it. You know that."

Bonehead accepted the cash. "Why you play it so squeaky clean? Other guys take the burger *and* the beer."

"I'll knock ten off your time you get me this guy in the next twenty-four hours."

"Ten?" Bonehead's forehead lifted so fast his entire scalp shifted. "Who the hell's that important?" he said.

"Get to work," Brandon advised.

"You look like something the dog dragged in," Brandon said, climbing back into the Jeep.

Resting his hands on the bottom of the steering wheel, Walt worked to control his voice; maintaining the face of calm in the midst of turmoil was critical to rank and authority within his office. "It took them all of fifteen minutes to reach Aanestead." The county prosecutor. "He's blocked the shoes, at least temporarily, until it's sorted out what my dog was doing in the house when I lacked a warrant."

"That was fast."

"He'll question you, Tommy."

"And I'll give him answers. I've known Doug a long time. Way before he won the prosecutor's job. He's okay. He gets it."

"You'll give him answers keeping in mind what we spoke about earlier."

"Keeping in mind that we have blood evidence on the shoes of a prime suspect."

"The truth is a piece of glass, Tommy. It's either whole, or cracked and broken. There's no in-between."

"There's windshield welding," Brandon said. "Where they suck that epoxy into rock dings and it's good as new."

Walt huffed.

"You think he'll let it through?" Brandon asked. "Let us keep the evidence?"

"Not without a fight. Wynn's going to put up a fight."

"Never known Doug to back away from a good fight."

Walt started the Jeep and drove off. The streets of Ketchum were quiet, the only action outside the few bars and restaurants that lined Main Street.

Brandon caught him up on Bonehead.

"You think it's good?" Walt asked.

"Felt like it."

"You've got some catsup." Walt indicated his own cheek and Brandon wiped his face clean.

"Could be the mountain man who did the Berkholders' place."

"That's not what you're thinking," Walt said.

"You testing me? Okay, could be the contents of Gale's wallet. We know the guy lived large and probably carried a wad. Could be our meth cooker. Could be all the same guy."

"That's what I'm talking about."

"It's not whoever's using the ATM card," Brandon said. "ATMs don't dispense hundreds."

"Now you're thinking."

"So it's two different guys."

"And we can assume whoever got the wallet, whoever either found the body or did him in the first place is the one with the card."

"So maybe our meth cooker breaks into houses for his jollies, or for food, runs into money after he makes his sale, and starts spending it around. Doesn't necessarily put him with Gale."

"Whatever his routine, he's important to us. He's a big piece of this. And according to Bonehead he's down here in town."

"Staying in town? Coming and going? He's got some money and he's living it up?"

"Or he's coming down at night to sell his goods and spend his winnings. I'll get Gilly some night vision gear and ask him to watch the trails," Walt said. *He owes me that*, he was thinking. Walt had given him a second chance, not reporting the forest ranger's drinking on the job.

"I told Bonehead I'd knock ten hours off his PS if we caught the guy."

"What'd he say?"

"Acted like it was Christmas."

"You've got to watch offers like that. They can backfire. Now he knows the guy's important to us. May try to take cash to keep quiet."

Brandon stewed on the reprimand, finding something to look at out the side window.

"Listen," Walt said. "It's good stuff."

"You're going to always hold this against me, aren't you, Sheriff?"

He wasn't talking about Bonehead.

Walt drove for five more minutes, crossing the bridge over the Big Wood just south of Golden Eagle, a mile south of the turnoff to Fiona's place, where he'd had to fight to keep from looking as they drove past.

"It is what it is," Walt said.

"And what is it?"

"Over," Walt said. "It's over."

Brandon crossed his arms and put his head back on the headrest and closed his eyes.

29

Walt dropped the girls off at the Rainbow Trail Adventure Camp, getting a hug from each as well as a wistful, puppy-dog look from Nikki that he didn't know how to interpret. He wasn't sure if this was the result of some male defect, or denial, or if there was nothing to make of it in the first place, a fine piece of acting by a daughter who wanted her mother back. Beatrice whined from the front passenger seat, wishing the girls weren't leaving, causing Walt to once again wonder if the dog wasn't channeling his own conscience. He hesitated there a little longer, considering calling them back to the car, playing hooky for a day and taking them to the park or for ice cream, or swimming in the public pool out at the high school. But they loved the camp far more than a day with him, or so he convinced himself in order to justify his driving off and leaving them for Lisa to pick up, which is what he did.

Except for a chaotic press conference that had gone passably well, and some news trucks out front in the office parking lot, the prior day had moved monotonously slowly as he'd weeded his way out from behind his desk and hoped for something to bust open the Gale investigation. The county prosecutor had determined that the existence of the lilies in Boatwright's garden, and the truck tires being the same manufacturer—Goodrich—as the impressions left at the crime scene were enough to win Walt a search based on probable cause. But he cautioned Walt not to be too hasty. There'd be formidable opposition from Boatwright's attorneys once Walt took it to the next level, and he wanted time to prepare. He also wanted to coordinate with the King County prosecuting attorney so they didn't accidentally jeopardize the Caroline Vetta investigation by coming off the blocks too early.

Each day that passed decreased the odds. The farther they got from the discovery of the body, the less likely the case would be solved.

Today passed much the same way: Walt feeling handcuffed by a cautious attorney and limited by circumstantial evidence. He called Fiona twice and left messages, fearing that she was avoiding his calls over embarrassment about the reappearance of the "stolen" Engleton truck, and let her know that he couldn't care less and was just happy to know Kira had apparently returned.

Fiona's refusal to return his calls annoyed and frustrated him, but the next step was hers to make. Hers to take.

With the girls asleep and the dishes washed, he sat down at the computer to catch up on e-mail.

The kitchen phone rang and Walt snatched it up.

"I found the guy's vehicle, Sheriff."

"Gilly?"

"I found the SUV. Avis sticker on the bumper. Plates still on it. It's Gale's rental."

"Where?"

"Well off trail or I'd have found it sooner. Was those night vision binoculars did it. Sun warmed the metal all day and the thing gave off a signature after dark. I'm standing here looking at it. You want me to open it up?"

"Don't touch a thing. Give me directions. It'll take me an hour or so. You sit tight."

"Got it."

He called Lisa and asked her to cover. Called the office and told them what he needed, including Fiona, and instructed them how to keep it off the radio, and how to release the vehicles one at a time, wanting to avoid a press stampede. Took a deep breath as he changed back into a freshly pressed uniform shirt.

He looked in on the girls just before Lisa arrived wearing a bathrobe with jeans. She looked tired and headed straight for the couch.

Walt offered his bed, saying, "Fresh sheets."

"How long are you going to be?"

"Take the bed," he said.

She nodded and trundled off, scratching her backside through the bathrobe and causing him to wonder if they didn't know each other too well.

Gilly Menquez looked small and pale behind the glare of headlights, squinting into the searchlight from Walt's Cherokee.

"This is good, right, Sheriff?"

"Very good."

"About last week—"

"Forget about it, Gilly. It's behind us."

"I got me a wife and four kids. Another coming."

"All the more reason not to drink on the job."

"You coulda had me fired."

"Just don't make it 'should have.' "

Gilly eyed him curiously.

"Never mind, Gilly. Just don't let it happen again."

"It won't."

Walt kept the smile off his face out of respect. Gilly looked all worked up, his face twisted like he might cry. Walt placed a hand on his shoulder, happy to have someone his own height, but wondering if Gilly's devotion was to the Blessed Mother or the bottle.

"This is exactly as you found it?" The man nodded, but submissively, and Walt was beginning to feel uncomfortable. Wanting to keep him busy, Walt asked Menquez to search the immediate area on the passenger side of the SUV. Walt took the woods to the left, awaiting

Fiona's camera and at least one deputy before entering the vehicle. He'd shined his flashlight through the glass to find the SUV was empty, keys in the ignition. The keys might come back with latent prints; he was eager to get on with it.

Flashlight in hand, Walt moved methodically through the forest undergrowth. He heard Beatrice clawing at the Cherokee's side window and wished he could let her out. Gale's rental had been abandoned in a swale between two treed ridges running east-west. Given the overhead canopy of evergreens, it seemed a miracle Gilly had ever spotted the heat signature, and Walt took it as a sign that the investigation had turned. Cases either turned for you or against you, and he'd grown superstitious over time.

He saw it as a wink of white, a color that didn't belong in the forest palette, approached it somewhat breathlessly, nearly called out to Gilly at his find.

He pulled back some fern, revealing the smooth, turned handle and grip of a baseball bat. Bent and reached down farther, pulling back the twist of green revealing the bat's wide end.

His heart was pounding now, really pounding, like he'd run a fair distance or hit the bench press. At first the discovery elated, filled him with a childish glee, cementing his theories and confirming his investigative excellence. He thought how impressed Boldt would be to discover that his own suspicions of Vince Wynn had not only been well founded but on the mark.

Just below the crown of the bat was a rust-colored smudge and what looked to be some human hair. He was looking at the murder weapon, and though he had yet to equate the truck's abandonment with the discarded bat, the timing and the logistics, the connection to Gale seemed inevitable. With any luck the case might be closed by noon, and the cameras and reporters could go home.

He donned surgical gloves, checking behind him. He'd lost sight of Gilly, off in the woods. And now, from well below, the first winks of arriving headlights. And behind those another set. His team would be here in a matter of minutes and, hopefully, Fiona among them— someone to celebrate the find with.

He dropped to one knee and was reaching for the center of the bat—keeping his contact off both the handle and the blood evidence—when the flashlight cast small shadows over the burned engraving—a script font—and three letters:

ton

He knew bats—Louisville Sluggers in particular— knew the placement of the logo and the location on the bat of certain brands or endorsements. This fit neither. Without giving it any thought his mind jumped ahead, trying to process which slugger this particular bat was named for, and why it might have been burned onto the bat so far down the head. He spun the bat slightly and the rest of the name appeared: *Engleton*.

A WOOD RIVER LITTLE LEAGUE ALL-STAR DONOR:
MICHAEL ENGLETON

Walt froze, the sound of the approaching vehicles growing louder. Off-balance and dizzy, he realized he wasn't breathing. The bat was supposed to have come from Vince Wynn's autograph collection. It was supposed to prove beyond a doubt that Wynn had taken the law into his own hands, just as he'd threatened to do.

The next image in his head was that of Kira Tulivich raising a bat and coming from the Engleton house toward Walt as he peered into Fiona's window. Kira Tulivich, so traumatized and victimized that she couldn't get through her keynote address without having a flashback that kept her from continuing.

The vehicles approached. Walt, hand on the bat, hesitated.

"The bat could have been stolen," he said aloud, quickly shutting his gob and thinking of the mountain man, or the meth cooker, or whoever had vandalized the Berkholders' place.

The bat firmly in hand now, he held it down, in lockstep with the movement of his right leg, as he marched hurriedly toward the idling Jeep. Beatrice went frantic with his approach. The headlights of the oncoming cars grew nearer.

Gilly Menquez appeared out of nowhere, at the rear of the SUV. "Sheriff?"

Walt stopped, keeping the bat screened from Menquez. "Gilly?"

"You got anything?" Walt didn't answer. "For me to do?" he added.

"Wave those cars down and keep them from contaminating the scene. Stop them back there as far as you can and tell them to kill their lights. Hurry it up."

Gilly took off running. A moment later, as the car lights went dark, Walt slipped open his Jeep's back hatch, switched off the interior light, wrapped the bat in a blue tarp, the same blue tarp they'd used to move Gale's body, and tucked the bundle behind his emergency backpack at the hinge of the backseat.

He told himself he was merely preserving evidence, was hiding it so that no one would know of its existence, so that there could be no possibility of it leaking to the press before he'd had it properly recorded and analyzed. So that whatever evidence it provided could be used effectively and properly before it was misused and abused in the court of public opinion.

He was not withholding evidence. Not doing anything wrong.

But then why had he hidden the bat from Gilly? Why had he secreted it in the back of his Jeep rather than record its location with a photograph—SOP for a first officer's discovery of any suspected murder weapon?

He shut the hatch as Fiona emerged into the glow of the Jeep's headlights. From behind her appeared Barge

Levy carrying a heavy backpack in his right hand. And then, a moment later, two deputies, one of them Tommy Brandon.

"Sheriff," Fiona called out, juggling two camera bags. She looked skeletal in the pale light. Fragile and pale and exhausted as she hurried ever closer.

"Ms. Kenshaw," Walt said, his voice breaking.

The digital clock on the kitchen microwave read 3:07. Walt was forced to decide whether or not to wake Lisa, and he'd ruled in favor of giving her a chance to sleep at least part of the night in her own bed. She drove off in her robe and jeans, bleary-eyed but grateful for the chance to get home.

With her out of the house, he pulled the blue bundle from the vehicle and walked it around to the privacy of the back door, never doubting for a moment that he might be watched. He'd long since learned two things in law enforcement: everyone carried at least one damaging secret, and there was no such thing as privacy.

With the blinds drawn, he carefully unfolded the tarp and stared at the bloody bat, wondering what the hell he was doing. He had a variety of excuses at the ready: he was protecting the investigation from a leak that could potentially strengthen Wynn's defense (though the inscription to Michael Engleton made that a difficult angle); he was keeping the first real significant evidence away from any chance of public exposure; he was sequestering evidence to allow himself to pursue a methodical investigation and interrogation of suspects—most notably, Kira Tulivich. Convinced that he was okay as long as he didn't contaminate or destroy evidence, he wrapped the bat carefully in cling wrap, then secured it with tape.

He hunted around in the garage and came up with an oversized cardboard box and cut it down to size with a razor knife and crudely shaped it to fit the bat. He used bubble wrap and newspaper and packaged the bat in the box, sealing it with more packing tape. He went online and filled out an overnight shipping label, printed it up, and left the package on the dining-room table as a shrine to his misbehavior.

Boldt had offered his help in speeding up the processing of evidence. The Meridian lab might expedite the work because of its association with a possible homicide, but Walt could overlook that possibility and send it to Boldt with a decent excuse in his back pocket. One day to reach Seattle, one day to process. He should have results in less than forty-eight hours, about the quickest he could expect it from the state lab in Meridian. But by putting it onto Boldt's books he maintained absolute privacy, something that could play heavily in his favor in the days to come. In the event the bat implicated someone of interest to Boldt in the Vetta investigation, then his use of the Seattle lab was further justified.

But he didn't sleep well that night. He tossed and turned, and what little sleep he found was marred with bad dreams and tangled plot lines that kept him barely

below the surface. He awoke irritable and tired and got
the girls off to camp in a cloud of silence they could feel.
Even Beatrice kept her distance, lying with her head on
her crossed paws, her eyes never leaving him.

"Stop it!" he called out to her across the room as he
cooked French toast. She blinked, looked away, then re-
focused on her master, his four-legged conscience refusing to let him go.

At ten a.m., Walt left the office without explanation,
telling Nancy only that he was heading home and would
be back in fifteen minutes.

Nancy associated such unexplained departures with
family or health issues, both of which worried her, as in
her mind she'd taken on the role of his guardian since
the divorce. She often handled personal matters for him
that had nothing to do with his job.

"Everything all right?" she'd asked, a question he
didn't have to answer given the expression he wore.

"Fine," he lied.

"If I can help," she added, causing him to slow down,
debating either a reprimand or an apology. She received
neither. He continued out the door, his eyes locked
ahead of him like a marching soldier.

"Sorry to call so early," Walt said, Boldt's face filling
the small window on his computer screen.

"Up for hours," Boldt said. "What can I do for you?"

"Am I that transparent?"

"You're using Skype," Boldt said, "instead of the phone. But I'm glad you called. Matthews had an explanation for us."

"Concerning?"

"First, why don't you tell me why you called?"

Walt kept his explanation of shipping the bat short and simple—he needed the lab work expedited. No excuse; no reasoning offered. He'd appreciate a phone call or e-mail the moment they knew anything. Boldt took it all in stride.

"Now you," Walt said.

"The girl at the nursery," Boldt said. "What was her name?"

"Martha Sharp. Maggie."

"Pot. Matthews says she's growing pot out there. She's working it at night when she doesn't belong there, which is why she was so sensitive about not being there after hours. She's doing this on her own to supplement her income. She lives alone, probably with one of her parents who is ill or relies upon her. We scared the hell out of her by nosing around, but the point is, Matthews thinks she probably saw something. With Gale, I mean. I described the interview and—this is her magic, Sheriff—she jumps in and starts to break it down for me. I know it may sound like hocus pocus, but this is what she does, and I've learned to trust her."

"Pot."

"Underground, maybe. Lights. But the point is: she was there. She saw something and is withholding it because she can't explain her being out there at all hours. Matthews said the approach is to get to her need for this money, identify and undermine her need. You establish the need, then you point out the ramifications to the need if she's busted for growing. The parent or sibling will suffer if she goes down. You trade burning her stash for what she knows, and everyone wins."

"And you'd go with this?" Walt asked skeptically.

"You'll meet her someday. Matthews. She's . . . well, she's one of a kind. I'd give this a seventy-five percent chance. She'd probably give it less than that, but that's how she is: modest to a fault."

"You'll call me?"

"The minute I hear from the lab."

Walt bypassed the sacred doctor-patient privilege by avoiding the doctor altogether and appealing straight to the hospital's comptroller, a man who served with Walt on Search and Rescue. The phone call took all of five minutes, and by the time he reached the nursery, he had what he needed without having to coax it out of Maggie Sharp.

"Your mother's dialysis," he said before even addressing the woman. Behind him deputies Milner and Tilbert leaned against the grille of their cruiser.

Maggie Sharp gnawed on a fingernail. Couldn't keep her eyes from wandering to the two deputies. She said nothing.

"Your employer need not know," he said, surprising her. "It won't be in the papers. You'll get off with some community service and even that will be kept off the books. Meaning no criminal record. This is a one-time offer. If the information you give me is good enough, if you tell me the truth about what you saw that night and don't try to give me the runaround, then my guys won't go tearing up every tree and plant and making a mess of this place. This is a critical decision you're about to make, Maggie. It has far-reaching implications that will not only affect you but your mother and all your loved ones."

As she stood stone still, tears burst from both eyes, though she did not sniffle or sob.

"I didn't know what else to do," she said. "It's so much money and without insurance . . ."

"Marijuana cultivation?"

She nodded.

"My guys will dismantle it, collect the plants, and we'll dispose of them. You will agree to two hundred hours of community service. You fail to keep your end of the agreement and there will be dire consequences. Are we in agreement?"

She nodded.

"You saw something. The dead man."

She nodded again.

"Tell me."

"A pickup truck." She hung her head and touched a knuckle to either eye, catching her tears. "I heard it . . . heard it hit something. It must have swerved to avoid an elk or deer, but I didn't actually see the animal. The pickup came off the road—this is maybe two in the morning—this side of the road and it stopped. Driver gets out. I'm watching all this from hut two. There aren't any lights in any of the huts. My stuff is underground."

"Show me."

Walt turned to his guys and waved them forward.

Inside the open-ended plastic hothouse, Maggie Sharp pulled back one of the shipping pallets used as floorboards between the various rows. Using a spade, she scraped away two inches of dirt, revealing a wooden hatch. An elaborate disguise that would have been impossible to detect. The hatch was six feet square and the hole beneath it contained well over fifty three-foot-tall pot plants heavy with reddish buds. There was an automatic watering system and a row of grow lights. The aroma was pungent.

As the deputies climbed down into the pit, Maggie Sharp pointed.

"I was standing right here."

"He or she?"

"He."

"Got out and did what?" Walt asked.

"Started looking around. Don't know for what. It was a long way, and it was very dark that night."

"The truck?"

"Had a light rack, I think. Maybe a ski rack. On the top of the cab."

The description fit Boatwright's caretaker's pickup

truck. He had no way to reconcile the Engleton bat with Boatwright's caretaker but for a moment he felt partial relief, as if this might work out okay for Fiona and, more important, Kira.

"Color?"

"Couldn't see."

"Make?"

"Pickup truck. That's all I can tell you. I don't think it was an extended cab, but it was really dark. I don't know exactly."

"Did he find anything? The guy looking?"

"He was outside the truck for, I don't know, a couple of minutes at least. Maybe he was peeing. Maybe puking. Maybe freaking out at hitting the game and surviving to tell about it. No idea."

"Just the one guy?"

"Didn't see anyone else. From that distance, backlit and all, headrests look like heads, you know? I only saw one guy get out. Don't know about inside the truck."

"He use a flashlight?"

"No, sir."

"And you say you heard him hit something?"

"Absolutely. That's why I came out of the hole. I heard the contact. I heard the tires. Saw the truck off the road."

She was facing him now, her eyes averted. Frightened. With every sound of destruction from the hole, she winced.

"So you didn't actually see him swerve off the road?"

"No, I suppose not. But I heard it all."

"A light rack."

"Or ski rack. Yes, sir."

"No extended cab?"

"Correct."

"Lights? Do you remember the taillights? Would you recognize the pattern, maybe be able to identify the make?"

She shook her head. "It's not that I'm not willing to try, but it was way far away. You want me to look at something, I will. Of course. But I doubt it."

The deputies started throwing the lighting equipment and torn-up plants up out of the hole. They were joking around down there. Walt didn't call them out for it.

"We're going to keep the equipment on file. Our insurance you'll keep up the community service."

"I will. I promise I will."

"This was a stupid thing to do, Maggie. Can get you twenty years in this state."

"Yes, sir."

"I'm not saying I don't sympathize with your situation. Wish I had an answer for your mother, but this is not it."

"No. I get that. I was desperate. I don't smoke it. I'll take tests or whatever."

"Random tests will be part of the agreement."

"Rotating the plants like that, I could make a couple thousand a month. It was just too easy, I guess. I'm not saying it was right."

"Twenty years," Walt said.

"I understand."

"You talk this up . . . if I hear about this deal from

anywhere, I'll have to charge you. Strictly speaking, I can't make a deal like this. We occasionally make exceptions. That door will close if you mention it to anyone."

"I won't."

"Report to my office tomorrow. Talk to a woman named Nancy. She'll have your community service outlined and some literature on how to apply for exceptional health care needs."

She hung her head and nodded.

"I'll want you to look at taillight patterns."

"Understood."

Walt called down into the hole, barking orders at his guys. He then drove straight to the county courthouse, knowing this time he would win his warrant.

30

Walt trained Beatrice by the side of the road as he awaited Barge Levy and Fiona. He enjoyed the dog training, found it relaxing, appreciated the need to repeat it several times a week, whether on a walk around the neighborhood, or more formally with some of the other Search and Rescue dogs. He heeled her. He put her on a scent, hiding a rag among the sage and rabbit weed. Beatrice responded with heightened excitement, pleased with and hungry for Walt's full attention. Basking in it. She practically flew into the scrub after the rag. Found it and barked until Walt released her. She heeled flawlessly, ever attentive of his slightest movement, ears perked, tail wagging high.

He kneeled and lavished her with praise and she reveled in it, as if this moment with him were all she lived for. And he loved her for it.

He picked some cheat grass from her hair and double-checked the pads of her paws for cuts. She sat without command as he checked her paws, head held high, her nose working furiously. She turned toward the arriving cars before Walt ever heard them.

He met Fiona's eyes through the Subaru's windshield and something immeasurable passed between them, something he was too out of practice to understand, but he thought she immediately picked up on the change in him and regretted he hadn't been able to hide his emotions better. It was something he would have to improve upon, and it struck him as odd that, as he entered this relationship, one of his first thoughts was how to hide what he was actually thinking.

And from her, a distant look of worry and concern, too complex for him to decipher, too buried behind a pantomimed, bright-eyed hello for him to know what exactly he was seeing.

Thought of the baseball bat wormed around in his abdomen, souring his mood. He felt slightly sick to the stomach. Light-headed. Beatrice whined and nudged him with her wet nose and brought him back from a few seconds of paralysis.

Levy's Volvo wagon pulled up behind Fiona and he leaned from the window and squinted and shouted hello. "All set," he called out.

With Fiona's window down as well, Walt moved to within earshot of both drivers and said, "The warrant is limited to the worker's truck but gives us plain sight, so Fiona, you'll get shots of everything you can. Barge, you and I will take the tire impressions. We'll ink them first, and if we get a likely match, then we'll impound the vehicle. We can pull full impressions later at the shop. All three of us are looking for any sign of a collision or damage to the truck, and Fiona will cover us by shooting the whole truck in detail while looking like she's just covering us on the tires. Any questions?"

"You mentioned the flower bed to me," she said.

"Yeah, that's correct. They redid one of the beds. Replanted it. If we see anything left of what they pulled up, I want that recorded. I'm going to ask the caretaker about that—where he dumps the garden waste. There may be a compost pile, which would make it plain sight anyway, but I may want pictures."

He tried to see something behind her eyes, to read her, to find some indication of what she knew about the bat, about why it would end up alongside Gale's rental. But he saw only Fiona, saw the two of them eye to eye in the throes of need and satisfaction, and realized he was too far gone to be objective. In the end, it might take a call to Boldt, some independent eye, to straighten him out.

They arrived at the gate and Walt called through. The caretaker met them, accepting the warrant through the bars of the gate, which seemed symbolic to Walt.

They drove through and parked, and Walt asked the

caretaker to stay away from his pickup truck as the man approached, saying they were welcome to look it over. He stood to one side and the trio went to work with a practiced efficiency. Levy had butcher paper and black acrylic paint in hand as he kneeled beside the front left tire. Fiona circled the vehicle, slowly taking dozens of shots.

"Sheriff?" Levy called.

Walt joined him.

"Sorry to burst your bubble. These are Goodrich all right, but Brandon's wrong about the model. They aren't Long Trail, they're Rugged Trail, a step up. Not the same tire."

"No way," Walt muttered.

"Afraid so."

"There's a light rack."

"Yes, there is."

"You're sure? The Gale crime scene impressions . . . could we have been wrong about those?"

"Very different tread patterns, Walt. I'm sorry."

"Well . . ." Walt's mind reeled. "We're here. Let's take the impressions and we'll have them on file."

"Got it."

Walt headed away but turned and approached Levy once again. "He could have switched them out."

"Certainly could have."

"New tires?"

"These? Not brand-new, if that's what you're asking. But listen, we all keep multiple sets. These could be his winter tires—they're serious tires."

"So the old ones might still be at his place."

"Or long gone."

"At the dump." The county trash dump out at Ohio Gulch had a tire dumping area. Walt wasn't past sending a team out there to look for a set of discarded Long Trails.

He joined Fiona. "It may come down to you," he whispered. "Any dents? Anything?"

"Looks in good shape to me. And clean as a whistle. *Real* clean for a gardener's truck."

Pickup truck owners in this valley were known for putting spit shines on their rigs. The spotless condition meant nothing.

"Every inch," he said.

"Got it."

"What is it you're hoping to find?" the caretaker called out.

"We'll know when we find it," Walt said.

"You do and it'll be news to me," the man said brazenly.

Walt wasn't accustomed to feeling desperate, but his eyes darted between Fiona busy at work and Boatwright's estate, with the growing sense of walls closing in.

"What was Caroline Vetta like?" Walt asked the man, seizing on the idea of blindsiding him.

"I don't know any of Mr. Boatwright's guests personally."

"Quite a looker," Walt said. "Kind of hard to miss."

"Wouldn't know."

Walt pulled the photo from his pocket, separating out

Gale's, which he returned to the pocket. "Jog your memory? Remember, we're here on a warrant," he said, hoping the caretaker didn't know his law real well.

"Mr. Wynn's friend. Yes."

"Nice lady?"

"I told you: I wouldn't know."

"What was your impression of how she got along with Mr. Wynn or Mr. Boatwright?"

"I wash the windows. I oversee grounds maintenance. I'm not paparazzi, Sheriff."

"Do you compost?"

"What?"

Walt appreciated the surprised reaction, appreciated the effect the question had.

"Around back?" Walt asked.

"In the aspen stand. East light. Early light. Get as much warmth on it as I can."

"Show me."

"You want to see my composter?" He seemed dumbfounded.

"If you don't mind? Actually," Walt said, now spotting the twin geometric shadows in the tight stand of aspens on the back side of the sprawling house, "I can see it from here." *Plain sight*, he was thinking. "Fiona?"

She joined him and they walked behind the house across a magnificent patio and past a bubbling fish pond. He had a dozen questions he wanted to ask her, but didn't want to blow the timing or sound suspicious. He needed to think about how to proceed.

"You're awfully quiet," she said.

"A lot to process," he answered honestly.

"The tires."

"Among other things."

"You think he switched them out?"

"I think it's possible. All I go on are possibilities."

"Got it."

"What are the possibilities our mountain man paid your place a visit?" He wondered why he'd suddenly started down this path, why he'd chosen to sound so certain of himself.

"We talked about this."

"Kira heard things."

"Kira imagined things."

Should he bring up the bat? The emergency room? Could he bring himself to believe any of what he was thinking?

Inside the stand of aspen the air cooled significantly. The two compost towers were green plastic with stackable sections. The lids to both were closed.

"Look over there," she said, pointing out toward the house.

Walt followed her arm. "What?"

"Huh!" she said. "Wonder what's inside?"

Walt turned around. One of the lids was laid back, open.

They exchanged a glance.

"I'm not deputized," she said. "It's why you wanted me to come over here, right?"

Walt said nothing.

"Thing is," she said, "we know each other too well. Personally, I think that's a good thing, but you're going to have to tell me if you think otherwise."

"I want to know you better," he said. "I want in. And I want to let you in. I want to reach that place that we're so far in that anything can be said, anything shared. I want to find that place where when one of us laughs, the other knows why, and when one of us is about to cry, the other is already reaching for the hankie. Like that."

"Hankie? Haven't heard that one in a while."

"I'm old-school."

"You are nothing of the sort. You are . . . dreamy. Thank you for that." She peered inside. "Blue and white lilies," she said. "You want pictures?"

He stepped closer. "Blue and white? I remember them as . . . yellow, when he was working on the bed."

"Yellow?" she said. "That would be my place. Leslie and Michael's. They have, like, five beds planted in yellow lilies. Unbelievably pretty."

"Your place," he stated, his voice raspy, his throat dry.

"You want me to shoot these?" she asked.

He nodded, unable to get another word out.

"You okay?"

He nodded again.

"Walt? Something wrong?"

His mind tried to stop his mouth, but it was over before he could stop himself.

"Everything," he said.

31

Walt stood, backlit by the glare of the Jeep's head-lights, his ghoulish shadow stretching far in front of him. Fiona parked her Subaru by the cottage and stood alongside him.

"Do you want to come in?" she asked.

"That flower bed is damaged," he said, his eyes on the freshly turned earth.

"The deer wreak havoc," she said.

He looked over at her, the harsh light playing across her face. "When did Kira go missing, exactly?"

"I don't know exactly. A couple days after the Advocates dinner."

"The right timing and she's in the clear."

"Do not go there."

"Believe me, I'd rather not. Occupational hazard."

"You don't really believe that? Kira, I mean?"

"Unfortunately, it's not about what I believe. It's what the evidence proves. You know that. And before it proves, it suggests. Right now, it's suggesting things I'd rather it didn't. I don't like any of this, believe me."

"It was a few nights after the Advocates dinner that she took off. That's all this is about. She was upset. At me. At having a flashback in the middle of her talk." She drew in a deep breath. "You know, I have this weird memory of you coming by here one night, but I'm not real clear on which night it was, or what was said."

"Nothing was said."

"Because?"

"Because you wouldn't open the door."

"That's ridiculous. If I didn't open the door it was because I wasn't home."

"Or it wasn't you. I saw someone on the couch."

"My door doesn't have a window in it."

"Yeah, I know that."

She crossed her arms. "Well, maybe it was me. For the record, I don't like guys peeping on me."

"For the record: I care about you. I was worried about you."

"Well, don't be. I'm fine."

"And Kira? Is Kira fine?"

"You're beginning to be annoying."

"You're beginning to piss me off."

"Maybe it's late."

"Maybe it is. I'd like to bring a team up here. I'd like

to eliminate her from consideration, and that's the best way to do it."

"Don't you need a warrant for that?"

"Do I?"

"It's not my property, Walt. I, or I guess you, can ask Michael and Leslie, if we can find them. They're in Tibet or Bhutan or something. She's on a meditation retreat, so who knows? It could be weeks. A month or more."

"It's to help eliminate Kira from—"

"I get it, okay! I understand it. I'm just saying that Michael and Leslie aren't easy to find."

"Find them," he said. "For Kira's sake."

"It's not that simple."

"It's not that complicated."

"It's late," she said.

"You want me to go." He made it a statement. "Your earlier invitation?"

"I don't think I realized how tired I was."

"Why—" He caught himself. There were questions he'd been wanting to ask her for some time now—her name appearing on St. Luke's emergency room manifest; her refusal to answer the door that night. He could have asked them anytime. He could have asked them now. But he held off because once asked, he couldn't take them back; once they were asked, he would have answers and he wasn't sure he wanted the answers. He couldn't recall a time that as sheriff he'd not wanted answers, the feeling so foreign to him he felt upended. She was protecting Kira, and for him to go after the girl meant he would have to go through her, and it was the last thing he wanted.

"Yes?" she asked.

"Let me help clear her," he said. "I want to clear her."

"I'll try," she said. "I promise."

"If she was threatened. If it was something like that—"

"Walt, she wasn't here that night."

"Yeah, but you see, that's part of the problem. The autopsy couldn't establish an exact time of death—the cold nights, the hot days. It screws everything up. We have a witness—"

He felt her tense and knew she tried to hide it.

"But it doesn't establish a TOD for us. Time of death," he explained. "We don't know which night it was. It's one of two. But you seem to think otherwise. Can you help me out here?"

"How?"

"Explain to Michael and Leslie how important this is for Kira. If they complicate this, it only makes things worse for her."

"I told you I'll try to find them. It isn't always so easy."

"I'm going to say something as a friend. Not as sheriff. Okay? For a minute let's say I'm not wearing the uniform."

"Okay." She crossed her arms more tightly. Any more and she'd have trouble breathing.

Collecting himself, he looked up into the darkness of the trees, the shadows from the headlights playing tricks on the eyes.

"I know you'd do anything to protect her. I understand that urge. But don't put yourself in the middle of
this. The law is real clear about that kind of thing. Believe
me, I don't want you or Kira caught up in this. But a
thing like this, it sorts itself out eventually, and there's no
going back and changing what was said, or done, before
it does. There's no changing that stuff."

"Some cases don't get solved," she said. "Some cases
go cold."

He felt his breath catch. A few seconds earlier he'd
been wondering if she'd somehow managed to substitute
her name for Kira's on the emergency room manifest—if
she was sacrificing herself for the young woman. Fiona
showed no signs of head injury. Had Kira taken off to
hide her injuries? Was she waiting for a bruise to heal
before returning? He'd been thinking he needed a look
at the actual medical records. But that had all evaporated with her pushing him off the investigation. Could
he let the case go cold? Could he do such a thing? A
month earlier he wouldn't have even considered such a
possibility.

"You're right, it's late. Neither of us is thinking
clearly." He stepped toward her and kissed her on the
cheek, but she stood rigid and unresponsive.

He whispered, "I hear you."

"I . . . My memory is all messed up." He saw now
that her face was stained with tears.

"Shhh."

She faced him and met eyes with him. She looked

frightened—terrified, was more like it—and he pulled her to him and held her.

"There's so much to tell you," she said.

"I'm here."

"I want to tell you."

"It's tricky," he said. "Some things may be better left unsaid." He wondered where that had come from. He couldn't—wouldn't—ask her to betray Kira. There were other ways he could do this. He could leave her out of it. "Get some rest."

"But I want to . . ." she said.

"Sleep on it."

She nodded, his uniform shirt damp with her tears. She clung to him as he gently pushed her away and walked back to the Jeep. He stopped and looked back at her in the headlights, wondering how he could let such an opportunity pass. Wondering who he'd become.

Bea licked him as he climbed in. He pushed her into the backseat and drove off, intentionally avoiding a glance into the rearview mirror.

32

As lead investigator on the Gale case, Walt was shown and was required to sign off on the case paperwork. The longer and more involved a case, the greater the paperwork. He was no stranger to bureaucracy. As sheriff, he was in charge of people management and budget oversight; he essentially ran a decent-sized company with a charter to solve crimes and keep the peace, work that was typically delegated to others. He and Nancy had developed a routine, a rhythm to the administration of his office that allowed him, as with the Gale case, to keep his hand in the work that interested him, while keeping the office work moving ahead. Like any worthwhile assistant, Nancy was crucial to the process. She knew what had to be done when, and saw to it, chasing him down for signatures and ensuring he attended the necessary meetings with the county commissioners and politicians.

He finished signing a stack of papers and slid the next in front of him, recognizing the top sheets as the inventory from Gale's rented SUV. He'd been so obsessed with his own handling of the baseball bat found outside the vehicle that, while he'd been briefed on the contents of the vehicle itself—including the victim's missing wallet, found under the seat; blood evidence, not on the headrest but near the ignition and on the steering wheel and passenger-side floor mat; and the car rental contract, discovered inside the console lock box—he'd not given a great deal of thought to any of it. The wallet contained no cash; the blood evidence had been collected and sent off to the lab, along with the rental contract to be processed for fingerprints. The vehicle's interior and exterior had been processed for latent prints, with little more than a few smears and smudges to show for it.

He flipped through the detailed inventory, making sure to read it carefully as he continued to think about his handling of the baseball bat, and how he was going to eventually add it to the same list. Boldt had promised quick lab work; he made a mental note to follow up on that.

He read past the line before stopping abruptly and backtracking. It was listed under contents of the wallet.

"Nancy!"

She knew that tone, and rushed through the doorway.

"Double-check this, will you? It's got to be a mistake." He spun the page around and indicated the line. "Someone screwed something up. I'm almost positive Brandon said the ATM withdrawals were from a Visa with this same bank. As in, this same card. It can't be in the wallet if it's being used to make cash withdrawals in town, can it? Sort it out, please."

"Got it." She took the page with her. But Walt came out of his seat and followed her back to her desk and hovered there as she located Brandon. Walt held out his hand for the receiver. She handed it over, disappointed in him for micromanaging. She and Beatrice knew how to get to him.

"Tommy? The ATM card. Gale's ATM card. It was a Visa with what bank?"

"Purchase Bank, in Mobile."

"You're sure?"

"Positive."

Walt cupped the receiver and said to Nancy, "Find out where Gale's effects are. Specifically, his wallet. The lab, I assume?"

Nancy returned to Walt's desk and carried a stack of papers back to her desk. She flipped through several and ran her finger along a line. "Yes. Still in Meridian."

"Ask them to e-mail us a photo of the card, will you? Both sides. And I want that card fumed or dusted for prints."

She held out her hand, wanting the phone back from him.

"Meet me in my office," Walt told Brandon, surrendering the phone to her.

Brandon tried to fit himself into one of the two chairs facing Walt's desk. He looked like Walt felt when volunteering to read to kids in kindergarten.

Walt passed him the inventory sheet, where a yellow highlighted line now jumped off the page.

"Son of a butte," Brandon said.

"Banks don't issue two cards with the same name on the same account."

"All I can tell you is that Blompier, I think it was, was the one in touch with them, and it was this card on this bank. Maximum cash advances a couple days in a row."

"And he was dead."

"Yeah, I get that."

"And the card is now somehow back in his wallet."

"I'm not saying I understand it."

"Blompier handed it right to me, and I missed it," Walt said, thinking aloud.

"Sheriff?"

"We were talking about cameras on the ATMs, how convenient it was that the ATM used didn't happen to have a working camera as part of its security."

"Okay," Brandon said.

"We were made aware of this during that poacher case. You remember?"

"Sure."

"So did Deputy Blompier. He mentioned it to me. Reminded me."

"You lost me, I think."

"All those trees, the forest as thick as it is where we found the rental—it occurred to me at the time that it was a miracle it threw off any kind of heat signature."

"Now I know you lost me."

"Gilly Menquez told me he found the truck because of its heat signature. The poacher case? Menquez handled that for the Forest Service. He knew that ATM didn't have a camera."

"Menquez?" Brandon couldn't believe it.

"We need a way to prove it. What about traffic cams?" Walt asked.

"What traffic cams? We don't have any traffic cams."

"You and I know that, but is that common knowledge?"

"If I knew where you were going with this, Sheriff, maybe I could help." Brandon stood out of the chair, making it look normal-sized again.

"Nancy!" Walt shouted, forgoing the intercom. "Get me Kenshaw."

"I'm on it!" she shouted back.

Brandon, his face a mass of confusion, pointed out the office door, miming his request to leave. Walt assented.

"Sometime today would be good!" Walt called out to Nancy.

"I said: *I'm on it*."

Walt addressed Brandon saying, "Find Gilly. Get him down here for a chat."

"Menquez? How am I supposed to do that?"

"I'm not asking, I'm ordering," Walt said.

His phone rang. She'd put him through.

Shaking his head, Brandon took off.

Walt answered the phone. "Sheriff?" Fiona said, sounding ever so professional.

"I need you," Walt said.

For the sake of security and secrecy, there was no window in the door of the office's Incident Command Center. But Walt felt as if he could see inside to where Fiona was working at his request. He stood outside the door as agitated as an expectant father, the prosecuting attorney's voice ringing in his ears. Finally, he summoned the courage to knock and let himself in.

"Why?" he asked her. She sat all alone in the room, dwarfed in what could pass as a lecture hall, her laptop connected to a large hi-def television screen.

"Why what?" she said, breaking her attention away from the screen.

"The Engletons turned down my request to search the property." He felt confused by the look of surprise on her face.

"I didn't know," she said.

"Why? Why would they do that?"

"I warned you: they're private."

"It's a murder investigation."

"It's their home. Their sanctuary. Leslie is . . . I tried to warn you. She's all about energy centers. Chakras. She would see this as a violation of everything she's built up there. The peace and tranquility. A bunch of men she doesn't know going through her things. It's just who she is. It's nothing personal or intentional."

"You actually believe that?"

"You think I asked her to refuse you?"

"I didn't say that."

"Your face just did."

"I need this search," he said, his frustration vented. "Kira needs for me to do this search."

"You're welcome onto the property. You know that."

"It needs to be a legal, authorized search."

"I contacted them. That's about all I can do."

"You could do more," he blurted out.

"You're welcome," she said.

He took a few steps closer, half the room still separating them.

"You know how this is going to look, don't you?"

"How's it going to look?"

"Are you protecting her?"

"Do you really have to ask that?"

"Is that your answer?"

"If you're asking would I go to great lengths to protect an innocent girl who's seen more than her fair share of things, then I would answer yes. After what she's been through, she certainly doesn't deserve to be dragged through something like this when her only crime is embarrassment. But if you're asking if I've actually done anything like that, the answer is no. But don't count me out, Sheriff. I will not allow anyone, not even you, to mess her up at a time she is finally getting her act together. Leave her out of this, please."

"I know this is difficult."

"You seem to be blaming me for the Engletons' decision when all I do is live there. You wanted to reach them and I reached them. Damn quickly, I might add. And this is the thanks I get!"

"Thank you," he said.

"That's better. Is there anything else? Because I was actually busy volunteering my time to help you with these images."

"I'm not the enemy," he said, speaking in a whisper.

"I've never seen you as such."

"If I can get ahead of the curve . . . Don't you get it?"

"Maybe not."

"Trust me."

"If you're suggesting I separate you from the badge when you're standing there wearing the badge, that's asking too much. I can't do that."

He reached for the badge pinned to his shirt. As he did so, a knock came on the door and he left the badge in place and turned to answer the door.

"A call from Seattle for you." Nancy looked beyond him to Fiona and then between the two of them. "I can tell them you'll return," she said.

"No," Walt said. "I'll take it." To Fiona he said, "It's good work. Stay with it."

Her flushed, angry face remained fixed on him, his back now turned toward her. "Yes, Sheriff," she said through clenched teeth.

Nancy held the door for him but knew better than to venture another look inside.

"Everything okay?" she asked, as they crossed the hall into Walt's office. "That looked a little . . . heated."

"Is it Boldt?" he asked, not answering.

"A woman named Matthews. She asked if we had Skype or video conferencing, and I told her I could set it up for you."

"Can you?"

"You don't have to sound so surprised."

"Impressed is more like it. Kevin does that stuff for me at home. Lisa, sometimes."

"She does too much for you," Nancy said.

They'd reached his office. Nancy came around his desk and took control of his keyboard, avoiding having to look at him, knowing she'd overstepped. The tapping of the keys sounded louder than normal.

"I shouldn't have said that," she said.

"You're entitled to your opinion."

"Am I?" She marched past him to his office door and shut it. "Okay then."

He wished he could take it back.

"Under the heading of none-of-my-business: you've become way too dependent on Lisa. I guarantee you she only charges you for about a third of her billable hours, because if she didn't, you'd be homeless by now, the amount of time she spends there. The girls have it bad enough being yanked back and forth. When they land on your side of the net, you should be there, not some paid-by-the-hour quasi-governess, aunt, babysitter. And she will never tell you that. She will never tell you how her own family needs her and how much you take advantage of her. You got the short end of the stick, Walt. No one's denying that. You needed Lisa to fill in while you got it together, and she did, and you did. But you spend too much time here. Much more than you used to, and I don't think you even see that. The job can fill some of the heartache, and no one begrudges you that, but you and me, we've been at this a long time together. All I'm saying is: it's time to move on." She drew in a deep breath and then exhaled. When he failed to respond, she said, "Click the green telephone in the open window. She should answer." She stood there for a second too long, huffed audibly, and let herself out.

Walt hadn't moved. He made an effort to breathe, shook his head, and moved toward his desk.

33

Daphne Matthews was a looker, given that computer video was anything but flattering. A dark beauty that carried an intensity in her eyes and an implied invitation in her somewhat husky voice, she piqued Walt's intellectual curiosity; he wanted to step through the screen and spend a couple of hours with her. He thought of her as Cleopatra—mysterious, seductive, fiercely intelligent—and she had yet to say anything more than "hello" and "good to meet you."

"The sergeant suggested I get in touch."

"Much appreciated."

"Anything new to add to the case?"

Walt walked her through some but not all of it, sensing she somehow knew he was withholding from her. Maybe she expected that from any cop.

He watched her arm move as she took notes about Bea's discovery of the blood evidence. Watched her reread and study those notes. Her eyes flicked up at him and back down. He could hear her faint breathing over the computer's thin speaker.

"Nothing worse than unsolicited advice," she said.

"Consider it solicited," he said.

"The sergeant's seriously interested in your case and believes there's both a possibility and probability that it may overlap with the Caroline Vetta investigation, which is why he asked for this meeting."

"I'm okay with it. Really. Sergeant Boldt and I . . . He was a welcome presence here. We worked well together, I think. He speaks highly of you."

"And you."

"That's nice to hear."

"He asked that I walk you through my sense of the victim and some of the things I've taken away from reviewing the case."

"By all means. I'm all ears."

"Okay. First, you're looking for a male between—"

"Because?" Walt said, cutting her off.

"Male? Because it was a single blow to the head that killed him."

Walt was suddenly aware of his own pounding heart and the sound of the forced air coming from the wall vent. Something so simple. Something he'd not considered. "A single blow," he repeated.

"Yes. The blow was high on the back of the victim's

head. A single, fatal blow, requiring, I would think, a substantial amount of strength. The medical examiner could help you there. You've cracked a few skulls in your time, I would imagine, Sheriff, haven't you?"

"I have."

"Then you know."

"I do," Walt said. "Honestly, I hadn't given it much thought."

"It's what I do," she said, trying to let him off the hook. "It's not inconceivable, I suppose, that a woman could deliver such a blow, but I play percentages. Statistics. And statistically we would put this into the male column. Another thing: a woman would likely deliver a blow to the side of the head, not the top down. Most women have not swung a bat or an ax as often as men, and they learn to swing a bat right to left. If they picked one up in self-defense, they would swing the bat right to left. Gale was struck high on the skull, straight down, like the person doing it was chopping wood. Listen, this is all speculation, I can easily be wrong and often am, believe me."

"No. It's good stuff. I'm with you."

"He'd be between . . . let's say early twenties and late thirties—again, in part due to the considerable strength it would take to dispatch a man of Gale's size with a single blow. He's strong, and he's fit. Gale is carrying a few wounds on his hands and forearms—possibly defensive. But I'm guessing those came after the blow. I'm thinking his killer sneaked up on him. Surprised him from behind. That carries its own implications: a hunter, a stalker. And the blow to the head was meant to kill, not wound. It was lights out, game over, from the start of that swing.

"As to Gale," she continued, "from what we can gather . . . from your contact with the Narcotics Anonymous member, his purpose for being in your area is, at the very least, unusual. Contrary to the image of vengeful paroled felon, in light of what we now know, I would suggest he was a remorseful, recovering addict. Typically such people working through the twelve steps are upbeat, even optimistic, remorseful, forgiving and in need of forgiveness. Can they turn violent? Of course. I'm not saying I can predict that one way or the other, but statistically I would not put Gale very high up the list of Caroline Vetta's likely killers, and I've told the sergeant as much. If he was there on a ninth-step call, then I think we need to see him more in the light of a reconciler. He would have come to apologize, to make amends, to atone. And the thing is, he's already internalized this. Already accepted his failures, which is central to his state of mind. He's turned control of his life over to another, and has likely distanced himself from that other man, the Gale of the past. No matter if a person like Caroline Vetta ranted and vented, blamed him, screamed, threw a tantrum, he would likely have two reactions: stand there and take it, accept it; or turn and leave. I just don't see him beating her to death, especially not in the capacity this crime was carried out.

"How does that inform your investigation?" she asked rhetorically. "It goes to state of mind of the deceased. Let's say he met with Caroline Vetta. Let's say when he left her, she was very much alive. Let's say he then learns of her death, her brutal death, and understands the system well enough to know he's going to be first in line. This puts him in a difficult, even desperate situation. He's assuming someone like the sergeant is coming after him. He still has the step calls to make. That may sound absurd, but recovering addicts get focused, Sheriff. They get into the program, and for some, it's all they know. All they live for. He's there in Sun Valley to get a job done. Maybe he trespasses on that agent's property. Maybe he's contemplating making contact, but also fearing the word is out ahead of him. His state of mind is fragile. He's in the process of rebuilding, redefining himself. Someone shooting at him. Who knows how he might react to that? My informed guess is: he'd walk away. He might return another day, far into the future, to make that step call, but he's not going to press it. Contact would have started and stopped right there. If the agent had then contacted him, would he have agreed to meet? I think so, yes. And remember: he's full of forgiveness and in need of forgiveness. Despite being shot at, I doubt he'd be suspicious of the meeting."

"He'd walk right into it."

"It's possible. The point being, he's in an almost naïve state. That first year in recovery . . . it's kind of a pink cloud. He could have walked right into anything, his guard down. And by the look of it, that must be close to what happened. Someone snuck up on him and dispatched him. He was a very big man. We both know it had to be a decisive blow and executed without warning. Gale had his back to the killer and did not expect the blow. I think both are important considerations for you."

Walt found himself jotting down notes. "Yes," he said. "Thank you."

"Have you found the crime scene?"

"We have not." *I was denied the warrant*, he thought.

"Consider this an act of stealth," she said. "I can't imagine the area was well lit. I would think there would have been obstacles to hide behind in order to creep up quite close, both unseen and unheard. The sergeant said you'd found his rental in the woods. But it's difficult, if not impossible, to sneak up like that in the woods."

"Maybe the killer was the one hiding, and Gale happened across him."

"A lot of things to consider."

"He wouldn't have necessarily known his killer, would he? Coming up from behind like that."

"I'd consider that two different ways: the first, it was a random attack; possible, I suppose, but a blow like that . . . a single, killing blow . . . implies intent. Second, if it was in a remote location where he didn't hear or see the killer, and I may be being a city girl here, but that suggests to me he was led there, invited there. It suggests, to me at least, premeditation."

"Someone he knew."

"I'm not always right. I'd be making a lot more money if I were."

He grinned at the screen, his own image displayed in a tiny window in the upper left corner. "It's helpful."

"I hope so. I don't mean to confuse your investigation."

"To the contrary."

"The sergeant and I . . . we're here if you need us. Available any time."

"If Boldt put you up to this, he must suspect it connects to Vetta."

"I can't speak for the sergeant."

"Did he tell you about the nursery? About our witness?"

"He did."

"And your opinion? Can I trust her? Can I trust what she saw?"

"She has everything to lose by lying to you."

"That's how I saw it."

"The dumping of the body. I'm not real clear on that. On the one hand we have a physically powerful assailant, possibly premeditated; on the other, a roadside dumping. We see such dumping along secluded highways, certainly. Easily accessible by vehicle. Someplace people don't frequent. I suppose this location of yours fits with that. But the way the sergeant described it, there are a lot more places over there to dump a body than alongside the valley's only traffic artery. From what your witness said, the driver of that truck didn't appear to dump something so much as collect something."

"That's one way to read it."

"The sergeant mentioned a carjacking. A viable scenario, certainly. Athletes carry baseball bats in vehicles. It would have presented itself. It fits with premeditation and the dumping of the body."

"But then we're faced with a single set of tire tracks. Just the one set. And if what she saw is what she saw, then that truck didn't dump him, and I don't even know what that means," he said, exasperated. "I suppose she got it wrong, the one set of tracks being the key."

"Possibly. Witnesses are, if anything—"

"Unreliable," he said. "We're going around in circles. Besides, I have a suspect. The blood evidence from Wynn's shoes is going to come back compatible with Gale. When it does, it's going to be about means, not motive."

"I wouldn't be looking too closely at Vince Wynn for this," she cautioned.

He didn't want to hear any more. He wanted to disconnect the call.

She volunteered, "Of all the people, Gale's agent would have known better than anyone the degree of threat Martel Gale represented. The kind of trouble he could make. He saw him through the assault trial. The conviction. He saw him on the playing field. All the trouble in the locker room." She'd done her homework. "Gale had forty pounds and several inches on Vince Wynn. Wynn showed his weapon of choice in his backyard: you don't hunt a lion with a BB gun. You don't take on Gale with a baseball bat. More like a double-barreled shotgun. I went over this with the sergeant. It took some convincing.

I realize the evidence—circumstantial and maybe otherwise—points you in a certain direction, and far be it
from me to contest evidence. But if I had to describe his
killer, premeditated or not, I would classify him as . . .
reluctant. I realize that implies contradiction, but the
other way to explain that single blow is as a crime of
passion—a final, life-ending, flash of anger and rage, so
intense that it required but a single strike. It happened in
a single strike, a blow perhaps never intended to kill."

"That is contradictory," he said.

"Maybe I'm just trying to cover myself." She laughed,
somehow finding it amusing.

Walt felt uncomfortable. He was thinking maybe a
woman could deliver a blow like that—an incredibly
angry woman—angry at men like Martel Gale who had
a record of violence against women. Never mind that it
had been a single blow—the human being was capable
of extraordinary acts of violence.

He wondered if Kira Tulivich had played high school
softball, or if her family home was heated by wood, as so
many homes in the valley still were. And if so, who in
her family wielded the ax.

34

After putting in a call to Royal McClure, and summoning his nephew, Kevin, to his offices, Walt returned to the Incident Command Center at Fiona's request.

"It's done," she said.

Walt sat down next to her and trained his eyes on the room's central, flat panel display.

"It's better up there on the wall," she explained, "because of the viewing distance. I didn't have time to make everything perfect. The stop action helps—it being all jerky."

She clicked the play button and Walt watched the three seconds of choppy video.

"Amazing," he said.

"You think so?"

"Is that even Ketchum?"

"A Seattle street. But I cut and pasted the signs in and they make it familiar enough to trick the eye, I think."

"Thank you."

"It was fun. A different kind of challenge."

"Do you mind showing me how to run it?"

"I can do it for you."

"Better if I do it," he said. "There's a psychology involved."

"Whatever you want," she said. She walked him through the operation of the video software, which turned out to be straightforward, and in turn caused him to wonder why she'd offered to stay and help out. The only thing he could think of was that she wanted to eavesdrop, to stay as current on the investigation as possible, and it troubled him.

"Where'd you go?" she said.

He grimaced. "Right here."

"I don't think so."

"A lot on my mind."

"You went cold all of a sudden."

He hated being so easily read. "Did I? It wasn't intentional."

Nancy saved him by knocking, and opening the ICC's door. "Kevin's on his way. I heard back from McClure and he's e-mailed your request. And Brandon told me to tell you he's here—the person you wanted." She knew better than to name names.

Fiona stood, looking down onto Walt, and said, "Good

luck. I guess. It being my laptop, I'll need it back, so I'll wait in the break room." She was fishing for his invitation to remain in the room with him.

"Thank you," he said, irritating her. To Nancy he said, "Okay. Have Brandon send him in. I want him one-on-one."

Gilly Menquez entered the ICC sheepish and confused, clearly overwhelmed by the room's size and the abundance of high-tech audio/visual equipment. He joined Walt at the front table where Fiona had set up her laptop. The video window on the overhead screen was black.

"What's this about, Walt?"

"I was hoping maybe you could tell me."

Gilly sat down in the chair Fiona had been occupying, alongside Walt. He kept his hands clenched tightly in his lap.

"I'm not sure what you mean by that," he said.

"I gave you a break, Gilly."

"I know that. Appreciate it, Sheriff."

"And how do you repay me?"

Gilly couldn't bring himself to look at Walt. "Don't know what you're talking about."

"Think before you say anything, Gilly. There are no lawyers involved at the moment. That can change."

Gilly dared a glance, but couldn't hold the eye contact.

"Are you drunk, Gilly? Right now, I mean? Have you been drinking?"

"Two beers. I swear that's all. I'm fine."

"I need you in your right mind."

"I said I'm fine."

"Okay then," Walt said. "That's going to go down in the statement." Walt scribbled a note.

"What are you talking about?"

"Are you going to mess with me, Gilly?"

"I swear, Sheriff, I don't know what you're talking about."

"Ten, fifteen years ago, a person in my position would have just beat the crap out of a person in your position. It wouldn't have been this way."

"I don't mean to make you angry, Sheriff."

"Some things we can't help."

That seemed to hit deeply.

"Are you going to tell me about it, or am I going to have to explain it to you?" Walt asked.

"I . . . don't . . . know what you're talking about."

Walt took a deep breath and spoke in a harsh, faint voice. "Damn you, Gilly."

Menquez ventured another look, but again couldn't maintain it.

"The first time I suspected something," Walt explained, "was when I saw how thick the forest was over the SUV—Gale's rental. You said you'd picked up the heat signature from it. I don't think so. If everyone hadn't descended on the site at once, maybe I'd have spotted your tracks by daylight. You knew that about me—my tracking skills. I should have understood how it was you failed to hold them all back from the scene. Should have seen through that."

"Sheriff, I . . ." He hung his head.

"Putting the ATM card back. That was quick thinking."

"I don't know nothing about any of this, Sheriff."

"But it was a stupid thing to do. You could have just thrown it out. Tossed it into a Dumpster. But I imagine that's when it began to unwind for you: how to make it look like you'd just come across Gale's rental, when in fact you'd discovered it much earlier."

"Don't know nothing about any ATM card."

"Blompier mentioned the poacher case. The ATM card. The lack of a camera in that ATM. *Your* poacher case, Gilly—the case *you* handled. There were only a few of us who knew that particular ATM didn't have a camera in it. You knew. That's why you chose it." Walt gave him a moment to absorb it all. "Not telling me about the SUV, that's not exactly a crime. Not something you could go to jail for. Lose your job, maybe. But not jail time. It's when you sobered up and realized how deep you were in this that you decided to return the card to the wallet, to let me find Gale's SUV. You thought that card being found still in his wallet might make things okay. But we've been onto the withdrawals since they first started."

A person couldn't lower his head more than Menquez was now. "I got no idea what you're talking about here, Sheriff."

"You sure that's the way you want to play this, Gilly?"

Walt reached for the laptop. "I need to clear this up. I need to know what you found when you first came across the SUV. I need a clean chain of evidence, and you screwed that up for me. I can't get that now, and you're to blame. But you're of value to me if you're willing to come clean and tell me exactly what happened, exactly what you found, what you saw. You're nothing to me if you play dumb like this."

Menquez remained bent forward.

"Have you lost your job?" Walt asked rhetorically. "I suspect you have. Are you in jail? Not yet. Cut your losses, Gilly. Play it smart."

"I didn't do nothing."

"Gilly . . ."

He leaned into Walt and whispered harshly. "You got nothing."

Walt dropped his fingers onto the space bar. The black-and-white video ran on the overhead screen, winning Gilly's attention. But it played too quickly for him to see it for exactly what it was.

Walt hit the rewind button and played the clip again.

The screen showed an elevated view of a quiet street with the signs of Ketchum establishments lining either side. There was an InterMountain Bank sign a block in the distance. The short clip played out as a series of stills—like from a bank's security cameras. A Forest Service pickup truck entered the frame, moved down the street, and pulled into a parking space in front of the bank.

"Recognize that truck? Traffic cams, Gilly. Did you know Ketchum has traffic cams now?"

Menquez's face went a pasty gray. He looked at Walt and back to the overhead screen as Walt played the clip again.

"You see the time stamp?" Walt asked. "Days before you claimed to have found the SUV. There's a time stamp on the withdrawal as well."

Menquez licked his dry lips. He looked like a beached fish.

"We can get you into treatment, Gilly. We can do that *before* all this comes out, so the Service will foot the bill for it. You'll come out clean and sober and on your feet, and maybe you even keep your job."

"I got kids. A family. I needed that money. I wouldn't have taken it."

"You've been drinking up your paycheck, Gilly. I see this all the time. This is nothing new to me. Let me help you."

"I didn't mean to screw things up for you. I found the truck. I swear I was going to tell you. But there was the wallet on the floor. The guy had written his PIN number on a piece of paper tucked into his wallet. I mean, how stupid is that? It's like he was asking me to do it."

"I need you to run it down for me. I need every detail exactly as it happened."

"Including the bat?" Gilly said.

Walt felt a bubble in his chest and did his best to suppress his surprise.

"How come no one found that bat?" Gilly asked. "That wouldn't have nothing to do with you, would it, Sheriff?"

Walt wasn't going to answer that. "Every detail," he said.

"Including the bat? Or am I supposed to leave out the bat? Then again, maybe this is up for negotiation. Maybe both of us have something the other guy wants. Maybe we both got something to hide. Maybe this works out for the both of us."

"I need to know exactly what you did," Walt said. "The chain of evidence is corrupted. It's not going to hold up in court, but *I need this evidence.* Do not play with me, Gilly."

"But then that bat's going to need explaining. That's evidence too, right?"

"You let me worry about that."

"I imagine you are worried about that."

"You don't want to go there."

"We're already there—you and me. I'm not going anywhere but to treatment and jail, isn't that right, Sheriff? Or maybe you're buying me my next drink and we get all chummy-like."

"I wouldn't count on that."

"I saw you go to the back of the Jeep just when everyone showed up. I didn't see you take nothing *out* of the Jeep, so maybe you put something in. You want to talk about evidence, Sheriff?"

Walt pushed the legal pad toward Gilly. "I'll give you thirty minutes. Every detail exactly as it happened. What you found, when you found it, what you did."

"I'm going to include tossing that bat into the woods," Menquez said, taking a deep breath. "That's right: it was lying there on top of the wallet. Didn't see the blood on it until I moved it. But when I did, I chucked it out of there. That goes down here," he said, tapping the pad, "unless you tell me otherwise."

"Did you see who drove the SUV?"

"No. Engine was cold when I found it."

"You said there was blood."

"A stain on the bat. I know dried blood when I see it, Sheriff. You track poachers for thirteen years, there's not much you haven't seen."

"The bat and wallet were on the floor. Anything else? Was there anything else of value in there?"

"Maybe there was, maybe there wasn't."

Walt sensed there wasn't. He pushed the pad even closer to Menquez. He needed a few minutes to get in front of the baseball bat as evidence. He hoped Boldt would answer the phone. "Exactly as it happened," he said. He stood and headed to the door.

"Whatever you say, Sheriff." Gilly Menquez gurgled up a laugh.

"Beggars can't be choosers," Walt said. He'd placed the call from his office phone where there would be a record of it. He felt like a juggler who kept adding balls to the circle he kept alive in the air. There was a limit to it all and he was quickly approaching it.

"They developed prints," Boldt said, half apologizing. "Three different sets. Last I was told, those prints were being run through ALPS. Not sure of the hang-up. Let me put you on hold."

The phone line went dead in Walt's ear. Thirty seconds gave way to a minute. Closer to two minutes before the line popped and Boldt returned. "The delay was with ALPS. Their e-mail went down. They've had the results, we just never got them. My guy made a call just now. No hits, I'm afraid. The guy said he can and will e-mail them some other way. I'll send them along when I get them."

Walt thanked him, and asked for the bat to be returned by overnight courier. "And all the paperwork, please."

"Chain of evidence." Boldt didn't miss much.

"I'd appreciate it."

"You spoke with Matthews."

"Smart lady."

"Hang on," Boldt said. "I just got them." Walt heard a keyboard tapping, and a moment later an e-mail notice popped up in the lower corner of his screen.

"That was fast," Walt said.

"She shared your conversation with me. I hope that's all right?"

"We're in this together," Walt said.

"You get anything back on the blood evidence?"

"Never went to the lab. Wynn's lawyer, Evers, put a noose around it. The shoes are still in limbo. We'll be lucky if we get them before the next millennium."

"It's got to be either your case or mine," Boldt said. "He didn't cut himself shaving."

"My deputy got a little overzealous. If they take a deposition, we're going to lose the evidence."

"Blood shadow," Boldt said.

"I didn't catch that."

"You're going to lose the blood evidence *on* the shoes," Boldt explained. "But then there's the matter of the shoes themselves."

"I'm afraid you've lost me."

"That's ironic," Boldt said, "because I think you may have just saved me. Do me a favor and send across the manufacturer and shoe size, will you please?"

"Happy to do it."

"And if nothing else, convince the judge that it's worth holding Wynn in town until the evidence is sorted out. I may need him to claim those shoes and I don't want him going anywhere. I don't want someone doing it for him."

"I'll make a couple calls. You going to let me in on this?" Walt asked.

"You'll be the first to know," Boldt said.

They ended the call and Walt opened the e-mail that included nine attachments, all high-resolution scans of latent fingerprints. The Automated Latent Print System was a national fingerprint database for felons in all fifty states. The fact that these prints had not kicked out identities didn't tell the whole story. Most states, including Idaho, also maintained databases of fingerprints of state

health workers, teachers, law enforcement officers, politicians, judges, attorneys, and even some ministers and
priests. There were national databases for federal employees as well. With the push of a button, Walt could initiate
additional database searches. The searches would then
generate candidate lists and the results would be scruti-
nized by hand by latent print experts. The results could
take anywhere from hours to days, sometimes weeks,
depending how Walt labeled the request, and the work-
load at the facility. Potential homicides moved to the top
of the list. Aggravated assault would move a request
down the list.

Two people lived on the Engleton property full-time.
One was a small woman just twenty-one, the other a
part-time fishing guide who had single-handedly res-
cued a drowning child from a raging river.

Walt typed up the request in the frame of the e-mail
message set to be forwarded to several departments, both
state and federal. His finger hovered over the enter key.

"Kevin's here." Nancy's voice, coming over the intercom.

Walt pulled his hand away from the keyboard and into
his lap. He pushed back his chair, the wheels squeaking.

35

Walt watched as his nephew worked on a Mac laptop on the opposite side of his desk. The physical similarities to Walt's dead brother—the high cheekbones, the nearly permanent five o'clock shadow, the perfect teeth, a darkly brooding rugged handsomeness—reminded Walt how much he missed the beers on the back porch, the softball games, their shared dislike of their father. He'd tried to step in to fill the void for Kevin after Bobby's death and would always wonder how much that had affected the failure of his own marriage. He and Kevin had been through some challenging times together. Looking at him now, his intense concentration, the singular focus, reminded Walt of Bobby even more.

Alongside the laptop lay a scaled color printout of a human skull, with curved arrows indicating a region on the top of the skull that looked like a jigsaw puzzle. There were measurements written in McClure's hand at the blunt end of the arrows, while their sharper ends pointed to the area of impact that had resulted in the death of Martel Gale.

"Regulation baseball bat is forty-two inches," Kevin said. He sat on the guest side of Walt's office desk, facing his uncle on the other side of the open screen.

"Okay."

"I'm doing this two ways—with and without a choked grip. Come on around."

Walt came around the desk and leaned in behind Kevin, his left hand on the boy's shoulder. The screen showed two animated figures, looking like mannequins against a plain background. Several boxes spread around the screen outside the center window held software tools, including one that contained two other, much smaller mannequin-like figures.

"On the right is your victim," Kevin said. "All six-foot-four and a half of him. A frickin' giant. On the left is the giant killer. The bat is to scale and I Googled the average arm length for specific heights. You gave me five-foot-four, so this guy on the left is five-foot-four. So check it out."

He set the screen into motion. The figure on the left—not "a guy," but Kira Tulivich, in Walt's mind—hoisted the baseball bat and, in frame-by-frame slow motion, brought it down onto Gale's head. Kevin used the mouse to draw an arrow at the area of impact and then pointed to the printout to his left.

"Not even close," Walt said.

"He's too short," Kevin said, referring to the Kira figure. "This guy was hit way up on top of his head. Even if I set it so he doesn't choke up," he said, adjusting the bat in Kira's hands and animating the action for a second time, "the bat hits the skull in about the same place, the problem being this guy just isn't tall enough to reach the top of the victim's head. So what I did was put him up a single step. Seven inches. Because maybe the guy with the bat's standing on a step when he connects with this guy." He repositioned the smaller figure. "And though it's better, it's actually *too* high, too tall. I mean if the victim is at the perfect distance away . . . sure. It can be made to work this way . . ." He moved Gale forward and this time, when animated, the bat landed squarely on the top of Gale's head. Walt shuddered, able to see beyond the world of computer-realized mannequins. "But if it isn't absolutely the perfect distance, what happens is a length of the bat connects from the back of the skull to the front, making like a trench instead of a pit."

"So, no good," Walt said.

"It takes a perfect storm," Kevin said. "That's all I'm saying. A step height and the perfect separation between the two. My guess, you could run this a dozen times and you'd be lucky for it to come out right once or twice. It's not a high-percentage shot."

"And the high-percentage shot?"

"That's different. Two options." Kevin replaced the Kira figure with another, taller figure from the toolbox. "Six foot. Six-foot-one. Wouldn't matter if it was two-handed or one. The length of the guy's arms more than compensates. Slightly choked-up on the bat . . ." He completed setting up the scene and put the new figure into motion. The bat was lifted high in the air and came down squarely with the end of the bat impacting the top of Gale's skull—exactly as McClure had suggested. "That's a frickin' bull's-eye."

"Six foot. Six-foot-one," Walt said, his voice giving away his relief.

Kevin looked over his shoulder and into Walt's face. "What's up with that?" He didn't wait for an answer. "I didn't say it was the only option, did I?" When Kevin got behind a computer he became arrogant. Walt considered reprimanding him but didn't want to get into it with him. "Here's the thing I forgot: tiptoes. When you really whale on a bat—" He scooted out, stood up, and demon-strated, rising to his tiptoes as he swung high overhead. "Okay?" Slipping back into the chair, he manipulated the laptop to replace the taller assailant with a slightly smaller one. The figure rose up onto bent feet and the bat came down, the impact perfectly reflecting McClure's notes. Kevin highlighted some areas and made the assailant stand once again.

Walt returned to his earlier thought: there were only two people living on the Engleton property. A minute earlier Kevin had all but ruled out Kira. "How tall?" Walt choked out.

Kevin moved the cursor arrow to the top of the head of the assailant figure, and steadied it there. A yellow box popped up alongside the arrow containing the measurement: 172.7 cm.

"Inches?" Walt asked dryly. He already knew the answer—his height when wearing a pair of boots.

Kevin asked the software for the conversion. A new number filled the box: 68 in.

"Five-foot-eight," Kevin said. "Or more precisely, five-foot-eight, but on tiptoe—six foot, six-foot-one."

Walt remembered kissing her. Coming slightly off his heels to reach her lips.

He thanked Kevin and politely asked him to leave, telling him he thought he could get him some compensation as a consultant, and Kevin saying how he didn't care about getting paid when they both knew otherwise. The kid was carting bags at the Sun Valley Lodge and delivering room service. How long was that going to last?

Walt shut his office door and returned to his chair and stared at the e-mail there waiting to be sent, his request for the fingerprint work. It wasn't a matter of thinking clearly. He couldn't think at all. The number, five-foot-eight, stuck in his head like a wedge, like a baseball bat to the top of his skull. Back to Kevin's perfect storm: a smaller person elevated on a step at just the right distance from Gale; a taller person killing the man easily. But it was the last option that wouldn't leave his thoughts, the last option that had been building like a tsunami inside him.

He hit Enter and the computer made a swishing sound indicating the e-mail had been sent.

"Some cases don't get solved," she'd said to him. *"Some cases go cold."*

At the time, he'd thought she'd been protecting Kira.

36

Brandon, his stocking feet up on the trailer's small coffee table, his hand in a bag of white corn chips, and his eye on the Mariners' fourth inning at bat, spoke through a full mouth.

"I think you two should talk."

Gail, paying bills at what passed for the kitchen table, didn't look up. "We talk."

"I'm just saying—"

"And I'm telling you we do."

"Maybe we need to think about getting a bigger place."

"Oh, yeah. That's going to happen. I can barely pay the electric."

"Maybe you need to think about what we talked about."

Still not looking up, she continued writing out the check. "Maybe you need to get some overtime."

"There's a freeze. You know that."

"Then some security work. You know how many people up here have bodyguards?"

"You want me working eighteen hours a day? Seriously?"

"There's nothing out there for me. You think I'm going to wait tables or something?" She pushed the pile of checks to the edge of the table. "You need to sign these."

Brandon's cell phone rang from the back bedroom. He struggled to standing, spilled the chips, and pushed past her to reach the phone before the call went to voice mail. It was the little nuisances that bothered Tommy Brandon—voice mail catching calls, lawn mowers that wouldn't start, birth control interrupting the act, the bathroom counter being cluttered with beauty products. He could leave the wars and the economy and illegal immigration to others. Just give him a remote control with a button that worked.

"Yeah?" he barked into a phone that looked toylike in his big hand. "Bonehead? Slow down! That's better. Now? You're sure? Yeah, it's worth something. Don't do anything. Don't say anything. Go back to flipping burgers and leave this to me."

He slapped the phone shut and right back open. Hit a speed dial key. "It's me, Tommy. Bonehead says our guy is at the Casino right now. A pal of his bartends there, called him. Suspect's got a burger and beer in front of him— Yeah, five, seven minutes, max . . ." He moved quickly down the trailer's narrow aisle and found the black windbreaker hanging on a peg by the door—SHER-IFF, it read on the back in bold yellow letters. He returned to the small bedroom, his ear pinched to the phone, and wrapped his gun belt around his waist, buckling it. "Okay, I'll call it in . . . I'll wait. I promise."

The phone went into his pocket. He kissed her on the top of her head as he swept past her. His hand was on the door.

"Later."

"Your vest!" she said.

He kept it behind the front seat of the pickup. He paused there at the front door for a second, thinking that only the ex-wife of a cop would have been able to decipher what was going on based on one end of a phone call.

"Yeah," he said.

"Be safe. Nothing stupid."

As he ran to the truck, he was wondering if this was how she'd sent Walt out the door all those years, if she hadn't simply traded him in for a newer model. It made him feel cheap. It made him relive a dozen conversations that the sheriff had started, some completed, some not. A *Twilight Zone* moment as he stepped into another life, a life different from the one he thought he'd been living.

"Jesus," he muttered to himself as he yanked open the driver's door and climbed behind the wheel. He pulled the door shut as he backed out. The tires yelped as he throttled down. He fished the Bluetooth device into his ear and got the phone dialing.

"Officer in need of assistance . . ." he said, running a stop sign and fishtailing out onto the two-lane highway.

He forgot all about the vest behind the seat.

"Just one?" Brandon mumbled to himself as a Ketchum Police Department cruiser pulled to the curb and parked across Main Street. Ketchum's nightlife scene was confined to this two-block stretch of bars and restaurants bookended by traffic lights. Tourists milled outside the establishments and jaywalked to join friends on either side. The Casino's A-frame, appropriately pushed a few yards back from the other buildings on Main Street, as if shunned by the mainstream population, was not for the faint of heart. Nor was it for the tourists. If Ketchum had bikers, this was where they'd go. It served as home for the hard-core drinkers, the barflies, and the locals who preferred tattoo-revealing T-shirts. The women wore their shirts tight and their lipstick red. Some nights you could bowl a frame down the center of the place, and then there were nights like this when it looked like a convention was under way. The Allman Brothers shook the exterior wall as Brandon approached the establishment's doorway, which was open to the night air.

His backup was positioned at the Casino's rear door in case the mountain man made a break, but he had no description to give the cop, no way for this guy to discern one person from the next. And when a cop—or in his case, a deputy sheriff—entered a place like the Casino, it would be like shining a flashlight under the fridge—the roaches were sure to scatter.

Brandon stepped through the door and pressed his back against a bulletin board covered in flyers for second-hand fishing boats and twelve-step groups. He kept the yellow lettering to the wall. Kept the windbreaker zipped to his navel, just high enough to hide the gun belt. At six-four, he had a clear view over the heads of the customers, five deep and crowding the bar, of the pool table in the back and the line of deuces to the right. Two guys sitting at separate tables had empty red plastic baskets in front of them, the deli paper stained with oil and catsup. Either could be the mountain man. Practically everyone in the place could qualify given the beards, the sweat stains, and the unkempt hair.

Brandon searched the three behind the bar—two guys and a girl—all moving calmly but at light speed, to address the needs of the customers. The beer taps remained on, a plastic cup or mug replacing the last and catching the next. *Horse piss*, Brandon thought.

He'd hoped for eye contact with one of the male bartenders, was surprised when the hard-faced woman connected with him and cocked her head just faintly to her left indicating the second of the two at the tables. Brandon didn't acknowledge, knew better than to connect her with himself.

Just for an instant, he remembered his vest behind the seat in the truck. Heard her voice reminding him. Just for an instant he considered going back to get it.

"Howdy, Deputy!" a male voice called out loudly from Brandon's left, offered as a warning to the clientele. It came from one of the bartenders, a guy named Stone whom Brandon had once arrested for breaking the windshield of his girlfriend's car with her mailbox, uprooted with a forty-pound ball of concrete on the business end. While Stone's warning didn't cause a mass exodus, some of those in the room froze, and a few slinked away. Both the men sitting in front of the red food baskets stayed rooted in their seats. Neither so much as looked up.

Brandon didn't move. He wasn't going to have a bartender dictating how this went down. He checked his watch: the sheriff could arrive anytime in the next few minutes. Maybe another backup or two. He liked those odds much better than two-to-one. He adjusted the Bluetooth in his ear, hoping it might ring, hoping the sheriff was close.

Despite Stone's broadcast, despite the wandering eyes, not many had landed upon him. Maybe no one cared; maybe those that did were now gone. What he didn't like was the collective cool of his two suspects against the far wall. Not so much as a twitch from either.

His Bluetooth purred. He touched the device and connected the call. "Yeah?"

"I have a runner in custody," the KPD cop announced.

"Lose him," Brandon said softly.

"Say what? He's cuffed and on the way to the cruiser."

"No, no, no. Lose him. Return to post." Brandon ended the call. *Moron.* The sin was not arresting the wrong guy, but leaving his post. He'd lost his backup.

He pulled the phone from his pocket and speed-dialed.

"Fleming," came the sheriff's voice in his ear.

"Your twenty?"

"Just passing the hospital. Five minutes."

"I make my move and the front door goes unguarded."

"Got it."

"My backup vacated the back. I'm wide open here."

"Do you see our boy?"

"Yeah. Could be one of two I'm looking at."

"Does he see you?"

"It's a work in progress, Sheriff."

"Hold tight, Tommy. You hear me? For once, hold tight."

"It's about to go down. I'd love to be wrong about that."

"Me, too. Two minutes away. I'll take the front."

"Out."

He slipped the phone back into his pocket. Felt the bulge of his handgun in the holster. Remembered the vest behind the seat in the truck. Was that what was stopping him? he wondered. Had he allowed Gail's warning to wedge into the cracks that held duty in place over the mortal fear that always existed? The noise of the place was getting to him. He found a mirror behind the bar that allowed him to monitor both men without facing them.

The man at the second table, the one farthest away, reached beneath the table, and Brandon's right hand sought out his own gun up under the windbreaker. The guy held a wad of bills, not a weapon, and Brandon saw what appeared to be a neat stack of hundreds with smaller bills in the fold. The man peeled off a ten and a five and left them on the table, returning the money to his pocket.

The man stood, and Brandon saw it too late. The guy fired a single shot into the ceiling. Everyone in the room ducked at the same instant. All but Brandon, all but the one man trained not to duck. He was reaching for his own sidearm as the second bullet was fired.

Brandon was jerked to his left. It was a hot, searing pain, but not overwhelming, the way he'd imagined it might feel. He felt his breath catch, instantly light-headed. Heard a car door out there somewhere and knew it was the sheriff. Wondered if the sheriff had heard the shots.

The man who'd shot him—their mountain man— swung a chair through the window alongside his table, raked a leg of the chair along the lower edge clearing the shards of broken glass, and jumped through and out onto the sidewalk.

The sheriff came through the door, taking one step past him, and rose onto his toes, immediately seeing the broken window.

"Here," Brandon coughed out, slouching toward the floor.

The sheriff spun around. "Damn it!" he said, holster-

IN HARM'S WAY 341

ing his weapon and reaching out to catch his deputy. "Some help here!" He reached for his radio clipped to his uniform. Brandon heard, "Officer down. Request ambulance . . ." He fought against the purple ooze at the edges of his vision, fought against the image of the muzzle flash from the handgun. That burst of light occupied his thought, had overtaken him.

"Stay with me!" he heard.

The sheriff? He wasn't sure where that had come from. His brother? A priest? No white light. No journey through his lifetime memories. Only that dark purple rim flooding in from the edges like a spreading pool of blood. That, and a penetrating cold. A cold like no other. The cold of fear. The cold of the unknown. Of outright terror. There was no warm wash of love. No angels. Just that cold dragging him down and unrelentingly pulling him out of sight.

Walt was heading to the Jeep to follow the ambulance to the hospital, when he glanced back at the Casino and the swarm of deputies now involved in the crime scene. He thought it ironic and unacceptable that when a deputy needed backup, one local cop showed up on the scene; but when a deputy was shot and wounded, the place was lousy with law enforcement. He had to turn that around.

Climbing into the Jeep's front seat, pushing Bea's wet

nose out of his way, he caught sight of the chair in the sea of broken glass out on the sidewalk. One of the bar staff, broom in hand, was just approaching the tossed chair.

Walt slipped out of the vehicle and shouted, "You! Stop! Yes, you!" He moved at a run toward the spread of broken glass.

"Stand back, please," Walt said.

"I clean up broken glass all the time, Sheriff. I'm good," the guy said. "I'll be careful."

"It's not that," Walt said, again amazed that a dozen deputies and local officers could be on the scene and none within shouting range, none paying any attention to the actions of their superior officer. Things needed to change.

"Deputy!" Walt hollered.

Three appeared within seconds: one from the other side of the broken window, and two from around the corner at the back of the club.

"Gloves," Walt said, addressing the nearest, Kramer, on the other side of the missing window. "I want this chair collected and bagged. I want it handled by the edges of the seat—not the back, not the legs. Are you clear on that?"

"Yes, sir."

"See if they have a clean garbage bag—"

"No problem," said the Casino employee, leaning the broom against the exterior wall. "You want me to get one?"

"Better get two," Walt said. "Go on." He explained to his deputy how he wanted it done, how he was to treat the chair as a murder weapon. That the deputy would personally be responsible to log the chair as evidence and then to transport it to the Meridian lab the following day for a full fingerprint analysis.

"And I want every shard of glass collected by hand as well. The glass on the sidewalk, and the broken glass in the frame. I want it placed in a bag—plastic—and sealed and labeled. It goes with the chair to the lab and they're to test for blood evidence." Pointing through the window, he said, "There's a toothpick in that food basket that may have come out of the mouth of our shooter. It's to be DNA-tested at the same time. Anything they get is to be run through every database known to man. One of our own was shot tonight, and while it doesn't look as bad as it might have been, we are *on this*. Cross every t, dot every i. No procedural screwups on this. You double-check everything you do before you do it. You do it right the first time. We owe that to Tommy. Are we good?"

"We're good."

"So someone pull some tape here and cordon off the crime scene inside and out. Somebody act like a sheriff's deputy for a change, would you please?"

The two at the end got moving, as did Kramer. Walt considered apologizing for the outburst. It was born more of concern for Tommy Brandon than the failures of his men.

But he didn't correct himself. He rushed back to the Jeep, hoping he'd put the fear of God into his team. Marveling at how Brandon's being wounded had so deeply affected him.

37

From the moment Gail entered Emergency, Walt sensed she blamed him for the shooting. She didn't say as much, but she didn't have to. The first look she gave him he interpreted as, "How could you?" and the second, "I'll bet you're just loving this." He didn't need a translator. He'd lived with her for over a decade.

She sat down well away from him in the small waiting area. He gave her five minutes. It took her less than three to stand up and move closer to him, sitting just one seat away.

"Was he wearing his vest?" She looked straight ahead, as did he.

"No."

"I told him to wear his vest."

"And you were right to do so. He should have been. It was in his truck."

"Did you catch the guy?"

"No. Working on it."

"Working real hard, I can see."

That didn't take long, he thought. "It collapsed his left lung. Missed the major arteries and blood vessels. They'll hold him a few days."

"As if you care."

"Wouldn't be here if I didn't. I know you're upset. You want to take it out on me, that's okay."

Her eyes flashed. He wasn't sure she'd heard him. "You're only here because it would cost you votes if you didn't look concerned about your deputies."

"But only you and I know that," he said, sarcastically.

The comment won a tick from her—she glanced hotly in his direction and then back to face the receptionist.

"Screw you," she said.

He had a half dozen retorts on the tip of his tongue. He swallowed them away. *How do you comfort someone you're still uncomfortable around*? he wondered.

"He's going to come through okay," he said. "That's what counts."

"How could you send him into something like that without proper backup? What kind of half-assed office are you running? What kind of superior would let his subordinates do something like that?"

"A lousy one," he said. "Might be as few as three days

if his lung holds. He's in good shape, good condition. That's in his favor."

"Bet you were hoping it killed him."

Walt jerked in her direction and she flinched, tilting away from him, but at the last moment he controlled himself and kept himself in check.

"You think?" he said, between clenched teeth. He stood, turned and faced her. She looked afraid of him. "I know you probably won't, but I'd like it very much if you would let him know that I was out here when you got here. That I'm thinking of him."

She hung her head. After a long moment she whispered, "I told him to wear the vest."

He thought she might be crying. "If Tommy started listening to someone else, that would be a first."

She cracked a smile and looked up at him through welling tears. "No kidding."

"He got lucky. We all got lucky. Believe it or not, this is one of the good days."

She nodded self-consciously. "How weird is that?"

"Tell him hello. I'll drop by later. I've got some stuff to do."

He walked toward the doors. They slid open automatically.

"I'll tell him," she called after him.

It caused him to catch a step. He stood there for a moment, his back to her. Then he continued on through the double set of automatic doors and into the chorus of frogs and night insects, switching on his BlackBerry, turning on his radio, and walking stiff-legged to the Jeep as incoming messages and e-mails began to light up his phone.

"My name is Michael." It was the third of seven voice mails Walt was set to retrieve. "I understand you want to talk to me. I am—*was*, whatever—Martel's sponsor. His NA sponsor, down here in New Orleans. Gimme a shout, you want to talk to me." The man recited a number that Walt scribbled into his notebook. Bea nudged him from behind, wanting Walt to drive. But the Jeep idled in the hospital parking spot. He faced four large framed photographs of happy, healthy people mounted to the hospital's brick wall. They were an illusion and he resented their presence.

"Back!" he commanded. Bea retreated, whining in protest.

He slogged through the remaining voice mails, making notes, his patience wearing thin by the time he returned the call.

"Sheriff Walt Fleming," he informed the man who answered.

"Michael. We go by first names only." He had a pronounced Louisiana drawl.

"I respect that," Walt said.

"I understand you were asking after me, Sheriff."

"I have some questions pertaining to Mr. Gale's visit

to Idaho. Was hoping you might . . . illuminate some of this for me."

"What's shared in the program is of a confidential nature. That is never more true than between sponsor and sponsee."

"I have nothing but respect for twelve-step programs. But in this case, given Mr. Gale is dead, and that you may possess information vital to the investigation, I have to ask you to drop the confidentiality."

"I'll tell you what I can tell you. I am not going to harm others, or put them at risk. That goes against the steps."

"If there's a killer loose, we're all at risk."

"Your point is taken, Sheriff."

"One of your members up here believed Martel," he switched to his first name to try to make Michael more comfortable, "was ninth-stepping."

"I have no reason to contradict that."

Walt then understood: Michael would rather deny or confirm something Walt said than offer information directly himself.

"There are two individuals in the Sun Valley area who are part of professional football and we believe may have been the intended recipients of Martel's goodwill."

"Is that so?"

"A team owner, and an agent. Martel's former agent."

"Interesting."

"Were you given any reason to believe one or both of

these men might have been who Martel intended to visit?"

"He may have."

"You don't sound convinced."

"You have a good ear," Michael said.

"Somebody else then?"

"Could be."

"A teammate?"

"In a manner of speaking."

"Not a football teammate."

"Very good."

"A different team: someone in the program."

"You're colder."

"You could just tell me," Walt suggested.

"We, those of us in the program, do not break the law, Sheriff. But nearly all of us have had contact with law enforcement. I'm not exactly a fan, if you'll pardon me. We cooperate with law enforcement when required. When asked. Volunteering is another matter, at least for me."

"So it's twenty questions." Walt hadn't meant to say that. It came out viciously.

"Something like that. Ball's in your court, if you want to look at it that way."

"Coming up here. That was about his atoning, his working the ninth step."

"That was my understanding. Yes."

"A different kind of team," Walt said, thinking aloud. "A relationship. Women, not men. Caroline Vetta."

"You see? You're good at this."

"Can you confirm Caroline Vetta?"

"I can confirm it was women, not men. I don't have names for you."

Plural, Walt thought. Caroline Vetta and at least one other.

"He mentioned Seattle and Sun Valley," Walt stated.

"Not exactly."

"Seattle and Idaho."

"Yes."

"Nothing to do with football."

"Everything in his life had to do with football."

"Did he see Caroline Vetta? Did he contact you?"

"He contacted me. We spoke every day. This was a big deal for him. An important trip. It's one of the hardest things we do. Also one of the most rewarding."

"And he told you how it went with Caroline," Walt stated.

"He never saw his Seattle friend. Nor did he mention a name. It was my impression he may have spoken with her, presumably by phone, but that their face-to-face meeting never took place." The man's drawl put emphasis on his verbs, making his speech sound foreign to Walt.

"Because she was killed."

"I can't confirm that."

"He called you after she was killed."

"When he called me the second time, he was in a panic. What you're saying would make sense, wouldn't it?"

"He panicked. He knew he'd be implicated."

"Once you've been part of it, you understand the mechanics of the legal system."

"That he'd be a suspect. That it was weighted against him."

"He never said that exactly, but that was my impression, yes."

"Michael, did he commit that crime? Did he do harm to Caroline Vetta?"

"They never met face-to-face. He wouldn't have lied to me. Especially about that."

"He was afraid."

"I believe he understood it was bad timing."

"You advised him to get out of there."

"I did."

"To move on."

"Correct."

"Did he suggest to you who might have done Caroline Vetta?" He heard the man's steady breathing over the sound of the idling car and Bea's raspy panting from the backseat.

"Not . . . directly, no."

Walt considered the careful nature of the man's answer.

"He wasn't scared," Walt said, guessing, "he was angry. He thought he knew who killed her."

"He was emotional. It's true."

"He did suspect someone?"

"That would be speculation on my part. I can't do that."

"Sure you can. I'm asking you to speculate. Believe me, I filter *all* of this."

"I believe his anger was directed at someone, at a particular person, yes. But I caution you, I do not know the identity of that person, nor did he give me any indication of who it might be."

"The trip to Sun Valley, a woman or this person?"

"Or both? I'm not sure I can answer that accurately."

"A woman," Walt said. "Like Seattle. He was ninth-stepping a woman, a former lover or at least someone he'd harmed in some way, something that required atonement."

"Idaho was mentioned in his original plans. So, yes, I'm sure you're right."

One of the four photographs on the side of the hospital showed a Hispanic child, several of her teeth still coming in, wide-eyed and smiling. For an instant that photograph bled into another: a black kid on a porch with nearly the same smile. The two photos were surprisingly similar. Then he recalled where he'd seen the photo of the black kid, and his hand holding the phone went out to the wheel and he pushed himself back against the headrest. "Oh, hell," he gasped aloud.

Michael's voice came thinly from the BlackBerry and Walt returned it to his ear.

". . . there? Sheriff?"

"Sorry about that," Walt said. "Dropped the phone."

"I don't know what else I can tell you."

"You'll be at this number?"

"I will."

"You've been very helpful."

"You don't sound too pleased."

"I'll be in touch." Walt ended the call and holstered the BlackBerry.

The photo mounted to the hospital wall was itself again, showing the cheerful Hispanic girl. But the other child's face—the one in Fiona's photo—lingered beneath the surface, poisoning him.

38

At eight p.m., Walt was watching the Disney Channel with his daughters, the smell of burgers and home fries lingering in the air. Nikki lay on the floor playing Animal Crossing on her DS while simultaneously watching the show, something Walt disapproved of but tonight wasn't going to make a big deal about. But it reminded him that as he made the transition back, away from depending so much on Lisa, that he had a responsibility to be consistent. The girls had learned to slip through the cracks, sometimes more like fissures, that existed between his way of parenting, Lisa's discipline, and their mother's basic fear of how to handle them. The girls had brokered these differences to their benefit, playing one against the other, citing established rules from another camp that likely didn't exist, and effectively playing Walt's guilt against him. There were at least two downsides to this: first, they got away with everything; second, they learned how to manipulate rather than face the music. He could cut them a certain amount of slack for the difficulty of their situation—the Taffy Twins, pulled and stretched in several directions at once—but for their sakes, it was time to lay down the law and see to it that, as much as humanly possible, Gail kept with the same program.

"Nikki, the TV or the DS, but not both," he said.

"Mom lets me."

"You want me to call her? If she says otherwise, it'll cost you the DS for the week."

She flipped the machine shut, stuck her lower lip out as she did so, and huffed as she pushed it aside.

"This show is boring," Nikki said.

"No it isn't," Emily complained. "I like it."

"Why don't you read, Nikki? After this show, we're going to read together. The three of us."

"Oh, Dad . . ." Emily complained. To her sister she said, "See what you did?"

"Did not."

"Did too!"

"Girls!" Walt said, raising his voice. "This show, then reading." He looked over at them thinking that these two children defined him more than his job, more than any of his accomplishments. At school events he introduced himself with "I'm Nikki and Emily's father." He thought that summed it up.

His computer chirped from the living room.

"Skype," the girls both said, nearly in unison.

"I'll get it," Walt announced. "But when this show's over," he said, already moving toward the dining table, "don't start another one."

"Yeah, yeah . . ." Nikki said, sounding entirely insincere.

He was going to have to work on that attitude of hers as well.

"Have you got a pen?" Boldt asked once Walt had logged on.

"I do."

"There can't be a paper trail right now, although that's being worked on."

"Did you get my e-mail with Wynn's shoe information?"

"I did. Thanks for that. More to come. Stay tuned."

"Ready when you are."

"These are the e-mail addresses on the list server: all people who requested to be notified of Gale's parole. Some, I'm told, had restraining orders in place. Others were his victims. He had a pile of assault charges by the time they put him away. There are twenty-two on here. I'll read them slowly. Here goes."

Boldt, head down in the video, reading glasses perched on the end of his nose, out of scale on his huge head and looking toylike, read the e-mail addresses carefully, calling out capitalization, underscores, and "dots," working patiently through the list.

Walt read each back. Some were easy to identify the

sender by the name, others wouldn't be difficult to follow up on because of the host server—the name of a football team or a recognizable company. Five were generic and therefore obscure.

"They're going to be tricky," Walt said.

"I could ask Buddy Cornell to chase down the real names. There's probably an e-mail trail in their system from these people, and I imagine at least some sign their names when sending a message. All he's got to do is chase down those e-mails and read them. As long as we keep this by phone, and off any kind of paper trail, I think Buddy will help us."

"I'd appreciate it."

"Let me check it out for you."

"I can Google the e-mail addresses as well. Sometimes that works. And I can cold-call the hosts. We've had to do that before and some of them are pretty cooperative."

"And we have CIs here," Boldt said, meaning criminal informants, "that are magicians when it comes to this stuff."

"Anagrams," Nikki's girlish voice said from over Walt's shoulder.

"Hello, young lady," Boldt said from the screen.

Walt didn't have to look over his shoulder because the camera view that showed his face in a small window also showed Nikki standing to his left.

"My friends' parents . . ." she said, "they make anagrams out of my friends' names so you can't tell who they are. 'Cause of all the creepy stuff you talk about at school, Dad. Maybe they're anagrams."

Boldt bit back a smile on the screen.

"Worth a try," he said.

"Looks like my daughters are going to help me," Walt said.

"Can't argue with that. I'll give Buddy a call as backup."

"Much appreciated."

"And thanks again for the shoe stats. I think we may be able to pull this off by tomorrow sometime, if you're available."

"I'm here," Walt confirmed.

They ended the call. Walt wrapped his arm around Nikki. "Okay, girl . . . looks like you just earned yourself a job. Double your allowance if you unscramble these names."

"What about me?" Emily complained.

"You take half the names. Nikki takes half. Nikki goes first. You both get the extra allowance, and reading time is delayed by half an hour."

"Hooray!" Nikki shouted, too close to her father's ear.

The girls took to the work enthusiastically, thrilled to be needed, he realized. It alerted him to a glaring omission in his fathering: he took care of his girls, but he rarely asked them to take care of him. As the computer printer whined from the other room, Walt realized it wasn't just the girls. He felt uncomfortable when others offered him their help—he looked at generosity as a debt, rather than as a gift. Even in the workplace, he had trouble delegating, pleased to have a deputy sheriff to handle that for him. He was sitting there contemplating the mistakes he'd made with Gail and was still making with the girls when Nikki delivered several pages of printout to him.

"We crossed out the ones that didn't make any sense," Emily explained.

"And we put arrows by the ones that sounded like names," Nikki said.

He looked at his watch: they'd been at it for just over an hour, content to eat up reading time. He'd been occupied with Larry King and stewing over his personality shortcomings.

He praised their effort, placed the pages down onto the coffee table, and headed into their room; the three of them spent forty-five minutes reading about five kids inside Disney World after dark. The girls went to bed reluctantly, which was typical for any night, especially in summer when the sun didn't set until nine thirty and the sky glowed faintly well past ten p.m.

He got a kick out of their effort, pushing the pages aside and reviewing some paperwork from his briefcase until well past eleven. Letterman was tearing into the administration's health care proposals as Walt packed it up for the night. He killed the TV and subsequently knocked the girls' hard work onto the floor, scattering the pages.

There was no explaining what the eye could see or the ear could hear. No explaining why Walt could look across a forest floor and effortlessly spot game tracks where others could not. No explaining how a musician could hear a flurry of notes within the confines of utter silence. Walt was bent over and scooping up the fallen pages as his eye picked first one word singled out with a hand-drawn arrow, then a second.

Shaw Ken

His eye darted around the page as his fingers found the sheet and brought it up to a reading distance, Walt still bent over the coffee table. Both entries had been crossed out, distinguished as nonsense words by either Nikki or Em:

A Fino

The cross-out was such that he could read the word as *Fine* or *Fino*.

The top of the page carried an extraordinarily long URL that combined the website and the search string. Walt hurried to the computer and carefully typed the address into the browser bar, his throat tight, his mouth dry, his heart pounding. He knew the answer but the investigator in him would not allow any jumping to conclusions, demanding precise evidence. He double-checked each letter in the long address, not wanting to input it a second time and, confirming its accuracy, hit Enter.

The screen went blank. Walt found himself holding

his breath as the web page loaded. He scrolled down the results, the page lying alongside the keyboard.

Fino

"No . . ." he muttered aloud.

The e-mail address "Anon.Weakfish@gmail.com" unscrambled to Fino A Shaw Ken. *Fiona Kenshaw*.

He looked back and forth between the page and screen in disbelief, trying hard to convince himself there had to be a mistake. Obviously, the girls had input the address incorrectly. But that reliable eye of his picked out the truth: all the double-checking wasn't going to change the results. Nikki and Emily had done a fine job of it.

He pushed away from the table. The chair legs caught and he nearly went over backward, throwing his legs out and recovering his balance. But he was unsteady on his feet as he stood and roamed the room, his eyes unable to leave the screen and the piece of paper carrying his daughters' handiwork. He paced. Hurried into the kitchen and popped a beer and drank from the can greedily as he continued to contemplate what it all meant. He knew what it meant, of course, but he couldn't allow it to mean *that*, so his effort was to reframe the evidence into something that made sense, offered an alternate universe.

He pried his eyes away long enough to glance at his watch: 11:28. He pulled the BlackBerry off his hip and held it in his palm, then sneaked a glimpse over his shoulder toward the girls' room. This was the collision of work and family, this moment and moments like it. The after-hours demands of the job and his allowing it to interfere.

He scrolled through the BlackBerry's address book to Myra's entry. His sister-in-law or Kevin would willingly come over and be in the house for the sake of his daughters if asked. Kevin was probably awake anyway.

He worked the device and his thumb hovered over the green key, now with Fiona's cell number highlighted. Then, not.

The list server evidence was not yet evidence—it would have to arrive in written form from either Boldt or Buddy Cornell to be of use to Walt's prosecuting attorney. Walt had mistakenly—stupidly, he thought—requested that Boldt pressure his people to authenticate the evidence, to deliver it formally. Could he now undo that request without sending up a red flag? Was he willing to do so for her? Did he dare jump to such conclusions without giving her a chance to explain things?

But he told himself he wasn't jumping to any conclusions. First had been Gale's NA sponsor telling him Gale was atoning to women, and Walt's recollection of the photo of the wide-eyed black kid on Fiona's wall, photos taken of Katrina victims: New Orleans, Gale's home city. Now the list server e-mail address providing a direct link between Gale and Fiona. Combined with Fiona's recent erratic behavior, Walt began to see his suspicion of Kira—and Fiona's reaction to it—in a new light. He thought back to his interview of Vince Wynn on the night of the backyard shooting, and Wynn's mention of having received an e-mail from the list server announcing Gale's parole, nearly two weeks late; he connected this, rightly or wrongly, to Fiona's going pale at the Advocates dinner as she got a look at her phone. Had she, too, received a list server e-mail that night? Had the man at the back of the conference room, the man Kira had mistaken for her abductor, Roy Coats, actually been Martel Gale? If Kira knew about Fiona's past it was conceivable she'd experienced a transference, making Fiona's anxiety her own, and not realizing the difference. The two kids working valet parking had described the man as a hulk of almost comic book proportions: that fit with Gale's steroid-induced enormity.

If he drove up to see her, what excuse would there be later for his not having used a ruling of probable cause to conduct a search of the property? He no longer needed the Engletons' permission for such a search. He had to shed his emotional response and think this through more carefully. Where did the evidence lead? What was hard evidence, and what amounted to speculation? What would his record show or suggest? Detailed records were kept of his e-mails, phone calls, radio calls, informal meetings, proper interrogations. Could he untangle that to keep charges off of Fiona? Was that what he wanted to do? Was that something he was willing to do?

He had prided himself over a career of public service at having never corrupted a case or allowed himself to be corrupted. The office had accepted donations of Hummers, RVs, boats, trailers, and cash— He had never once taken so much as a gas can or a dime for himself. He'd had ample opportunity to screen friends from drunk driving charges or excuse parking tickets. Never had done it. But Fiona was different. Not only could he forgive a woman from defending herself against the likes of a Martel Gale, but after nearly two years of avoiding women in the wake of his marriage's collapse, he'd now found the one woman he was willing to risk himself with—and here was his repayment. It seemed quite possible she'd bludgeoned a man to death.

His thumb cleared the phone's search field and typed an "F" into the blank bar. Hovered there.

But his cell phone calls were a matter of public record. He looked toward the kitchen phone. His home calls could easily be subpoenaed. His work calls. His e-mail. He cursed into the room: his *life* was a matter of public record.

He caught sight of the computer. Nikki had a Hotmail account she used for instant messaging. He'd set it up for her. He knew the password. He stepped toward the dinner table, recalling that Skype allowed the user to place phone calls anywhere in the world.

Including six miles up the highway.

39

Walt asked Fiona to step outside the cottage and led her up the hill to the edge of one of the dimly lit, yet oddly colorful flower beds where he'd dragged a pair of her lawn chairs. Beatrice patrolled the forest, snapping twigs and snorting when she caught something up her nose.

"Why the cloak and dagger?" she asked. The nearest floodlight was a good distance behind them at the corner of her cottage. Their long shadows stretched in front of them, following their motions, their faces dark.

"I can't see you very well," she said.

"That's probably okay."

"Walt?"

"This is tricky for me," he said.

"*What* is tricky for you?"

"I've never done anything like this."

"Like what?"

He let the hum of the crickets answer her. An old tree house hung between two firs on the far side of the flower bed filled with yellow lilies. Its presence suggested the children the Engletons never had, and for Walt it hung there like sadness.

"An investigation like this—probable homicide—is either straightforward or elliptical. When it's your case, you hope it'll be easy. Fast, and easy. When they drag out, they often go unsolved."

"This is about your case."

"And what happens is, some of the evidence is hard, some soft. Some you can take to court, some not. And then there's this gray area where evidence is soft when it first comes in but then firms up as the lab gets it or the chain is laid out properly. It's this no-man's-land where as the investigator you know something but can't legally prove it. At least not at the time. It's a dangerous and difficult minefield to negotiate because if you misstep, maybe you alert your suspect or the suspect's lawyer to what you have, and they're in front of it before you actually have it."

"Is your circumvention intentional?"

"Making matters more difficult," he said, as if not having heard her, "is that any of us can be made to testify in court as to what was done or what was said in any given circumstance. Including this one. Including me. For once in my career, maybe I don't want to get on the stand.

"There are databases—all sorts of databases out there now—for everything from fingerprints to DNA," he continued. "Felons, sure—known criminals. But also government employees, federal and state. Teachers. Military. Idaho maintains a database of the fingerprints of victims of abuse. In case a body should ever be found, or a kidnapping or abduction takes place. It's voluntary but, especially with minors, parents nearly always give their consent." He paused, allowing that all to sink in. "Just now, on the way up here . . . it's been one of those days where all the data comes in at once. I just picked up a voice mail from the lab. The way it works is the computers do the yeoman's job of searching the database, and then people take over, carefully studying the promising matches.

"Minors, victims of abuse under eighteen, *are nearly always in the system*." He made that as concrete as possible. "I need to ask you . . . on the record . . . so I need you to consider your answer carefully . . . Are you aware of the whereabouts of Kira Tulivich?"

"Do you mind if I get a glass of water or something?"

He told her he didn't mind. She brought them both lemonades a few minutes later. She placed hers in a cup holder attached to the lawn furniture and drew patterns on the sweating glass.

"You've won my attention," she said.

"I need you to answer the question."

"No. I don't know where she is. But I'm guessing you

found her prints on something." She made it a statement.

"I can't confirm or deny that, though I'd like to," he said. "What I *can* tell you, because it's soft evidence, is that I received the list server database, the e-mail list for people at possible risk from Martel Gale."

She drew a deep inhale through her nose, keeping her vision set straight ahead.

"If I'm going to help you," he said, reaching over and touching her arm, "and I want to help you because I care about you, I need to know. I need to know it all."

A minute or two passed. For him it felt much longer.

"Please. It's not the sheriff asking."

"I tried to stop my picture from running in the paper. I tried to get you to help me. I knew someone would see it. I knew he'd find out about it." She said nothing for a long time. He thought back to how he'd interpreted her attempts to stop the photos of the rescue as false modesty. If only she'd explained back then . . .

"The emergency room," she said. "I woke up with a lump on my head and not much memory of what happened. So as you've put this thing together, I've tried to figure it out from my side. I keep hoping something will help me remember. But so far, not so much."

He felt awash with relief. She had decided to talk, not close him out. He'd feared the latter. "Probably better if we talk hypothetically whenever possible," he said. "It won't always be possible."

"I'm not asking you to protect me."

"I didn't say you were. And you don't have to ask. But hypothetical is still better."

"But what I'm telling you is that I don't know. I don't think I can help you."

"An e-mail address—an anagram of your name—is on the list server for those at risk from Martel Gale."

"I'm sorry I didn't tell you." Several more minutes passed. Beatrice came out of the dark and lay down next to Walt; he reached down and scratched her head. "I didn't want you to know. Not you. Not anybody. Especially not you, not given . . . you know. *Us.* I was afraid what you'd think."

"You and Gale."

Her shadow faintly nodded on river rocks edging the garden. "It was supposed to be behind me."

"It still can be."

"No. Not now." She waited for what seemed like minutes. "I came here to get away from all that. Him. To get away and stay away. Kira . . . she and I, we share that. It's what allowed me to reach her in the first place, to help her find her way back. It could have been me giving that speech at the Advocates dinner, Walt. Marty—Martel— was . . . awful. People like that, they're insidious. You're afraid to leave. You know you can't stay. Stuff like that, a situation like that, it's a lot to go through. A lot more to get out of. But the worst of it is the labels people put on it, and how others see you once those labels are put on you, and I didn't want that. I wanted a clean slate. With you, of all people. You're in contact with that stuff. I didn't want you knowing. I didn't want you seeing me that way."

"Wouldn't happen. Won't happen."

"Easier said than done."

"You think I haven't seen this stuff? I'm telling you: it won't happen. I'm not that guy."

"The bottom line is, I was selfish. It was wrong of me."

He worked to control his breathing. He was both angry and scared. Scared that he would succumb to seeing her as she feared.

"I have to protect her," she said. "She doesn't need this. This is my problem, not hers. If she had any part in it . . . well, listen, he deserved what he got. I'm not putting her through this again . . ."

"It's not her I'm looking at," he admitted. "That's where the conflict comes in."

She gasped and turned her head fully toward him. "Seriously? But I assumed . . . I thought . . . She took off right after it happened. I just assumed . . ."

"Some of the most important evidence is still soft, Fiona. That's why we're talking. Why I'm here."

"Meaning? Help me through this, Walt. I don't know where we are, much less where we're going. Why *are* you here?"

"Because for the first time in a long time, I'm afraid to be right. I would do . . . I will do . . . nearly anything in my power to help you. Protect you. Keep this off you."

She continued looking off into the dark.

"When you found him. In that pile of stuff, that debris . . . When I saw him . . ."

He recalled how wrecked she'd been, how he'd put that off to the horrific condition of the body, not its identity.

"That—out there by the road—was the first I'd seen of him in twenty-six months and nine days," she said. "At least *I think* it was him. Let me ask you something: did his killing happen on the same night as my accident? Is that what you mean by you're not looking at Kira? The timing makes sense?"

He said nothing, weighing how to answer her without damaging them both down the road. He'd never been in this position. New territory.

"The timing didn't escape me," she told him. "And I could already hear the questions: Why hadn't I called in the breach of the restraining order? Why hadn't I at least told you or someone else about my connection to him when I had the chance? I'll tell you why: I panicked. My secret was still safe. My identity, my role in the trial, was sealed by the court; not even you could uncover I was the one who testified against him. I knew that much. No one could possibly connect the two of us. All I had to do was keep my mouth shut and let him be dead. But as it turns out, I underestimated the investigator. Should have known better."

"Have you done anything to protect Kira?" A question that had to be asked, but as it came out of him, it sounded more like an accusation.

"I beg your pardon?"

"Forgive me for even asking, but you said you couldn't let her become a suspect. What did you mean by that? Did you do something to protect her?"

"You think I messed with the investigation."

"You control our record of evidence. I just need to know—"

"My pictures? Are you kidding me?" She turned back. "That's unfair."

He searched for the right words, wondering how the law defined conspiracy.

"Unfair . . . of me," she said, correcting herself. "Did I consider it? Hell, yes. I printed the truck tires after it was returned to the garage." She left that hanging there like a knot of bugs around his head. "They're the right brand. The same tread. I couldn't be sure if they matched or not. I didn't see anything to say they did, but I have to admit I considered what I'd do if they did. I thought . . . I realized I could probably switch out the photos in your office. I mean, it's all electronic. You probably would have given me access if I'd asked. Did I consider it? Yes. Did I do it?"

He breathed a little easier. The logical next question, he couldn't ask: *Where were you that night?* A simple enough question. *Explain your head injury that's on record at the hospital.* In fact, he nearly asked both of these. But he stopped himself, knowing the code that would bind him if either answer proved revelatory. He not only didn't want the answers, he didn't want to have to lie about having asked them, if it ever came to that.

"I'd seen her nearly come after you that night you were poking around the cottage. It's not like there was blood or anything in my house. There was nothing in there, my place, to suggest . . . I thought maybe it had happened outside. And if so, I had a pretty good idea who'd done it."

"The lilies," he said. "The pollen wasn't from Vince Wynn's." Not fifteen feet in front of them, like a carpet beneath the tree house, was a flower bed of yellow lilies. "The body was dragged through a flower bed of lilies. Dragged up a hill—way up a hill—and dumped. Rolled off and down a scree slide into some avalanche slash at the side of the highway. The evidence we have supports that scenario. It just took us a while to piece it together. That's what we call hard evidence."

"Her taking off without a word. Not answering my calls. Taking the truck when that's totally off-limits. I know her, Walt. It's just not like her. But listen to me: she can't take this. Do you understand? She won't survive this. If she did this . . . if she's put through something like this again . . . She is beyond fragile right now, has been for a long time. She's young."

Should he tell her again that he was no longer looking at Kira? He thought not. He sipped the lemonade to open his throat.

His ability to refrain from and resist corruption through several terms defined him. It was not only a matter of pride, but a matter of identity. So ingrained in him that to contemplate otherwise made him feel physically sick. He searched for a way to do this without doing it. To remain true to himself but to limit collateral damage. *To protect and serve*, he thought.

"The idea behind what I do," he found himself saying in a whisper of a voice, "is to serve the public, to do so equally, uniformly, to treat people fairly and equally, the idea being that you make society safer. I accept that that's a naïve attitude, but there you have it. Safe to live and work and to limit or eliminate fear. As much as it's a cliché, fear is in fact the real enemy. Fear limits us all. The fear of illness is often much greater than the illness itself. The fear of crime is the same way. So I'm supposed to keep the crime down and to bring in those who commit crimes when they happen, and those two things are supposed to work in concert."

"I realize how hard this must be. I'm so sorry, Walt."

He drew in another lungful of air like it was his last. Exhaled. "Harder on you, I know. I can bend the laws, Fiona. I can't break them."

"Understood. And I don't want you to have to do either."

"It's supposed to rain tonight," he said.

"Walt . . ."

"Bear with me," he pleaded. "A lightning strike can set an area on fire. Spark a little wildfire that burns an acre or two before help arrives. You're pretty high here on this knoll. And you're what, about a mile from the

East Fork station house? They'd probably respond in under ten minutes. Five minutes, more like. Five minutes *from the time of the call*."

"Walt?"

"The thing about a small fire like that . . . you'd have to have the right winds so it didn't hit any buildings. Not much wind tonight, not at the moment, which is good. The thing about blood evidence in the wild? It stays there for a long, long time. It's recoverable weeks, months, sometimes years later. Rain doesn't do much to it. Snow. Ice. But wildfire . . . fire's the one thing that destroys it."

An owl screeched from deep in the woods. Bea lifted her head but thought better of it. He heard Fiona swallow and noted her lemonade was still in the drink holder.

"I see," she said.

"It's a two-edged sword," he cautioned. "When a fire's called in, of course they respond, but we do, too. We're on the property. We have access at that point."

"I can't possibly do something like that."

"Who said anything about you doing anything?" he said, as if it were the farthest thing from his mind. "It would be entirely improper for me to suggest such a thing. I was simply talking about lightning strikes in general. If a fire started out here, obviously you'd call it in. And they'd be up here *quickly*." He dragged himself up out of the chair. Bea jumped to her feet.

Fiona remained seated. "I worked so hard to put all this behind me." She spoke straight ahead as if the forest were listening.

"When the evidence firms up—and it will—we're going to act on it. It's what we do."

"The thing is," she said. "A guy like him. He ruins things forever. They talk about second chances, but there are none. People warned me, but I didn't want to believe it."

"Even after a fire, you put a little water on it and a forest grows back again. Sometimes prettier than it was. I imagine the same is true for flower beds."

"Were you listening to me?" she asked caustically.

"What's important here is whether or not you're listening to me," he said.

"Is that right?"

"Yeah, that's right."

"What you're asking—it's impossible."

"I'm not *asking* anything," he said. "I thought I made that clear."

"Telling me, asking me, whatever."

"Shit happens," he said.

"Do not go there. Do not even think that. That's not you. You do something like that and it'll be there between us forever. It won't bind us. Don't fool yourself. It'll be there between us, something you'll regret, something you'll always hold against me. Promise me you won't do this."

"Focus on what we talked about."

"I know what you're asking. I just think—"

"Don't think!" he said. "There's a time for thinking and a time for doing."

"Is that right? I don't think so."

"Don't make this into something it isn't," he cautioned. "Remember what I said about investigations. About evidence. Striving to better, we often wreck what's well."

"Don't lay that on me."

"I didn't lay anything on anyone. I'm paraphrasing Shakespeare: 'oft we mar what's well.'"

"You blame me already."

"I don't blame people, I arrest them, Fiona. I have no plan to make any arrests in the near future."

"No plans right now," she qualified.

"Right now," he said, going along with her, "I've got nothing in terms of hard evidence."

The owl called again and a coyote followed.

Chills ran up Walt's spine.

"Feels like rain," she said.

"I've got to go. I left Kevin at the house, and it's late, even for him."

"Too late?" she asked.

He came up behind her chair and lowered his head next to hers from behind. He kissed her on the left cheek, kept their cheeks touching until he felt the wetness of her tears. Wiped her right cheek with his thumb, pressed their heads together.

"You are not alone," he said. "Trust that."

She shook her head, their cheeks slapping.

"I mean it."

She nodded, sniffling, fighting a losing battle.

"Go," she whispered.

Walt clucked for Bea and the dog jumped up, holding obediently by his side until together they reached the Jeep.

40

Walt thanked Kevin for sitting his sleeping children, as he walked him to his car.

"How'd all that baseball bat stuff work out?" Kevin asked, as they stood outside on the front porch. The summer insects were in full throat, the smell of fresh-cut grass and burning charcoal lingering in the air. These were the nights Walt lived for, but this particular one he wished he'd never been through, his head reeling.

"Hmm?"

"*El Kabob?*" Kevin said, making a motion with both arms, bringing them down sharply from overhead.

Walt shuddered, wondering how he was going to handle this. *Some cases go cold.*

"That work is confidential, you know?" He delivered it as a rebuke, and regretted it immediately.

"Whatever. I was just asking."

"It's a work in progress. I appreciate your contribution."

"This isn't a press conference."

"Sorry. I'm kind of preoccupied."

"Would never have noticed," Kevin said sarcastically. He didn't seem to want to go. It was nearing one a.m.

"Everything good?" Walt asked.

"Sure, I guess."

"Your mother?"

"Same. A head case."

"She means well."

"Been thinking about asking Summer up." There it was, the reason for his delay. Summer was a girl Walt knew well, a girl that had nearly gotten his nephew killed. And yet he liked her. They both did.

"For a visit? That's a good idea."

"Thing of it is, I can't exactly ask her to stay with us. Mom has, like, totally taken over the other bedroom, and hell if I'm sleeping on the couch and parading around in my skivvies, and even if we got the other bedroom happening, there's only the one bathroom for the two rooms, the one in the hall, and that would be, like, totally not cool."

"She could stay here," Walt said, knowing where this was heading.

"With the girls! Yeah, that's what I was thinking. Take care of the girls for you—we could do that together. You think? Seriously?"

"There are not a lot of high school kids who would want to stay at a sheriff's house. You'll want to clear it with her first. I wouldn't hold my breath if I were you."

"She doesn't think·like that with you."

"I put her father in jail."

"True." It was as if he'd forgotten. "Yeah. Well. But I could ask, right? You're offering."

"I am."

"It would only be a couple days. Three or four days." He seemed to be talking himself into this, or needing encouragement.

"Long way to come for a long weekend. Ask her for the week. With your working and all, it's not as if you'll have a ton of time together."

"I'm hoping I can juggle my schedule."

"That might work."

"Seriously, though: you don't mind?"

"I don't mind. Happy to do it."

It was as if the sun had come out in the middle of the night. He smiled widely and stayed on his toes a beat longer than he had to, balancing up there, extending his arms as if he might take flight.

"Smells like rain."

"It does."

Walt remained on the porch and watched him drive off, waving once as a final thank-you.

As he was heading inside, his BlackBerry buzzed, announcing the arrival of a text message, a rare thing for him.

Call me when ur up—B

Walt called Brandon's cell.

"Damn! Didn't mean to wake you, Sheriff."

"No, Tommy. I'm up."

"What are you doing awake at this hour?" Brandon asked.

"I could ask the same thing."

"You aren't lying in a bed with a hose stuck in your chest."

"No, but I feel like it. How you doing, other than the hose?" Walt asked.

"Appreciate your hanging around here. Gail told me."

"Was worried about you, Tommy."

"Doing fine. They're going to fill up the flat tire, and I'm walking out of here. Like maybe tomorrow, if I'm lucky. Any sign of my shooter?"

"We're on it."

"So, nothing."

"He took off. I'm optimistic. Forest Service is scouring the camps west of the highway below Cold Springs. Guys like this, they get in a rut. He won't go far."

"Smack him around for me when you catch him."

"Yeah, that's my style," Walt quipped. "What's up, Tommy?"

"Wanted you to check the property room."

"For?"

"Not much to do here but watch the tube or stare out the window."

"Yeah . . . ?"

"So I was looking out the window and saw this hawk circling."

"Tommy, I don't mind the call, but it *is* late."

"So you suppose there's any chance that's what the truck was about? Not a deer, but the hawk?"

Walt heard the sounds of the night like a hum in his head.

"Not sure where you're going with this, Tommy."

"Hawks feed on carrion. Like roadkill. Wouldn't be the first time we've seen a wreck caused by mowing over a hawk or eagle."

"Does that change anything?" Walt asked.

"Truck hits a hawk and skids off the road."

"So what?" Walt asked. He checked his watch, suddenly feeling extremely tired.

"The driver knows what he hit," Brandon said, speculating. "Maybe there's some of it smeared on the windshield. He skids off the road, but gets out. Your witness gave us that."

"I'm listening." Indeed, Walt was perched forward on the edge of the bench.

"The truck, the tracks we found, had nothing to do with Gale," Brandon proposed. "He never saw the body. His attention was on finding that bird."

"The bird . . ."

"Flight feathers," Brandon said.

"I'd like to say I'm following you, Tommy, but I'm afraid I'm not."

"Who gives a shit about a dead bird?" Brandon asked. "Sure, maybe he wanted to go back and stomp the thing for sending him off the road like that. But I don't think so. I think he wanted the flight feathers."

Walt shifted the phone to his left ear. "Flight feathers," he repeated.

"Light rack on the roof of the pickup. What kind of fool is that?"

"Search and Rescue, maybe." Walt said, taking issue with his description. "A volunteer firefighter."

"Or just your basic backwoods asshole."

"Lovely."

"A tricked-out pickup truck? A backwoods yahoo."

"A hunter?"

"Now don't go putting down hunters," Brandon said.

"This is your theory, Tommy. *Whatever it is.*"

"Not your everyday hunter: a *bow* hunter."

Walt heard himself breathing into the phone. "The feathers."

"Dude!" Brandon said. "The hawk runs the guy off the road. Driver knows what he hit. Finds himself off-road, maybe sees the hawk flapping away in the mirror. Heads back to check out his victim—"

"Our witness confirmed that," Walt said, recalling the woman at the nursery.

"Any bow hunter knows it's a felony to collect feathers from a wild bird. But this one ran him off the road. This one asked for it. He isn't about to risk the fine by taking the whole bird, but he lifts a couple feathers. Who's going to notice?"

"You are," Walt said.

"We can check it. Right? I collected that bird. It's in the property room fridge."

"So the BOLO should include an inspection of the front grille."

"Could be easier than that. A pickup sucks a bird in the grille, it's not going off the road. But if the bird hits the windshield, that's another story."

"A broken windshield."

"A red-tailed hawk? Going fifty or sixty, it's like hitting a freaking rock."

"Window welders. Window repair shops."

"A pickup with a light rack," Brandon said. "That ought to narrow it down. We catch this guy, maybe he saw Gale, maybe not. But he's someone we want to talk to."

"It'll be good to have you back," Walt said. The first raindrops fell in huge splashes on his front walkway. Lightning flashed high in the sky to the north.

"Keep me posted, Sheriff. And just in case anyone asks: daytime TV sucks."

"I'll pass that along."

Walt was at the foot of his bed. He had his shirt off and was stripping down to his shorts when he heard the distant grind of heavy machinery. Living just two blocks from the town's firehouse, he knew exactly what it was. He crossed the room, grabbed his radio off the dresser, and called dispatch.

The fire was north. Mile 125. Cold Springs drainage. A BCS patrol had been dispatched. Walt had his pants buttoned and was reaching for his gun belt as he simultaneously called Kevin.

Fifteen minutes later, Kevin returned, wearing pajama bottoms and a T-shirt. He climbed from behind the wheel of his beat-up Subaru and passed Walt on the front porch without a word.

Walt hurried to the Jeep.

41

Pulses of blue and white lights flashed in the treetops as Walt merged the Jeep into the phalanx of fire trucks and emergency vehicles. Fiona, wearing a T-shirt and full-length pajama bottoms, stood at the door to her cottage, arms crossed against the chill. Her hair down and tousled, she looked both tired and frightened, her attention fixed up the hill where rising whiffs of smoke still faintly clouded the air. Four firemen, clad in turn-outs and armed with pickaxes and shovels, were chasing down the last vestiges of fire, the buried, smoldering plant roots that could hold fire for days.

She didn't see him arrive. But when he told Beatrice to stay, Fiona must have heard his voice and she turned toward him, her solemn expression like a veil. He took away only this: she'd heard him over the shouts and pumps and diesel engines; she'd recognized his voice with only the single word spoken. Somehow, this gave him hope.

The fire had consumed an acre of hill, singeing the bark of the fir and pine trees, destroying the flower bed where Walt had stood with her only hours earlier. It left behind a black carpet of charred pine straw and the gray ash of what had been lawn grass.

Another sheriff's office cruiser rolled in, only seconds behind him. Two deputies: Blompier and Chalmers. They clambered out and looked to him for instruction.

"Search the main house. Confirm it's vacant."

He walked slowly to her, wondering what he was going to say.

"I swear," she said, beating him to it. She hung her head, shaking it side to side. "I know how this looks, but it isn't true."

"I didn't say anything."

Lowering her voice to where he could barely hear, she said, "Tell me you're not involved, Walt. If you did this for me—"

"Me? I'm not involved."

"Seriously?"

"Do you honestly think I'd do something like this?"

They studied one another in the flashes of colored light.

Was he to believe this charade? After their discussion about this very act? Or was she playing out the hand he'd dealt her? Attempting to keep the cover story going?

"A lightning strike," he said.

She said nothing, but snorted her derision. Her arms crossed more tightly, she lifted her head, wearing a look of incipient terror.

"I was asleep," she whispered, though defensively. "It could have burned the cottage . . . I could have . . ."

A shudder passed through her head to toe.

For a fleeting moment he was tempted to want to believe her, but the moment passed.

"You called it in?" he asked.

"I smelled it," she said. "Idaho air-conditioning. Without that . . . who knows?"

Few homes in the area carried any kind of air-conditioning. With forty-degree summer nights, the trick was to throw all your windows wide open and chill the house down and shut it back up again before eight a.m. A well-insulated house could remain cool the remainder of the day.

"Might have saved your life."

"That's what I'm saying."

He kept waiting for the wink or the nudge, but it wasn't forthcoming. She wasn't going to give him so much as an inch of rope.

"Okay, then," he said.

"You don't believe me?" Spoken as if it had just occurred to her.

"Of course I believe you."

The flashing light continued to play across their faces. She looked at him searchingly. Probing.

"I should get on with it . . ." he said.

"Yes."

"Get a jacket or something. It's chilly out here."

"I'm fine," she said.

"It's cold. Get a jacket," he repeated, heading off to a firefighter he recognized as the one in charge.

"Any ideas?"

"Storm strike," the man said. He was tall and broad-shouldered and had a deep voice. "Best guess."

"Yeah," Walt said.

"It's usually a tree takes the strike, but I'm no expert."

"Got it," Walt said, wanting to leave it right there. "Anything you need from us?"

"We're good. Another thirty or forty minutes. I'll send some guys back up here in an hour or two to make sure there're no flare-ups. You might tell her, so she doesn't scare." He jerked a shoulder toward Fiona.

"Will do."

Walt turned back downhill.

"Sheriff?"

"Yeah?"

"Shape of the fire doesn't add up, in case you care. We should have a pear shape running uphill like this. But if you'll notice, it's flipped upside down. Since when does fire run *downhill*?"

"That *is* or isn't significant?" Walt asked. "You didn't mention that when I asked."

"It's different, that's all. Significant? It's not like I can put down a lightning strike to arson. Right? But it's unusual. In case you care. That's all."

"Of course I care," Walt said a little too defensively.

"Not something we see very often, if at all."

"I got it," Walt said.

"Okay. Okay." The guy huffed, turned, and swung his pickax into the ground, spraying ash and soil. Walt couldn't be sure, but he thought he heard him say something under his breath: "Asshole."

Worst of all, he thought he probably deserved it.

"Sheriff?" Deputy Linda Chalmers called out from the front door of the main house. Deputy Blompier stood just inside the house in silhouette.

It took Walt a moment to see the person wedged between them, the shorter girl, her arm clasped tightly in Linda's hand. Took him yet another fraction of a second to process that it was Kira Tulivich. His mind made the identification, and then his eyes tracked over to Fiona, whose surprise appeared too genuine to be anything but. Barefoot, Fiona walked half on tiptoe as she crossed the driveway. She looked up the hill to Walt and back to Kira, mirroring him.

"Found her in a room off the wine cellar," Chalmers explained as Walt reached them.

"A safe room. Hot plate. Chemical toilet. The works," Blompier supplied.

"What safe room?" Fiona said, reaching them.

"Blompier, your jacket," Walt instructed. The deputy peeled off his jacket and Walt placed it around Fiona's shoulders. She tugged it around herself tightly and seemed to shrink.

Kira, looking tired, could not take her eyes off Fiona. It was this heated, locked stare of hers that interested Walt. It wasn't a look of daughter to mother, or friend to friend, but one of incredulity, concern. That was it, he thought, the girl was afraid for her, projecting sympathy. Had Kira overheard them talking at the garden? Had she lit the fire? Had she killed Martel Gale, as the evidence suggested? Walt had no choice but to act upon the evidence.

"Kira," he said, his voice subdued, "I'd like you to come down to my office with me for a talk."

"Now?" Fiona complained. She tried to win Kira's attention.

Walt spoke up immediately. "Yes. Now. For the time being I'm asking, but it can get more complicated than that."

Kira's focus remained on the sheriff. "Sure. I can do that."

42

Walt wouldn't have offered any visitor a personal explanation; any one of his deputies or the desk sergeant could convey the procedures and practices well enough. But the woman sitting alone in a row of chairs, separated by a table holding *People* magazine and copies of *Western Sheriffs' Association*, was not just any visitor.

"Since when don't you video an interview?" Fiona said angrily.

"We are videoing the interview," Walt said calmly. "It wouldn't be approp—"

"Oh, bull."

"—for you to be in the room."

"It's one in the morning."

"It is."

"You should do this tomorrow."

"Let's not get into this, okay? I'm doing what I have to do. Kira is here voluntarily."

"So what? You think it's a conspiracy?" she choked out. "Really, Walt!"

"Of all people, you've been around this enough to know the way it works."

"You try not to judge," she said.

"That's right."

"That's a pile of crap."

"It's voluntary. Exploratory. You think I'm incapable of keeping an open mind?"

"I'm like her guardian or something. I need to be in there with her."

"She's not a minor."

"You notified her parents?"

"That's up to her. I don't believe she has."

"An attorney?"

This was a sticking point. A matter of investigative leverage. "She has not requested a lawyer, and there's no reason she should. She has not been charged with anything. This is exploratory."

"Walt," she chided.

"I'm sorry you came all the way down here. I don't mean to shut you out. Please know that." He remained on his feet, avoiding the chairs. He did not want to get into this with her.

"You can't conduct this interview without an attorney present. She doesn't know any better. Why won't you look at me? Look at me please." He turned. "Oh, Jesus," she said. "You'd actually do something like this?"

"Like what? It's voluntary. It's necessary."

She stood and lowered her voice, taking his forearm in hand and squeezing. "You think you're helping me somehow? Is that it? I can see it in your eyes."

How was that possible? How could she nail his thoughts so perfectly? He wanted back behind the restricted door and into his world, but her grip only tightened.

"Listen to me," she said in a tone he would have rather not heard. "If you put this on her, I will be forced to . . . I will not let her be charged with this."

"She hasn't been charged, Fiona. But this—the way you're acting, isn't helping anything. Let me do my job. *I know what I'm doing.*" He let that sit there a second.

"But maybe you've forgotten who you're doing it to."

"We have evidence—hard evidence—that has to be accounted for. For all your good intentions—and I believe in them—there's a process. A procedure. We're just at the start of that. She answers these questions honestly, she walks out of here for now. If an attorney gets into it, it will prejudice the interview. That's when I get backed into a corner and things get tricky. Let's not get there. Let's avoid that."

"You're setting her up."

"I am absolutely not setting her up!" He'd raised his voice. It reverberated against the high ceiling. The receptionist on the other side of the window kept her head down.

He lowered his voice to a hush. "Listen to me. I care for that girl, and I care about you. At some point you have to trust me. I happen to know what I'm doing."

"She's innocent."

"Good. Then there is nothing to worry about."

She started for the doors, turning to look back at him once and put an exclamation point onto her disgust. Then she reconsidered. "No," she said. "I'm not going. I'm not giving you that. I'll be right here. Waiting. I'm not going anywhere."

"Suit yourself," Walt said, heading back through the door that cloistered him.

He mumbled to himself as he strode down the hall toward the first interview room, where he would find Deputy Linda Chalmers behind the video camera. Truth was, there was nothing to operating the camera; he asked Fiona to do the recording as a way to slip her extra income and get a chance to see her. She had begun to seep into his work and his decision making in ways like this, and he saw it for what it was—trouble—while still feeling no desire to change it. He opened the door and looked at the young woman on the other side of the table, frightened, unsure. Deputy Blompier sat in the chair to the left, by the wall. Walt took the only other chair facing Kira.

"You okay?" he began. Something transformed in him the moment he took his chair. A voice in his head said "game on." *Establish a rapport. Mimic language. Control emotions. Manipulate.*

The empty chair to her left, the chair intended for an

attorney, called out to him. Was he supposed to charge
her and fill that chair for her, to give up the slight advantage he held by her not being represented? Did that help
anyone?

Kira held a fixed stare of bewilderment and fear. He
reminded himself beguilement took on many faces, came
in all sizes and ages. Whether or not she might attempt to
play him, he couldn't tell. Her dazed expression seemed
real enough. But one learned in the narrow confines of
these interview rooms to put away interpretation, to
ignore the suspect's beauty or the tattoos or the lack of
language skills and to drill down. So he took a second to
make himself comfortable in the chair, his decision made.
He took a deep, calming breath and exhaled, placed his
forearms onto the table, a man determined, his body language as practiced, as important, as each word, each
inflection. He lived for such moments.

He glanced over his shoulder. Chalmers gave him a
nod: tape was running.

"Do you want a glass of water or a Coke or anything?"

"I'm okay, thank you."

"You understand why you're here?"

She nodded. "To talk."

"That's right. Do you have any questions?"

"I don't get it. Why me? What'd I do?"

"Why do you think you're here?"

"That guy getting killed and all."

"You're referring to Martel Gale."

"I guess."

Walt opened a file folder and slid a photograph in front of her. He'd had two choices: an NFL photo, or the crime scene—half the guy's face eaten off. It wasn't out of the question that in certain interviews he would have chosen the crime scene photo, but not here. Not her.

"Have you ever seen this man before?"

She nodded.

"It's important you answer aloud," Walt said.

"Yes," she said.

"Please describe the circumstances of the last time you saw him."

"The only time I saw him, you mean."

"The only time, then."

"You were there," she said. "It was the night of the Advocates dinner."

Walt caught his breath but maintained his composure.

"I'd seen . . . She'd showed me . . . Never mind. I knew who he was, that's all."

Walt hesitated, facing a fork in the road. He knew who she was referring to. *Some cases go cold.* He felt obliged to pursue the identity of "she," but understood not to. He was painfully aware of the camera aimed at the back of his head.

"You knew who he was," he said, making it a statement.

"The football guy."

"You follow pro football, do you?"

"Not exactly."

"But you recognized a linebacker who's been out of the league for several years. Can you explain that?"

"I knew who he was. I don't remember how." As her eyes lowered to the desk, and her shoulders caved forward, he thought even a first-year graduate student could identify the lie from her body language.

"Seeing him . . . Was that when you stopped for a second in your talk, your address, your speech? You're right: I was there, and I remember your . . . interrupting yourself."

"Might have been."

"Seeing this man caused that kind of reaction? Why is that?" Why couldn't he bring himself to just ask her the identity of the woman she'd referred to? Why did he insist on dancing around the edges?

"Roy Coats," she said, naming the man who had brutally assaulted her a few years before. Walt winced at the mention of the man, his memory still holding on to the grainy webcam images of the violent sexual abuse this young woman had endured. His brain lacked the delete button he sometimes wished it had. "I don't get exactly why. I don't expect you to get it. But when that guy opened the doors back there and looked inside, it wasn't him I saw, it was Roy Coats. That happens to me pretty much all the time. In Atkinson's, out on the street. Can be anywhere. I just see him. He's looking at me that way he looked at me. Like he knew what he was going to do to me, and me having no clue. Like that. Like people look when they know a secret you don't. And it makes me physically sick. Like I'm going to puke. I want to scream. I want to scratch his eyes out. Castrate him. Kill him." She looked up from what had looked like a trance.

Walt felt a jolt. Neither of them had wanted her to say that word.

"Not that I ever would," she added quickly. "I didn't mean it that way. Look: that was the only time I ever saw the guy. I'm telling the truth. That one time in the Limelight Room. I hadn't seen him again until just now when you put his picture down here." She reached out and touched the photograph. "That came out all wrong."

Yes, it did, Walt thought. "Roy Coats," Walt clarified. "You wanted to kill Roy Coats."

"Exactly. But he's dead. Look, I know that. Okay? I know he's dead. But what your mind knows and the rest of you feels are two different things. And that particular time, I saw Roy Coats and all that stuff came back."

"And that's the only time you saw Martel Gale?"

"Yes."

Walt pulled the photo back and returned it to the folder. The job turned sordid too often. At times like this he wondered: why him? Why law enforcement? Why expose yourself to this stuff? "Where do you live?"

"I'm staying, house-sitting at the moment, up at the Engletons' place."

"The residence of Leslie and Michael Engleton."

"Yes."

"In the main house or the guest cottage?"

"Fiona lives in the guest cottage. I'm house-sitting the main house."

"Fiona Kenshaw. Our crime scene photographer."

"Yes."

"For how long have you been residing at the Engle-ton residence?"

"They're on this trip. You know, for like the whole summer. I've been there . . . I don't know . . . two months? Another month or so to go."

"You and I have seen each other there," Walt said.

"Yes."

"You came after me with a baseball bat in your hand."

"Yeah. Sorry about that. There's that guy in the woods around there. That guy you're looking for. It was dark. I didn't know it was you. You looking in the window and all. I thought you were a peeping Tom or something."

Walt felt himself flush, an uncontrollable reaction.

"Tell me about the baseball bat."

"I don't know. It's Michael's, I guess. He has a bunch of them in the sports thing out in the garage. Fiona and I . . . we both put one by the door. You know. In case that guy came around."

In fact, Walt did not know, had not heard. He didn't recall seeing a bat by the door to Fiona's cottage. Had there been one? Had it been moved? Had it been left in the rental car? Dangerous territory. He steered slightly away.

"What purpose did the bat serve?"

"You know? When you're scared. Like that."

"To strike an intruder."

"Not that I ever have, or would. But, yeah, I guess. Closest I ever got was hitting you. And I didn't do that. I can't even kill spiders. I have to ask Fiona to do that. Call her over to the house. Nothing seems to bother her."

Why did it have to keep coming back to Fiona?

"If a man like Martel Gale came onto the property unannounced and you saw him in the dark. A big guy. Huge guy. If he turned on you. If he scared you, any reaction on your part could be considered self-defense. Do you understand that?"

"I get what you're saying, but that's not what happened."

"The thing about a voluntary interview . . . well, for one thing we're recording all this on video, as you know. For another, none of us can take back what we say. It's incredibly important that you tell the truth the first time. The very first time. That you stick to the truth, no matter how hard it may be to speak of it. The law . . . it isn't black and white the way you might think. That's not the way it actually works. We think of it that way: right and wrong. In practice, it works a lot differently. A guy comes onto your property uninvited, comes on there at a time there's some guy vandalizing neighborhood properties, maybe late at night when it's hard to see clearly. He surprises you and you defend yourself"—she was shaking her head violently side to side—"especially a person, any person, with a past that makes overreaction understandable. It's all viewed differently. Each case is viewed differently."

"That didn't happen."

"I'm just saying, you want to stick to the truth."

"I am. I didn't do that. It's not like that. I saw him once at the Limelight Room. That was it. Only then."

And a few minutes later, Fiona left the room without notice, Walt thought. He'd followed outside and had quizzed the kids working the valet parking. They'd all but identified the visitor as Martel Gale.

"We . . . my deputies . . . conducted a search of the Engleton residence. We found no baseball bat by the front door of the main residence," Walt said. He left out that none had been found at the cottage either. "We located the ones in the sports cabinet, as you've mentioned. But nothing by the front door. Can you account for that bat's whereabouts?"

"No idea."

"Has it been missing?"

"No idea."

"Why's that?"

"I have no idea where I left it. That night I saw you? I don't know what I did with it. I could have left it outside, for all I know. Anyway, it's not like I was hanging around in the main part of the house. I've been in the safe room."

"And why is that?"

She looked as if he'd slapped her.

"Did you leave the residence for a while?"

"I did."

"In what vehicle?"

"I'd rather not say."

"I'm afraid I have to ask you to answer the question."

"The truck. I'm not supposed to drive the pickup truck. Okay? I get it. I blew it. But I drove the truck. I went over to Yellowstone like Fiona said. But the campgrounds were full, so I slept in the truck a couple of nights, and couldn't stand it, and came back here."

Like Fiona said. "You were in communication with Ms. Kenshaw during this absence?" He hated dragging her back into it. Could he find a way to just end it?

"No, I wasn't."

"But you just said—"

"She was bugging me. Okay? Leaving messages and stuff and, I don't know, it was like my parents or something. I just wasn't interested."

The answer felt rehearsed. She'd expected that question long before the interview had begun. It knocked him back on his heels. How much of this had been rehearsed? How much had he missed because of his own interest in the outcome of the interview? Would he pick up things in replaying the tape?

"If you're trying to get me to say something about Fiona, I'm not going to."

Walt's chest tightened. Could he instruct Chalmers to shut off the video? Could he call a break to the interview?

"What would I want you to say about Ms. Kenshaw?"

She locked eyes with him. "I'm not going to say it," she said.

"Tell me about that night," Walt said.

"What night?"

"Late the twelfth. Early morning the thirteenth."

"Nothing. There's nothing to tell."

"Someone came onto the property—drove an SUV onto the property." Speculation was part of any interrogation, but he knew he was on thin ice. "If you didn't see him, as you've stated, you must have heard him. You could hear cars arrive, couldn't you?"

"There's a bell that rings. It's one of those electronic eye things at the gate."

This was new information for Walt.

"When a vehicle enters," Walt said.

"Yeah. That's how big the house is. You can't hear squat in there. The gate's like in a different zip code. Without the bell you'd probably never know someone was out there."

"Late night the twelfth."

"I told you: I didn't see him."

"But you heard a bell."

"The bell rang a few different times. It wasn't like I jumped up to see what was going on."

"Wasn't it?"

"No, it wasn't."

"So you were used to visitors late at night?" He realized what he'd said—what he'd asked—too late.

"I saw your car out there a couple of times. Your police car."

He closed his eyes and took a deep breath, glad that

his face was off camera. He never had trouble thinking when in these rooms. An interview was supposed to sharpen his wits, engage him. The deeper he dug, the faster the sand poured back down in, burying him. He reminded himself he was not the one being interviewed. He reminded himself that he didn't need to react to or explain anything. He was the one in charge.

"So you're suggesting you did in fact look outside when you heard that tone."

She looked stunned. "Maybe . . . I guess so."

"You did or you didn't look out that night? Late night the twelfth, maybe the early hours of the thirteenth?"

Her eyes told him the whole story: concealment, fear, an overwhelming sense of emotion.

A knock interrupted him. He could have screamed. He was never to be interrupted during an interview. He collected himself, nodded, and let Blompier open the door for him.

"Sheriff," his receptionist said with urgency in her voice. "Peter Arian's here."

Arian, a young public defender who was recently winning far too many cases as far as Walt was concerned, could only be there for one reason. But Walt played along.

"So?"

"He says he's representing Ms. Tulivich."

Walt shut the door.

"Ms. Tulivich, did you contact a lawyer? We were not aware of—"

"No, I didn't."

Fiona! he realized. Anger competed with resignation. He felt the wind knocked out of him. Mindful of the video, he kept his cool. "You'll excuse me for a moment. The interview will now pause," he said for the sake of the video.

Sandbagged by a possible suspect. He thought he'd identified a seam to exploit, a way to let the system do his work for him. Fiona had just turned all that on its head.

"But if there's a lawyer here—"

"It doesn't work like that. I'll be right back."

Out in the hall, he told his deputy, "Show Ms. Kenshaw to Interview two, will you please."

"Fiona?" the deputy clarified.

"Interview two," Walt repeated. "Mr. Arian will see me in my office."

"Yes, sir."

He waited for the choreography to play out. Closing his office door, he met with Arian first.

"Sheriff, I'd like to see my client, if you don't mind."

"She's not your client, Peter. She has not called for an attorney and you cannot solicit clients in this building. You know the rules."

"It's one a.m. and I'm here to see Kira Tulivich."

"Take a seat at reception if you want, but you won't see her until I'm done speaking with her."

"Her guardian appointed me—"

"Kira Tulivich is not a minor, and you know it."

"She's been under the care and responsibility of—"

"Take it up with the courts if you want, counselor.

But not here. Not tonight. She's here voluntarily and she's staying here voluntarily."

Arian stood. "By tomorrow, it's a different playing field, Sheriff. Shorter field for me. Longer for you. You might want to think about that. I don't like getting out of bed at one in the morning. Affects my mood in the morning."

"Take an Ambien. You'll sleep like a baby." Walt opened the office door. "Good night, counselor."

He then joined Fiona in Interview 2. She looked smug and confident, but it was a fragile veneer.

"You're pissed at me," she said.

He stared her down, unflinchingly.

"I had to," she said. "She's entitled to representation."

His eyes darted to the soundproof door, ensuring it was shut tightly. "Do you really think the right thing to do is to play me? The two of you? I take it you have an end game in mind. You mind cluing me in on what it is *exactly*?"

She glared back at him. "What's that mean?"

"There's a dead body in the hospital cooler and I need answers. You and Kira are right in the middle of this."

"You think I killed him?"

"You're protecting her. She's protecting you. Do you actually think I can't see that? Do you actually think you can keep this up? It's a homicide, Fiona. It doesn't get any more serious than this."

She squinted. "I'm worried about you."

He slapped the table. She jumped back.

"Homicide! I'm talking about the fire. I'm talking about a baseball bat from Michael Engleton's collection. I'm talking about you and Kira doing this dance that's growing really old and is not going to hold up. You want *attorneys* involved? You'd rather have Peter Arian handling this than me? Jesus!" He breathed deeply, trying to calm himself. "You two had better get in front of this. I had a plan—one you've just made a hell of a lot more complicated. I hope to hell you have one, because this thing is coming apart on you—on *both* of you."

"You think I set that fire? Are you still playing like you didn't do that for me? You want to talk? Talk."

"Me?" he asked incredulously. "This is me we're talking about."

"And I'm supposed to believe you?"

He reached across the table and took her hand in his. "Now. Right here, right now. You look me in the eye and tell me you didn't set that fire."

"I didn't set that fire."

His mind raced. "No way," he mumbled.

"I . . . told . . . you . . . I . . . didn't."

"Kira? Do you think she could have overheard us?"

"From inside that house? I don't think so, Walt. You can't hear anything from in there. It's a fortress. And if she was in the safe room—a room I didn't even know existed!—you really think so?"

"You should never have brought Peter Arian into this. You send him packing. I can work this out *if you'd just let me*."

"Let you railroad Kira? I don't think so."

"'Some cases go cold,'" he said back at her.

"What?"

"You said that to me."

"Did I?"

His patience tested, he fought to stay in his chair. "Yes, you did. I'm attempting to bring charges against her. You have to stay out of this."

"I will not stay out of it. I will not allow that. She's been through—"

"This is my job. My world. Stay out of it."

"Is that an order, Sheriff?" All life had gone out of her. She leaned away from him, nearly tipping over the chair.

"If I can't push Arian off the base, if he gets to her, then my game plan is over. At that point, you two will need to get in front of this." A mechanical silence hung between them—the eerie whisper of HVAC. "Terry Hogue's the best criminal lawyer in town. You call Terry."

"What plan," she said. "You said you have a plan."

"Had," he corrected. "I said I *had* a plan. With Arian in the mix, the evidence is going to come out, and that's coming back to bite her."

But a worm started drilling through his head: the unidentified prints on the baseball bat; Fiona's insistence she hadn't set the fire; the probable height of Gale's attacker. The bits and pieces began to come together in unexpected ways.

"The fire was not a lightning strike," he said. "You don't talk about something and two hours later it spontaneously combusts. Do you see how it plays out if it's forced to play out? Kira goes off the rails at the Advocates dinner. She's unstable. She takes after him like she almost did to me that night. Then she takes the truck and runs. Comes back and hides. Overhears us, and sets the fire. There is evidence to support most of this. My plan . . . Well, at least I had one. I hope you do."

She was squinting and blinking and looked as if she was either going to cry or pass out.

"You okay?" he asked.

"I need a minute." She sat there breathing deeply. He wasn't sure what to do—an uncommon feeling in him. "I need to see Katherine. I need to talk to Katherine."

"Who's Katherine?"

"Katherine," she said, as if that answered him. Standing from the chair, she hurried toward the interview room door.

"Don't walk out on me," he said.

She glanced over at him, turned, and was gone.

43

"It was like a door opened, or something," Fiona said.

"Okay." Katherine crossed her legs and brushed the front of her blouse.

Fiona had been made to wait a half hour while a client finished her session. Katherine had pushed back the next appointment to accommodate Fiona's arrival.

"Will you hypnotize me?"

"Perhaps there's no need. Tell me about it."

"Walt mentioned . . . He started talking about that night. And I don't know . . . like I said, it was like a door coming open."

"It happens. Do you want to tell me about it?"

"I'm not sure what there is to tell."

Katherine offered her a sly but affecting grin as if she knew there was much to tell.

"He *was* there," Fiona said.

Katherine said nothing. Did not ask her for a name. Barely moved at all.

Fiona felt at the center of a windstorm, leaves and sticks swirling, each with a message written on it. Words. Names. Parts of sentences. Like a magnetic word game for the refrigerator, a hundred thoughts or glimpses of thoughts awaiting some semblance of order. Her instinct was to try to stop it, to try to grab hold of one or two and begin organizing them, but the more she reached, the more the cloud moved away from her.

She felt the tears spring to her eyes before she knew what was happening, before she had a chance to protect herself from them. The leaves moved closer. "What a bastard," she whispered dryly.

"You're safe here," Katherine said.

"Prick."

"Take your time."

"He just arrived, you know? Unannounced. All of a sudden, just there at the door, like I expected him or something. Such a prick. So typical." She sniffled and dragged her wrist across her nose, creating a snail line. Katherine leaned forward and offered a tissue. Fiona saw it more as a flag of surrender and refused it. "I didn't know why he was there. I thought maybe to kill me. You know? After the trial and everything. But it wasn't even him. Not the Marty I knew. Had known. Whatever."

She looked out through the blur: Katherine, with her expressionless face. How did people do that? Sit there, impassive, while the other person eviscerated herself? She might have been waiting for a cake to finish baking. If she'd had knitting . . .

"I backed inside, and he followed without invitation. When he spoke, it was like it wasn't even him. Like he was channeling someone else. I couldn't process it all. Round peg, square hole. Him, soft-spoken and polite. Me, loud and demanding. I told him to get out, and he stopped and turned around. This is Marty we're talking about. The Gale Force. I told him to wait, and he stopped, and it was like I controlled him. Me, controlling him. Try that one on for size. He stopped again. 'What are you doing here?' I said, and he spoke to the door, not to me. His back to me. His hand on the doorknob. Maybe he didn't want to be there. That's what was going through my head: this guy shows up and he doesn't want to even be here. And it was like he was reading my thoughts—I always thought he could. He tells the door how he's part of a program and that part of the steps of that program—And I cut him off. Scornfully. Abusively. Marty Gale reformed. As if. And he waits me out, politely, I might add, and then starts into it again like it's something he'd rehearsed, and maybe he had for all I know. How it's something he's got to do, for me and for him. For both of us. Wants me to know this is not a gift, not a negotiated truce, but a requirement to his sobriety, and how what it amounts to is an apology.

"He says that word," she continued, "and as he does, he looks over his shoulder at me. Delivers it like a spear into my heart. An apology. Marty. You know how long I'd waited for that? For that one word: apologize? All the shit I'd been through with him. The hell. The endless hell of it all. And me too weak to leave, and him too overpowering to allow me to. Too Marty. Too unpredictable and dangerous. And here it is, and it's not 'better late than never.' Never would have worked for me just fine, thank you. Apologizing. Turning toward me now. Tears, real tears, streaming down his face. How he didn't know the guy he'd been, how the things he'd done—" She pursed her lips and realized her eyes were clear now.

"I think he stepped toward me. I must have stepped back. Whatever happened to him happened after that. Maybe once I fell, he came to help me. Maybe K— Maybe someone showed up and saw him bent over me like that. How should I know? What a bastard."

"Is that where your memory stops?" Katherine said.

"It's not like I remember hitting my head. But yeah, I'm assuming that's what happened. Why? What? Are you saying I didn't hit my head? Are you saying . . . ? That my memory stops there because I did something to him? Is that why you're looking at me like that?"

"Like what?"

"Don't give me that crap! Like that! Like you're looking right now."

So Katherine looked away. But the seed was planted and Fiona sank into a well of despair. A dark, cold, unmerciful place.

"I thought you were supposed to help me," Fiona said.

44

"You want to talk to her again, you're going to have to charge her." Peter Arian carried confidence in a way that disarmed juries and wooed judges. A surfer through college, he was Armani-ad handsome. Even at nine a.m., his eyes had a Hollywood sparkle. He spoke like a southern Californian despite his San Francisco roots.

The thing was, Walt liked Arian. Thought if he'd been a lawyer instead of a lawman, that he might have come out much the same way. He'd occasionally teased the young lawyer about switching sides and joining the prosecutor, but all he'd ever won was a laugh.

The bare hills outside Walt's office were electric with the morning sun. He wished he were hiking.

"I want to see the evidence involved."

"I respect your situation, Peter. You're good at what

you do and we both know it. But you do not want to go the evidence route. This is one time where, in the best interest of your client, you should just walk out the door and leave this to me. I like Kira."

"That's not happening."

"Let me talk to her again this morning for an hour or so. Alone. Everyone's a winner."

"Walk me through the evidence first." Arian issued a penetrating look meant to intimidate, but it fell short. "Make a believer out of me."

"Don't do this. You know that's not going to happen."

Walt's intercom sounded.

"Sheriff, when you have a minute."

Walt wasn't superstitious by nature. There were cops who were: guys who turned their wallets a certain way in a back pocket, wore their shield upside down or carried a talisman. There were guys who checked the calendar in the morning and determined their activities on the whims of numerology. He wasn't one of them, but the interruption served the same purpose. Something about the timing, something about that look on Arian's face, something indiscernible, impossible to put a finger on, that weird kind of something that made him act in a way that he felt was inconsistent with his own actions. Nonetheless, he did it. He held out his hand, waited for Peter to shake it, and motioned him toward his office door.

"The evidence," Arian said, "or no interview."

His mind made up, his hand forced and his plan with

it, Walt said, "I'm going to brief Doug." The county's prosecutor, Doug Aanestead. "We'll take it from there."

Arian looked wounded. He forced a grin—more of a snarl—and made for the door.

"That's a bad call, Sheriff."

"The bad call was the one Ms. Kenshaw made to you, counselor."

A knot formed in his stomach. It was one thing to find yourself out on a limb, another thing entirely to crawl out there willingly. He blamed Fiona; he blamed himself for seeing everything through the distorted lens of emotion. He felt foolish and vulnerable and knew perfectly well it was the small decisions that determine success or failure, more so than the bigger ones. He was typically rooted in procedure, so this feeling of flying by the seat of his pants left him queasy. A feeling of regret overcame him. Regret for digging so deeply in the first place.

He returned calmly to the other side of his desk, picked up the phone, and followed up on the intercom interruption.

"Wood River Glass," he was told, "replaced a cracked windshield in a Ford F-one-fifty on the afternoon of the thirteenth. Truck has a light rack on the cab."

He did not want to deal with the missing pickup truck right now, but he also did not want to overlook any chance at new evidence. He intended to find Doug Aanestead and make his case.

"Do we have a name?" he asked.

"Dominique Fancelli. Of eighteen—"

"Alturas Drive," Walt said, supplying the address.

"Well . . . yeah," spoken with a mixture of disappointment and astonishment. "But if you knew that—"

"Lucky guess," Walt said.

"Yeah, right."

"Issue a BOLO for the F-one-fifty," Walt instructed. "And have a patrol do a drive-by, real quiet like, of the Fancelli residence. If that pickup's in the drive, I want to be notified immediately."

"Got it."

He allowed himself a faint smile, the satisfaction of a small victory. He didn't want to misstep. He'd have to check with the prosecutor about how to approach this as well. Ironically, the law was the reason he most often lost a case.

He called Tommy Brandon because it was only fair: Brandon had made the connection to the red-tailed hawk—a bow hunter—in the first place. It felt good to possibly deliver on a favor, and for Lisa of all people.

Brandon answered on the first ring as if just sitting by the phone waiting for his call.

"Do you feel strong enough to drive about a mile south?" Walt asked.

"What do you think?"

"I think you just got out of the hospital."

"I told you: the soaps don't cut it for me."

"Be ready to move. I'll call as soon as I know anything."

"The pickup truck?"

"Yeah. Did you ever see *Little Big Man*? The movie with Dustin Hoffman?"

"It's one of Gail's favorites," Brandon said.

No, it's one of my favorites, Walt felt like correcting. *She just happened to have been in the room at the time.* But he let it go.

"The Indian scene," Walt said. "The one where he's dying. Or trying to?"

"What a great scene."

"'Sometimes, the magic works,'" Walt quoted.

"Yeah, I remember."

Walt blocked from his mind the second half of the couplet: "Sometimes, it doesn't."

45

Doug Aanestead reviewed the evidence from behind the twelfth hole on the Valley Club's upper eighteen. He and his golf partner allowed three other groups to play through, each one increasing the man's impatience. A light breeze curled the edges of the papers in the open folder, causing Aanestead to wrestle with its contents. His putter was gripped between his knees, the handle sticking out somewhat phallically.

"Honestly, Walt, I don't love it."

"Is that right?" Walt understood the risk of his current, and only, plan. The plan he'd wanted to play out on his time frame, not Arian's. But here he was.

The law could be your friend or enemy, and for the past several days Walt had been working up a way to convince Aanestead he had a pretty good case against Kira.

Like Walt's, Aanestead's was an elected office. Walt was counting on that.

"It'll be damn unpopular, indicting this girl. Hell's bells, she addressed the Advocates this year. We were both there."

"We were."

"She's something of a local hero."

"We have the bat," Walt reminded.

"A bat that's carrying three sets of prints. She's already admitted to handling the thing. And taking a drive to Yellowstone? That's not in the code that I know of."

"No."

"What about Fiona?" Aanestead asked. "She see Gale around the place? She confirm any of this?"

Walt couldn't afford to lie. Aanestead had a competent staff. The man was ambitious, was said to have his eye on the state attorney general's race. He would vet this thoroughly.

"Ms. Kenshaw showed up at the emergency room early the next day. A blow to the back of the head. She's a little fuzzy about the details. Says she fell over a footstool."

Aanestead looked at him askance. "Have you questioned her? Formally questioned her?"

"I wouldn't if I could. She's not of sound mind. Anything she says, anything we get from her would be tossed out because of the existing medical condition. When the effects of that blow wear off . . . But who knows when that might happen?"

"She's saying she doesn't remember? That's certainly convenient."

"Her prints are not the ones we found on the bat. She didn't take off unannounced and return to hide in the basement."

"The Tulivich girl's had a tough time of it, for Christ's sake, Walt. She's scared of her own shadow. We go after her, we'd better be damned sure we know what we're doing, and I don't see it in here."

Walt kept a straight face. "There's the forensic evidence," he reminded. "The pollen. He was on the Engleton property."

"We all know juries love this shit. But judges take more convincing. And I don't see anywhere in here a lab comparison of the flowers up at the Engletons' to what was found on Gale. Do I?"

"That kind of lab work can take weeks." In fact, Walt had been refused the collection of evidence by the Engletons.

"Not my problem." Aanestead handed the folder back to Walt and eyed the thirteenth tee. "You play, don't you?"

"Yes."

"We ought to knock it around together sometime."

"I'd like that."

Aanestead glanced at the thirteenth for a second time. His partner looked ready to explode as yet another party reached the twelfth green.

"What about Fancelli?" Walt asked. "I followed a

pickup truck thinking it important to the Gale killing, only to have a deputy figure it differently. But I can use it. We can use this to our advantage."

"You'd be going out on a limb. I would doubt that federal law's been tested for some time."

"There was that class-action suit against Northwest Generation in Wyoming."

"That was birds frying on high-tension lines, not some bow hunter plucking roadkill. It's federal law, not state."

"But it's on the books."

"Yes, it is. But untested."

"You see where I'm going with it."

"I do. It's creative, and I think important. A scumbag like that, you take him down however you can."

"That's the point." Translation: the voters would approve.

"I'll not only back you on this Fancelli thing," Aanestead said, "I'll hold a press conference and lay it out there and hope that helps us get a foot across the finish line."

Surprise.

"I'll want you by my side," he said.

"Not a problem," Walt said.

"You want my guys to leak it?"

If the press were notified, it might mean Fiona was sent to photograph the arrest. Walt shuddered at the thought.

"Probably better off not."

"You sure? Hell of a card to play, a front-page piece

showing a guy in cuffs. Talk about prejudicing the jury pool." He punched Walt lightly in the shoulder. Things were getting too friendly for Walt.

"I'll notify your office when we have him in custody. How's that?"

"How soon are we talking about?" He didn't want to be caught on the back nine by reporters. Wouldn't look right.

"I can hold off for about an hour," Walt said.

"You're a good man, Walt," Aanestead said, grinning widely. He leaned in close. "Twenty bucks a hole, and with Tim it's like taking candy from a baby. But you didn't hear it from me."

"My guys'll call your office once we've got him," Walt repeated.

"I'll want you by my side."

"Understood."

"You're going to need a hell of a lot more before you'll have me signing off on Tulivich. She's a dead end, Walt. Nothing but trouble."

"Okay." He tried to sound disappointed, while inside he was celebrating the man's predictability. It wouldn't be the first time the evidence came up short despite having a suspect in the sights.

"I wouldn't go there unless you have the dead guy sitting up and pointing a finger at her." He smiled. Perfect teeth standing out against the wicked tan. Walt was looking at the next attorney general, and both men knew it.

"It may go unsolved," Walt warned, again keeping the celebration out of his voice.

"Hell of a game," Aanestead said, holding his club, but looking Walt in the eye somewhat suspiciously. He'd picked up on Walt's relief.

"Hell of a game," Walt echoed.

46

Walt focused intently on the small log cabin in front of him. One of twelve homes in a subdivision dating from the 1980s, it was log with forest green trim and asphalt shingles. Two mountain bikes sagged next to the front door, along with a pair of work boots and a dog bowl. The F-150 was parked in the driveway. Lisa's house was one to the left, a charming home with wooden flowers painted primary colors in a line across the lawn. Strung between two of the flowers was a small sailcloth banner reading Alturas Day Care. When she wasn't taking care of his kids, she was running the day care.

Walt didn't see Lisa's house. He barely saw the Fancelli place. Instead, as Brandon sat quietly in the seat beside him, his arm in a sling, Walt saw only the horror of what Lisa had witnessed; he heard the slapping of the bed frame against the wall as she had heard it; he felt sick, as she had felt.

"It's not like he's going to give us a hard time, you think?" Brandon ventured.

"We need him."

"How's that?"

"Our witness, Maggie Sharp, puts his truck there that night."

"So this is or is not a takedown?"

"Sorry to disappoint you."

"What the hell, Sheriff?"

"We need to work it."

"And I'm here because . . . ?"

"You love this stuff."

"True."

"And I have a warrant, a search warrant to execute. But for now we have to execute it without his knowing what's going on. Keep him thinking it's about bird feathers."

"So plain sight for now."

"Exactly."

"Which is where I come in."

"Now you've got it," Walt said.

"And you sweet-talk him."

"I'll do my best."

"And if it doesn't get that far? If he bolts on us?"

"We can't afford that," Walt said. "That's why we're here. That's why it's you and me instead of anyone else. We can't scare him. We can't let him know the real reason we're here, or the card we can play. It's not an arrest.

We're lucky to have found him. You're the only one I trust to understand how to play that. The other guys, knowing the crime, might allow that knowledge to get the best of them."

"I understand."

"So be cool in there."

"Despite the fact this guy's a bastard of the first order and I'd like nothing more than to make his arrest as uncomfortable as possible. Maybe dislocate a shoulder or two."

Walt's guys occasionally played the resisting arrest card, the same as in any other cop shop, took their frustrations with the system out on the suspect, made sure the arrest was as painful as possible, since the system tended to coddle suspects: jails with television and fresh food; an hour a day outside; gym equipment. A few of the suspects deserved the black hole and everyone knew it. Arresting deputies felt it their responsibility to punish the person right to the edge of what was tolerated, and sometimes a touch beyond.

"Not this time, Tommy."

"Understood."

"You're the one guy I trust."

"Got it."

Brandon took the back side of the home, going around the far side, looking for windows without screens on his way to cover the back door. He stood at the corner with a view of a potential escape window, but within a few steps of the back door. He clicked his radio once.

Walt, waiting at the front door, heard the radio click and knocked and rang the bell within a second of each other. The Wood River Valley was not a place residents checked outside before opening their doors. A beautiful girl opened the door. She wore a loose shirt that obscured her figure.

"Your father here? Dominique Fancelli?"

Maybe it was Walt's use of his formal name. She stood staring, clearly unable to speak. She nodded. "Stepfather," she finally managed.

"Would you tell him the sheriff's here, please? Sheriff Walt Fleming."

"'Kay." She filled her lungs. *"D . . . a . . . d!!!"* She then hesitated, swallowed, and added, "Sheriff's here to see you!"

Walt thought her face grew more ashen as the *clomp* of footfalls approached. More sullen. He understood the risks involved by his coming here. If there was any suggestion, any indication she had spoken to the police about her situation, it could mean a beating or even death. Walt's mission was to get as much as he could from the man, and then to separate the two and make sure things remained that way. As Fancelli arrived at the other side of the screen door, Walt reached up and pushed the button on his radio mike twice. Brandon now knew Walt had made contact. Even so, his deputy would not leave his post until and unless a second signal was sent.

"Dominique Fancelli?"

"Yeah?"

Walt did not need to introduce himself. "I have a few questions concerning your Ford F-one-fifty."

Dionne's face relaxed considerably. The furrow left Dominique's brow. "Is that right?"

"You mind if I come in?"

Fancelli pushed open the screen door, but he stepped outside instead of allowing Walt in. Walt thought the move shrewd and an important indicator of who he was dealing with.

"Shut the door," Fancelli told his daughter.

The girl did so, but her expression, behind her stepfather's back, was one of intense curiosity and no small degree of fear.

Walt elected to play his Brandon card. He clicked his handset three times, and Brandon rounded the far corner of the house and approached them. Brandon slowed at each window, looking inside. Even wearing the sling, Brandon's size and demeanor were intimidating. He was a person you paid attention to, kept one eye on, in any given situation. The big dog, poised in the corner, his eyes taking in everyone in the room. He approached the front of the F-150 slowly and, when he had Walt's attention, nodded slightly. That motion affirmed he'd seen evidence of the bird strike and filled Walt with additional confidence.

Fancelli was appropriately distracted. "What's up, Sheriff?"

"Deputy Tommy Brandon," Walt said, introducing the two.

Tommy nodded at the man, but kept six feet away. *If a stare could burn*, Walt thought.

"What's going on?" Fancelli greeted Brandon.

Brandon said nothing in return.

"Mr. Fancelli—"

"Don."

"We're occasionally put in the position of seeking a statement from a civilian, a citizen, on a voluntary basis. We're not asking that you get involved, but to be forth-right, it's not out of the question that at some future date you might be deposed or even asked to give testimony at a trial. If you were opposed to that, we would do every-thing in our power to protect you and prevent that from happening."

The effect was as he'd hoped. First, he'd distracted the suspect into believing their arrival at his front door had nothing to do with his own actions; second, they'd instilled in him a sense of their dependence on him, lending him a false self-confidence.

"What's this about?"

"We believe your Ford F-one-fifty may have swerved off the highway on the night of the twelfth, or early morn-ing of the thirteenth."

Fancelli managed a convincing deadpan, though his eyes darted nervously between Walt and Brandon. "Yeah, that's right," he said.

Walt concealed his calming exhale, having worried he might have to fight the man on this part of the story.

"We had a witness," he said, just to place one nail firmly in place.

"Is that so?"

"ID'd your truck," Brandon said in his deep baritone.

"A fox was into some roadkill. Swerved to miss it and lost control."

"It happens," Walt said, secretly impressed the man could seem so nonchalant. He was learning more about Fancelli than Fancelli would have wanted him to know. This was the testing phase: the chance to probe the suspect in an effort to decode him. Find the right code and you could unlock all the walls erected in front of the truth.

"So you were driving," Walt said, continuing. "You were behind the wheel?"

"It's my truck."

"You came to a stop and you left the vehicle," Walt said, watching as that piece of information caught Fancelli off guard. "Now, most guys I know would move to the front of the vehicle to see if there was any damage done."

"I didn't hit anything," Fancelli volunteered. "I said there was a fox in the road and that I swerved to avoid him."

"Yes, you did," Walt said. "My point was that most guys would get out of the vehicle to check for damage. I mean, why get out at all? Why not just drive back to the highway?"

"I still don't get what this is about."

"Did you leave the vehicle running?"

"What does that have to do with anything?"

"Your headlights. It has to do with your headlights."

"My headlights are fine. Both headlights are working."

"That model, F-one-fifty, even if the engine's turned off, the headlights remain illuminated for sixty seconds. It's a safety feature to let you reach your door."

"What's with the headlights, Sheriff?"

"You got out of the vehicle and walked back behind it."

"This," said Brandon, "according to our witness."

"Yeah? So what? Scared the shit out of me, running off the road like that. I had to take a leak. You think I was going to take a leak in the headlights? So I got away from the truck. Big deal."

"Makes sense to me," Walt said to Brandon, who nodded. "It's of no never mind to us."

"Could have fooled me," Fancelli said.

"The point being you were *behind* the truck—"

"And the headlights were on," Brandon said, chiming in.

"Yeah? So?"

"So," Walt said, "you approach the truck from the rear as you return to the cab. Can you see that?"

"I suppose."

"We're interested in what you saw as you returned to your truck."

"You lost me."

"If you saw anything, anyone, in the general vicinity of your truck as you returned to the cab."

"Such as?"

"Anything at all unusual?"

"Not that I recall."

"We need you to think about this. Need you to tell us anything you might have seen that might have struck you as out of the ordinary."

"I didn't see anything. I took a leak, got back in the truck, and drove back to the road."

Walt kept his shoulders from slumping with disappointment. He retained his impassive, slightly bored expression—a public servant doing his job.

"Are you a bow hunter, Mr. Fancelli?"

"What of it?"

"Would you have applied for bear tags for the past three years?"

"No law against that, is there?"

"Not to my knowledge," Walt said.

"Okay then."

"Did you take the Ford into Wood River Glass for a windshield replacement on the afternoon of the thirteenth?"

Fancelli's veneer cracked. His brow tightened, his eyes narrowed, and he dismissed Brandon as if he wasn't there. His full attention was now fixed on Walt. He'd identified the enemy and he tracked it with a hunter's eye.

"What's going on here?"

"Do you remember what you told the mechanic? The worker at Wood River Glass? What you told him had caused the damage to your windshield?"

"I ate a rock."

"Are you aware that shops like Wood River Glass take pictures of damage for insurance purposes?"

"No."

"Some do," Walt said. "The ones that want to get paid."

"So?"

"Have you ever heard the expression, 'Why do it the hard way when there's an easy way'?"

"What's your point, Sheriff? I gotta get back inside."

"You sure it was a fox, Mr. Fancelli?"

"Maybe I'm mixing it up with another time I was run off the road. I think that's right. Did I say fox? It was a bird. A bird hit my windshield."

"What kind of bird?"

"How would I know?"

"Maybe it landed somewhere behind your truck?"

"Maybe you saw it," Brandon said, "when you were taking that piss."

"There was a dead hawk there," Fancelli said. "You think it was the same bird? What does any of this matter anyway?"

"We'd like to see your arrows, Don," Walt said. "You hand-make them, don't you?"

"How the—? What do you care about my arrows? Someone shoot someone or something? It wasn't me."

Walt withdrew the search warrant and handed it to Fancelli. "We have a warrant to search the premises." He nodded to Brandon, who pushed past Fancelli and entered the home.

Walt caught a glimpse of Dionne. She'd been standing right by the door, listening to everything said.

"There was a body!" Fancelli blurted out.

Walt tensed. "Excuse me?"

"There was a body in the bushes. A guy. Big son of a bitch."

Brandon stopped and turned, now inside the house.

"Where are we talking about?" Walt asked.

"In front of my pickup. That night."

"You saw a body?"

"I did."

"And did you call it in?"

"I didn't. No."

"Because?"

He looked confused. "We could cut a little deal, right?" Fancelli proposed. "I saw the body. I've got what you want, so maybe you cut me some slack."

"Regarding?"

"You know damn well."

"I need to hear it from you."

"The feathers. I took some hawk feathers. Okay? Thing was dead. It's a stupid law anyway, you ask me. I took a couple flight feathers. Your warrant. That's what you're looking for, right? My arrows. You won't find them in there. I've got a workshop in the garage. My gear's in the garage. I tell you about the body, you cut me some slack on the feathers. Deal?"

"We'd have to see the feathers first," Walt said.

"Sure, no problem."

Fancelli led Walt and Tommy Brandon to the small garage in back, and inside to a corner workbench where an array of material was collected. The air was stale. Some moths worked frantically against the glass, trying to escape.

"So let me get this straight," Walt said, inspecting a piece of one of the hawk feathers not yet used, "you didn't call in the body because you'd taken the hawk's feathers and didn't want to get involved."

"Listen, I thought about calling it in to nine-one-one or something. But you guys trace all those calls, right? Am I right? I just didn't want to be involved."

"The hawk feathers were more important to you than the dead man." Walt made it a statement.

"I know that sounds stupid."

Walt waited for Brandon to be in position behind Fancelli with his one good hand.

"Dominique Fancelli," Walt said formally. "You're under arrest for violation of the Fish and Wildlife Act."

Before Fancelli could think, Brandon had a strong hold of one arm. He turned the man effortlessly toward Walt, who cuffed him.

"What the hell is going on here? I thought we had a deal!"

Walt spoke over the noise. "Call in the team. I want them to take this house apart, nail by nail."

Fancelli suddenly looked terrified.

"What the hell are you doing?"

"My job," Walt said, catching sight through the garage door's rain-gray windows of the forlorn face of Dionne Fancelli, who looked as if she wanted to disappear.

47

The two women faced each other in sumptuous opulence in the first of three living rooms in the Engleton house. Peter Arian sat to the side in a padded needlepoint chair that creaked when he moved. He'd called Fiona over to the house, requesting her help in "reaching" his new client, who had so far refused to answer any of his questions. It was late afternoon, the hottest part of the day, and the shades were drawn against the sun, denying them the glorious views of Bald Mountain to the west.

"Hey, K," Fiona said.

Kira pursed her lips.

"It's okay."

"No, it's not. I think I got you in trouble."

Arian seemed to know better than to interrupt, or to

take notes, or to react in any way that might cause his client to clam up. He was a human mannequin. But his eyes found Fiona and attempted to deliver something that she found difficult to interpret.

"You remember that I was having problems remembering what happened?"

Kira lifted her eyes to look across at Fiona, but said nothing.

"I've made some headway in that department."

Kira appeared concerned.

"In a good way," Fiona said. "The way I look at it, the truth can't get us into trouble. You know? It is what it is. What happened, happened. That's all we're after here: the truth. What happened. It's no big deal."

"It is if it gets you in trouble."

"Do you think that's going to happen?"

Kira looked over at her attorney, then at Fiona. "Yes, I do."

"I wouldn't worry about it."

"You would if you were me," Kira said.

"Why is that?"

"Because . . . you know."

"Tell me."

"I left the bat there."

"Where?"

"Outside the door. That night the sheriff came, and I sneaked up on him and all."

"Which door?"

"The front door. Here." She pointed.

"Okay. And what about the bat?"

Kira's eyes darted to Arian, then to Fiona. "Well, it isn't there anymore."

"The thing is," Fiona said, "he's on your side. Our side. Whatever he hears, it doesn't matter, because he represents you."

"What about you? Who represents you?"

"I'm not the one who needs a lawyer," Fiona said.

Kira lowered her head.

"K?"

"What if you do?"

"Need a lawyer?"

She nodded.

Fiona checked with Arian, who nodded ever so slightly, encouraging her to pursue this line.

"The night of the Advocates dinner, you recognized him, didn't you?"

She nodded.

"Marty was there. You saw him. You told me that later, and I didn't believe you, and now I know I should have. I apologize for that."

Kira shrugged her shoulders.

"I just . . . It just didn't seem possible."

"I froze."

"I must have walked right by him. You realize that? I got that e-mail and I left right away, and if I didn't walk right by him, I came incredibly close. None of this would have happened. None of this would have been the same if he'd found me there. He was looking for me."

"That's what I was afraid of. That's why I froze."

"All these years. Well, you know how afraid I was of him. You're the only one here I've talked to about any of this. Your thing with Roy Coats . . . We shared stuff, you and me. I know you want to protect me, but you can let go of that because I remember now. Something Walt—the sheriff—said. I don't know. It was like it all came back to me. Like something unlocked. Katherine says it happens. She told me it would happen, and I didn't believe her. But it happened. I don't have it all back. She says it takes time. But what I remember, I remember clearly. He was there . . . he came here to apologize to me, Kira. Not hurt me. But to apologize. He freaked me out. I was terrified of him. And him apologizing like that. I think I freaked out and stepped back and probably went over the stool and hit my head."

"But I saw you with the bat," Kira blurted out, as if forgetting about Arian. "I saw you hit him."

"Me?"

"On the head. From the back."

"Me?" Fiona gasped dryly for a second time.

"In front of your place. The two of you."

"But . . . you saw *me*?"

"What was I supposed to do? I didn't want you to know I'd seen. I didn't want anyone to know. The car took off. The guy's car. It wasn't him driving, that was for sure. Not after that. I got in the truck and left. I didn't know what else to do."

"Me?" Fiona repeated. "You saw me?"

Kira was crying. She lowered her head.

Fiona came around the coffee table and sat down next to her and held her. Kira sobbed. "I didn't want to get you in trouble."

Fiona fought back her own tears. "But I thought *you'd* done it."

"Me?!" Kira leaned back and explored Fiona's face. "Seriously?"

"And Walt . . . He thinks we did it together. That we're covering for each other."

Kira burst out laughing, tears still falling. "He what?"

"I know."

"Seriously?"

Fiona nodded.

"What do we do?" Kira asked. Then she looked to her attorney.

"There's evidence," Peter Arian said. "From what I'm hearing from you, I'm assuming it's the baseball bat. That could be damaging. The sheriff wouldn't give me that, so we're better off now that I know. And they haven't charged you. Either of you. I'm assuming the prosecuting attorney called off the sheriff, and for good reason: he didn't like the evidence. Or, it could be that they're awaiting more lab results, or witnesses. Or it could be your standing in the community. You're something of a celebrity," he said to Kira. "They may simply be waiting for it all to come together. That's important for us to consider. What's equally important is that both of you lay out exactly what you remember. That you write it down exactly as you remember it. I will be the only one in possession of those documents. If charges are filed, I can apply for access to the evidence. If the sheriff is building a case against the two of you, that's more complicated and will take more time. At some point he'll attempt to get one of you to turn on the other. It's a pretty straightforward approach. I will need to be there for those interviews."

"It wasn't me outside the cottage," Fiona said. "I'm willing to bet I was inside, lying on the floor unconscious, although I don't know that for sure."

"That's a big bet," Arian said. "I'm not sure that's a bet you want to make."

"Well, it wasn't me," Kira said. "I saw it. I didn't do it."

"No other cars?" Arian asked Kira.

"Not that I saw. And I didn't hear the gate beep."

"They can make a case that it was one or the other of you, or that, as you say the sheriff is thinking, that it was both of you, and you're covering for each other."

"But it's not true," Kira said.

Arian's face sagged. "This is the law we're talking about. Truth is only one small part of the equation." He waited a moment for this to sink in. "Your parents have asked you to stay with them?"

Kira nodded. They'd discussed this earlier on the drive up. "But I don't want to."

Fiona spoke up. "Kira, you should do it. Maybe this is the chance you've been waiting for."

"I don't want to see him."

"What if your father's changed?"

"He doesn't change."

"We all change," Fiona said, "if others give us the chance to."

Kira nodded faintly. "But only for tonight."

"Don't be too quick to judge," Fiona advised.

"I don't want to leave you."

"I've got stuff to work out," Fiona said. "Stuff to write down. I'll be all right."

"I can drop you off," Arian proposed.

"I'll get my things," Kira said, standing and reluctantly letting go of Fiona's hand.

"What do you make of all this?" Fiona asked Arian when they were alone.

"Do you believe her?" he asked.

"Absolutely."

"And how do you know you went over a stool? What if your injury occurred outside your cottage?"

"You think that didn't occur to me?"

"Do you think it's possible?"

"Did I hate him that much? Yes, I did. Could I do something like that? Never."

"Never's a big word."

"Never," Fiona repeated.

Arian dug out his wallet, and from it, a business card. "In case you need me."

"I don't."

"But in case you do," he said.

Fiona accepted the card.

48

A Disney Channel Original Movie played from the living room as Walt worked the computer at the dining-room table. Tied in to his office's server, he was finishing up the report on the Fancelli arrest. He'd already been in touch with AUSA in Boise, who'd promised Walt the Wildlife Act charge would hold. Walt believed that with some backroom discussion he might get Fancelli the maximum sentence of a fine and a year in jail. Small payment for his real crime, but at least something.

The search of the Fancelli home had failed to turn up any suggestion of child molestation or abuse—no souvenirs, no videos—but the man's arrest included a mandatory DNA swab—this had been the golden ring Walt had been reaching for—and he hoped within the week to use that sample to prove the paternity of his daughter's unborn child. Fancelli would be going away for a lot longer than a year. As he wrapped up the report, he was feeling good for a change and thinking that this was one of the good nights.

"Hey, Dad," Nikki called from the living room. It had to be a commercial break because typically they didn't know he existed if a show was on.

"Yes?"

"I thought you were going to build us a tree fort."

A family issue that arose every six months or so, Walt had resisted the idea of a tree fort because of the enormous work involved and the likelihood of it turning out to be only a passing interest. He realized, more important, that this was gender bias on his part. He thought of tree forts as a boys' realm, and was convinced his daughters would quickly lose interest, a conviction he now questioned.

"You're right," he answered. "I think I forgot all about it."

"Can we build one?"

Now Emily was sitting up and looking at him excitedly as well. "With curtains and a bucket to bring stuff up?" she said.

He wondered if a tree house was part of the show they were watching. They were easily influenced.

"Curtains? Why not?" he said.

"When?" Emily shouted far too loudly.

"How soon?" Nikki added.

The questions hit him as a fist in the chest. Everything

came down to time. It was the one commodity that fell short and left him feeling cheated, as well as the one doing the cheating. Never mind that he had no time for himself; he gave his daughters short shrift and even his job occasionally suffered. He considered himself an excellent time manager, and yet how was he supposed to find the four hours to erect a tree house with his daughters? And if he couldn't find four hours to be with his kids, what did that say about him?

"This weekend," he answered.

"Seriously?" Nikki said, suddenly the spokesperson for the two.

This change caught her father's attention. Of the two, Nikki had retreated far more deeply into herself following the divorce. Her elevation to spokesperson, and Emily's willingness to allow it to happen, held profound significance for him.

"Seriously," he answered. "This Saturday."

To his surprise, the girls exploded off the floor, throwing their hands high in the air and dancing around, causing Walt to realize how much he missed the obvious. Their excitement had little or nothing to do with a tree house.

"Saturday," he repeated, watching how it spurred even more celebration. He wished he had a camera. Wished he could preserve forever the elation on his daughters' faces, wished he understood the complexities of fatherhood better, and resolved to do just that.

With the idea of a tree house now firmly rooted, he

began to imagine what backyard tree or trees could be used, as well as the structure's overall design. A tree house was no simple undertaking, and Walt was no do-it-yourselfer. He Googled "tree house plans" and uncovered a half-million hits. He scrolled down through, then changed his mind and clicked on the "Images" link at the top of the page to see what he was in for.

There on the screen was a small thumbnail photograph of a structure that matched the last tree house he'd seen: the one in the Engletons' woods. The one he'd been sitting near when he'd suggested to Fiona that a small fire would clean things up nicely.

His house phone ringing interrupted him, and he rose to answer it with reluctance. Anyone who wanted to reach him called him on his mobile, so he assumed this was either for the girls, or a telemarketer. Both options left him grumpy. He answered the phone, "This is Walt," and paused.

"Sheriff Fleming?" It was a high, timid voice, with a Hispanic accent, and Walt's first thought was how she'd gotten his unpublished phone number.

"Speaking."

"My name Victoria Menquez. I am married to Guillermo. You know Guillermo. He work for Forest Service."

"Yes, Mrs. Menquez."

"My Guillermo, he no come home."

Walt had been led into a search for Gilly once before; he felt the taste of sarcasm lingering on the tip of his tongue as he swallowed it away.

"I'm sure he's fine," Walt said. "Have you called his friends?"

"He not fine," she protested. "He said he do something for you when he left this morning. This is why I call you. Why he not call? Why he not come for supper?"

"Me?" Walt blurted out too quickly. The last thing he needed was to be dragged into a pub crawl looking for Gilly Menquez. He was about to suggest looking under "Bar" in the Yellow Pages when he gained some control. "The Forest Service," he said. "He must carry a radio or something?"

"I call. No answer. Only recording. Office opens eight a.m. I know when office opens." She was the one reverting to sarcasm. He glanced at the kitchen clock. It felt later than it was. The soundtrack of the Disney movie was bothering him; too much laughter for his present conversation.

"I think you should try some of his friends."

"You are his friend, no? Guillermo say what a good man you are."

That stuck like a bone in his throat. "Listen, Mrs. Menquez, if I'm going to be honest with you, I would suggest you call his favorite taverns. My hunch is, that's where you'll find him."

"But he said he was working for you."

"I wouldn't know anything about that, I'm afraid. I haven't seen or spoken to Gilly—Guillermo—in over a week."

"Said you were looking for someone, that he could find him. My Guillermo, he can find anyone in the woods. Says you are almost as good as him."

A bubble of laughter rose in Walt's throat but he choked it back. "That's what he said?" Walt asked. "That I was looking for someone?"

"He made a mistake, Sheriff. He know that. He told me. And I told him: 'You make a mistake, you fix it.' That is what he was doing in the woods today. He was fixing it."

Then the collision happened, as it so often did for him. Like one idea can't get out of the way of the other, so there's nowhere to go but into each other. And suddenly two thoughts spawn a third. It was this—the Google image overlaid with the lovely, lilting speech of this woman—that drove Walt to sign off the call as politely as possible.

"Hit the record button," he called out, advising his daughters. "You're coming with me."

He called Myra from the car, the girls strapped into the backseat, Beatrice's tail smacking them both as it swished back and forth. "I'm heading up your way," he told Myra, before his sister-in-law could get a word out. "I need to leave the girls with you for a few minutes. Can you handle that?"

"Walt? I—"

"Can you do that for me?"

"Of course."

"Ten minutes."

• • •

"Lock the door, and stay near the phone."

"Walt?" Fiona said.

"Better yet, just get out of there."

"I will not." She paused, the telephone connection crackling. "We need to talk."

"Later. Right now, you need to get in your car and get out of there. No, no. Stay. That's good. But lock up tight. Do you have a weapon in there?"

"If you're working on scaring me, you're doing a fine job."

"You do or don't have a weapon?"

"I own a handgun."

"But—" He caught himself. How had he never asked her this question earlier? Who went after a guy with a baseball bat if there was a handgun in the drawer? He couldn't help himself: "Have you had training?"

"Walt, what's going on?"

"I'm coming onto the property. On foot. I've called for backup, but there was a drowning in Carey. Anyway, for the time being, it's just me. Do you know how to use that handgun?"

"Yes."

"Then keep it close. And don't do anything stupid: it may be me coming through your door."

"Who else would it be?"

"That's the point," he said. "Anything out of place

there recently? Anything missing? Clothes, maybe? Underwear?"

"What's got into you?"

"Should I take that as a no?"

"I haven't thought about it."

"Well, think about it." He guessed he was still five to seven minutes away. He liked keeping her on the phone, liked hearing her voice so close.

"I haven't lost anything. Kira and I leave each other little gifts. You know: cookies. Wildflowers. It's a girl thing."

"Any lately?"

Her pause was far too long.

"Fiona?"

"You're coming straight here? Come straight here, will you?"

"Fiona. Talk to me."

"I'll get the gun now, like you said. I've already locked up."

"You were going to tell me something."

"No, I wasn't."

"I think you were."

The mobile connection sparked and crackled. Reception wasn't perfect on this stretch of the road. Walt's Jeep approached and passed the area where Gale's body had been found. Broken yellow police tape flapped in the light glow of the headlights.

"He *is* dead, right? With his face so badly— What if it wasn't him?" Walt's question about the gifts had in fact jogged loose yet another memory: Gale entering her cottage carrying flowers. She'd found them, withered and dry, on the coffee table after returning from the hospital, believing them to be from Kira. But she now knew Kira had taken off by then. They couldn't have been from her. Only him. The idea of that monster bearing a gift of flowers was almost too much to take.

"We ID'd the body," he said. "No worries. Sit tight. I'm on my way."

He pulled off the highway but took the right fork toward the Berkholders' instead of going left toward the Engletons'. He drove twenty yards, killed his lights, and coasted to a stop, shutting off the engine. Beatrice was made to heel and understood from the urgency of the whispered command that this was not a training session. She responded appropriately: silent, attentive, holding close to his left leg, her nose and eyes working overtime. Together, the two moved quickly through the dark.

Up the hill, the Engleton flagpole showed in silhouette against the illumination of the night sky and the richness of the Milky Way. Also in silhouette, to the right of the flagpole and farther still up the hill, a strongly geometric shape revealed itself—the northeastern corner of the Engleton tree house.

Minutes later, Walt hopped over the rail fence alongside the gate and Beatrice slipped through, catching up to his leg and heeling obediently without further command. Walt stayed in the shelter of the planted aspens that formed grove after grove as the driveway climbed up the knoll. He reached the end of the drive, where it widened into a turnaround and parking area connecting Fiona's cottage to the main house's garage, and a path leading to the front door. He crouched here and waited, settling his heartbeat and getting control of his respiration, his left arm over Beatrice's back as she panted at his side.

He rubbed the dog's head, rewarding her, and as he stood, gently placed his hand on the outside of his left leg, reinforcing the heel. She followed him to the right, around the back side of the house, rather than across the inviting, open space of the turnaround. He passed more beds containing the yellow lilies reminding him of the fire, then his conversation with Fiona near the tree house. He held to shadow, Beatrice at his side, moving silently.

Walt stayed low as he finally reached the southeastern corner of the main house, facing the scar of burned earth directly in front of him, then moved up the hill, the tree house now immediately to his right. A pine rail ladder was attached to one of the three fir trees supporting the tree house, a sizable structure fifteen feet off the ground. He signaled Beatrice to stay and then moved in a stealthy crouch to the base of the ladder and began to climb. Beatrice followed his every action, her nose rising with each ladder rung.

It was a trapdoor entrance leading up through the tree house floor. Walt paused just beneath it. He fished out his Maglite and Beretta and, marrying the two while holding to the ladder, used his back to push and throw open the trapdoor. The Maglite's bluish halogen beam flooded the lavishly decorated space, past posters, curtains, a hand-hooked rug, crumpled tissues on the floor, a child-sized table littered with half-eaten food and open soup cans, and landed on Gilly Menquez, stuffed awkwardly into the corner, his tongue purple and grotesque, his eyes open and unmoving.

Walt threw himself up into the space, spinning, preparing for someone on the other side of the elevated trapdoor, but the space was empty. He caught his breath as he scrambled to Menquez, still not quite believing the tree house was empty. The flashlight's beam caught the overhead vaulted ceiling, a tiny loft, and the rope ladder leading to it.

Gilly Menquez was warm to the touch. No more than thirty minutes dead. Probably closer to ten or fifteen. Walt called it in as calmly as possible over the radio, but there was no return, the radio's signal lost to the contours of the geography. He tried his phone and got through.

"I want the highway entrance sealed," he explained to his dispatcher. "Ambulance and coroner to the residence. Every deputy available is on the manhunt. We want Greenhorn covered and a team to watch Cold Springs. Contact Roger Hillabrand and have his place locked down. This guy could be out there. Could be long gone."

The bottom third of Gilly's boots were soaked. Brown mud filled the space between the heel and sole. There was a piece of velvet leaf caught in the cuff of his khakis, along with pine straw and flecks of bark. But it was the amber beads of field grass that won his full attention.

These, along with the cheat grass stuck to his socks. You didn't find grasses in the forest, only in meadows, and one meadow in particular came to mind: Gilly had returned to the high mountain campsite they'd discovered, the same campsite he'd been keeping an eye on when he'd drunk himself into a blackout. Walt could picture Gilly, an expert tracker, starting there and working his way down to the Engleton estate. Could picture him finding his way directly to the tree house, could only imagine his surprise when he'd thrown open the trapdoor ahead of him.

As he came down the exterior ladder, he slipped a couple of rungs, catching himself at the last second. Seeing this, Beatrice lunged, but did not leave her spot. He saw her and, reminded of her value to him, returned to the tree house, carefully retrieving two of the discarded tissues without touching them himself. A moment later he presented the tissues to Beatrice's discerning nose and issued a single command: "Find it."

The dog, a bundle of repressed energy, took off at a shot, nose to the ground, executing her bizarre loops and double-backs at the base of the ladder at astounding speed. Wagging excitedly, she faced her master and paused expectantly. She'd caught the scent.

"Find it," he repeated, motioning into the woods. Beatrice raced off into the darkness and Walt followed, his mobile phone already dialing Fiona's number.

"What's going on?" she said before even identifying him. "Are you here?"

"I need you to listen carefully and do exactly as I say," he said. "Are you with me?"

"Okay."

He hadn't checked her Subaru. He hadn't cleared the main house. He was trusting Beatrice but knew some slight possibility existed that the dog might be following Gilly's scent and not the killer's.

"Do you lock your car?" he asked.

"What the hell?"

"I need you to stay with me, Fiona. I need you to answer my questions and do as I say."

"Why are you breathing like that? What's going on?"

"I'm in the woods above you. Do you lock your car?"

"No."

The car was a likely hiding place. If the killer had spotted Walt's approach, had left the tree house while Walt had circled the main house, he could be anywhere—including in the back of the Subaru, awaiting a hostage.

"Your doors and windows are locked?"

"Yes. You're scaring me."

"Good. I want you alert. My people are on their way. It may take them a while. They're coming in quietly, on my orders. Do me a favor and don't shoot one of my deputies. But if anyone tries to break into your place, shoot first and ask questions later. You got that?"

Silence.

"My guys will not break into your place. Certainly not without announcing themselves. Are you with me?"

"What the hell's going on, Walt?"

"It wasn't Kira," he said.

"I told you that!" she said indignantly.

"The guy . . . our mountain man. He's been living in your tree house."

Her gasp was audible through the phone.

"At least part time. He's been up there."

"The tree house? *Our* tree house?"

"Stay put. My guys are maybe ten minutes out. Are you with me?"

"I won't be a victim again, Walt."

"It's not going to come to that."

Beatrice's continuing up into the forest pulled Walt in that direction. He could call her off, return, make sure Fiona got in the Subaru and that the Subaru was safe.

"I'm just saying."

"We won't let that happen."

"We?"

"You and me."

The silence was protracted. Walt felt it in his chest.

"Okay," she finally said. "Okay."

He signed off and holstered the BlackBerry and followed the sound of Beatrice up ahead of him. She was focused and determined, and it was her level of concentration that returned him to the task at hand. Swallowed in the darkness of a thick conifer forest, navigating more on instinct than vision, led by the sounds from a dog he had come to trust and depend upon, he drove himself on, half blind, half terrified, determined to push Fiona from his mind, but finding it impossible. Higher and

higher they climbed, Beatrice leading him along a meandering game trail. They were moving quickly, Walt light
on his feet and nearly silent, and he wondered if they
weren't closing the gap on Menquez's killer. The man
might or might not know Walt was in pursuit; might or
might not be experiencing remorse over killing Menquez. Walt imagined him justifying taking the baseball
bat to the head of Martel Gale. But strangling a Forest
Service ranger, whether panicked or not, had to weigh
differently. Walt imagined him desperate, irrational, and
in search of some way out of his actions. He didn't picture the man a lunatic despite his having jumped through
a window at the Casino. The break-in at the Berkholders' had been cleverly planned and disguised as the work
of a bear; that wasn't the mark of a lunatic.

He and Beatrice were really moving now, Walt at a
near run, Beatrice stopping ahead, waiting, and then
bolting on. When Beatrice allowed him to catch up, her
body craning forward over her front paws and every inch
trembling, he knew they were close. He patted her head
and chest and thrust his palm out marking her to stay.
Worked forward through some underbrush as quietly as
any man or animal could move. Believed himself invisible, faster and more capable than his adversary, no matter how much the person considered himself a mountain
man. This, right now, was Walt's domain, a place where
he thrived, a place with which he identified and drew
upon for his own identity. Leave the conference rooms

and the relationships to others; give him the pitch-black forest and the motivation of a killer on the loose.

By the time he got a look at the meadow, it was empty. The BlackBerry vibrated in his pocket. He ignored it and it stopped. Starlight gave the grassy field a blue hue, its abandoned campsite like a scar in the distance. Walt reached through the chokecherry, taking hold of a clump of field grass, the ripened seeds falling away; seeds he'd recovered from Gilly's pants cuff. The cheat grass played out in the driest portions of the meadow in oblong shapes: kidney beans and a hook nose. Walt broke out and entered the meadow but stayed low and held to the boundary of where the forest formed a wall of shadow.

He clicked his tongue once and Beatrice came padding up behind him faster than he could have expected. A single hand motion, and she heeled. Given his angle, Walt was able to look behind, struck by a darker swath in the still sea of grass: a person, alone, moving from very near where Walt had crouched and in the direction of the abandoned lean-to and campfire. He stayed perfectly still as his eye sought other anomalies. He easily spotted the beaten-down path used by the occasional hiker, the path he and others had used to approach the campsite. He could imagine Gilly there now, having picked up on some markers in the woods, following expeditiously, the way of any tracker. Excited. Driven forward with purpose. Given the line leading that direction, he pictured Menquez's killer somewhere up near the lean-to, or by now well beyond, following the trail that led up and over the ridge and into Greenhorn Gulch.

Walt caught the flicker of headlights through the trees below and to his right. *The ambulance*, he thought. He faced a choice of trying to start Beatrice on the scent again or heading out on the same trail on which he and Brandon had followed the amorous backpackers. He tried to think like his adversary, or if not think, react like him. What would the headlights mean to him? Danger, or curiosity?

The man had revealed himself as brazen, staying at least some of the time in a tree house within a matter of yards from two women. Did his clubbing Martel Gale suggest an attachment to Fiona? Had Walt perhaps been in store for the same outcome when Kira had interrupted his peering inside the cottage windows? Would the arrival of headlights arouse curiosity? Could the killer resist the gravitational pull to see if his kill had been discovered, and if so, the reaction?

Walt resorted to what had gotten him here, to the one thing he could trust. He pulled the tissue from his breast pocket, placed it for Beatrice to sniff, and commanded once again, "Find it."

49

"You can't go up there!" Fiona called out as the ambulance driver put his foot on the ladder's first rung.

"Excuse me?" the man said.

The man's partner, the medic, approached from the far side of the ambulance. "Lady, we've got a shift change in forty-five minutes. We've been on twelve hours. We've been instructed to do a job here and I'd appreciate it if you didn't interfere."

"To recover a body," she said, an educated guess on her part. Walt had said his people were on their way. He'd warned her to stay put. But she had to know. Given the ambulance had arrived under no siren or lights, given that Walt had left the area immediately after coming out of the tree house—for she'd watched the whole thing—added up to the obvious.

"And you are?" the ambulance driver inquired.

The medic was new, or he'd have recognized her. "Me?" About to give her name, she revised her answer. "Crime scene photographer. You can't go in there until I'm through, and I haven't started."

"You can identify yourself?"

"Wait here," she said to the medic. "Don't move," she instructed the driver at the base of the ladder.

Stall, she thought. She returned with her camera bag and her wallet, displaying her sheriff's office ID.

"You want to take some pictures, go ahead and take them. But you've got five minutes."

"More like a half hour," she said.

"I told you, we got a shift change in forty," he said. "Listen, if this was a big deal the place would be lousy with deputies—am I right? It's a body bagger, that's all. We got the call, we do the job."

"And I've got to do mine."

"And I'm giving you five minutes. Four, now that we've used one jawing it to death. Hold up," he called out to his buddy. The driver stepped away from the ladder.

Fiona slung the camera bag over her shoulder, walked to the ladder, and climbed.

With each rung she feared what she might find.

50

With the advent of a siren coming closer, but still far in the distance, Walt's blood pressure rose. He had specifically ordered otherwise, and it was only as the siren passed and faded to the north that he realized the cruiser was on another call. Beatrice loaded herself with cheat grass as she spun her loops in the meadow, snorting and hurrying to pick up the lost scent, Walt looking on from a distance, not crowding her, but prepared to follow. As he looked up, he saw thousands of acres of national forest, acres that by now the mountain man knew well, had exploited for the past few months. It gave the man a decided advantage, whereas Beatrice provided Walt a counterpunch.

Hindsight was nobody's friend, least of all his. He could see now the unspoken pressure he'd put on Gilly

Menquez to deliver; he would have to live with the outcome, while Gilly would not. Could begin to see how
he'd allowed the evidence to form unwarranted suspicions, wondering how much of his own feelings had colored those suspicions. Standing alone in the meadow, he
felt an urge to cry out, a need to beg forgiveness, though
from whom he couldn't be sure.

He withdrew his BlackBerry and checked the missed
call. Dispatch. He double-checked his radio; still not
working even with the added elevation. He called in, his
temper getting the better of him.

"Emergency Services," answered the outwardly calm
woman's voice.

"It's Fleming. Where's the backup?"

"We have an ambulance on site, Sheriff. As to the
patrols . . . It appears all but Huxley rolled to Carey on
that drowning. Huxley was the other side of Galena.
He's on his way south to your twenty."

Budgetary concerns had lowered his swing shift to six
officers in four cruisers. He cursed the commissioners
for pulling the dollars out from under him, and his own
deputies and dispatch for allowing a patrol void to occur.
It wasn't the first time a group of bored deputies had
bunched up.

Walt's office rang the Ketchum Police Department as
well. "Ketchum?"

"Four-car pileup with fire and injury at the saddle
intersection. Two patrols on site. We need your ambulance up there A-SAP. I called them off just now."

Walt hadn't seen the headlights leaving, his attention on Beatrice.

"I need backup, Gloria."

"Yes, sir."

"I need those areas blocked and searched as we discussed. This is a homicide suspect, Goddamn it," he flared, revealing a rare display of emotion. "I want every on-call deputy up here. I want anyone and everyone we've got, right now. Do I have to spell it out for you?"

"Copy that. Initiating the call tree."

It was a not-too-subtle stab at Walt by a very alert dispatcher. Gloria knew her stuff and he'd been wrong to dress her down. All that had been required of him was to order the call tree instigated. His outburst hadn't helped anyone.

"Thank you," he said.

It caught her off guard.

"No problem, Sheriff."

"Make it happen," he couldn't help adding. He disconnected the call.

His flashlight followed Beatrice's apparent random looping as she began to define the pattern and Walt knew to move in her general direction. However her olfactory process worked, it eventually led to a smaller, tighter pattern from which she shot out in a straight line, suddenly fixed on the scent. That moment quickly approached, and as she got a faceful of the trail left by the killer, she looked back to make sure Walt was paying attention. She actually looked proud of him as she found him coming up behind her and she tore excitedly to the edge of the meadow, looked back once more, and dropped out of sight. For a moment Walt lost his equilibrium: when he'd last seen her, she'd been nose to the ground, aimed back down the hill toward the Engleton estate.

51

Fiona had taken more than the five minutes allotted to her for the recording of the remains of Guillermo Menquez. So she was surprised to hear the ambulance engine start, and the vehicle drive away when she'd been expecting a reprimand.

"Hello?" she called down through the hole left by the open trapdoor. "Hello? Are you there?"

In truth there wasn't anything more to photograph. She'd taken a dozen pictures of the deceased and another dozen of the tree house interior, overcome by chills most of the time, both to be alone in the presence of a dead body, and to realize someone had been *living* up here. It looked like it; it smelled like it. There was little doubt that the structure had been used as a hideaway, and the thought that it was but a matter of yards from her cottage and the main house made her sick to her stomach.

As she came out of the tree house and back down its ladder, she looked over her shoulder to see a tiny light up the hill, winking at her as it descended steadily through the forest.

She clung there to the ladder and reached for her phone to call Walt, to confirm this was him headed toward her, but didn't have it on her. She'd left it in her bedroom, along with the handgun. Suddenly the cottage and the main house looked different to her, given the evidence of someone living in the tree house, given the dead body up there. She considered the safe room where Kira had hidden herself, but couldn't bring herself to enter either the home or her own cottage. The flashlight was heading through the forest at a run, heading down the hill, heading toward her.

Now she heard her ringtone from within the cottage. She took two steps in that direction but stopped, picturing someone hiding in there waiting for her. The phone's dull ringing continued through three more cycles and went silent. The phone . . . The gun . . . The flashlight, no longer seen.

No way she was going in there.

She looked up. Maybe the safest place was in the tree house, standing on the trapdoor to keep it from opening, but not if it was the killer's lair, not if she had to hole up with a dead body. Hadn't Walt once said the best place to hide was out in the open? She spotted the stack of split firewood, and beyond, another stack of the unsplit rounds. A trail led up into the woods from just beyond the pond. Where would she feel safer: wandering an empty house the size of a hotel, or tucked away in the woods with her back against a tree? The flashlight had to be Walt. He couldn't be more than ten minutes away.

She left her camera bag at the foot of the ladder and hurried to the stack of logs, jumpy and agitated and feeling like someone was constantly a few feet behind her. Glancing over her shoulder nervously. Scared of her own shadow.

She reached the stack of rounds and there was a baseball bat stacked among the logs. Kira's missing baseball bat, probably placed there by one of the gardeners. Or maybe it was the bat from outside her own cottage. She wrapped her hand around it and squeezed tightly.

It felt right.

52

Walt followed Beatrice down the hill at a jog, their routine familiar to both: she would go out ahead of him, locked on the scent, then return to within a few yards of him to make sure he was still with her. As he broke out onto a defined path, Walt switched off the flashlight and fitted it back into its loop on his gun belt. It was dark in the woods, but the path revealed itself as a pale ribbon and Walt followed it effortlessly, slowing only occasionally as it turned or twisted around a rock out-cropping or became darkened with a tangle of exposed roots.

As much as he appreciated being on the scent, as much as he understood a killer's bizarre need to return to the crime scene, he took little comfort. Fiona was not answering her phone. This fact alone drove him toward the Engleton place at a dangerous pace, nearly keeping up with Beatrice, and by doing so, encouraging the dog ahead at a full run. He pushed her faster; she pulled him along. But he was no match for her. She took his pursuit of her as some kind of game and quickly outpaced him.

Two minutes passed, Walt charging down the descending path. Five. Beatrice's absence—her failure to return to him—began to weigh on him. Had the sense of game won out over her obligation to follow the scent? Had he confused her with his running? He couldn't be sure, the woods unfamiliar to him, but it felt as if he would arrive at the estate any minute.

Beatrice yipped. It was a cry. A painful cry, and it set into him a sense of panic and dread as if one of his daughters had called out. *Beware when the hunter becomes the hunted.* His first and only conclusion was that the killer had somehow known the dog was trailing him, that Walt, by challenging the dog, had driven her headlong into a trap—that that yip had been Beatrice's final moment, one last desperate attempt to warn Walt.

His response visceral and immediate, his foot speed increased exponentially, running blindly now, all out. It was more than a connection between them, it was a bond, Walt to her and her to him. It was something in his blood. The kind of something that couldn't be explained to another human being without sounding foolish, even childish. The love of family. The love of forever.

Her yip rang in his ears. Burned. A baby's cry in the night. A call for help. His eyes blurred, watery from the run, or from tears, or from both. He wiped them away but all was a blurry, darkened landscape, the path's lighter shade swirling and shifting, suddenly a river beneath his feet.

A geometric shape among it all: the Engleton roof.

And then the pain.

It ripped through both legs at the shins. He hadn't seen a log across the path, but he went down face-first, losing the gun as he reached out to break the fall, his head flirting with unconsciousness in an effort to escape the pain. It seared from his broken shins, up through his knees, his groin, his stomach and exploded into his head as he cried out a sickening, agonized shriek.

Blackness loomed at the edges of his consciousness as he rolled over and drew his knees into his chest, writhing and gasping for air. *Breathe through it!* he told himself, as impossible as it was. He could ill afford to pass out. From somewhere through the fog of pain, Fiona appeared on her knees, a baseball bat in hand. Even with the evidence so blatant, it took Walt several seconds to connect the bat with the excruciating pain in his legs, and only then in what amounted to total disbelief. She was mouthing, "I'm sorry . . ." beneath the intense ringing in his ears and the waves of his own internal groaning.

Then, from behind her, came the mountain man like a specter. He emerged through the darkness, drawn by Walt's shriek or out of some sixth sense that made him aware of Fiona's presence. Whether a lunatic or a calculating murderer who understood the value of a hostage, he moved straight for Fiona, who was herself too absorbed in her own mishap to have any awareness of him. But it wasn't Fiona he wanted.

She screamed and rolled away, releasing the bat as the man seized hold of it. It hung at his side like the bat of a hitter stepping up to home plate staring down the pitcher—Walt.

Whether traumatized or demonized, vengeful, or drugged and demented, both men knew what the mountain man intended to do with the bat as he took another step closer. Fiona, who had scooted away on her back, thrusting herself along the forest floor by digging in her heels, who had moved a good five yards away, also saw the future—where the next ten seconds were headed. Whether to protect him, or herself—Walt couldn't fathom such thoughts, still gripped in his pain—she rolled to her knees and began sweeping her arms through the pine straw, in what at first appeared such a lame and odd behavior. *The gun*, he realized in a flash of lucidity. She was going for his gun.

Movement caught the edges of Walt's wavering peripheral vision. Beatrice limped onto the path holding her right front paw aloft, her expression—did he imagine it or actually see it clearly in the dark?—one of remorse and grave concern as her master lay writhing in the dirt, a camouflaged giant glowering over him.

Walt, who couldn't hear anything beyond the rush of his own blood past his ears, who sensed Fiona clambering in the underbrush, raking left and right in search of his handgun, who saw Martel Gale's and Gilly Menquez's killer turn toward the woman, clearly sensing she presented the greatest threat, managed a single word to rise up through the pain.

"Defend!"

Beatrice squealed again as she lighted onto her injured paw, bounding some four feet through air like a projected missile—a dozen bared and flashing white teeth.

53

Walt found the wheelchair an embarrassment, never mind a necessity. The orthopedist told him that despite the lack of any fractures, he wouldn't walk for a week. He spent as much time as possible behind his desk, because it hid his disability, his condition forcing him to reassess what formed his self-identity.

Nancy came in to wheel him. "I can do it myself," he barked.

"You're going to be a delight in your old age, you know that?"

"Maybe I won't get there."

"Not if you work without backup."

"That was supposed to be my fault?"

"Was there somebody else out there in the woods

with you? Did I miss something?" She grabbed the wheelchair's handles and Walt didn't object. She rolled her eyes behind his back.

"Yeah . . . well . . ." he said, lacking any decent retort. He hated her sometimes.

"You sure you're up for this?"

"I'm fine." He loved her at other times.

"It can wait."

"No, it can't. I can't. He can't. It has to happen now."

"Yes, boss."

"Shut up."

"Yes, boss."

She delivered him to Interview 1, as charmless and bland as Interview 2, but one door closer to reception.

He thought it some aspect of Intelligent Design that he should be the one conducting the interview and she the one behind the video camera. All they lacked was Beatrice, currently bandaged and on the floor of his office asleep. She'd taken a piece of cheat grass in the pad of her front paw, had run on it, leaped on it, and driven it in so far that Mark Aker had to remove it surgically.

The accused, in the jail's blue jumpsuit, won the Charles Manson look-alike contest. Curly black, tangled hair. Unshaven. Basset-hound brown eyes. Peter Arian had wisely ducked this one, letting a wet-behind-the-ears public defender by the name of Crawford sit in the attorney's chair. Crawford worked to lose his neophyte's startled look, making him appear to be the one accused of homicide.

"Sheriff," Crawford began, "my client objects to any alleged victim of his—"

"You! Shut the fuck up," said the accused. Handcuffed, he couldn't add the punctuation he would have clearly liked.

Walt appreciated the reprimand. Crawford was now officially a spectator. The attorney glanced in the direction of the video camera and Fiona, but then thought better of making any further protest.

"I don't care who you are," the accused stated dryly. "Why should I? It's not like I killed you." He smiled. He might have had decent teeth once. He looked directly at Fiona, and therefore directly into the camera lens. "I wasn't going to let him push you around. Him knocking you down like that."

Walt had some housekeeping to take care of: name, age, current residence; but he let it go for now. Fiona had been warned not to engage with the man.

"Is it running?" Walt asked her.

She nodded.

"You can leave the room."

She slipped from behind the tripod and past the wheelchair. She leaned down and whispered, "I wasn't pushed." Walt nodded. She closed the door gently. Her presence had accomplished what he'd hoped; he wasn't going to put her through anything more.

Walt said, "You shot one of my deputies. We have your prints off the chair you threw through the window, and they're going to match your prints at booking, and that's going to buy you a long, long time in maximum. The State of Idaho doesn't take kindly to people shooting its peace officers. So you might as well tell me everything."

To Walt's surprise, Randy Dowling then confessed to the two murders and Brandon's shooting. He'd killed Gale in a fit of rage at him pushing Fiona and hurting her—the way it had looked from his vantage point behind a living room window. "My own wife walked out on me. You probably know that much, am I right? Me being the loser I am? That's what you're thinking, am I right? Takes the kids with her. All because of money. Because I lose my stinking job. I'm a CPA. I'll bet you know that. A guy like you knows everything, right? You bet you do. But you don't know me. I'm not the guy you think I am. College of Central Utah. Top twenty-five of my class. You know all this, I'm not telling you anything new. I'm putting it down on tape. I was this guy," he said, pointing his two cuffed hands at Crawford, who recoiled. "Even looked like him. You'd a bought insurance from me, the way I looked. But a guy that big pushing a fine-looking woman like that one. Gave him the old Louisville Slugger up top of the head. Beaned him. Thought it was lights out till the prick got up and came at me like Frankenstein. Jesus. Like trying to chainsaw a sequoia. Guy takes these steps toward me, and me, I'm backing up lockstep. I couldn't believe he'd gotten back up. His eyes are staring straight ahead—I swear he doesn't see me—and right as I think he's about to do me, he drops to his knees and then face-plants into the garden. Down for the count. Like a zombie. Night of the Living Dead. I couldn't believe it."

Walt had witnessed other confessions where the guilty party proved himself eager to purge, but honestly hadn't expected it of this one. He'd initially appraised the man's wild looks, deciding he had an ignorant lunatic on his hands. When Nancy had brought what little they could find on him, Walt had ordered it double-checked. But now the man was confirming what they'd learned about him. Somewhere down the line he'd be deemed a victim of the economy by a sympathetic press or a politician seeking additional funding. A poster boy for all that can go wrong.

"You cooked meth," Walt said, seeing it as a conversation starter.

Crawford leaned forward but not for long, his participation shortened by a woeful look from Dowling.

"And damn near every penny went into an envelope I slipped under the door of my wife's mother's place. I can take care of my family. We sure as hell aren't food stamp people."

"The tree house."

"I got tired of running around, you know? Your

RIDLEY PEARSON

people—people like you, like that other one—scouring the woods looking for me. You know how that feels? You get treated like an animal, you start acting like one. You drove me to that place. You, and people like you. Couldn't leave well enough alone. You know how many people are out in these woods, Sheriff? More than you think. And come to find out these other people have tree houses nicer than a lot of people's homes. Including mine. What's with that? You think I *liked* it out there? Shitting in a hole? Getting sick from the water? What kind of country is this when you can't even drink the creek water? How'd we let something like that happen?"

"So you killed him?"

"Mostly I slept days and moved around the woods at night. Safer that way. Fewer of your kind. Except for that one. A drinker, that one. I'd had my eye on him before. No real threat to me. Not until he pokes his head up in that tree house like it's *Groundhog Day*. Scared the shit out of me! Wanted to take my tree house away, I'm thinking. So I kicked him—kicked him in the throat, turns out. Grabbed him by the hair. Hauled him up. Musta broken a bone or something in his throat. Voice box, maybe. Guy went purple on me. Didn't mean for it to happen that way. I'm not a killer."

"There are two men dead."

"Yeah, but that just kind of . . . happened."

"What happened to those men?" Walt asked.

"I just told you."

"You killed them. Martel Gale and Guillermo Menquez."

"If you say so."

"It's you saying so, Mr. Dowling, not me. Are you saying you killed them?"

"I killed them. I dragged Gale up the hill and dumped him. I'm not proud of it, you understand. I'm not like some sicko or something, you know. I'm not one of them. I didn't *like* it. It wasn't like that. It just . . . happened. You think about it: it was bound to happen. A person like me. You and everyone like you did this. You're the ones made it happen."

Dowling was still ranting about the economic inequalities of the valley as Walt let the door shut behind his chair.

Fiona had her back pressed against the wall across from him, her expression severe.

"So?"

Walt shook his head. "The lunatics are easier."

"He didn't confess?"

"Oh, no, he confessed. No resistance at all. Gilly messed us up by taking the ATM card. This guy, he took Gale's cash out of the wallet. Left the cards. Gilly came along and hijacked the ATM card. We thought we were looking for one guy, when it was two."

She said nothing. Uninterested.

"Lunatics?" he said. "I meant they're easier to live with. To sleep. A guy like this? He's going to haunt me."

"Because?"

"Because he was avoidable. You don't need to be haunted too. The least I can do is shelter you from that."

She squatted so she could face him eye to eye. He found the pose vaguely sexual and reminded himself once again that he was on dangerous ground with this woman.

"I'd like that," she said.

He'd forgotten what it was he'd said.

"For the past I don't know how many years, I've wanted nothing but independence. To take care of myself. To protect myself—defend myself—whatever. To be reliant upon no one. To trust no one."

"Sounds lonely."

"About as lonely as a divorced man with two young daughters, I imagine," she said.

"No arguing that."

A female deputy entered the long hallway and Walt looked at her, and she stood and put her back against the wall to allow the woman to pass. To her credit, the deputy passed without a glance. Walt thought Fiona looked sexy against the wall like that, too.

Trouble.

"This is extremely complicated," he said.

"Yet incredibly simple," she countered, allowing a smile onto her face.

"But complicated." He had to have the last word.

"My point being, I wouldn't mind someone sheltering me from some of the stuff. Just as long as that someone allowed me to shelter him in return. I won't be a kept woman, but I'm not an open relationship type."

"You're racking up the points," he said.

"In the good column, I hope."

"In the very good column," he said.

"We take it slow," she said.

"Look at me," he said, indicating the wheelchair. "What's it look like to you?"

54

"Home again, home again, jiggity-jig!" shouted Emily. More enthusiasm than she'd showed in a very long time. Their father confined to a wheelchair, the two girls had taken it upon themselves to make dinner—microwaved, prepackaged meat loaf and stovetop mashed potatoes—and were incredibly proud of their effort.

"You know Fiona," Walt said.

"Of course!" the girls said almost in unison.

"She's going to hang out tonight. Help me out. Maybe help get you guys in bed and then take off."

"No problem," said Nikki. "You want to help him or us?"

Fiona considered her options. She placed Walt's briefcase into his lap and entered the kitchen with the girls.

He feigned complaint and wheeled himself into the dining room, following up on an e-mail to Skype Boldt.

"You heard?" Boldt asked when his visage appeared on screen.

"Heard what?" Walt said. "I thought you were calling about Dowling."

"I am. Indirectly, I am," Boldt said gruffly. "But since it came from your office, I thought you'd probably already heard."

"It's been a busy afternoon."

"Lab results came back on the blood from Wynn's shoes: Caroline Vetta's blood type. DNA comparison's next. A couple days out. But if I was a drinking man, I'd be popping the bubbly."

"Vince Wynn?"

"Lover's quarrel. He couldn't stand that she'd moved on. Pulled a Steve McNair in reverse."

"Did he reclaim the shoes? I thought you needed my help with that?"

"Blood shadow," Boldt said. "We had a blood shadow at the Vetta scene, an empty shape of a shoe print in an otherwise sea of blood. That shoe shape is distinctive. Exclusive. It was Wynn's brand. That gave us the warrant we needed. His sweat will carry the DNA we need in the shoes. He's toast."

"Vince Wynn," Walt said, still in shock.

"Now I can justify my expense coming over there," Boldt joked. "And just for the record, I wanted to pass this along."

"Go ahead."

"Your father called."

Here it comes, Walt thought.

"Was crowing proud as a peacock about how his son—*his son*—solved a multiple homicide. And no, Walt," Boldt interrupted before Walt had a chance to speak, "it was not to compliment me on whatever role I had in it. It was to tell me about you. It was to brag *on you*."

Walt let the words swim around inside him. Found it no use to fight the curl at his lips.

"No kidding," Walt said, allowing astonishment in his voice.

"None. And I knew you should hear it from the horse's mouth."

"I appreciate it."

"I thought you would. Proud as a peacock, I'm telling you."

"Means a lot."

"Yes, it does." *More than you know.* "Well," Walt said, "Vince Wynn."

"I know."

"You were looking at him all along."

"Don't do that," Boldt said. "Don't take away from your moment."

"Am I that transparent?"

"We've all had fathers. Fathers and sons. It ain't easy."

"No."

"But . . . I don't know . . ."

"Yeah, I'm with you."

"I'm outta here," Boldt said.

"Don't be a stranger."

"Back at you. You need me on the witness stand, I'm there."

"You're just looking for another excuse to use the expense account."

"You know me too well."

The screen went blank.

Walt stared at the royal blue.

"What was that about?" Fiona called out from the kitchen. "Anything important?"

Walt considered how to answer that. Caught his own reflection in the blue and the glass of the monitor. His reflection was still smiling.

He reached up and turned off the monitor.

Turn the page for an exciting preview
of Ridley Pearson's latest thriller

FOREIGN EXCHANGE

Introducing John Knox and Grace Chu

Now available in hardcover
from G. P. Putnam's Sons

FRIDAY
SEPTEMBER 24

"Edward" Lu Hào, a slim, well-dressed Chinese man, stood on the roof of a subcompact car the size of a toaster, peering over a ten-foot-high concrete block wall and into the parking area outside an aging tannery.

There was almost too much at play for his senses: the acrid smell of tar, the clamor of dump trucks and road surface rollers, the din of Chinese spoken in machine-gun staccato.

Lu Hào had been schooled from an early age about the role chance and fate played in one's life. If he hadn't driven past that particular fuel station at that exact time, he would never have recognized the foul Mongolian, a man he knew from his deliveries over in Shanghai; would never have followed him here to this remote place. Would never have witnessed the meeting where three

men went into the factory building and only two came
out. He had watched through a crack in the hanging
doors as the smaller, younger of the three had argued
with the gentleman and then been bludgeoned by the
Mongolian.

A moment later, back outside, the Mongolian shook
the hand of the well-dressed, portly Chinese gentleman,
who then walked over to a black Audi four-door sedan
and was driven away. As the license plate flashed in the
glare of a floodlight, Lu gasped: the first character was
沪—"hu"—followed by the western letter "A" which,
when combined, indicated a government pool car. A
high-ranking official. Why here, a hundred kilometers
from Shanghai?

Trembling now, Lu Hào clung to the wall like a para-
site, refusing to let go. Refusing to move and risk attract-
ing attention. Terror rippled through him: opportunity,
risk, reward. Chance. Fate.

What was it to be? He wished he could forget what
he'd seen. Wished he could sneak off in the subcompact.
Was about to do just that when the Mongolian, inspecting the paving job, jerked his head up quickly in the
direction of the yard's far corner.

Lu Hào looked in this same direction.

By the gods! The wink of a lens trained over the wall.
A sizable video camera with only a pair of hands—*white
hands*—seen holding it in place. A *waì guó rén*—a for-
eigner!

Lu Hào dropped from the wall like a stone, fumbled

for his keys and was into the car in a heartbeat. *No more!* He would determine how to best use this information later, when he could be calm and reasonable. He might appeal for help.

He might go the temple and burn incense.

But for now, he'd get the hell gone, return to Shanghai, and hope by all things good and gracious that he'd not been seen, too.

THURSDAY
SEPTEMBER 30

Lu rode his lovingly restored CJ-750 motorcycle, its side-car seat covered by an oilcloth tarpaulin hiding a duffel bag that minutes earlier had contained cash. A good deal of cash. The kind of cash Edward Lu Hào needed in order to repay his father for his own foolish mistake. But now the duffel was nearly empty—a few thousand *yuan* was all that remained. He returned his eyes to the street. To glance away from Shanghai traffic for more than a second could prove suicidal.

13 . . . 12 . . . 11 . . .

The middle lens of a Shanghai traffic light was an LCD timer that counted down to the light change, giving motorists on both sides of the intersection time to at least consider the traffic laws. Not that anyone obeyed them. The traffic laws in Shanghai were observed more as guidelines than rules.

Lu revved the bike—a thing of beauty, a sound like that. He drew a few curious looks his way.

4 . . . 3 . . . 2 . . .

Hundreds of waiting vehicles crawled forward. A Darwinian exercise commenced in the wide bike lane to the right: motorcycles assumed the lead, followed by motor scooters, electric bikes, and finally bicycles. Not a horn sounded. Not a curse was thrown. Everyone knew their place.

Lu turned off Ya'nan Road, a major ten-lane avenue, and traffic immediately lessened. A few more turns, and he entered a time machine: Shanghai as it was a century before.

Laundry hung like colorful prayer flags from bamboo poles jutting from apartment windows. There were more pedestrians than vehicles on the street. He slowed, straddling the motorcycle's sonorous rumble. A delivery man had dumped a half dozen water jugs off his motor scooter, stopping traffic.

Lu swung right again down a narrow street lined with stalls. Old, toothless men in white undershirts commandeered second-floor windows. The spirited laughter of a mah-jongg game echoed down the lane, mixing with an out-of-tune piano working through Gershwin.

He caught movement from his left: a man running toward him at top speed, head down. An ambush, forced upon him by the spilled water jugs. The lane was a choke point. He glanced to the sidecar and the hidden duffel containing the money.

His attacker led with his shoulder, connecting with Lu and knocking him off the bike. Two more men appeared. They grabbed hold of him. He was dragged, face down, barely conscious, and thrown into the back of a micro-van where yet another man slapped duct tape over his mouth and pulled a plastic tie around his wrists.

Then everyone started shouting at once.

Clete Danner wore the motorcycle helmet's mirrored visor down to hide his Caucasian face. He bent into the handlebars to disguise his size—there weren't many Chinese six-three and two thirty. When the threat came from Lu's left, Danner vaulted the bike and, in an infinitesimal misjudgment, caught the toe of his right shoe on the frame. He overcompensated, suddenly finding himself off balance and thrown back on his heels only a few meters from the van.

A *nunchuck* came at him like an airplane propeller, its aluminum cylinder striking his raised right forearm. He felt a bone snap. He swooned, and a deep purple overtook his vision.

He cocked his right leg and kicked. The *nunchuck* connected with his upper thigh, but the man holding it went airborne, slamming into the metal frame of the van and sliding down unconscious.

His assailant was hauled inside. There was much screaming in Mandarin.

The van's motor strained at high revs and coughed exhaust from the tailpipe. The van backed up, knocking Danner over. His helmet bounced off the asphalt. Everything went dark.

A second or two—*more?*—had passed. It was followed by pain. The broken arm. The bruised thigh. His concussed head.

He was dragged into the van, the smell of sweat, oil, and blood overwhelming him. The van doors banged shut. A flurry of angry Mandarin as the van took off. His helmet was ripped off his head.

"Waì guó rén!"—he heard.

He knew he could not possibly be part of their plans. He'd had Edward Lu under surveillance for months. Where had these guys come from? His cover was now blown. The entire operation was blown.

The pain subsided, replaced by a deep and welcome silence.

From #1 *New York Times* Bestselling Author
Ridley Pearson

KILLER SUMMER

Sun Valley, Idaho: playground of the wealthy and home to an annual wine auction with enough rare bottles to lure high-rolling connoisseurs from across the country—as well as an inspired and ingenious team of thieves after a particular collection. Sheriff Walt Fleming's attempt to prevent the heist uncovers a far more sinister plan. Outsmarted, and forced to play catch-up, Walt finds his mettle tested when the crime suddenly turns personal and the stakes ratchet higher. With his private life unraveling, undermined by unforeseen obstacles, Walt walks a dangerous line, struggling to remain above the law he's sworn to uphold.

Ridley Pearson
KILLER VIEW

"Put *Killer View* on your summer reading list."
—*St. Louis Post-Dispatch*

When a skier goes missing from a Sun Valley mountaintop, Sheriff Walt Fleming's crack search-and-rescue
team becomes a target. Waist-deep in snow and knee-
deep in lies, Walt suspects that people of great wealth
and power—including a former state senator—want to
keep him where he started: out in the cold.

THE *NEW YORK TIMES* BESTSELLER
THAT WILL LEAVE READERS BREATHLESS

Ridley Pearson
KILLER WEEKEND

Controversial New York State Attorney General Liz Shaler is announcing her candidacy for president at a high-profile convergence of media heavy hitters. Also in attendance is an assassin with a brilliant and foolproof plan . . .

M647T0210

Penguin Group (USA) Online

What will you be reading tomorrow?

Patricia Cornwell, Nora Roberts, Catherine Coulter,
Ken Follett, John Sandford, Clive Cussler,
Tom Clancy, Laurell K. Hamilton, Charlaine Harris,
J. R. Ward, W.E.B. Griffin, William Gibson,
Robin Cook, Brian Jacques, Stephen King,
Dean Koontz, Eric Jerome Dickey, Terry McMillan,
Sue Monk Kidd, Amy Tan, Jayne Ann Krentz,
Daniel Silva, Kate Jacobs...

You'll find them all at
penguin.com

***Read excerpts and newsletters,
find tour schedules and reading group guides,
and enter contests.***

Subscribe to Penguin Group (USA) newsletters
and get an exclusive inside look
at exciting new titles and the authors you love
long before everyone else does.

PENGUIN GROUP (USA)
penguin.com